Michael Duggan, who writes under the pen name of Michael Taylor, started work as a secondary school teacher in Shepherd's Bush, London, which was in a very tough boys' school. After 8 years of teaching, he applied to study medicine and went to UCL on a 5-year course. Being a graduate after two years and passing the 2nd MB exam, he was eligible to join the clinical course at Cambridge, which was 18 months (half that of UCH), he applied and was accepted and so, he went.

Having qualified, Michael commenced working in obstetrics and gynaecology and then switched to being a GP for 31 years. During this time, he became the county chief forensic medical examiner, was approved under the Mental Health Act, as well as serving as a JP for three years.

I dedicate this book to my colleagues who continue to work in the NHS despite the interference and indifference of governments.

Michael Taylor

THE WATCHER, THE MECHANIC AND THE DOCTOR'S WIFE

21st April 2024

To Dea Lizzie

c love from

the Duggan

(The Real Author).

AUSTIN MACAULEY PUBLISHERS™

LONDON * CAMBRIDGE * NEW YORK * SHARJAH

A CIP catalogue record for this title is available from the British Library.

ISBN 9781035834686 (Paperback)
ISBN 9781035834693 (ePub e-book)

www.austinmacauley.co.uk

First Published 2024
Austin Macauley Publishers Ltd®
1 Canada Square
Canary Wharf
London
E14 5AA

I would like to acknowledge my parents, who encouraged me to study medicine, my teachers, who guided me through it and my patients, who, in good faith, let me apply it.

I am indebted to my aunt, who helped pay for my studies to my friends for their support; and to my wife and family, who put up with me despite my frequent complaining.

The Preface

This story is about a university student of medicine and what happens to him when he embarks on his clinical medicine course at Cambridge. It is intended to entertain the readers and possibly educate them about the realms of medical training in recent years. It may also acquaint them with the consequences of an ineffective rule of law.

The story describes a dangerous time, when only the most able were called upon to make the difference between the survival and the destruction of our way of life.

There is the sex, there are the drugs, there are the crooks, the skulduggery, the police, and the doctors with the lives they affect. It presents a guide through clinical medicine and a rare group of practitioners, who try to make it work. They strive in the face of a cash strapped, impotent government, a befuddled public, an ill-led, over-managed, underfunded NHS, depending absolutely on the goodwill of its professionals.

Medicine is a life of extreme personal and conscientious academic application. It involves lifelong study and occasionally, moments of euphoria, when once in a while, it facilitates the saving of a life by human effort and learning pitted against the pervading ravishes of disease.

Author's Notes

At the time of the events in this book, in most UK Universities, medicine was a five-year course. At London University, it consisted of two years of pre-clinical studies in Gross Anatomy, Histology, Physiology, Pharmacology, Biochemistry and Neuro-Anatomy. This was followed by an examination known as the 2nd MB examination. This exam had to be passed to commence the Clinical Training course most commonly lasting three years, in a hospital attached to the university. At University College London, that hospital was UCH (University College Hospital).

In clinical medicine, Clinical Students are taught how to examine patients in different clinical specialties and how to manage those patients' relevant diseases.

Cambridge was an unusual university, in that they had a much shorter clinical course of eighteen months for graduate students, enabling them to qualify much earlier than elsewhere. They had a similar two-year pre-clinical course leading to the 2nd MB exam, like other universities.

However, after that, their students could undertake a year of study in whatever subject (usually, but not always, relevant to medicine), they wished. This led them to a degree level examination to obtain the Cambridge Bachelor Of Arts degree, B.A. (Cantab). After that, if they wished they could then pay the university a fee and be awarded a Master of Arts degree, M.A. (Cantab). Either of these two degrees enabled them to enter the shorter clinical medicine course there.

Cambridge Bachelors' degrees are considered, by some, to be at a level equivalent to other Universities' Masters Degrees. As a result of this, the Cambridge clinical students who had gone through the Cambridge system had M.A. degrees in various Arts/Medical/Science subjects, before they went on to study clinical medicine at the clinical school and Addenbrookes Hospital, or various hospitals attached to medical schools elsewhere.

Several had also progressed to higher doctorate degrees and were experts in their various fields. Following that, these higher degree graduates went on, like the others, to study clinical medicine for eighteen months, before taking their medical finals to qualify as a doctor with the M.B., B.Chir. degrees in medicine and surgery.

1

"Good morning, ladies and gentlemen, welcome to the University of Cambridge, School of Clinical Medicine. I am Thomas Hawkins, Dean of this medical school."

'The Hawk', as we came to know him, looked serene on the stage of the William Harvey lecture theatre. Clinical Dean Hawkins was like a film star, eloquent and most elegant, in his dark navy blue pinstriped 'Brioni suit'. He was at the height of his career as a professor in one of the world's greatest universities and a consultant Neuro-Radiologist in one of the top teaching hospitals. He oozed confidence and goodwill, as if we were all part of the same and exclusive club. We were its newest members, overflowing with enthusiasm and mutual benevolence. He held us all in silence and you could have heard a pin drop.

"You have all achieved a great deal to be here, selected with distinguished academic records at your universities from all over the world. You are *La crème de la crème* of academia and set to embark on the most interesting and privileged part of your training in the most important profession in the world."

We inhaled unanimously, fully expanding our chests in total agreement with his exultations, like proud post coital cocks in a farm yard full of hens; in which we were soon to observe, we were.

"Henceforth, you will see and treat people who are vulnerable and who will have faith in whatever you say and do. They will allow you to explore their bodies and minds and for the most, they will obey unequivocally every behest you make of them. For some, you will have powers to cure them extending the gift of life. To them you will be most special and above ordinary mortals.

"With those powers and rights comes a great responsibility. You are already graduates in medical sciences and know the meaning of the 'work ethic' but now you will experience it daily to earn that privilege, as we fashion and shape you into doctors of medicine.

"You acquire here the Cambridge Badge you will take with you all over this planet and possibly to others in the future. You will never know everything and never cease to learn every day for the rest of your lives.

"This onerous prerogative will grip your senses, wake you in the middle of the night, motivate you, spurn your indulgences, spur your consciences and drive you until you die. These are exciting times in medicine and I am certain that you will enjoy this subject until your demise. You have been selected for this privilege and from now you will be tested and be found worthy to take on this mantle.

"Make no mistake you are going to work more than other students anywhere and when you don't work you will need to rest and rest you will, if you are to succeed. You will work harder than ever before to absorb the level of knowledge required for this Cambridge course of clinical medicine.

"With every step you take, there will be those who will scrutinise your every move, encouraged by over-demanding governments left and right, avaricious of your incomes and jealous of your entitled influence on your patients.

"If you falter at any step, they may ill-perceive your good intentions and cut you down like avenging angels to take away those privileges we bestow on you here.

"They may closely monitor your good objectives, so do not falter and allow them to interlope between us. They are not of our genre, few are numerate, and even fewer are literate; most answer to their health service managers, who care little for your welfare and others answer to their electorate and the inadequacies of acquisitive government policies.

"While you are here, you are both members of this clinical school and graduate members of your various Cambridge Colleges and you have responsibilities to them both. You cannot be a member here without being a member of a college and you owe us both allegiance.

"I wish you good fortune in your endeavours, but remember, we who are your mentors and examiners are also your sponsors in this profession. Your tutors and I are here to help you and my door is open to all of you."

The dean was ebullient and awe-inspiring. He clearly believed we were "on his team" and was emotionally moved by every word he pronounced.

We had arrived at the academic hub of the universe and were joining his exclusive club. Momentarily, I wondered whether I might not live up to the confident expectations and faith he was placing in we naïve but enthusiastic academic human beings, but then secretly inside I wanted to blurt out: "Let's get on with it, Dean, I'm ready for this!"

I had no idea how this 'club' was to unexpectedly change my way of life. I knew I was capable, having already been a graduate and also passed the pre-clinical medical course from London University, which was no mean feat and where I had always been classed with the highest achievers. Now, I was at one of the most eminent schools of learning with the academic best in the world. All my life, I'd wanted this and at last, it had arrived.

I looked round the lecture theatre at my peers. There were around a hundred of us, of several different races and creeds. We were mainly whites, with only two students of colour, several Indians and a large group of Chinese. We didn't know at this stage that this day was to be possibly the last day we would see our Chinese student colleagues, apart from in our academic groups; if academia was a racial trait, they had it and almost to a man, they would be spending all of their other free time studying in the library. As a group, they had swallowed the work ethic hook, line and sinker. In fact, they'd swallowed it right up the line to the fishing rod!

Certainly, at my pre-clinical course in London, they had almost universally achieved the highest academic results of the year. I secretly wondered how they would fare here at Cambridge, competing with the academic best!

The dean continued to expound on his aspirations for our behaviour.

"To be a doctor, in the public eye, you have to look like a doctor.

"You will be conservative in your dress.

"You will not have inappropriate piercings and nor have any tattoos inscribed on your bodies.

"You will not break the law and you will respect its officers.

"You will attend all lectures and not be late.

"You will show care for your patients and be exemplary in your behaviour towards them, to other healthcare professionals at this hospital and to the British public, whose taxes pay for this establishment and your education."

'The Hawk' thanked us for our attention and exuding goodwill, he left the stage, followed by a posse of professors, consultants, college fellows and senior registrars, who would soon become our mentors, lecturers and tutors. They would teach us the clinical skills to examine patients in the surgical and medical disciplines that incorporated their specialties' relevant ills and afflictions.

We filed out of the theatre behind them and arranged ourselves outside on three tiers of benches for the Annual clinical school Photograph, with tutors at the front and we students surrounding them.

Eaden Lilley photographs are a very great tradition at Cambridge. This photographic company had for generations recorded the achievements of new undergraduates in their year groups and in their glory at Cambridge University.

In the centre was the, *Regius Professor of Physic* who was also the Vice-Chancellor of Cambridge University. He was the most powerful man in the university, second only to royalty and was the Queen's personal physician.

In this company, there was none of the joviality of our earlier undergraduate pre-clinical photographs, I'd experienced at University College London. No-one dared to run round the back from one end to the other, appearing at both ends of the picture.

The writing was on the wall and we had just been welcomed and initiated into the sub-club of 'almost doctors'. We were sedate, like athletes waiting for the starting gun to launch us into action! The wide-angled panoramic lenses were clicked open and photos were duly taken, fulfilling family expectations and providing me with the evidence that I'd made it into Cambridge University's Faculty of Clinical Medicine.

2

Straight after that, we broke for coffee and I went to seek out the men who had come up from our pre-clinical studies at UCL. The place was a melée of students gathering around various clinical tutors. The Cambridge students already seemed aware to which tutor they'd been allocated and everywhere small groups of them were already encircling their Masters for the next 18 months, with introductions all round.

I was pleased to see Paulos, a Greek Cypriot research scientist and a good friend from the London pre-clinical course and with whom I had planned to share my college flat in Cambridge. He was happily holding court with three of the other London graduates. Paulos, had already achieved a PhD prior to studying medicine. We discovered that he'd actually had to re-sit our pre-clinical 2nd MB finals during the summer holidays to be eligible to get onto the clinical course here. I was relieved to see he was here, having passed the exams and made it over the hurdles.

I joined them quickly and asked how he'd got on with the re-sits, but to my surprise, he didn't actually know. The results were published that morning and he hadn't yet rung up to find out how he'd done. He said that if he failed, then at least, he would have the photograph to remind him of his only day as a clinical medical student.

The five of us made our way to the notice board to seek out our academic groups and discovered we'd been split up. We agreed to meet for lunch, keen to find out if Paulos was here to stay. We wished each other luck and went on our merry ways to meet our tutors.

My tutor was Dr Stephen Walker, a Medical Senior Registrar in Dermatology; so, I was to learn how to examine clinical systems on patients with skin conditions. Oh hell, I thought, all those horrible sticky diseases!

Dr Walker was a handsome man in his mid-thirties and an expert in the use of lasers for treating skin nasties. I was to learn a great deal from this man. He rapidly replaced my horror of the potential disfigurements caused by skin diseases, with an intense interest in and respect for the largest of the body's organs. He showed us how the skin helpfully displayed many outward signs of systemic diseases inside the body, providing us with useful and subtle clues to the range of pathologies beneath.

He spoke.

"Good morning everyone, I'm Steve Walker and I'm your clinical tutor. With my help you will learn how to examine patients. You will become able to apply all those medical sciences you've been acquiring for the last two years of pre-clinical medicine that led to the 2nd M.B. examination, which you have all just passed at your various universities."

I thought of Paulos, who might not be in that happy position.

"The principles of physical examination that you will acquire here, will become ingrained in your head and become second nature to you. From now on, wherever you are, you will see people and think to yourself that person over there has a certain illness or another and if you pay very careful attention here, you may be able to get the diagnosis right. You will carry this with you for the rest of your life. So let's get on with it."

"Pass round this box and take one blue book each. This is your own personal guide to clinical examination, provided free to you by the clinical school. It fits into the pockets of your white coat, which you can collect from that rack over there. Also please find your blue name badges on the table behind you and pin them on your left lapel. You will wear these white coats when you attend patients on the wards.

"Please change the coats weekly at the hospital laundry in the lower floor. You are no longer scruffy university undergraduates; in 18 months you will be doctors, so you must look the part. These coats and light blue badges identify you as clinical medical students and without them you will not be allowed on the wards to attend and clerk patients."

"Please remember to be exceedingly polite to the ward staff, especially the staff nurses, the ones with the big hats, and more especially to the ward sisters, in the dark navy blue tunics. Both of these persons can make your student life and your life as a junior doctor, hell on earth. So don't upset them, be nice to them, but not too nice, because all nurses want to marry a rich doctor, so be aware and very careful with them."

We donned our nearly doctors' uniforms and sat in front of our tutor, who passed round a box of stethoscopes with one for each of us. We all pushed in our ear bits, making us feel even more like doctors.

Dr Walker interrupted, "This is to listen to different bits of the human body, not just the chest, but the heart and all sorts of lumps, bumps and other interesting bits and pieces."

"Before you listen with these, pay attention. You will always look first and hard. Notice as much as you can before you touch anybody. You will be privileged to be allowed to touch people but always remember; 'Eyes first and most, Hands last and least!'"

"Well, actually, almost last. First, we look to 'Observe' as much as possible. You will learn that the way a person appears displays a great deal about their health and their diseases."

"Then we touch and feel very carefully for any lumps and bumps that might present themselves. This is 'Palpation' and patients feel reassured when we do this to the relevant part they're complaining about.

"Then we tap on the relevant area. This is called 'Percussion', and it can tell us if the part is full of air, full of fluid or even solid. If we think it's full of fluid, we press it to see if it's soft and fluctuant and whether it spreads out in every direction as we press it; then we shine a torch on it to see if it's full of fluid and the light passes through it. Finally, we listen with the stethoscope. This is 'Auscultation' and can tell us all sorts of things, which you're going to find out over the next few weeks."

He pointed out the bell and the diaphragm parts of the stethoscope.

"These are for listening to sounds of different frequencies, mainly relevant to listening to the heart's valve sounds and other flow abnormalities. You will always examine patients in this order."

We were keen to practise listening but Dr Walker continued, "Before you examine a patient you need to question them, listen to their answers and write them down in their patient notes. Patients like to see the doctor show interest in their problems. This is called 'Clerking the patient' and involves taking a history from them of their presenting complaint, its duration, its effects, as well as their other relevant histories, including their previous medical history, their family histories, work history, drug history and age. This gives us the information we will need to help diagnose and treat them."

"Right then, you've heard enough from me now. I suggest we adjourn for a lunch break and during it, I'd like you all to read the first two chapters of your blue clinical school book. As doctors, you must always make sure that you break for food so that you have fuel inside to run your human machine. Afterwards, we will meet up on Ward 8 South, at 1500, where we will try to put into practice your first day of clinical medicine. Remember to put on your white coats and badges or you won't be allowed on the wards."

We were totally gripped by this man and excited by his warm and confident aspirations for us who were his clinical group and couldn't wait to actually lay 'hands on' a real patient and put all that pre-clinical stuff into practice.

My pulse was racing as I hurried to catch up with my fellow London grads in the clinical school Student Union bar. I'd forgotten that poor Paulos was yet to discover whether he'd actually passed his 2nd MB and made it to the course at Cambridge. I found him in the bar, looking euphoric and loudly giving court to our pals. We were all elated and I was mightily relieved to discover he had indeed passed and we were both about to embark on this second and rapid 18 month clinical part of our way to become doctors.

3

Near the appointed time, I gathered with the rest of my clinical group at the bottom of the main Addenbrookes Hospital lift/stairs.

Dr Walker rapidly approached us saying, "Come on then you lot, up the stairs. A most important attribute of a doctor is stamina!"

He led the charge up the 8 flights of stairs and onto the ward. As we filed in puffing behind him, he asked, "What's another important attribute of a doctor?"

"Empathy!" called out one of the girls in the group.

"That's right," he reassured us, "and also, but possibly more important, you will all need a very good memory, just to retain and recall the amount of knowledge necessary to practise medicine. I've always found it useful to make up lists, but there are also many simple ways to remember, such as acronyms/reminders to help you deal with the vast amount there is to learn. You can make a note of these as we meet them over the next few months."

Still puffing, I thought to myself, well the first thing on my list is to start working on my stamina! He waited for stragglers at the top of the stairs and we flocked onto the ward behind him like disciples, which we actually were.

As we trailed along the ward bays, we attracted the attention of the nurses working away with their light blue pinstriped tunics, black stockings and high pointed hats.

I sensed they were thinking, "Not another bunch of nuisance students!"

In their eyes, we probably had less status than the 'laboratory rat', but we had to ingratiate ourselves with them to be in a position to access patients and learn the rudiments of clinical medicine; not to mention any other benefits their un-popping uniforms might reveal inside.

Progressing down the ward, there were six bays with curtains pulled around the beds. Dr Walker reminded us that patients were our respected allies in the diagnosis and treatment of their diseases. We must nurture the special privileged and professional relationship that we have between us. He called out our names allocating us each to the bays and we approached them with trepidation.

All of us were trying desperately to remember the order of the various headings for clerking and the questions with which we had to probe the patients, for the relevant details of their conditions. I guessed that we were very anxious about what terrible and hideous skin diseases were about to be revealed to us.

With a deep breath I pulled aside my allocated cubicle curtain and stepped inside. There before me was not some hideous pathological monster, but a tall slender blond and exquisitely beautiful young woman dressed entirely in an NHS dressing gown. I gasped and swallowed with my tongue stuck dryly to the roof of my mouth from the adrenaline pumping through my veins. I'd really like to probe her, I thought to myself.

Now, there I was, an ordinary working class bloke and not some 'Effeminate type', featured frequently by the BBC or Channel 4, thrust anxiously in among these predominantly upper middle class, highly academic Oxbridge students. What could I do, but stare in admiration at this paragon, with both eyes popping out of my head and my jaw wide open.

"Hello," she said with a smile that would melt the anger of an avenging angel, "I'm Sally Rawlings, I gather you'd like to ask me some questions."

"Yes," I blurted out, "I would!"

"Where do you want me?" she retorted.

'If only I could tell her,' flashed across my mind with almost simultaneous images of a sadly disappointed Dean Hawkins rapidly focusing my mind back onto the task in hand.

I swallowed to unstick my tongue and blurted out, "Could you please tell me what brings a girl like you to a place like this today, I mean to the hospital today?"

"Well, I have psoriasis."

I'd never heard of psoriasis. It couldn't be a very serious skin disease and I couldn't take my eyes off her as she looked entirely perfect to me.

I fumbled my way on; trying to remember all the other questions I was supposed to ask her about her name, address, her date of birth, her marital status and occupation.

She told me that she was a twenty-six year old, unmarried actress and an understudy for another very famous actress, who was appearing in a West End play.

She was her double, if not even more beautiful! She lived quite nearby, close to the Cambridge Railway Station.

Eventually, having completed taking her medical history, rapidly noting her replies, I finished and sat there just looking at her.

"Well?" she asked after what seemed like an age.

"Well what?" I stammered.

"Well, aren't you going to examine me?" she replied.

"Yes, yes of course!" I quickly exclaimed raising my arm to usher her towards the couch.

She rose gracefully, gently separated her gown, allowing it to fall superfluously to the floor, revealing the perfect body of the Venus Di Milo, except Sally had both arms! The dean didn't exaggerate when he said we were privileged. There was a noticeable pause and she smiled as she caught me staring at her perfect and curvaceous figure. I swallowed repeatedly as I followed her towards the examination bed, which she mounted in one fluent movement.

"Am I all right like this?"

My mind was racing trying to keep up with my heart which was pounding in my chest and doing a hundred-metre sprint.

"Yes, you're perfect just as you are?" I hoped that she appreciated my double entendre.

She showed me that she had very small plaques of skin thickening on the backs of her elbows, which she said, was a classic sign of psoriasis, but they were miniscule on her otherwise consummate body.

I asked if she minded if I examined some other parts of her and my hands shook as I lifted her left breast and placed my stethoscope on her chest. She gasped as it touched the skin over her heart. I looked at her as I listened to her heart and chest revelling in my tutor's advice of 'eyes first and most and hands last and least!'

She was exquisite, as we caught and held each other's gaze, I forgot what I was there to do. I suddenly thought I must be taking ages to deal with what I thought was in her case, a fairly trivial condition. I thanked her sincerely for letting me examine her and she said that she thought I'd done it very well. I circled her phone number in her clinical notes in front of her and she noticed.

"May I give you a call, just to check up on your treatment, you understand?" I hurriedly chanced.

"Yes, you may. I'll look forward to it," she said reassuringly.

With that, I left through the curtain blinds and retreated more confidently out of her cubicle, like the cat who got the cream! I was the last to return to my tutor, where my fellow clinical students were already presenting our cases. I thought to myself, 'Time really does fly when you're enjoying yourself!'

On my turn, I presented my patient to Dr Walker, in front of the other students in my group, with an inner glee that was obvious to everyone.

I commenced, "My patient is 26 year old Sally Rawlings, who is an actress complaining of some areas of thickening of her skin." I confidently went through the history and examination, thinking I had this one sown up, but my glee was to end abruptly with Dr. Walker's comment.

"Is that it?"

"What else did you find?"

"That's all she had," I retorted.

"Anyone want to tell him?" my tutor replied.

All of the Cambridge graduates there put up their hands bursting to tell me what I'd missed. One of them was waving both his hands at me from behind Steve.

"Her hands?" Steve exclaimed.

My lovely patient was there, chosen to see if I could be distracted and I was. I missed her fingernails which also showed another sign of her psoriasis, with some slight lifting and flaking.

'Onycholysis', a classic sign of Psoriaisis, and I'd missed it! I was so distracted by the rest of her perfect anatomy, I'd sadly neglected part of the instructions on the 1st page of our blue clinical clerking book and looked a complete amateur in front of the others. Bugger that, I won't let that happen again, I'll make sure I look at everything, with my eyes first and most!

We medics spent the rest of the afternoon and the following day working through the rest of the volunteer patient 'Guinea Pigs', history taking and examining with a view to seeking all the clues that were there for the finding.

Steve Walker told us not to collaborate, but of course we did. After all, treating patients is all about multi-disciplinary team work!

During those two days, I looked out for and spotted Sally Rawlings on a number of occasions and couldn't get her out of my mind. I was happy to see her return my gaze. I called her on the second evening and we arranged to meet the following Friday, her night off. The date was for a Chinese meal at the local restaurant in Mill Road, which was close by her house.

She was delightful, totally fun-loving, vivacious and confident in conversion and perfect in her movements, where she seemed to float across the ground. Perfect that was, except for using chop sticks, where her adroitness left her bereft. The chop sticks beat her but happily gave me the opportunity to rescue and surreptitiously touch her, but this time in a social way, not confined by my early attempts at professionalism.

As I held her hands on the sticks, she managed to pick up a piece of tea-smoked chicken but dropped it before reaching her mouth. She turned up towards me, laughing and I couldn't stop myself from closing in on her fabulous mouth with a longing and all-consuming kiss, which she returned like for like.

We didn't stay for desserts, she insisted on paying the bill and we raced back to my college flat and left a trail of clothes from the front door all the way into the bedroom. We christened the bed till the early hours and then again a short while after as she stroked my body, re-arousing my hunger for her.

She had a perfect physique, in perfect proportions. Her succulent breasts stood to attention as I salivated over them, round and round with my tongue as she sighed in responsiveness. Despite the substantial Chinese meal, she was ravenous and fully indulged her desires and my appetites, leaving the *Kama Sutra* in a poor second place for imagination; until we finally lay together in a sublime exhaustion. Stamina, I thought, mine wasn't too bad after all!

We awoke late, made love again, just to reassure ourselves that the night before hadn't just been the occasion. I didn't want to drag myself away but she'd already run off to make coffee, over which she confessed that her commitment to acting had left her with little time for a serious and long-term relationship and that she hadn't tasted any passion for some time. This puzzled me because she seemed to be exceedingly good at it but it also somewhat suited me with my as yet unknown, clinical student workload.

We parted agreeing to call and meet up when her desires and her next London theatre leave coincided with my freedom from clinical school studies. I felt a bit disappointed that she was almost a touch 'matter of fact' and slightly pragmatic about our parting, because she was absolutely gorgeous. My heart wanted more of her, but my head said enough and she seemed resolute in her commitments to acting. So, I was happy that our love-making had cleared my head from any such distractions and enabled me to concentrate on my clinical work to come.

4

Following our first two days of introduction to Clerking and Clinical Examinations, Dr Walker demonstrated patient examinations of the various human anatomical and physiological systems and then made us practise on each other, including the art of phlebotomy (blood-letting from the Greek Phlebos-vein and tome-incise/cut), to obtain blood specimens for pathological analysis.

In the afternoons, we would attend the wards with him to review his dermatology patients. We rapidly learned how patients with certain skin conditions were often afflicted with diseases of other systems like the nervous system, the musculo-skeletal system, the endocrine glands or of the red blood filled mucosa that lined the passage ways throughout the body.

There was some evidence that these diseases were caused by patients' own immune system, where our own body defender cells had somehow been directed against ourselves, to destroy our own healthy cells by mistake. In particular, it was shown that the patient's B and T lymphocytes were those defender cells that had been turned to attack the patient's own body.

In many cases, these 'Autoimmune' Diseases(1) were more common in certain populations, in fair or red haired and fair-skinned people with light complexions and blue, green or grey coloured eyes as well as being more common in women. I thought these factors certainly applied to some extent to the beautiful blond Sally Rawlings.

It had also been noted that in some cases of fair-skinned identical twins, who were genetically the same, but where only one of them had an autoimmune disease; it must be that some external agent, encountered in the environment, by the twin with the illness, had caused them to develop the autoimmunity, but the other non-encountering twin didn't.

It was also thought that the external agent (possibly a bacterium, a virus, a drug or even a type of food, but more probably a virus), may have reacted with certain inheritable cell membrane markers to prompt the immune cells to attack various parts of their own body.

It occurred to me that if the megalomaniac Adolf Hitler had known this, he might not have pursued his perverse idea of a pure Aryan race. He'd obviously never heard of the evolutionary benefits of "Hybrid Vigour". It was discovered with the onset transplant surgery that these cell membrane markers were a means of identifying cells as being our own and not foreign to us. They have become known as tissue type markers.

These were early days in the discovery of autoimmune diseases and over the next thirty years, over eighty different types of such disorders were discovered, affecting our tissues including, endocrine glands, such as the Thyroid and Pancreas, our skin, our joints, our muscles, our nerves, blood cells and their vessels, our reproductive cells and our connective tissues (which hold our bodies together).

I thought the dean was right. These were busy times in medicine and with so much research work being done here in Cambridge, we were again highly privileged to witness it and hopefully become part of it. Yet much more research needed to be done to find answers to the questions posed by these diseases.

I thought there's much more to this dermatology business than just sticky and itchy rashes.

The pace of work at the clinical school was hectic, 09.00 to 18.00 was a usual day, with a snatched lunch, if you were lucky; but days were often earlier and later and as we were to discover, including weekends and holidays. The long summer breaks enjoyed by other university students didn't apply to us on our shorter accelerated course. We had a two week summer break and had to work most weekends.

I was surprised at the end of the first day when I drifted towards the student union bar to discover that all the new medics there were graduates from other outside universities. I learned later that all of the Cambridge students had gone home to work. They may have known something we didn't.

They clearly knew how tough it was going to be and didn't want to waste their time socialising and drinking beer. Still, we second M.B. graduates from other universities were happy to be there and celebrated in the usual medical student way, in the bar!

We were very lucky in having Dr Walker as a tutor as he gently corrected our failings, when we made glaring mistakes and reinforced our successes, when we did well. Our first month of the acquisition of clinical skills very quickly passed and we had rapidly become very confident in the examination of the various systems and the instruments we used to test them.

After the first six weeks, we were again split up, away from our clinical tutor and allocated to consultants in various specialties. I was delighted to be allocated to General Surgery, which I always thought of and pictured to be my medical career's raison d'être.

We were told to report to main operating theatres at 08.00 the following morning, where we changed into scrubs, to assist in the morning operations list and meet our surgery tutor, who would introduce us to the literally sharp end of medicine. We turned up brimming with enthusiasm for surgery and were greeted by a very tall, very fit and exuberant Liverpudlian Senior Registrar called Mr. Rafftery.

He seemed to know everything about the discipline of surgery and made us want to learn more by his infectious enthusiasm. He introduced himself cheerfully and drew our attention to the very important difference between surgeons and physicians. He emphasised how surgeons could stop diseases in their tracks, cut out a tumour or other noxious malady and reverse the course of deadly diseases by their dexterous surgical interventions.

He stressed that when doctors first qualify, they are called 'Doctor', but when they see the light and work very hard to qualify as a surgeon, they can then be called 'Mr' again. He pointed out that in earlier times, the village surgeon was also the village barber and that was why they were called Barber Surgeons and have a spiralling red and white pole outside their shops, representing the former bloody aspect of their profession.

He continued, "Physicians know a great deal about disease, but are too hesitant and slow to try anything for their patients, whereas, we surgeons may not know as much about disease, but we charge in and operate on anything and anyone at any time. We never let the sun set on pus. We drain it as soon as possible!"

I knew that this 'devil may care' attitude certainly wasn't the real case with Mr. Rafftery. He was a bright, sensitive, cordial and perceptive person, who drew information from we 'new apprentices', without the over-bearing pomposity of the prototype 'Carry on Doctor' surgeon in the form of the 'Lancelot Spratts' of this world.

He was universally popular and we students queued up for his theatre lists and jovial ward rounds. He truly reinforced my desire to become a surgeon.

Through this man and by the end of our surgical attachment, we 'newbies' had settled down into the routine and hectic life of a clinical medical student. We'd covered miles every day, running between the Addenbrookes 10th floor surgical wards, operating theatres and tutorials back in the clinical school.

Not to mention the monthly 'collegiate soirees', gowned up for post-graduate dinners in our various colleges. These were quite sumptuous evenings where we met with the postgrads from other subjects, in our college graduate middle common room, consumed lots of port and then paraded behind the senior tutor, in graduate gowns and a column of twos across the old court into our ancient graduate dining room. This delighted the tourists who took copious photographs of we privileged academic few.

I met my college tutor once a month and enthused clamorously about surgery over a large glass of claret in his study. I told him about my enthusiasm and he suggested that I apply for a scholarship at the Royal College of Surgeons. He was a neuro-anatomist and a former army surgeon. I took his wise advice and applied. Quite soon after and following a few anatomical examinations and searching interviews, I became a scholar at the Royal College of Surgeons, which included four yearly payments as a student and a fifth payment, provided I passed the membership examinations to join the Royal College of Surgeons of England. I was so proud, thinking I was on my way to become a surgeon, not realising how gruelling the training was to be.

During our attachments, we had also been exposed for the first time to have close dealings with a group of other professionals called 'nurses'. They were dressed in their crisply starched uniforms, with silver buckles denoting their training hospital and dress colours that denoted their rank and high-winged Addenbrookes' hats. They tended to the patients, alleviating their illnesses. We had been told to be nice to them and carefully aware of them.

We had especially learned to be nice to the ward sisters and staff nurses. These creatures could make the difference to our ward attachments by pointing out interesting cases and procedures, facilitating our experiences as well as our contacts with patients, by occasionally acting as 'chaparones'. Through this means, we could clerk and examine patients for the next daily ward round, where consultants and senior registrars would grill us about them, weeding out our knowledge of their condition and its management.

While being nice to some staff nurses and complimenting them on their high-winged hats, my flat mate and I were invited to go for a swim in the pool at the hospital social club. We politely accepted and that evening, we met up in the pool. We were shocked when a flock of five of them evolved from the changing rooms at the allotted time.

I said to myself, *Blimey,* those straight and starched uniforms really covered up their curvy bits.

They looked much better in their cosies! We mingled much less formally in the relaxed climate of the pool and the social club bar afterwards. After a few beverages, it was suggested that we might like to join them for a coffee back at Granchester House, the nurse's home, where they rested their weary heads. How could we refuse?

As we ascended the lift to the 8th floor, I manoeuvred my way next to Staff Nurse Susan Griggs, whom I'd been admiring at a distance for the previous days on the surgical wards. Whenever she had caught me staring at her, she reciprocated with the warmest smiles, melting my surgical resolve and hardening my anatomical extremities.

That evening, in the pool, we had both glanced more intensely, occasionally brushing against each other in our feigned indifference. This was making the blood course through my veins and my heart race faster, supporting those expanding extremities. She was lovely, warm, well-built and a vivacious brunette with a broad smile, a haughty laugh and huge and inviting brown eyes. I was melting.

We arrived at the Nursing Home 8th floor and three of the girls split off to their own flats, leaving me and Paulos with Sue and her flat mate Debbie. She was a tall slim blond divorcee in her late twenties. Paulos and she were already on good terms, laughing at their own shared individual conversation between them.

I thought to myself, 'It's remarkable how fate sometimes intervenes to make things happen!'

As we moved into the flat's hallway, she and Paulos were already displaying some of Desmond Morris' naked-ape-ritual-mating behaviours as they peeled off into her bedroom on the right of the hallway.

I said almost in a whisper, "Well, that seems to leave only us."

Susan laughed and said, "Do you really want a coffee?"

"Later," I whispered as she moved in so close that I could feel her chest heaving and her ravenous mouth closing in on mine to suck on my tongue, like a mega-watt vacuum cleaner!

The next moment, she retreated, pulling my arms forwards into her room and glided us towards her bed in the corner. She closed the door behind us with her toe.

God bless the NHS, I thought, nurses certainly know a lot about anatomy and physiology, as I pressed myself into her and she felt my ardour against her belly.

She retreated a bit, pulling off her sweater, revealing her voluptuous naked breasts heaving rapidly. She came back reaching for my belt buckle and breaking open the top of my jeans, she wrenched out my manhood in all its engorged glory. She knelt before me and almost swallowed the phallus in one gulp, sucking and rubbing it towards explosion.

I thought I was about to burst when she stopped and unzipping her skirt, pulled me down on top of her fabulous body. I pushed her thong to one side as I sunk into her, right up to our pubic symphyses. She was hot, wet and wonderful, wriggling like an eel, caught on a giant fishing hook, her moans becoming louder and more frantic as our thrusting coalesced into a mutual frenzied orgasm, with me pumping her full of life's fluid and her body gyrating in spasms.

My God she was fantastic, grinning like a Cheshire cat, she held me clamped tightly between her thighs and I didn't want to move, replete in my desires and empty of semen. I thought, "working on the Addenbrookes 10th floor must have done wonders for her stamina as well".

I fell asleep in situ to be awakened by the sunrise and her kissing my face, neck and other erogenous areas.

I felt myself stand up to be counted and again I pumped her pelvis as if that morning was my last one on earth.

She gave me as good as she got, as we fell apart minutes later, exhausted and utterly replete.

It was 05.30 and we could hear alarm clocks rousing her colleagues. It was time for me to go, before their hall of residence burst into life with the stampede of nurses rushing to change-overs on their wards, where they caught up with developments overnight. I needed to be out before the stairways filled with them cutting off my discreet retreat.

I reached my flat in 15 minutes and discovered that Paulos had left Granchester House about an hour after we arrived. I did wonder what had happened and guessed he'd brief me later.

Nurses had to be on duty at 07.00 and we medics attached to surgery at 08.00, so we all had to move, which I did with a warm feeling in my head, my heart and more especially, in my loins!

At 08.00, I walked on to ward 10 South, greeted my fellow medics and bid "good morning" to the nurses in general and Susan in particular! She and I both had a rosy post coital flush! My colleagues had no inkling of our secret and I hoped they wouldn't notice. I wondered whether her juices were still running and lubricating her movements round the ward. I pitied some of the medics who were busy flirting with her. They had no idea what we were both looking so pleased about!

They might have guessed something was going on when the nurses started including, we medics in their tea break, but they failed to spot the casual glances and extended eye contact between staff nurse, Griggs and I.

We knew we had to be careful. There was a 11 o'clock curfew for males in Granchester House and an ancient deputy matron living on the same 8th floor, who'd bypassed sexuality many years earlier and was intent on catching her nurses with males after hours. She professed that this was to dampen their ardour and refocus their minds on nursing. We knew it was just rancour!

I had already just escaped her one morning, as I was leaving Susan late and waiting for the lift, I heard the matron approaching on her broomstick. In one instant, I leapt through the fire escape door and sprinted down the stairs to be out of the building before her flight landed.

I wondered how long our luck would last, when Sue announced that her mum and dad, who lived nearby, were going away for a break and we could go there and be alone, without any disturbances. So, there we went, for a night of unbridled passion without flat mates, matrons or early alarm calls.

What she didn't quite mention was that her dad was a senior officer in the Royal Air Force and lived on a nearby airbase, still in for a penny! Next evening, I found myself being driven through the security gatepost at an RAF station just outside of Huntingdon. She drove round the base, parked in front of a block of large detached houses and we entered her parents' home. I was very nervous, but she was completely relaxed, no doubt very much at home.

She said, "Help yourself to a drink" and left me alone in the living room.

I poured out a large vintage port, which was the only drink I recognised of the large multi-coloured selection in the cabinet. I was half way down it when she came back into the room in black lace underwear, displaying her curvy contours. She looked fabulous.

I couldn't do anything else but stand to attention and salute her in the most appropriate manner. She laughed out loud unzipped my flies and taking hold of me by my rigid salute, led me off to the bedroom.

She was totally uninhibited, wild with enthusiasm, louder than just loud, utterly released and hollering like a cayote. Hell, I thought someone might call out the guard, call out our fighter command or launch our nuclear deterrent! Certainly, her neighbours must be thinking, 'Young Susan seems to have grown up a lot'.

We collapsed into rhythmical orgasm as our parasympathetic nervous systems gave way to their sympathetic colleagues, leaving our genitalia floundering in our elaborated juices; each of us exhausted in the other's arms.

I dropped into a deep sleep, to be roused not long after, by Susan, in a panic mode.

"Wake up, wake up," she uttered, shaking me back to life and rushing to the window.

"It's my parents," she gasped, "I thought they weren't back till the weekend. You'd better go quickly; my dad won't like this. He thinks I'm pure and a virgin. He wants me to marry one of his flight lieutenants."

She gathered up my clothes and handed them to me as I raced towards the stairs. I exited the back door as her parents came in the front. I stopped to hurriedly put on my pants in the freezing cold and dressed in the back garden, thinking, 'Even Matron was better than this. How am I going to get out of here and what will happen if I'm brought back to the clinical school in handcuffs by RAF MPs?'

'Don't panic', I thought. I figured I wouldn't risk walking out through the base front security gates, in case they challenged me. I decided to stay close to the houses, out of the street lights and made my way to the perimeter, where maybe I could climb the fence.

Happily, it was a dark and moonless cloudy Autumn night. I climbed the eight foot perimeter fence and dropped over, landing softly on the muddy roadside grass, but with a long walk back to Cambridge. I hitched a lift and an hour later was recuperating in a hot bath back in my college flat.

I was lying there comfortably, savouring every exciting moment of the evening, when Paulos burst forth through the front door with Susan's flat mate, Debbie. They were laughing loudly and clearly exuberant. I called out and they fell silent. Paulos poked his head round the bathroom door.

"I didn't think you'd be here," he almost grouched.

I apologised and said, "I didn't think so either, don't worry, I won't disturb you, just pretend I'm not here."

They did and kept me awake all night pretending!

5

That brief ecstatic hectic evening was the end of my loving relationship with Staff Nurse Griggs, though I did sincerely hope that our paths might cross again later. My surgical attachment ended shortly afterwards and I'm glad to say I anticipated my examiners questions in our end of course assessment and achieved a pass with flying colours, despite the absolutely delightful distractions.

Susan feigned illness to her parents and had to stay at home until she 'recovered'. I wondered if they found the half glass of port I left in the living room that night. Maybe Susan knocked it back to rapidly sooth her sudden panic.

Michaelmas term at Cambridge was coming to a close and we students retreated to the clinical school to enjoy the Christmas Graduation Ball, for the leaving students in the year above, which I happily attended with a group of my fellow medics.

We went back up to university for the Lent term in the new year, refreshed and eager to continue with our clinical training. After a week of clinical examination revision with Dr Walker, we separated again off to our new attachments in various specialties, absorbing all the relevant skills for each. This was an intense period of study and clinical practice that would hone our skills in patient examination.

My next attachment in Respiratory medicine, was on a cancer ward, where we saw lots of lung cancer patients, all of whom had been smokers. We listened to their obstructed, wheezy and phlegmy rattling chests. We watched the specialist physiotherapists patting their backs into coughing up wads of thick green often blood stained phlegm and saw their chests being drained, by Senior House Physicians.

We learned that you have to wait a while to make sure the local anaesthetic had worked. Then you can cut through the skin, cut through the intercostal 'spare rib' muscles and reach the pleural membranes underneath. Pleural membranes are in a double layer and surround the balloon-like lungs.

In lung cancer, they can be invaded by cancer cells and fill up with fluid, leaked from damaged blood vessels. The fluid presses against the lungs, preventing them expanding with air, so they have to be penetrated to insert the tubes to facilitate drainage and enable the lungs they surround, to inflate.

The weak and cachexic skeletal patients were in enough pain from the metastatic spread of their cancer, without inflicting any more pain by rushing to cut them open! Draining the pleural cavity gave them a few more days of relief without the severe shortness of breath, just before they all died.

The medical profession in general wondered why our usually patriarchal government was doing so little to intervene in the slaughter of these patients. The general medical opinion was that smoking raised lots of taxes and mainly knocked off the older smoking and ill-informed low achieving classes. The huge revenue from taxes and massive savings from lower pension payments didn't motivate the government's intervention to reverse this.

We were quite sure the government would deny this. I took some comfort at the thought that Sir Walter Raleigh, the Tudor Privateer, who brought tobacco back to England from the American Indians, eventually had his head chopped off.

After this medical attachment, we all embarked on a two-week intensive course of pathology (2) lectures, in which we had seven lots of one hour long lectures a day with a five minute break between them and half hour break for lunch.

Cambridge pathology is a very intensive course and a very difficult examination in finals, alleged to be more difficult than the actual Membership of the Royal College of Pathologists Examination, which is the qualifying examination to become a Consultant Pathologist. It is also said that Pathologists know everything about medicine but all the patients are dead before they see them so it's too late to use their knowledge to do anything to help them!

On the first morning, at the beginning of the first lecture, on urine testing, the consultant lecturer asked us all to take a sample bottle and pee in it. On our return he was extolling the diagnostic virtues of urine, in providing us with insight into many diseases. He held up his specimen, commenting how the colour, bouquet and taste demonstrated information about dehydration and with that, he dipped in a finger and licked it, bidding us to follow suit.

Many of us naively complied with his example, at which point, he preached that pathology was about the study and observation of disease processes and had we observed him carefully we would have noticed that he had licked a different finger to the one he dipped into his sample!

After the first week, it had become apparent to some of we ex-London University Medics that a particular group of Cambridge students, who were not only very bright but were also very arrogant, had volunteered lots of answers and proffered loads of questions, throughout the whole of the first week, unnecessarily prolonging our lectures. It was decided between us to test whether their sense of humour matched their arrogance.

Forged letters, from the dean, were typed on his headed note paper. These letters were sent to the most arrogant students, requesting them, for relevant research purposes, to collect their early morning urine samples, each day for a week and for them to deliver the correctly labelled bottles to a box outside the dean's office on the fifth day, Friday.

This, they proudly undertook, eager to obey the dean. However, on Friday, faced with dozens of bottles of urine, for no particular reason, the dean realised it was a prank.

The medics left the dean's office with their academic feathers ruffled, becoming even more furious when the pranksters pinned a message to the notice board saying, "Happy April Fool's day, we've been taking the piss!"

The medical student's union immediately put out a public reward for information leading to the identity of the perpetrators; who happily, were never apprehended! No-one ever found out how the dean's headed note paper was obtained.

Throughout the whole year, the different tutorial groups from our intake, were sequentially attached to various pathology consultants. Following the intense pathology lecture series, it was our group's turn to have this experience. I was attached to Professor Morris Greenish, who was the Professor of Pathology himself and a top Home Office Pathologist to boot. He was a great man and a brilliant teacher and I learned a great deal about the study of disease from him.

One day, he was undertaking a post mortem examination and I was assisting him. He had been demonstrating lots of pathological signs in the previous few days and I was quite keen to learn from this wonderful and highly distinguished man. The deceased on this occasion was a poor woman who had committed suicide by throwing herself into the river Cam in early January. The river had then become frozen until it thawed out, just a few days before, when she floated to the surface and was brought to the Addenbrookes' Mortuary.

As the Prof was working away removing organs as part of the process of finding the cause of her death, he removed the spleen and holding it up he asked, "What do you think we will find in there, my boy?"

Jovially, I replied, "Sticklebacks sir!" in response to which, he threw it at me!

Apart from that minor sticky incident, I enjoyed my attachment in this discipline immensely. I learned a great deal about disease. I liked very much and got on very well with the good professor. I didn't know it at the time, but later on in my career I was to enlist his expertise to put right an injustice to a good friend of mine.

My next student sojourn was in the Addenbrookes Casualty (Accident and Emergency) Department, where we were following a very enthusiastic, and highly informed Senior House Officer (SHO), called Roger, who was also a Cambridge 2nd year post-graduate and an alumnus (former student), of my college.

We followed him around the department watching him deal with the everyday lacerations, fractures, bruises and many other, usually trivial, illnesses and injuries that the majority of the public felt warranted a free attendance in the Emergency Department, although very few were really emergencies.

Suddenly, a multicar road traffic accident was announced over the tannoy system and Roger and his colleagues moved into the admitting area enthusiastically but calmly awaiting arrival of the casualties.

Our man took delivery of a patient, who had struck another car at high speed and had been projected through his front windscreen, sustaining multiple quite extensive lacerations to his face, scalp, neck, chest and arms.

The doctor took a rapid history from the conscious patient of what were fairly apparent and obvious injuries, briefly examined him and started injecting his multiple lacerations with lignocaine local anaesthesia.

He dutifully explained to us students the dangers of local anaesthesia whether mixed or unmixed with adrenaline and the high risk of cardiac arrest by lignocaine over-dosage.

As he did so and almost on cue, the patient suddenly collapsed before us. Roger, who was of West African origin, visibly pallored and looking worse than the dead patient, pressed the cardiac arrest crash bell. Within 30 seconds, we were surrounded by a large group of physicians, who set about resuscitating the poor patient.

We medics stood back and let the doctors do their thing. We were impressed by the professional and disciplined way the on-call team dealt with the situation. The medical registrar directing events in a resolute manner, clearly issued instructions for drug infusions to the rest of the team, culminating in an 'all clear' command/question followed immediately by a 300 joule defibrillator shock to the patient's chest.

Happily, the patient's heart restarted and with some assistance, settled down into the normal steady and regular so-called 'sinus rhythm', with the patient waking up moments later.

We were highly impressed to witness that at one second the patient was alive and talking, a second later he was dead and a few minutes after that he was back among us, asking us what had suddenly happened and saying that he could hear us talking throughout this terrifying experience.

I thought this was actually what A & E or Casualty was really about, with skilled physicians and surgeons, often resuscitating dead people arriving in ambulances. I noticed this was very common among unfit middle-aged men, often brought in dead from golf courses, where they went from being sedentary office workers, all week to suddenly undertaking 18 holes of golf, when they should really have stuck to the 9 hole course.

Some medical staff had become slightly cynical about the choices made by the public in their sporting activities at the weekends. The results of which ranged from sudden deaths in seriously overweight golfers, to trivial time-consuming injuries in large numbers of seemingly sensible adult men, commonly those playing in amateur soccer matches.

Every time they came in, the doctors would say, "Why don't you play a sensible game like snooker where you won't injure yourself?"

This became the norm for many occasions, until one day, the Casualty Sister sent the duty doctor to a cubicle to see another sports injury case. The doctor walked into the cubicle already preaching out the usual dogma about playing the safer sensible game of snooker, to be confronted by a man with the side of his head battered and lacerated by a snooker cue.

The nurses hooted with laughter. After that, the medical advice varied more appropriately. Interestingly, it was very obvious and notable that the incidence of injuries was much higher in soccer players than it was in rugby players, considered by most to be a far more physical sport!

We clinical medical students were all exposed to a vast range of casualties throughout this interesting attachment. Some patients' situations were tragic and moving and some exceedingly happy, but to we students, all were exhilarating and the whole attachment was a highly fascinating experience.

Having completed our attachments in A&E, we became eligible to undertake locum house doctor positions, where as senior medics, we could work as stand-in doctors, providing we were adequately supervised by our qualified superiors. We didn't get time for this during our attachments to surgical and medical firms. However, we could during our rare free weekends, our holidays and our electives which essentially were our times off, so we could do as we wished, as long as it was considered part of our medical training.

My first locum position was as a house physician for a weekend, as the incumbent doctor had gone on his holidays and as usual, medical staffing hadn't been able to find a locum. This was during my "elective" in cardiology. I'd opted for this specialty to get to grips with this highly technical and important discipline concerning cardiac dysrhythmias and ECGs, in particular. An ECG is a picture of the electrical activity of the heart.

I'd learned about leaky and scarred cardiac valves, with my tutor Dr Walker. He taught us which bits of the stethoscope were used to listen to them and the individual noises they made. I felt confident to listen to any lesion I would hear. I'd had plenty of opportunity to listen to sick hearts during this period and was pleased when the Consultant Cardiologist, an ex-Cambridge man, asked me to undertake the locum.

The doctors were very cynical about the Medical Staffing Department's attempts in obtaining cover for doctor's leave periods. Although doctors had to give six weeks' notice of any pending leave, medical staffing could never find replacements!

'Had they really looked?' we wondered.

'No!' we thought and it usually ended up with colleague junior doctors having to work many extra hours to provide internal cover.

I was to be working with Dr Hernandez, the medical registrar, who came from Goa. He was a highly experienced physician and certainly taught me well throughout my elective and especially during my weekend on-call with him.

We'd had nine admissions over 72 hours and I went to bed exhausted at 02.30, early on Monday morning.

At 05.50, my bleep went off and it was a GP calling from a town nearby, where he was attending in a convent. He said that one of its nuns had been unwell with severe tight chest pain and he was sending her in by ambulance, with a possible diagnosis of heart attack. My own heart was racing as I leapt up out of bed and called Dr Hernandez immediately with the news. He didn't seem quite as excited as I and asked me to let him know when I'd actually clerked the patient!

I rushed down to A&E to await the ambulance. I waited and waited for about three hours, until at 09.00, Dr Hernandez called me asking what had happened to her. I said that she hadn't turned up and he thanked me and advised me to go and take some rest in the doctors' mess, as I had by that time finished my shift on-call and my locum period.

As I was about to leave through the ambulance reception area, I saw two penguin-like figures, who turned out to be nuns, waddling across the car park heading towards A&E, so I turned back to the receiving area. They duly checked into casualty and were ushered through to me, in the crash room cubicle. I discovered that the nun with chest pain had sent away the ambulance that came to collect her from her convent and she then went to Mass and finally waited for her colleague to get ready to give her a lift to hospital.

I pointed out that I'd been waiting for her for over 3 hours and was gently remonstrating with her about not using the emergency ambulance when she ought to have and she suddenly collapsed, dropping to the floor in cardiac arrest. I was still quivering as the Dr Hernandez and the Cardiac Arrest Team charged into the area, ripped off her habit and commenced CPR (Cardio-Pulmonary Resuscitation).

I watched aghast and was wondering how I was going to explain to the dean that during my elective, I'd bullied a nun and caused her to drop dead and effectively murdered a bride of Christ.

Dr Hernandez ushered me away, saying, "Go and get some rest and don't worry we'll discuss this later". I returned to the hospital's on-call accommodation and exhaustedly fell into a deep sleep.

Unhappily, when I returned to the ward, I learned the Arrest Team had been unable to resuscitate the good sister, which amplified my guilt for remonstrating with her.

Dr Hernandez placated me saying that it was no-one's fault that she died and that she was very old, with a very old failing heart and had probably gone straight to heaven. That was the first time a patient of mine had died and the emotions it elicited have stayed with me ever since.

I learned a great deal about cardiology on that elective and how its principles were applied in real life. I was mostly impressed by the unassuming expertise of my medical colleagues; by Dr Hernandez, an unceasing worker, who taught me so much and also our good-humoured, eloquent and most elegant consultant, who patrolling the cardiac ward at lunchtimes, seized the salt condiments on the patients' dinner trays and threw them into the waste bins.

These people positively enhanced my medical knowledge and professional self-esteem and as my elective closed, I returned to Cambridge as a confident "Almost Doctor".

I later discovered that the casualty officer, who had injected the lacerated patient and who was a very decent chap, gave up medicine to work on the stock exchange, where he became very very wealthy.

While attached to Accident and Emergency, we were taught how to stitch up wounds by the Casualty nurses, with dissolving absorbable sutures first in the fat layer for the deeper wounds, followed by non-absorbable smooth plastic superficial sutures to the skin layer. We felt very important doing this, as patients were very grateful for putting them back together often saying "thank you, doctor" for our trouble. This made us feel highly accomplished!

We observed how dedicated, competent and effective the relatively junior doctors were in the A&E department. We saw that they were rushed off their feet, because there weren't enough of them to deal with the huge numbers of patients attending.

We learned that it was a free service and most frequently open to abuse by the non-thinking and non-paying public. We universally thought a small fee would perhaps make them think a bit more, but such a change would require a braver government.

6

Back at the clinical school, we met up again in Tutorial Groups and Dr Walker, had us make a list of what we thought were the most important clinical things we'd learned from our electives. These were discussed across our group and usefully, I noted what I needed to study from the experiences of my peers. Again, I pondered about team work in medicine, and thought how fortunate I was to be a member of an elite team of 'Us against Disease'.

During this revision period, the clinical school was visited by a group of medical students from the Hadasser Medical School at the Hebrew University in Jerusalem. We'd been told to be polite and friendly to these fellow medics, whose professor was a good friend of our Professor of Surgery.

A Reception/Party was arranged for them in the clinical school. We were amused to see all the Israeli Medics were dressed in Military Uniform and were mainly females. We quickly discovered although medical students, they were all also serving officers in the Israeli army. They'd come to see how medics were trained in England and how we, in particular were trained at Cambridge.

They also hoped to see how our Professor of Surgery performed some advanced liver operations because he was an expert and to see Addenbrookes, which was a specialist centre of excellence for liver transplants. These female medics were almost to a woman highly fit, young and very attractive. They very quickly integrated with we native students, facilitated by a very economical bar and the music of 'Dire Straights' blaring in the background.

Paulos and I were particularly struck by two of the young beauties with deep brown eyes, long raven black hair and dark olive skin and we invited these ravishing lady lieutenants to meet up the next afternoon to show them around and give them a guided tour of the city. They accepted enthusiastically and we met up at my college where I'd arranged to borrow one of the students' punts.

They were most impressed by this and the quick visit to the undergraduate bar, where the drinks were also very economical and where no money was exchanged. Instead we had to sign for them and the bill was put on our termly 'college bills'. The notion of an undergraduate social account impressed the girls enormously that we were trusted with such credits.

Resting on these laurels of superiority, Paulos and I suggested that we might cancel the rest of the city tour and that they may like to visit our flat for coffee and manoeuvres of a slightly less military nature than those with which they were accustomed. We hoped to teach them a little about life in the UK and the freedoms we enjoy and in particular, not having to worry about being shot at, bombed or blown up!

That night my dark eyed beauty called Adina, taught me all about unarmed combat and repeatedly wrestled me into submission. I gave up in the end and surrendered everything, wishing for peace on earth and goodwill to all women!

The next day, Friday, the girls were confined to work by their duties, and preparation for their Sabbath. We were in our tutorial groups going through our various clinical situations we'd encountered on our electives. My group were very keen so I was a bit delayed when I met up with Paulos. As we'd missed our rendezvous, we decided to try and find our Israeli lovelies. We asked the Dean's secretary if she knew of their whereabouts and were delighted to discover they were housed in Darwin Post-Graduate College down on the corner opposite Queens College and the Backs.

We rushed down there as fast as his Porsche could carry us through rush hour Cambridge. We passed the porter's lodge with a flash of our student I.Ds. and he happily told us where the visiting students might be found in the Union Bar. We made our way there posthaste to discover our two delicious Israeli medics looking bored and bereft of any entertainment. We felt it was our duty to save them and squeezing them into Paulos' open topped motor, sped back to the clinical school disco, where we attended to their every wish.

It all passed too quickly, with other medics asking where the other Israelis were hiding and Paulos and I doing our very best for Anglo-Israeli relations. We left as fast as possible rushing them back to our flat to mutually explore our most interesting anatomical markers. It was all for the sake of diplomacy, medical co-operation and the fact that they were both exquisite beauties. Paulos and Daniella rapidly peeled off into his room, where no doubt, they continued their anatomical prospecting.

Adina and I quickly followed suit and she led me into my room, where she proceeded to disrobe me, while simultaneously massaging the uvula at the back of my mouth, with her tongue. She was already sighing as I fell between her thighs sinking inside her. She started gently thrusting her pelvis into mine and was slowly increasing her speed and power, before reaching her screaming climax. My seminal vesicles pumped until they were drier than the Sinai desert. I collapsed into her fluid filled loins, where she over flowed like the river Jordan. I fell into a deep sleep until I was awakened by Paulos. He'd just returned from Darwin College. He'd very kindly driven them back before the college curfew when the gates were locked at the porter's lodge.

He said, Adina had insisted on pulling the duvet over me before they had to leave. She also left me a note, explaining that she had to go as her company were leaving England next day. She thanked me for befriending her and hoped that the fates might lead us together some time in the future. Me too, I thought to myself. What a woman!

If the Arabs ever thought of invading Israel again, they better think twice! I felt a great pang of regret, as Paulos left me alone with my thoughts of her beautiful face. I felt highly protective towards her and wanted to run off to find her and bring up ten children in an Israeli Kibbutz, until Paulos brought me back down to earth with:

"There's another disco next Friday, we better go early so we can pull some more crumpet!"

Good old Paulos, ever the Greek philosopher!

Two days later, we were back having a revision session at the clinical school. By lunchtime, the work had been unrelenting and I was quite worn out when we broke for lunch. I met up with Paulos in the reception area and went off to the Addenbrookes Canteen to restore our energy supplies. We were caught in the hospital lunch rush hour and the tables were packed, so we squeezed onto one full of hospital admin' staff.

They budged up and one of them laughingly exclaimed, "Watch out girls, here come the medics."

Indignantly, I said, "How'd 'you know we're not doctors?"

Unanimously they retorted, "Because of your blue badges."

Paulos defensively replied, "Actually, I am a doctor, a proper doctor with a PhD," which is a higher degree than most medical doctors' M.B.B.S. degrees.

Which was true but not unusual in Cambridge medics, who were all usually highly qualified and highly intellectual.

After that rapid put down, the ladies realised they had been a bit harsh and their attitudes softened. We got on very well and discovered they were secretaries in several different medical and surgical departments. They soon had to leave to go back to their offices, so we invited them to come to the 'End of Electives' disco at the clinical school the following Friday, not really expecting them to do so, but in fact, they did, all six of them!

On Friday, we were a bit nonplussed when they all walked in, but happily, they bought the first round of drinks, as we were 'only students. We discovered that these ladies were great sports, fun-loving and most professional. They told us that they had to know a great deal about the various specialties in which they worked, possibly more than we medics did!

They were very vivacious and confident in their group, questioning us with interest on the medicine, we had learned so far and certainly, they led the way on questions, drinking and dancing. Importantly they were very generous buying the drinks most of the evening.

I imagined that their pay scales were probably somewhat higher than the nurses we had entertained prior to this. Whatever the reason, we were soon becoming very merry in their company. Paulos and I felt a bit outnumbered so we tactically 'homed in' on the two prettiest and danced them away from their mates.

My choice was a girl called Anna, a tall blonde surgical secretary with a great figure and a smile to match. We danced, joked and laughed our way to the end of the evening, with her mocking my dancing and me enjoying every wonderful movement of hers. She gave me lift home and embraced me warmly outside my flat.

"Would you like my phone number?" she offered politely.

I laughed at her honest and straightforward enquiry, which actually sounded quite natural and innocent.

"I thought I was supposed to ask you for that," I replied.

This time she laughed, "I'm sorry, I bet that sounded terrible, I didn't mean to be so forward."

I was happy she was. I thought I had better stop this and asked, "Would you like to come out for dinner tomorrow?"

"I would but I can't, I already have a date, but we could make it another time, if you'd like."

"Ok, that would be great, I'll call you on Sunday."

As I exited her car and made my way into the flat, I thought bugger! I didn't take her number and it's not surprising she has another date; she could easily get anyone. That put the mockers on a fabulous evening.

I felt sad as I rattled about alone in the flat that night, Paulos didn't come back and had obviously scored again with her colleague!

I woke late the next morning and decided to work the weekend and prepare for my next attachment in the Department of Venerology, dealing with patients with sexually transmitted diseases (STDs).

The preparatory handouts we had been given, instructed us to research a new condition called 'the Acquired Immune Deficiency Syndrome', or AIDS for short. I'd never heard of it and decided to go to the Library at the clinical school to find out all about it. On arrival there, I found that there were quite a few other medics with the same intention as me. They had collared a librarian, who was running off a list of all the references on a virus called the Human Imuno deficiency Virus and on the Aids, so I put in my request and decided to check my pigeonhole.

To my great delight, I came across a note from Anna with her phone number. She'd broken her date and wondered if my offer was still available. My heart leapt on high as I skipped down the stairs and used the phone at the clinical school entrance. She sounded excited as we arranged to meet that evening. She would pick me up, as well. I was elated as I left the medical school, the AIDS could wait and I could no longer concentrate on academia.

I jogged back to my flat feeling great. I thought as an 'almost doctor', I'd better smarten up for this date, so I shaved, sang loudly in the shower and emerged in smart casual clothes just in time to greet her on our landing, as she rang the doorbell. She looked adorable with the warmest of smiles, in high heels, a very mini 'mini-skirt' and a smart top.

"Well, where are we going? I hope you didn't mind me leaving you a note in your pigeonhole. Do you think I'm being forward again? I'm not really like that," she enquired rapidly as we descended the stairs not allowing me to respond.

I suddenly realised I hadn't booked anywhere and it was Saturday night in Cambridge.

"I know, what about a drink in the Queen Edith Pub? It's just down the road and we can walk and no, I'm really happy you left me a note and I don't think you're being forward. You're being sensible and rescued me from a boring evening of books."

We walked slowly to the pub, discussing our origins and backgrounds. She enthused about how she loved working in neurosurgery and how brilliant her boss was, both to work for and as a doctor. She thought we medical students must be very clever too, to be able to deal with all it takes to become doctors.

She was so easy to talk to and the walk to the pub passed very quickly. I was feeling very happy and hoped the pub served good food, as I didn't want to look stupid for inviting her out to dinner and not booking anywhere. Happily the pub 'came up trumps', with good beer and good food and she topped it off by being really good company.

Annie, as she liked to be called, was fabulous with all that it encompasses. Her job as secretary to one of the Consultant University Teaching Fellows, meant that she knew a great deal about the lives of clinical medical students and was thoroughly familiar with our work commitments on the wards and in academic study. I found her conversation during dinner fascinating. She was vivacious, highly alluring and anatomically highly desirable.

As we walked to my flat, she took my hand, without hesitation and we walked back as if old friends arm in arm. On reaching the landing, I opened the front door and as I followed her in, she turned and pulled my face towards her giving me a gentle embrace on the lips, which seamlessly became more longing and passionate, but still with an enduring gentle tranquillity. I could feel myself eagerly stirring, pushing against her, as if we were opposite poles of a body-sized magnet!

Her mouth was exploring every part of my face and neck and I felt light headed with my senses consumed by her embraces and the overwhelming erotic bouquet of her perfume. I felt I was salivating, like a carnivore about to devour its delicious prey. Suddenly, she stepped back and looked at me with my swollen manhood exposed *in flagrante delicto*. She was staring at me with longing in her eyes as she breathed through her open mouth.

I was about to explode as I took her hand leading her to my room and we undressed each other as slowly as we could possibly control.

It was a natural progression to embrace and make love gently and caressingly at first, embracing her neck, her shoulders, her luscious breasts and soft flat abdomen. We fell back against each other, on the bed, with my phallus fixed against her. She ran her fingers over its rigid and wet glans, guiding it over her pubis and lowering it to her vulva.

She gasped as it collided with her clitoris and bathing it in her warm juices, she let it sink into her, gripping it with her taut pelvic muscles. We oscillated back and forwards, gaining more strength and urgency until we totally lost control and burst forth in a mutual clamorous crescendo. I filled her with my copious wash of living seed and her pelvis rocked, receiving it. We collapsed into heap of ecstatic perspiring flesh and fell asleep against each other.

We awoke early that Sunday morning, before the university church bells started to peal. We lay there in each other's arms and talked about everything, where we came from, what we'd done, how we'd got there, what we were doing and what we wanted to do.

She hailed from the Midlands and had a faint lilt in her accent. She confessed she had been trying to consciously exclude it from her conversation.

I said jokingly, "I don't blame you!"

She irked at that and said, "I know, I hate it, everyone's so posh here, I feel inadequate, when I open my mouth and sound like someone from a Birmingham Fish Market!"

I said, "You sound fine to me. They just have to look at you and whatever you say would be all right."

She pulled me to her, kissed me passionately and I felt aroused! It was one of those moments, when everything comes into focus and you feel what's important to you and what isn't. I was certainly having some very important feelings in my nether regions.

She said she had to hurry as she had to get to church and that she was a Catholic and Mass was due to start in an hour.

I said, "Don't panic, it's only 8 o'clock, we must have loads of time yet."

That wasn't the case, she had loads of commitments and within half an hour she was up, showered and exiting by the same door where she had enraptured me several hours earlier.

As we embraced on her leaving, the opposite door on the landing just happened to open simultaneously and Mrs. Hobbs, our neighbour evolved, eyeing up Annie as she said, "Good morning Michael, I see you've had a lovely night!"

"Thank you, Mrs. Hobbs, and how's Mr. Hobbs?"

"He's OK but you did say you'd come and have a look at his leg," she replied.

"OK, I'll call across later," I replied as Annie hastened down the stairs.

I was left bereft of this perfect being, who had floated into my complex and controlled life, as a medic, conquered me and then rushed out of it, to go off to church, totally out of my sphere of influence!

Suddenly alone, I thought there was nothing left to do but get back to medicine and swot up on this new disease I'd never heard of, just in case I was cornered by the Venereologist, in the V.D. Clinic, in the morning.

However, first I had to go and see Mrs. Hobbs' husband's leg.

Mr. Hobbs, who was in his late 70s, and had been the college gardener, until he'd retired about ten years earlier. He was also a descendent of a great English Cricketer. He had the gruff voice of a smoker who 'rolled his own' since childhood and had the chest and heart to match! He was also under the hospital for an ischaemic leg, wherein the blood supply to his extremities was poor, due to the furred-up blood vessels of this old smoking man.

He liked talking to Paulos and me as it reminded him of the good old days, when he would be-friend the college undergraduates and often let them into college, via the college garden gates after curfew, when the main gates were locked. This kind gesture was traditionally accompanied by a small fee of one Guinea. It enhanced such friendships and avoided being dragged up before the college senior tutor, to be more seriously fined for not keeping college hours!

Mr and Mrs Hobbs knew that I knew a bit about dermatology via my tutor and from time to time asked me to check that 'they knew what they were doing up and at that hospital', which of course, they did!

His left leg had an ulcer on the heel and he had been attending the dermatology clinic for weekly dressings. To Mr. Hobbs, my job, as a clinical medical student and member of the college, was to keep an eye on these hospital doctors, who weren't all Cambridge men and therefore, in his eyes, were not to be trusted.

He proudly bared his wound and I inspected it and the new growth of regenerated healing granulation tissue. I reassured him it was making progress and having redressed it, diplomatically exited to return to my studies on the AIDS.

This new illness called the Acquired Immune Deficiency Syndrome, which left its victims dying from what would usually be easily treatable trivial infections, seemed to be spreading across the West coast of the USA like the old London plague. There were very few research papers available at the time and the clinical school Librarian had already accessed all of them for us, so it was easy for me to acquire the relevant knowledge to equip me for tomorrow's clinic.

I discovered that AIDS as it was to become known, hijacks T lymphocytes cells which protect us from infections. These T-cells undertake cell mediated immunity, recognising and killing both foreign organisms and included killing primitive cancer cells attacking our bodies. This AIDs disease kills T-Cells and dramatically reduces our defences, making us vulnerable to infections we would normally overcome and a particular type of skin cancer known as Karposi's Sarcoma.

Public Health Bodies over the world were beginning to notice that many of the victims of this syndrome were intravenous drug addicts and/or members of the homosexual community.

It was observed that drug users would often share the paraphernalia necessary for their drug habit including the use of needles for I.V. injections. Also it was apparent that there was a very vulnerable degree of high promiscuity among the homosexual community and that this somehow, probably through unprotected intercourse, made them much more vulnerable to this syndrome. I read all the papers and went to bed excited about Annie and prepared for my attachment in the 'Clap Clinic' in the morning.

7

At 08.30, we collected together in Clinic 1A in Addenbrookes Outpatients, to be greeted by Dr Khan, the Consultant Venereologist. He led us into the lecture theatre and ran us through a horror slide show of photographs and x-rays about the range of conditions, which we were likely to encounter during our short two week attachment. He gave us a succinct and very interesting lecture on all the unspeakable conditions we can inflict on each other when we make love.

Also, he ran through a range of different and peculiar stories that patients might invent for presenting with their 'Winkies' and 'Vaggies' having such painful smelly discharges or sagas of how they slipped in the bath and fell on the soap, which appears to have lodged in their bottoms and just won't come out doctor. These patients were unfortunates from right across the social strata. They ranged from workers out on a Saturday night, to the local vicar, who fell for one of his pretty parishioners, not realising that in the past, several other members of his flock had grazed there as well.

Dr Kahn's last words were, "Just be prepared for anything because you will see it here and don't forget to wear gloves and change them between patients. We don't want any of you catching anything and inadvertently sharing it across the university population!"

We silently pondered how he had become so cynical.

It was a most fascinating attachment with, as Dr Khan had said, all sorts of people attending. I was amazed at the general level of promiscuity and extra-marital affairs among the Cambridge population, including a Catholic Priest, who took 'brotherly love', literally!

Of course, I didn't tell Annie, about the priest. I saw her most evenings as there was quite a lot of freedom in this specialty. I felt our relationship was different and somehow much more intense than others. She was just so lovely and I felt totally at ease in her presence. I vacated my college flat and moved into her house with her. We made love like rabbits and she was ravenous for my attentions.

I'd been a regular at the gym, played a lot of football and was generally in good physical shape, but she made me develop several new muscle groups in our love-making. I liked to watch her dress in the mornings. She started with her suspender belt and then bent over to draw up her stockings one by one. There were a number of occasions when I dragged her back to bed making her late for work. I was captivated by her and she was physically perfect.

In those moments, I felt totally happy and it seemed to flow out of me naturally to say to her, "I love you."

To which she replied, "I love you more."

Well! With that answer, I couldn't just let her finish dressing. So, we hugged and it ended up making her late for work again.

On the last night of our attachment in venereology, I'd attended the late clinic to deal with the commuting extra-marital 'shaggers', who'd in all likelihood picked up the Chlamydia bug infecting them from the young girls in their office. They'd probably gone into London every day, carrying their pelvic bugs from the partners they'd been sharing their favours with, back in their commuting Shires.

I'd taken multiple swabs from all their relevant parts and screened them for this new and relatively unknown deadly Aids plague and left the clinic quite late, after seven. I was already late to meet Anna who was waiting patiently twenty minutes away in the clinical school bar.

I decided to cut through the University Faculty Offices, on the 2nd floor and take the lift to the lower ground floor, which was underground and go via the tunnel from the hospital to the clinical school by the back door.

I walked gingerly through the closed corridors of the University Department of Obstetrics and Gynaecology, as I wasn't supposed to be there. Then I was suddenly startled to hear what sounded like someone in distress, with some distinct sounds of emotion; someone was definitely upset and crying.

As I approached the sound leading to the academic unit in the Sanctum Sanctorum of the Professorial Offices, the sounds became more distinct and seemed to come from the professor's office itself. I approached in trepidation, as I had no knowledge of this erudite, highly esteemed, world expert on women's medicine and surgery. The office doors were open, and I peeked round the corner to recognise the good professor, clearly distraught and in tears.

I felt I had to say, "Are you alright Prof?"

He raised his head, recognised I was a clinical student and instantly apologised, saying, "I'm sorry, I've just had some very bad news about my family."

"I'm so sorry to intrude on you, I heard your distress from the corridor and thought I should see what was happening. What's wrong?" I asked, as if I might be able to help.

"Well, it's my son, his wife and my grandson have gone missing, somehow believed kidnapped, in Somalia, where they were Christian Missionaries. Our Foreign Office in London have just told me it's possible that they won't survive, as Britain doesn't make deals with such kidnappers and they are not very high up the valuable list for any prisoner-exchange procedures. They said they would do what they could, but were not too hopeful for a happy outcome."

I thought, 'Oh God! That's dreadful. Here was this wonderful highly valued expert in his medical field, torn away from his professional life by a group of ignorant and moronic so-called revolutionaries, who decided to steal away his family probably for ransom; when they had done no harm to them whatsoever!'

I was outraged at the visible distress caused to this popular, cultured and highly sophisticated man of learning!

I didn't know what to say that might comfort him; I thought of President Lincoln's famous letter to the mother of five fallen soldiers, who were brothers, during the American civil war and thought better of trying to assuage his grief.

Instead I said, "Prof, we don't know how much our government can do for ordinary citizens, at times like these and what influences they may bring to bear on these animals that assault our people abroad."

At that, he suddenly looked up knowingly and said, "Thank you, my boy. We must have faith and pray for divine intervention. I would ask you not to tell anyone anything about what you have witnessed here today. We don't want this sort of thing to become public knowledge; there are a lot of idiots out there who might try to imitate these events and cause havoc in the thinking community, where we belong."

I assured him of my silence and went on my way down the lift to the tunnel back to the clinical school. I emerged to find Anna holding court, surrounded by a group of my peers, chatting her up. My sudden appearance dampened their ardour and they gradually dissipated, leaving us alone together.

I had totally forgotten about the content of my chance meeting with the professor and thought I' better leave it that way. It was none of my business but inside, I wished him all the luck in the world and actually prayed for him as I made my way through the tunnel. It's funny how in times of disaster, we turn to a more powerful being to ask for help.

Generally, we medics at Cambridge, brushed over the existence of a divine being, stating that we knew that there must be some sort power we can call God and 'She' was in the year below us in the university! I didn't really believe that.

I couldn't wait to get back to Anna's place and restart where we left off and drown in her pelvis, which I knew was pure and clean and all mine. She wasn't soiled with any of those nasties I'd been dealing with for the last two weeks. I adored her, her perfect face and figure, her naivety, her charming charisma and keen sense of humour. This which made her highly popular with my peers and despite her innocence, not at all intimidated by their haughty intellects.

After the Clap Clinic, my next attachment consisted of two weeks in public health. The first week was made up of lectures at the clinical school on the benefits of various measures like national vaccination schedules and smear protocols, national radiology screening programs for breast cancer, smears for cervical cancer and other killer diseases.

The second week was in the community, attached to its services such as district nurses, McMillan nurses and Community Medical officers. I found the first weeks of this particular course to be fairly common sense, but was surprised to learn how generally low the uptake of these measures had been among the British population. Unhappily, the course was cursed by statistics, which appeared to fascinate the various doctors who were there to try to enthuse us with their meaning, in the overall medical scheme of things.

I was delighted when Anna suggested that we might sneak away for a package deal of passion in Benidorm, during the last two days of the second week of the course and the weekend; and so, we did.

I thought that the small hotel high on the Northern edge of town, would probably have to buy a new bed by the end of the holiday, when we'd finished with it. We'd made love every day, in every position possible. One day, we were making love on a raft anchored in the bay when a powerful speed boat raced past and nearly launched me over the side. Late one evening, we went for a walk along the beach and even made love in a small sailing boat that had been dragged up beyond the high tide level!

I reckoned, I was totally azoospermic by the end of the holiday and Anna was a full reservoir, brimming to her top in semen. She would have been a great sperm donor that week. She couldn't wait to take my love juices and seemed to ache for sex, no sooner had we orgasmed, when she was mmmming and aghing again, moving her hands over me, stretching my manhood into its full height for her to drain again!

Apart from meals, I hardly left the room because I was anxious to avoid the ever-present sun. I couldn't return to medical school with a tan, when I was supposed to be with district nurses in the community in the dark and dismal weather of the city.

On the very few occasions, we left our room to actually go out in amongst the locals in Benidorm town, I was struck (with my most recent public health hat on), that almost all the local Spaniards I saw were cigarette smokers. Everywhere we went, the local population were puffing away on "fags". They must have a terribly high incidence of lung cancer and chronic obstructive airways disease.

One evening, as we were in line for the dinner buffet, one of the other hotel guests leaned forward. In a hushed voice, he said that he had been watching me always sitting in the background and never being noticeable. He asked if I was 'one of those crooks living on the Costa del Crime?'

I thought he might be a policeman on his 'hols', so I told him that I wasn't avoiding the police, but was simply avoiding the sun and the dean back at my university. I explained that I wasn't really supposed to be there and that we had sneaked away for a few days to be together as much as possible.

He replied that he could see why. I imagined he'd spotted Anna sunbathing all alone, and quite understandably been watching her getting an almost all over tan, without any male companion there to watch over her. He didn't know I was watching her as closely as possible, from the 10th floor, while she was getting steadily more tanned and I was recovering from my total sexual exhaustion.

That brief episode made us giggle for the rest of the trip.

8

The following week, we medics embarked on our senior surgical attachments. I was very happy to be back in surgery and eased back into the clinical school, with only a few friends knowing that I'd been away. I wondered whether my clinical tutor Steve Walker, a dermatologist, may have noticed the slight rosy glow on my face, but he never mentioned it.

My first senior surgical discipline was a further two weeks in Ophthalmology at the Addenbrookes old site in the city centre, opposite the museum. Apart from one or two interesting lectures on the theory of this subject, we students felt it was not a good use of our time as there was very little space in theatres to watch the intricate procedures undertaken to preserve vision and we had been informed that it was not to be examined in finals.

Still, it gave us free time to enjoy punting on the Cam and picnicking in the spring sun. As a student, I had free access to my college's two punts, Hermes and Endurance named after the two British warships which had taken an active part in the Falklands War, some months earlier.

We were young, we were fit and we had access to the excess funds, which the government paid for us to be members of the Students Union. We spent it well, enjoying every moment that spring and summer in the city had to offer.

There were several parties in the medical student Union bar, frequented by we medics, administrators, nurses and various junior doctors. At one such do, I was having a very pleasant conversation with a pretty girl, while Annie was at the bar. I hadn't met the girl before.

All of a sudden, an older man approached, touched the girl on her shoulder and interjected grumpily with, "Come on, we're going."

I responded, "Hang on a sec, we're talking."

She looked up and replied, "Sorry, I'd better go" and before I could make any response, she'd left, just as Annie returned to the scene.

I said, "Blimey, he was a bit rude, making her leave like that."

"Who was?" asked Anna.

"That bloke over there," I pointed out the interloper.

"Oh yes, that's Mr. Everard, the consultant surgeon. He can be a bit brusque. That's his daughter you were speaking to."

"Well, you're right he was really brusque." I was suddenly very glad I hadn't been too brusque back to him.

My next medical attachment was in paediatric medicine. It was usual that we had two weeks away in a district general hospital and another two either back at Addenbrookes attached to the Professorial team or in other hospitals across East Anglia.

On the first day at the District Hospital in North Herts, six of us arrived on the ward, and met the Consultant Paediatrician, a South African called Dr Jim Hyde. He was an excellent doctor and teacher. We joined him, his Registrar and Senior House Officer plus a group of Paediatric nurses and together we undertook a rapid ward round. As we stood at the foot of each child's bed or cot, Dr. Hyde gave us a 'world-wind' lecture about their particular conditions.

In the space of about an hour, he gave us a thorough encyclopaedia of information about the course of paediatric children's diseases and management of each child. It was a hell of a lot for us to take it all on board. Finally he told us to select a patient, find out everything about him or her and the management of their condition. We would then present our patient to him and our colleagues on the last day of our attachment.

This work was to be an episode of private study to enable us to become familiar with research, by delving into scientific journals and discovering everything we needed to know about our patient's condition.

I chose a little baby who was failing to thrive. He was fair-skinned, blue-eyed and had blond hair. He had short stature and the great big abdomen of someone who wasn't absorbing his nutrients from his small intestines and thereby not growing normally.

The undigested and unabsorbed nutrients remaining in his small bowel then passed into his large bowel, where the bacteria living there, digested them and grew on them making a great deal of their waste product gases mainly Methane and Hydrogen Sulphide. These gases collected in the baby's colon and contributed to flatus, which is passed as 'wind'.

The baby's belly, distended by the gases, was swollen like a drum. The child's diseased ileum (small bowel), had been biopsied showing atrophy of the villi through which digested nutrients are normally absorbed from the gut into the blood. Normally, these villi projections stick out like sausages into the small gut lumen increasing the surface area for the absorption of the nutrients out of our digested food intakes.

His condition was called Coeliac Disease and again, I'd never heard of it. We all went off to the library to research our patients' conditions, where I asked the librarian for help. She was called Sally and was very demure and a most attractive lady and sounded most enthusiastic when I asked for her help.

And, help she did. She was so brilliant and thorough that she not only taught me all about the condition, she also discovered a number of other newer research tests for diagnosing it as well, which I duly noted and presented enthusiastically on the last day of our attachment.

The consultant praised me for my thorough investigation and eloquent presentation, of course, I didn't mention all the help I'd received from Sally, the lovely librarian.

We all thoroughly enjoyed this attachment and discovered that paediatric medicine is a whole different discipline to adult medicine, with its own different clinical presentations and disease courses. Dr Hyde enriched us and enthused us all with this new knowledge as we slotted in smoothly to his dedicated team. One important learning point we took away with us was that children can get very ill very quickly, but if they're going to get better, they also get better quickly too.

The district general hospital made us very welcome too. We were allocated convenient on-site rooms in the hospital accommodation, saving us commuting and enabled us to quickly retire to our rooms to do some work in the early evenings and partake of the hospitality of two local pubs just five minutes down the road. Anna also had come to stay with me over the weekends, which made things even more enjoyable.

At the end of the attachment, Annie and I travelled back to Cambridge together early on the Monday, while the other medics went off to their placements in other hospitals in East Anglia.

Unhappily, I had failed to account for the busy traffic of the 'Monday rush hour' and having dropped off Annie at the department of neurosurgery and then found a parking space, I arrived late on the paediatric ward at Addenbrookes.

The other students there had already been allocated patients to clerk and when I arrived, there was only one left, with about 2 minutes to spare before the professor arrived for his 'Ward Round'.

It was reckoned that the Professor of Paediatrics was the most powerful man in the University and no-one in their right mind would want to upset him, lest it had serious effects on their future career!

I rushed down the length of the ward, thinking I was the person about to be going out of my mind to upset him, being late and knowing nothing about my patient. Then I saw my patient, an 18-month-old baby with fair skin, blue eyes and the distended belly of mal-absorption. Praise the Lord!

Just as I said hello to his lovely mother, also blond and blue-eyed, the Prof descended onto the ward with a huge entourage consisting of the paediatric nursing sister, other paediatric nurses and junior doctors flocking around him. He walked straight down the ward and right up to my patient.

I reckoned that the other students were all thinking that I was in the quagmire, right up to my neck. They thought that they were about to witness the demise of my career before it had started. My downfall was imminent! How would I ever get out of this dilemma? They didn't know what I knew!

Prof said, "Whose patient is this?"

"Mine, sir," I replied.

"What's wrong with him?"

"Mal-absorption, sir"

"And what are the causes of this mal-absorption state?"

I reeled off all of the several causes that the librarian and I'd investigated during the two weeks of my previous attachment.

"What investigations would you like to do to elucidate a diagnosis?"

Again, I reeled off the usual management but also added the new tests the wonderful Sally had found for me earlier at the North Herts District General Hospital.

The Prof said, "Well done, my boy, I'd like you to do them. The Crosby Capsule biopsies we've taken have missed the affected areas of his ileum. Let's see what you come up with!"

The other students and the Prof's entourage were standing gazing with their mouths wide open. As none of them had been we me in Stevenage, the fortnight before, they had no idea what I'd seen at the Lister Hospital, during that attachment and must have been thinking what a swot I was.

Over the next few days, I duly carried out the tests and they all came back positive for Coeliac Disease. The baby's mother thought I was a genius and the

Prof, who was also very pleased and almost agreed with her, subsequently awarded me a prize for my research in Paediatrics.

He called me to his department and invited me to present the case at the Medical Grand Round, held weekly in the William Harvey lecture theatre. This gathering was a seminar for consultants from the whole of East Anglia. I would be the first clinical medical student to present a case at this esteemed conference. It's funny how against all the odds and quite by accident, things can work out!

The previous speaker at this conference was to be from the professorial team in the Department of Paediatrics, and had been the man who researched the correct dosages of a drug (a steroid called Surfactant) capable of facilitating premature babies' lungs to expand. (3) This doctor worked on how much steroid was necessary and the best time during pregnancy to give it, to enable premature babies to make enough of that surfactant, so I was in good company!

There were two snags with the Prof's invitation. Firstly, there wasn't much time to prepare the case for the next Grand Round and secondly, it was to occur the lunchtime after the evening of my college May Ball!

Such May balls are not to be missed at Cambridge; they are the pinnacle social event of the college year and alumni from earlier years arrive from all over the world. Tickets for this all-night event were very sought after, as many famous past students from every walk of life, including actors, politicians, biologists, including Nobel Laureates, were after them.

They turn up suited and booted to indulge themselves in sumptuous partying throughout the night till sun up. I could not miss this event, despite the Grand Round, as it was the most popular gathering and definitely not to be missed.

I charged round to the clinical school, trying to make slides with the technicians at the audio-visual aids department to load up into their projector. Annie was kind enough to type up my relevant notes and I just had time to read through them once, before I climbed into my dress suit and set off for a fabulous evening of my college ball.

May balls were traditionally held by colleges, in the month of May, but over the passage of time as the syllabus content of courses increased leading to examinations at the end of May, so college balls were relocated to happen after exams in June. Though they're still called "May Balls".

As expected it was phenomenal, with sumptuous food, champagne and every sort of beverage you could imagine. There were several famous bands and dancing went on over the campus, till the sun came up in the morning. I saw several famous celebrities from the world of television and theatre.

I remember leaving my college's Old Court at dawn and walking back with Annie to crash out on her bed to the whines of electric milk floats, as the city woke up for business.

I aroused with a start and the sun burning into my eyes and a base drum pounding in my head.

Hell, I was late, there was just an hour to get to the lecture theatre, where I was giving the lecture! My temples thumped as I tightened my college tie, put on my white coat and Annie drove me like the wind to arrive with moments to spare. The Prof was introducing me and the patient's condition, where repeated biopsies had failed to provide a diagnosis.

I climbed onto the stage, the audience fell silent and I croaked into my presentation. The Visual Aids people had done a marvellous job, the slides worked and after a while I managed to project my rattily voice so they could understand what I was saying.

I ran through my revision of all the causes of mal-absorption and the inadequacies of the current method of Coeliac diagnosis by Crosby Capsule Biopsy sampling of small bowel.

I expounded how these newer methods of investigation would supercede the current state of affairs. I came to the end of my presentation and asked for any questions. Thank God, there weren't any.

The Prof then returned to the stage, congratulated me for the work (entirely undertaken by Sally the librarian at the peripheral hospital in Stevenage), and presented me with an envelope, containing the paediatric research prize, which was a cheque. Then someone started to clap which spread across the audience and it was over. I'd made it!

As I walked towards the exit up the aisle through the audience seats, Steve Walker, stood up and said, "Well done."

Annie walked up and hugged me, I felt like I'd just won the Nobel prize!

I asked her, "Can we go home now?"

She said, "I've got my car outside, let's go," where we fell asleep wrapped together and exhausted by the last 24 hours of burning the candle at both ends and in the middle!

9

At this period of summer, we were free to use this brief interval to enjoy ourselves in medicine, before the examinations waiting for us at the end of Michaelmas term in December and the exhausting hectic life of a junior hospital doctor after that.

At this time, my flat mate Paulos was heavily into the local private Colleges of Higher Education, where English as a foreign language was taught to dozens of mainly gorgeous women, commonly from Scandinavia. This meant our flat was quite frequently flooded with several blond and rampant lovelies, who joined us at our student parties and as often as possible, ended up coming on our trips up the river Cam, in one of my college punts.

We'd fill the craft with food and wine and punt up the river to picnic on the meadow at Granchester. We engineered it for them to fall off the punt, as they were totally uninhibited and would strip off to dry their clothes, displaying their wares for all to enjoy. I have to say, I often felt very tempted by these beauties, feeling I ought to be doing my best to re-kindle Anglo-Viking relations, which was highly justifiable considering how their ancestors had raped and pillaged through the English countryside in the 8th and 9th centuries!

During this decadent and abandoned time, I was surprised to receive a letter in my pigeonhole, from the Professor of Obstetrics and Gynaecology, asking for me to make an appointment to see him as soon as possible, which I did immediately. I was most anxious as I approached his offices, wondering what he might want.

The river Cam at the picnic meadow in Granchester

I was mightily relieved when a smiling Prof opened his office door ushering me through to armchairs in his ante-room where a tray of tea and crumpets awaited us. His secretary poured the tea and the Prof thanked me for my prompt

attendance and more-over for my silence about the events I had witnessed some months earlier. He was delighted to tell me that he had heard a few days earlier that his son and family had been released and were on their way home.

I was delighted also and could see the glow of relief in his eyes and I thought to myself, maybe there is a God after all.

He thanked me again and wished me luck for the forthcoming examinations at the end of term. I left feeling elated for him and strangely also for myself, as everything in the world felt right and the 'just' had won!

As the Autumn of our second year advanced, we students again returned from our discipline attachments. I'd just completed an attachment in Obstetrics and Gynaecology at the Newmarket Hospital, the town of the famous Race Course. There, I attended many obstetric deliveries with the midwives, some in the birthing pool where the about-to-be mothers could wallow in the warm water until the natural pains of labour focused their minds and reminded them what they were really there for.

I was concerned but also keen to see how the new born babies reacted to suddenly being caste out from their mother's womb into the pool. I needn't have worried of course, because the pool was maintained precisely at body temperature and the babies were still connected to the mother's circulation by their placenta and umbilical cord and could still receive enough nutrients and oxygen to comfortably survive via this connection.

It was in this attachment that I saw many pregnant wives of the itinerant horse racing Jockeys, who migrated from race course-to-race course riding for their various owners and trainers. This effectively meant that their wives, who were also peripatetic, often didn't get to see a doctor during their pregnancy.

Sadly, I saw such a case at Newmarket, when a young wife from Northern Ireland, where the diet is commonly deficient in Vitamin B9 (Folic acid) and, there is a high incidence of failure of closure of the foetus's central nervous system neural tube at either end and quite often at both of its two ends. This patient had not had any scans of her pregnancy and presented in late labour at the Newmarket Maternity Ward.

Sadly to say, her baby was born with no frontal lobes to its brain. A condition called Anencephaly, where because of this vitamin deficiency, the upper end of its neural tube didn't close and as a further result, its surrounding membranes (meninges), didn't close either and thence its skull bones didn't grow and close and because of that, its scalp didn't grow and close also. Leaving the child with a flat uncovered central nervous system, where you could poke fingers into its mal-developed brain.

Following Newmarket, I was back again in Cambridge attached to the Obs and Gynae professorial team, where we were introduced to the senior registrar, Mr. Paul Bradley. He taught us a great deal about Obstetrics and Gynaecology. I grew to like this interesting subject as it was both a surgical discipline as well as a medical one. At the time, I didn't know that this subject would have a large part to play in my life and medical career.

After O & G, we returned back to the clinical school for a week long revision course, before a further week with our clinical tutors to revise the skills of examination. During this time, there suddenly appeared on the final year notice board a notice from the Professor of Pharmacology, inviting us all to attend a tutorial at his college on the following Sunday. It advised those of us whose surnames began with A – L to attend from 10.00 am till Noon and the rest from 13.00 till 15.00.

There was a nominal charge of £20.00 to be paid to the college porter at the gate. The tutorial was not compulsory but advisable as the good professor not only set the final examination in therapeutics but also marked it. Almost all of we final year students attended. I have to report that it was an exceedingly good and most comprehensive lecture and guess what, most of it came up in the final examination, which I happily passed.

These revision courses culminated with our final written exams in the Examinations Hall in the centre of Cambridge opposite Peterhouse College, where we were examined in several 3 hour question papers on every aspect of clinical medicine.

The long and short case practical 'Viva' examinations took place in the clinical school later that week, where outside medical and surgical professors from favoured universities around Britain and the world, came to explore whether we knew enough and were ready to be let loose on the public as doctors.

We were given times to meet at the appointed case staging positions. There were two examiners for each case. We had all worked extremely hard for these finals and I felt I had done well in the written exams. I was fairly confident, waiting for my turn to go in for the surgical long cases.

As I entered the room, I was horrified to see Mr. Everard, who some months earlier had interrupted my conversation with his daughter. He was the internal examiner at that station. The external examiner directed me to examine the volunteer patient's neck. I looked at the female patient from the front for about 3 seconds (I remembered, 'eyes first and most'), and was relieved to see she had swelling in her neck from an enlarged thyroid gland.

"Well?" Mr. Everard interjected in a stern voice from where he stood immediately behind the seated patient.

"Would you excuse me, sir?" I politely asked as thyroid glands usually have to be examined from behind and I felt that he had tried to put me off course by his position right behind the patient. Mr. Everard moved aside and gave me access to the patient, but I could sense his antipathy!

The external examiner continued to ask me about thyroid diseases and their surgical management, which I was able to answer thoroughly. Then Mr. Everard stepped in again and grilled me about the anatomy, the innervation and the blood supply of the thyroid, the larynx and other structures in the neck. I did my best but was unable to satisfy him about some of the vagaries he was pursuing. After a very brief pause, he said, "Ok that's enough, thank you".

My long case was over.

Afterwards, I thought about it and discussed it with my college tutor. We decided he was after the embryology of the neck, which is a bit steep for clinical surgical finals.

I should have known by his attitude and unfriendly manner, that he would fail me, as he had the unquestioned power to do so. Still, I was hopeful that the average from my good written papers and the outside examiner would carry me through despite this misanthropic bastard!

I didn't have long to wait and three days later, I learned the worst. He had indeed failed me and when I was not only a surgical scholar, but considered it my best discipline within the medical school curriculum. I'd passed all the Medicine papers, but was devastated as I found my results in my pigeonhole. There was generalised jubilation from those who'd passed everything and solace among the many who hadn't.

As well as my results, I was curious to find two notes, one from my college tutor and one from my clinical school Tutor inviting me to meet them, that afternoon in the middle common room of my college.

I was despondent as I approached the room. My tutors greeted me with warm handshakes. Recognising my mood, Dr Walker, my medical school tutor told me that he knew that the present Professor of Surgery at Cambridge had also failed his surgery finals and look how well he had done! They pointed out that I should keep up my studies and re-take the surgical exam in six months in order to obtain the two Cambridge degrees in medicine and surgery.

They also said that I shouldn't delay and that as a surgical scholar at the Royal College of Surgeons, I could take the joint examinations of the two Royal Colleges, known traditionally as 'the Conjoint', which was another way to qualify as a doctor in England, dating back to the 18 hundreds. They advised that I should obtain the relevant forms and have the dean sign them immediately endorsing that I was worthy to take the next sitting. My college tutor poured out three large glasses of port and they toasted my success, which went a decent way towards lifting my spirits and calming my fury!

The next sitting was to be in February, which was after I was due to start my first house job. It meant that I could no longer embark on this job due to my failure in surgery. However, I duly sat the 'conjoint' exams and happily passed with flying colours, and noted that the surgery paper of the Conjoint, known as the M.R.C.S. exam, was much more involved and detailed than the Cambridge exam that I'd recently failed.

However, I sailed through the Conjoint, to at last become a qualified doctor, but without a job. My job had been taken by someone else, since all posts had to be filled for the start on the 1st of February. I returned from London to Cambridge intending to do locums to keep the wolf from the door.

I arrived back in the clinical school to search the notice board for locum posts that were usually advertised there. I was once again surprised to find a note in my pigeonhole, but this time from the Professor of Obstetrics and Gynaecology. He was again asking me to call in at his study as soon as possible.

On arrival there, he greeted me enthusiastically and more like a friend and his secretary produced more tea and crumpets. He congratulated me on qualifying as a doctor. He was genuinely pleased that I had joined the worldwide club of doctors.

Without prompting, he said, "I gather you have missed your first house job".

"Yes sir," I replied disappointedly, unaware of how he could possibly know such things. The doctors' club really did stretch far and wide, and blimey I thought, I only found out that I'd passed the day before!

"Then you mustn't worry; one of our SHOs has recently moved to his next post and his replacement hasn't arrived, so you can take his place. I've read your report from your elective, your consultant there, is an old alumnus of mine and a good friend. He rates you highly and I know you, so you can come and join the professorial team and work with us until your next house job starts in August! We will also arrange paid study leave, so you can work for your surgical 'resit' in June, which you will of course pass, to get your Cambridge degrees! I will make sure that the stickler general surgeon isn't an examiner next time, just to eliminate bias."

"You will be most welcome in our Obstetrics and Gynaecology Department, a discipline where modern medicine is complemented by life-saving surgery. We are surgeons, but some of our main roles involve ultra-modern medicine and we are at the pinnacle of research into infertility, where we are foremost in the world and also where we combat cancer with the latest tools known to mankind. You are indeed privileged, but we think you are worthy; so, swot up some gynaecology tonight, ready to meet the team in the morning."

I could hardly believe my ears and wanted to hug this great man! I felt highly honoured. He was taking a great risk in employing me in a job I wasn't qualified to do, as I hadn't done my year 'in the house', and therefore, wasn't even a fully registered doctor (4).

"You'll be well taken care of and strictly supervised, so don't be anxious. You'll learn a great deal of medicine and surgery; you'll be among friends you can trust and who will trust you and you can do it. Would you meet me tomorrow at 08.30 in the Clinic 2A in the outpatient's department?"

"Yes," I gasped. "Thank you, sir, thank you, I'll be there."

I floated two feet above the pavement, back to my flat in Queen Edith's Way, unable to absorb the enormity of the privilege this man had bestowed on me. I was a failed surgical scholar, qualified by the "Back door" Conjoint and given one of the most prestigious jobs in England, working for a professor at Cambridge.

'Please God, don't let me screw this up!'

I called Annie from the phone box on the corner. I was trying to be cool and invited her to come to my flat straight from work, as I couldn't wait to hold her and share my joy. I wanted to celebrate with her and Paulos.

However, when she arrived and I told her, Annie, practical as ever said, "No let's wait to celebrate till the weekend. Now, I think you should go into your study and read that book you have on Lecture Notes on Gynaecology, so you won't be overwhelmed when you deal with your patients tomorrow."

So I did, until I fell asleep over my book, awoke in the early hours, drove to her flat and slid quietly into bed beside her, where she congratulated me thoroughly.

10

Next morning, I arrived at Clinic 2A, early to be greeted by the senior registrar Paul Bradley, who parked me at my desk at the front of the clinic and gave me a list of patients, who were mainly follow-ups.

He said, "We're starting you off gently. Don't worry we've all had our first day and survived it. If you're uncertain about anything, just ask!"

The clinic was in a large oblong room with the Senior House Officers (SHOs), at the front, registrars behind us, then senior registrars and finally the consultants on the professorial team, followed by the Prof, at the very back, sitting at his massive desk on a large leather swivel chair.

I wasn't a Senior House Officer; I was merely an unregistered House Officer in the missing SHO's seat. As such I wasn't allowed to prescribe controlled pain killers like Pethidine which was commonly used for women going through the pains of labour. You can imagine how anxious I was feeling; the Prof was putting himself out on a limb employing me and I didn't want to let him down.

I worked my way through my list, with mainly common-sense decisions guiding me, until a married couple approached my desk and nervously asked if I could help them with their particularly embarrassing problem of painful intercourse, which was making their married life most stressful at the moment.

Never having heard of or imagined that problem before, I asked them to wait while I went to ask the Prof's advice.

I walked to his desk at the rear of the clinic and asked him about the management of this couple's problem. He beamed a great smile, leaned back on his big leather chair, put both his feet on the huge leather topped desk and replied with, "My dear boy, far better to have dyspareuned than never to have pareuned at all!" He then briefed me on the management of dyspareunia or painful intercourse and sent me back to my patients, all the wiser.

I knew I was going to enjoy working for him immensely and my other five consultant bosses in the professorial team. I was acting as one of four senior house surgeons and between us we would be on call every 4th day and every 4th weekend, attend Consultant Clinics, assist at theatres' operation lists and look after the patients on the gynaecology wards, preparing them for surgery and caring for them afterwards during their recovery.

The Gynae' wards were in the old Addenbrookes hospital, opposite the City Museum. My on-call room was right next to a roundabout on the A10, which was quite busy all night and making it almost impossible to sleep. We had powerful bleeps, where the operator could converse with you. One night when I couldn't sleep, I checked there were no problems on the Gynaecology ward and drove to Annie's house and climbed into bed beside her.

I was just falling into a deep non-rapid eye movement sleep when I was rudely awakened by the hospital switchboard calling me on my bleep to go the ward. I reluctantly slid out of her arms, quickly dressed and rushed to my car. I was driving back towards the hospital at an insane speed when suddenly the sky behind me lit up with the flashing blue lights of a large blue and white traffic police car. I rapidly pulled over and the cop car swerved alongside the kerb in front of me, as I stepped out.

"Where d'you think you're going then?" "D'you think you're in the grand prix?" the very large traffic police officer said, as he leaned up against my vehicle, with me squarely in his sights.

"No, sorry officer, I'm very sorry if I was speeding, I'm a doctor and I've been called into the Old Addenbrookes Hospital for an emergency," I exaggerated.

His mouth dropped open.

"Oh! All right then quick, jump back in your car and follow me," he retorted.

I leapt back in to my car and he screamed off down the road, with all his lights and claxons bellowing and me hotly in pursuit behind him. We jumped all the lights and screeched to slow outside the hospital main entrance, with the gate porter's eyes popping out as we passed his lodge without stopping. I rushed in and up the stairs praying the cop wouldn't follow me up to the ward.

Instead, he shouted, "Good luck doc," and was gone.

When I reached the ward, I discovered the so-called emergency was simply a lady who had some post-op pain and had gone off to sleep, by the time I got there. My God, I thought the bloody agency night nurse dragged me out of Annie's bed for this rubbish. I remember how my tutor Dr Walker had warned us that nurses could make your life hell, if you upset them. She probably only called me to get a look at the new 'SHO'.

I determined not to let that happen again and was as nice as possible, to keep the buggers on my side. I also wrote every post-op patient up for painkillers and anti-vomit drugs just in case they needed them. It was a sharp learning curve to grasp, but we doctor quickly realised who the good nurses were and would only call you in a real emergency. The trouble was that the fools outnumbered the bright ones and the agency nurses far outnumbered the permanent more stable nurses, because of the lousy insulting pay the permanent ones earned.

I had come to like this discipline of gynaecology, which was a medical and surgical specialty. I must admit I found the surgery more exciting than the medicine, but these were exciting times in medicine and the Professorial Unit at Cambridge was foremost in the Investigation and Treatment of Infertility and Cancer. We were trying out theoretical stuff at the forefront of science and intervening with surgery to both save old lives and make new lives.

One Saturday morning, I came on duty and was doing a ward round to become acquainted with the patients. This round was with the Ward sister and the SHO who had been on duty all night admitting patients. We circulated around the old oblong shaped ward and were dealing with the penultimate patient.

Because we were approaching the last patient, who was in the bed next to the nurses' station, the sister asked a student nurse to remove the patient's dressing pack from her nether regions, so that she would be ready for examination. She'd been admitted with heavy vaginal bleeding during the night before.

The student nurse drew the curtains around the bed and in the next minute, there was an almighty scream, as the several pints of blood pooled in the patient's pelvis blasted the vaginal packing out across the bed, spraying the nurse from top to bottom and lifting the surrounding curtains backwards.

I rushed to the bedside, grabbed a dressing pack from the top of the cabinet and shoved it into the patient's groin attempting to stem the blood flow. The young patient was a very pale grey with an un-recordable pulse and blood pressure. The sister called the crash team, while my colleague and I put canulae and drip lines into her other arm and both her feet.

We took her straight to theatre and Mr. Bradley, the senior registrar who was on call, undertook a laparotomy, laying open her lower abdomen. We found that at the top of her vagina and beyond it, her anterior descending uterine artery had traumatic tears. Her boyfriend (who turned out to be her pimp), apparently had

71

repeatedly rammed a Pepsi Cola bottle into her, during a public display of her anatomical pelvic talents.

That morning, the patient lost her womb, one ovary together with its fallopian tube and her fertility, but we saved her life. The patient had been admitted from A&E, in the early hours, having complained of unexplained heavy P.V. (Per Vaginam) blood loss.

My colleague, who believed her story of enthusiastic sex, put a canula and fluids into her arm, packed her vagina and admitted her for investigations next day. He lost faith in the veracity of the British Public after that and learned to examine every patient very carefully and systematically for himself.

I was getting used to the routine of seeing patients in clinic and admitting them for later surgery. We routinely undertook complete pelvic clearances for patients with cancer. It was good being part of the Prof's team, not only undertaking exciting stuff, but undertaking it with experts usually in a safe and relaxed environment.

One afternoon, I was assisting the professor in a hysterectomy operation, with the radio playing music in the background. The news came on and we heard that a lady police officer had been shot and killed outside the Libyan embassy in London and that Metropolitan police officers had laid siege to the building. They had been unable to enter the embassy to arrest her killer, because he or she was inside the large house, which, as it was Libyan territory, had so-called Diplomatic Immunity.

This was quite shocking news to everyone in the operating theatre including me, and I loudly protested my incredulity that our police were prevented from storming the building to arrest the perpetrator. I berated the government for making the police hold their positions and for not being bolder. I loudly advocated buggering diplomacy and charging in there to catch the murderer of an innocent unarmed police officer.

I didn't notice that the Prof didn't say anything or express any opinion on the situation. I thought that he must be only too grateful for getting his son and his family back from another situation in a country not that far from Libya. I felt justified in my view, which was also the consensus of the rest of those present in theatre that day and by that evening, possibly most of the country.

The hysterectomy was our last case that afternoon and I felt a bit ashamed to be British as I walked back to change in the surgeons' room. I started to get out of my scrubs for a shower when the Prof walked in to change.

He sat on the bench opposite me and quietly said, "I understand how you feel about these dreadful events. That poor innocent young woman, brutally killed by those cowardly uncivilised bastards! However, you are quite wrong about this situation."

I replied, "What do you mean wrong? We should seize the culprit, it's common justice! That's what would happen in their primitive country, if the boot was on the other foot!"

"It might, but on the other hand, it might not. Look, we can't talk about this here. I think I know you sufficiently well by now. If you really would like to learn some more about our country and British diplomacy and why you aren't right about Britain not standing up for justice; perhaps you might like to join me this evening for dinner on 'High Table' at my college. Can you call in at the Porters Lodge at Downing College at 7 o'clock?"

"Errr, yes sir," I stammered. "That would be very kind of you."

"Good then, I'll see you there and come dressed appropriately, it is high table."

With that, he left the changing room and I was left there somewhat at a loss for what to say, but as I was alone, it didn't matter. I suddenly realised that this great man had invited me, from lowly origins, to join him for dinner to teach me about British diplomacy. As I dressed alone in the surgeon's room, I wondered about what had just been said and where this might be leading!

11

Somewhat bemused, I showered quickly and left to rush back to my college flat to change into something smarter. It tickled me to think that although I was a newly qualified doctor via the "Conjoint" finals, I was technically still a student and member of a Cambridge College, not having graduated and due to re-sit surgery finals in June.

Despite that, I was being paid more than my peers, still living in a spacious and privileged highly subsidised college flat and had just been invited out to a high table college dinner by my boss, the excellent professor. Little did I realise that my life was about to change dramatically, as I sat somewhat numbed in the back of my taxi to Downing College to sit at high table; not bad for a working class lad, from a small country Grammar school!

I arrived at the porter's lodge with five minutes to spare and introduced myself.

"Come in, sir and I'll let the Professor know that you've arrived and do take a seat," said the very large man who greeted me in a very genial tone.

He picked up the phone to do just that in an even more affable voice and signing off, he said, "Yes, sir. I'll send him over."

He turned to his colleague and said, "Be a nice chap and show the good doctor over to the Prof's rooms on Stair 11, would you?"

"This way sir," his colleague, who had a military bearing, continued and led me out of the Lodge onto a huge quadrangle where the luscious green grass was cut short enough to play snooker on it.

We marched straight-backed down two sides to the opposite corner and up a flight of ancient oak stairs to the first floor where the room numbers and occupants' names were hand painted in Roman letters and numerals. He banged on the Prof's door and was summoned to enter.

He stepped in and announced, "I have your guest here Professor, shall I bring him in?"

The Prof answered in the affirmative and I was duly shown into a sumptuous suite of rooms, where the walls were panelled in highly polished light oak wood from floor to ceiling. The lighting was subdued and the Prof was at the far end of his living room. He turned holding two large glasses of red wine and walked towards me.

"This is the college claret, a very good year I think you'll agree. It's one of the perks, when you get to my position in the pecking order! I thought we'd have an aperitif before we go to high table in the graduate dining room. Sit down, my boy and make yourself comfortable. Now then, what were we talking about earlier? Oh yes, we couldn't really talk in the surgeons' room, those walls definitely have ears and we don't want anyone knowing our private business, which is, in fact, very private business!"

"Do you remember when you came across me in the hospital, that evening, as I had just discovered that my son and his family had been abducted in Somalia?"

"Yes sir," I replied again, slightly wondering where the conversation was going.

"You were very comforting towards me at the time. You tried to ease my situation, like a good doctor, by reassuring me that our government might be able to make great efforts towards securing their release and that we didn't know all the diplomatic steps that go on behind closed doors, the connections and levers they might exert to protect our fellow countrymen, in the general running of things and particularly for my son."

"I recognised qualities in you that evening that will one day make you a great doctor. Also, do you remember that happy day, when I called you to let you know that my family had indeed been released and we were celebrating it in my rooms? I saw how happy you were, as your exuberance, like mine, was clearly visible on your open face. This is what has influenced me to offer you a position on our team, which you very wisely accepted. Your supervisors have told me how well you are doing and I'm very pleased I was able to take you on board!"

"Today, I wasn't very surprised at your reaction to the terrible events that occurred in London, with the murder of the young police woman and the anger you expressed at our government's impotence to punish the culprits. That is why I feel it may be an appropriate time to make you more aware of aspects of our country, to which you have previously not been a party. Do you love your country, and would you call yourself patriotic?"

"Yes sir!" I blurted out, "I didn't mean to sound so disparaging about Britain. I was just really angry about the utter waste of the life of that young police officer, at the hands of those uncivilised so-called diplomats. I was also angry that our hands are tied by diplomacy and we can't do anything about it!"

"Yes, I thought so. I want to tell you something. I'm aware that you are able to keep a confidence, as you already have about my son's kidnapping. What you are about to hear you will have to keep as secret for the rest of your life. Can you swear to me now that you will do that?"

I could see he was deadly serious about what he was about to impart to me and I replied, "Yes sir, I will."

He leaned across the table and said, "My son wasn't released. He was tracked down by some of our country's agents and located in a place, where he was confined by these terrorist or bandit groups."

"A team of specialists were sent out from one of our ships in the Med, dropped by helicopter on a moonless night, at a distance from the terrorist position, which they observed, infiltrated and secured my family's release and that of several other captives of various nationalities. While this was going on very quietly, the remaining team members proceeded to slaughter most of the bandits without mercy.

"They captured several of them, including a number of Europeans, who were active members of the IRA. The bandit camp was totally destroyed. Their equipment and weapons were also captured along with documents and information deemed relevant to our country's security. The specialists, their equipment, the rescued captives and terrorist prisoners were rapidly picked up and delivered safely back to one of our navy's ships, waiting in the Mediterranean.

"So you see our government can be very active in defending our citizens. Furthermore, plans are already in place to identify the culprit of today's brutality and in time the individual or individuals concerned will also be dealt with swiftly and without mercy."

I was totally 'gob-smacked', and didn't know how to reply. I must have looked shocked with my mouth open as he continued, not allowing me to interrupt.

"I invited you here tonight to give you a further opportunity. That is, if you want it. If you do, it will change your life forever. If you decide you don't want it, then you may walk away and forget what you have heard here, never to repeat it to anyone! Shall I go on?"

At that point there was a loud knock at his door and I said, "Shall I get that?"

He put his hand on my arm and shouted, "Come in."

My mouth dropped even further open as a very tall and elegant man in his late middle age walked through the door.

"Good evening, Charles and hello to you, young doctor. I am the Master of this college and the Vice-Chancellor of our university. I have heard a great deal about you and know that you are a member of our clinical school. I'm very pleased to see you here this evening. You come highly recommended by my friend here, which is no mean feat! Is that the claret, Charles? Mind if I join you?"

The Prof stood and poured another large one.

"Welcome James, you're just in time, I was just about to start and I'd just asked our colleague here if he wanted me to continue telling him about our other role outside of the university and the NHS." He turned to me looking very serious.

"Good, then let's continue," interjected the other great man in the room, as he laid his large arm on my left shoulder.

"Would you like me to continue?" said Prof.

"Yes, yes I would like you to continue," I almost blurted out.

"Well then, let's begin. The Master and I and a number of other individuals, some of whom you may already be acquainted with, work for the government outside of our commitments to Cambridge University and the National Health Service. We work for the Intelligence Community in the government's Department of Defence. We undertake specialist jobs for which our medical training has equipped us. The roles themselves may not always be medical but our training makes us uniquely qualified to carry out such matters as quickly and quietly as possible.

"We believe that you have the qualities to be part of our team. We are not directly part of the military. We might be described as a sort of an Academic Gentleman's Paramilitary Association. You won't be in uniform or have to learn to march up and down. However, you would have to have some military training, mainly for your own personal safety, on a just-in-case basis. It is highly unlikely that you would be involved in any battlefield operations and apart from a smattering of training. You won't be involved with the military, unless you want to be, but that would be on very rare occasions. However, you may be involved with certain aspects of local police work that may involve co-operation with the military. We're all on the same side."

The Master added, "We usually deal with very rare esoteric civilian situations, that require the utmost secrecy and expeditious action. Your life may be very rarely at risk, so long as such events can be planned, but no guarantees can ever be made as to how events may unfold! We must now ask you again, would you like to become part of this secret and unrecognised team that works quietly for our country? Do not answer now, we are almost late for high table. Think on it over dinner and we'll retire to the senior common room for your response, over a glass of college port. For now, here's to Britain!"

We chinked our large glasses, I gulped down the college claret and was silent. We left straight after by Stair 11 and strode unquestioned, straight across the sacred lawn to the post-graduate dining room, where everyone stood and clapped as we entered. The great hall dining room was also panelled with timber, but it was polished golden Yew, and very palatial. At the far end was a huge table also of golden Yew with twelve huge luxurious chairs, in place around it.

We sat down and joined the other Dons and guests who were dining there. As we sat down, the other post-graduate students sat also. I felt very important. On high table we each had a waiter, who stood directly behind us and delivered our various courses throughout the excellent fare. Every time we sipped from our glasses, they topped them up, without asking. After grace, in Latin, what followed can only be described as a sumptuous feast, but my mind was racing with the enormity of what I'd just heard and I couldn't focus on the resplendent dishes before me.

My head was still spinning as we adjourned to the senior common room for coffees and college port, brought up from their extensive wine cellars and chambréed to perfect room temperature. We sat in deep leather chairs as the college waiters poured our drinks, decanted from ancient Vintage Port bottles with the Downing College label and passed them correctly to the left, from person to person.

Prof was the first to break the silence, "Well, my boy, how do you feel about our proposition to you?"

I leaned forward in my chair, "I am honoured by your belief in me Professor and Master, I accept your offer with great relish, thank you."

"Bravo and well done!" roared the Master. "Welcome aboard!"

The Prof smiled sedately, looking very pleased. I felt elated, wondering how fate had brought me into the company of these two great men of our time and what that encounter might have in store for me in the future.

Prof continued and elaborated on his earlier comments.

"This great university has been tainted in the past by the treacherous behaviour of a small undistinguished group of five of our former alumni. I'm sure you are aware of this and I don't have to denigrate this meeting by reiterating their names and activities."

I thought I could recall, only from reading it in the news, that sometime in the past a number of very prominent society individuals, all of whom were Cambridge graduates had been suspected of spying for the USSR. The most eminent of whom was actually the head of MI6, our own spy service. They had been recruited during World War 2, when the world was at war against the atrocious Nazis and it was more acceptable and quite common among young idealistic university intellectuals to become members the Communist Party. The NKVD (forerunners of the KGB) nurtured these young intellectuals in the high ideals of the communist dogmas of those times, against the decadent inequalities of the West and recruited them into their service. I wasn't aware of the numbers or names, but I wasn't going to interrupt the good professor.

"We are a group of highly qualified specialists that help our government in unique and highly sensitive ways for which we are equipped to deal. The diversity of the roles we undertake for our country is vast, but they all involve duties in the interests of Britain, and in our minds, they go some way towards exonerating the subversive behaviours by some of our past alumni. Such duties may be anywhere, but they are usually in Britain or in Europe itself. You will have your own career as a doctor before you, in whichever branch of medicine you choose but we will of course take a keen interest in you, wherever you go and we will be watching over you, in an almost paternalistic manner."

"Although you will not be employed in the usual sense of the word, you will be paid a generous retainer into a separate and confidential account at the Queen's bank, where we have somewhat of an influence, as its leaders and many of its directors are Cambridge alumni. This account, as I say will be secret. You need not declare it to any accountant and we expect you to keep it secret. You will also be given a generous payment whenever you undertake a specific duty for the state. Eventually at your retirement, you will also receive a further pension for your special service to our country."

"As a doctor, you will of course be subject to certain ethics and governance by the GMC, but additionally, as a member of our service, you will have a very strict code of conduct and you will behave in a highly responsible and silent manner. You will not draw attention to yourself and you will be answerable for your actions. When called upon you will make yourself available to undertake whatever is necessary to achieve the interests of the state."

"You will make every effort to remain physically and mentally fit. You must set aside some time each year for training in self-defence and in the use of personal weapons, so that you will be competent, should the need ever arise. This training will be residential and conducted by the military at relevant training establishments. You may on occasions, work alone, or with other similarly trained civilian colleagues but also, you may undertake jobs alongside other branches of the military or those of law and order. This work will of course be most secret and you will never be able to discuss it with anyone. Now that's rather a lot to take in at one briefing, so I think we should probably call it a night. Don't worry about what you have heard here, you will have lots of time to ask relevant questions later. We are very happy that you have chosen to accept our invitation."

"Waiter will you summon one of the duty porters and ask them to give our good doctor a lift back to his accommodation?"

"Yes, Professor," the waiter replied pivoting around on his heels.

Before I left, he advised me that things would now proceed at their own pace and that I should carry on as normal and that I would be contacted in the fullness of time for induction training. In the meantime, I would continue to be an acting Senior House Officer in Obstetrics and Gynaecology, currently practicing Gynaecology at the Addenbrookes Old Site and that I should not speak of any of this to anyone.

I thanked them and bade them both good night and left with the porter. We marched almost in army style round the lawn perimeter back to the porter's lodge and the big man there gave me a lift straight round to Annie's place. The porter asked me for the address, but didn't make any small talk on the way back. I don't think I could have said much anyway.

I was stunned by the evening's events and revelations. I'd been entertained to a feast of a dinner, by two eminent professors who were not only senior figures of the university, they were also senior figures in the country's secret service as well. I pinched myself to see if it was real!

12

My brain was still racing as I let myself in to her house, which was in darkness. I had no idea of the time. I climbed her stairs two at a time.

As I entered her bedroom, she turned over towards me and greeted me with, "Where've you been? I'm freezing. Come here, I need you to keep me warm. Quick!"

I almost ripped off my clothes, spreading them all over the floor.

I felt my manhood stirring below, as sliding into bed beside her, the high table and high secrets went straight out of my head. She reached out placing her open hand on my buttocks pulling me into her, where I sunk wantonly, slowly raising her to a back-arching fever pitch, until she washed over me.

Well, she did ask me to keep her warm! I fell asleep in her arms, a panting perspiring mound of flesh immersed inside her.

As the weekend dawn arose over Cambridge, I awoke to the feel of her toes gently massaging my manhood back to life.

She eased herself towards me nibbling my neck and whispered, "Ummm, what did you do to me last night? I just exploded. My muscles are aching. It's never been like that. Let's…ummm…do it again!"

She slid down my abdomen and gripped my expanding phallus between her lips, washing its head with her tongue, exploring my urethral opening with its tip. My enraptured nervous system was alive to a million pleasurable sensations. My taught body shuddered and I sprayed her again evacuating my last remaining stores! I sunk into the deep sleep of repletion, my every sinew undone by endorphins.

We finally roused around noon and I pondered about what had happened the previous evening. Its most serious reality felt somewhat dulled by the private intimacy of our love-making. I was surprised by my feelings of total relaxation and the duration I had slept, not connected to the stark realities of the real world outside.

I answered Annie's curiosity about my late arrival, in every sense of the word arrival, with an alibi of a monthly college dinner, which she accepted without reservation and no guilt on my part whatsoever, after all, though not my college, it really was a monthly college dinner and it was 'pro patria'.

She was full of excitement about the weekend, but I couldn't relate to or share her enthusiasm, despite the passion of our earlier love-making; which had cleared my mind, I was very pensive wondering about how this new role into my way of life would affect my life in general, my civil status and my relationship with this woman. Could I get married? Indeed, would I want to get married?

Annie was wonderful, but there were too many unknowns. How would it affect my career in medicine? What would my career in Medicine be? I hadn't yet decided what I wanted to do. Yet now these two very eminent and powerful men were about to make a huge difference to my future. They had been very open with me and made me an offer to help my country and I had accepted.

Christ, what have I done? My mind was racing, there she was in front of me looking very lovely and being very happy, asking repeated questions about various trivia, like lovers do! I just couldn't concentrate on them and felt I had to get out of the house before my head exploded.

"I've got to go," I blurted out that I'd forgotten to write up some notes in one of my post-op patients records. "I needed to do it before one of the other docs write in her records and realise, I forgot."

I pecked her on the cheek and ran out the door before she could inhale to answer me. I drove back to my college flat, which I still had the benefit of and where I knew I could be alone and think through the extraordinary events of the evening before.

These men had selected me because they had faith in my integrity, abilities and my patriotism. They were highly placed members of the British Establishment, clearly very well-connected. They could make or break my career in Medicine. They clearly cared about my welfare; the Prof had demonstrated that on several occasions. I should feel honoured that I'd been selected. Yes, I did feel honoured. They wouldn't knowingly place me in danger.

No, they wouldn't. I wouldn't let them down. No, I wouldn't. Suddenly things started to clear in my head and I started to relax, as my anxieties about the unknowns faded away. I was fit and young with my life ahead looking exciting and rosy. I drove back to Annie's, elated to enjoy the rest of my weekend off with a fabulous woman!

We drove into the centre of the city, parked in my college car park and walked to the shopping Mall, where Anna insisted on buying new lingerie in her namesake's underwear emporium, that specialised in such enjoyably feminine and louche undergarments. I tried to insist she didn't need this stuff to turn me on, she just had to look at me to make my intentions rise! But she insisted it made her feel good to look so good and she really did look so good!

Afterwards, we walked to the 'Airman' pub opposite Kings College nearby and imbibed a few real ales and food in the historic atmosphere, where bomber and fighter pilots from the local air bases had relaxed during the air war for Britain. The pub was full of noisy tourists and we couldn't converse very well, so we gulped down the good pub food, picked up her car and sped back to her house where she treated me to a fashion show of her latest boutique wear.

It didn't last too long as I couldn't watch her display without being overwhelmed by desires and in no time, we were rolling over her living room floor entwined in each other's limbs and going hell for leather.

We slept and I awoke early to attend the Sunday morning 8 o'clock round on the gynae' ward at Old Addenbrookes, where the duty doctor handed over the admitted patients from the previous night. The night had been quiet, so I was able to discharge all those patients due to go home and set about admitting and clerking patients for the theatre list on Monday.

The young lady of the night who'd lost her fertility, was waiting to leave with her pimp. She thanked me graciously and I advised her to avoid Coca Cola in future. They both left the ward rapidly without looking back. I wondered if they knew how lucky she had been not to have rapidly bled to death and to survive those very dangerous and stupid party displays.

I settled down into the busy routine of the Gynae Surgical Ward, which was fairly hectic, examining the admissions, taking samples to cross match units of blood for each patient on the morning 'Ops List'. We wrote up drug charts, checked on the patients' needs, wrote discharge summaries and grabbed a bite to eat before the nurses bleeped us again to exert their powers on us for some trivial reason that would have certainly waited until we'd finished lunch.

I decided that I had to be even nicer to them, so they at least thought about it before bleeping me. I returned to the ward and seeing my chance, I joined them in the ward kitchen as some of them were taking a coffee break. They were very welcoming, moving around their table to give me room to sit. I asked their names and re-introduced myself as the new Professorial SHO. They looked impressed and asked what made me choose that specialty. I didn't mention the Prof rescuing me from unemployment and said I liked the mixture of both medicine and surgery in Obstetrics and Gynaecology as well as the opportunity to undertake research working in the Prof's academic unit.

I was smiling enthusiastically and trying to show interest in their conversations and quickly discerned which of them were good at their job and actually thought before disturbing my daily duties with some things they could have dealt with easily. I had already learned not to complain or show any anger, when they were incompetent and to praise them as much as possible, whenever they did something right. This paid dividends and facilitated my undisturbed sleep, while some of my other colleagues really didn't fare so well.

Easter was rapidly approaching and Annie mentioned she was thinking of taking a break. She asked if I'd also be off for the bank holiday and whether I would like to go with her to visit her relatives in the Midlands. I said I'd investigate and get back to her. So, I went to the Infertility Lab in the Medical Research Counsel building, found Mr. Bradley and asked him whether our team was going to be on duty.

He smiled and said, "Well, I'm not but you are. You're actually going to be on a duty of a different kind. You're due to report to the guardhouse at the military Academy off the A30 in Camberley, next Monday at 09.00. I was going to talk to you about it later today, but since you've asked; let's go next door to the clinical school, find a discreet corner in the post grad' dining room and discuss it."

Shocked, I gasped, "So, you're part of it as well?"

"Yes, I am," he countered. "Let's go, we've got lots to discuss!" as he led the way out.

We sat facing each other in the corner of the room.

"Well Mike," he said in a low-pitched voice, "Prof would have told you we'd be in touch and here we are. You're no doubt a bit surprised to encounter me in this role, but as you've discovered, I am part of all this and in deed I am to supervise your induction training, so you'll be seeing a lot more of me than so far. If you have any other plans after the weekend, you'd better postpone them posthaste, because your training is scheduled to start as soon as possible, which means next week."

"I won't be there with you, but you will be in the capable hands of a Sergeant-Major or possibly a warrant officer who will be looking after you and some other officers. You will have the nominal rank of Captain and theoretically be one of the highest ranking of the group, but we don't really observe ranks in our sort of roles as you're there to learn how to look after yourself. So treat the Sergeant-Major or warrant officer with extreme respect, as your mentor and guardian angel. What he imparts to you may one day save your life and those of others."

"Initially, you will be there for a week, but you can expect to go back there intermittently throughout your career in the security service. You have a car, I know. Let me have your registration number and a pass will be waiting for you in the guardhouse at the entrance, when you arrive. If you call in later at the Prof's office, we will give you your orders.

"These are secret materials, which you will keep entirely confidential. The Prof is away next week at a conference in London. You may use that as your cover with your colleagues and friends. I do not have to tell you that no-one must ever know of the real reason for your sudden departure from your position at the Old Addenbrookes site.

"The Professor will cover your absence as his assistant on this week away. From next Monday, you will be a paid member of her Majesty's Security Services and will have a bank account with her bank. You will receive details of the logistics of your new employment on your return. Keep your receipts for re-imbursements through Marion, the Prof's secretary. Yes, she is also a service member."

"In her office, she will go through the Official Secrets Act with you. We have made different oaths and commitments, so you won't have to sign it, but you will be expected to be bound by it.

"You will need to take your gymnasium gear with you, as a lot of your work will be quite physical. You will also be slightly on trial on this, your first outing, but we have great faith in our decision to approach you and we are certain you won't let us or your country down. You may socialise with the other officer trainees on the course, but do not under any circumstances discuss who you are or why you are there.

"You may not be the only member of our group in your class there, but of course, they will not reveal themselves to you. I wish you luck and look forward to seeing you on your return. You may contact me about any problems you may have about our services both surgical and security. However, you must always remember to discuss these with me in the first person, as walls have ears!"

"I'm not sure what the Prof has already told you about our service, but I'm here to fill in the details, answer your questions and give you wise advice. I will try to anticipate what you need to know, but if in doubt just ask. There's no such thing as a silly question in our game. You will want to know what our game is. Well, we are not spies, like MI6; we won't be going out looking for useful information for the good of the realm.

"We're also not really part of the security service MI5 and don't catch and prosecute foreign agents. We are specialists, because of our medical training but separate from these security services. However, we may work alongside both, as well as the Special Branch part of the police force. We are armed for our own security purposes because of the dangerous individuals we may come up against. However, we aren't usually called upon to use our weapons."

Praise the Lord, I thought to myself.

13

The dawn was breaking as I silently slid out of bed and quickly washed. I returned to the bedroom to dress and Annie had woken up. She embraced me as I dressed and I had to tear myself away from her. I said I'd call her as soon as I could, conference permitting and would be back as soon as possible. I set out on my secret journey to Surrey, keen to avoid rush hour traffic and being late for the Non-Commissioned Officer, who awaited me at the army guardhouse.

The journey was arduous down the A10 to London, round the overcrowded North Circular road with its multiple traffic lights almost invariably red, frequently stuck behind disastrously slow drivers, dropping off their commuting partners. Poor bastards I thought inwardly. How lucky I am to be a doctor, with the most interesting job in the world, still naïve and unaware of what the government had install for me.

On the North Circular, I noticed that the drivers who seemed to want to queue; block up the outside overtaking lane, where there was never anyone to overtake; pull out at roundabouts and then suddenly stop, or wait until there was nothing coming for half a mile before they actually pulled out; mostly seemed to be lady drivers!

I made a mental note to ask the Prof about that. Then, suddenly, I'd made it to the A30 This was very busy by then, with loads of commuters and winding roads where you couldn't safely overtake the poor workers driving like Lemmings, at a snail's pace to avoid getting to work a minute too early.

I imagined they weren't at all like me, highly keen to work at this new adventure and eager to show my capabilities. After what seemed a lifetime, I finally arrived at 08.40, covering the frustrating hundred and forty odd mile journey in just over three and a half hours, which wasn't that bad considering the state of the roads and the two and a half hour 'rush hour'.

I pulled into the vast car park, under the watchful eyes of numerous cameras. They like their security here, I thought to myself as I manoeuvred into a very tight parking space. All this space here and still the totally inadequate sized gaps to park your car. The car parking spaces in the UK haven't changed for aeons, probably down to some government idiotic regulation, even though cars have grown enormously.

I rushed along, almost bursting into the guardroom, where several very large military police men were banging on typewriters. One looked up and went back to his typing, most had big typewriters with golf ball-like letter-bashers, but I noticed a couple of the soldiers had these new word processing machines with electronic screens, attached to printers, where you could go back and change everything before you finally ran it off on a printer, or sent it off electronically.

Finally, the typing M.P., a corporal, left his desk and approaching the counter addressed me.

"Can I'elp you, sir?" he grumbled out without looking in my direction.

"I hope so," I replied, handing him my carefully sealed orders that Marion, the Prof's secretary had handed me a couple of days before I left.

He unsealed them and scanned them, then suddenly he leapt to attention and sharply exclaimed, "Excuse me, sir, would you like to come this way, sir?" as he opened up the counter to show me through to a back room, where a middle-aged man looked up, his battledress shirt was adorned with lots of multi-coloured ribbons over his left breast pocket.

"This gentleman is for you, Sarn't Major," barked the corporal.

The seated soldier replied, "Thank you, Corporal. I'll take him now."

With that the corporal stamped his feet together, saluted, about-turned and marched out the door.

The Sergeant-Major slowly stood up, to his full height of about six foot six. As he stood, his shirt didn't move because of the stiff razor-sharp creases running down its front. The creases continued down his trouser legs and ended at his highly polished army boots, in which I thought I could probably see a reflection of my face.

He marched over towards me briskly. Under his arm he had a beech swagger stick with a silver cap on the end. His wide powerful shoulders tapered to a slim waist enclosed in a green webbing belt. On his right wrist was a leather band with the insignia of a regiment which I later discovered was the Irish guards. He came to attention in front of me and saluted.

I was awestruck and didn't know what to do, so I proffered my hand, which he ignored saying, "Would you like to follow me, sir?" as he spun round and marched out the back door with me in hot pursuit, half-walking and half-running to keep up.

He led me to a group of large wooden huts, signed outside as 'Officers Quarters'.

He stepped onto the veranda, opened a door and said, "This is your room, sir. The Officers' Mess is outside to the left. If you give me the keys to your car, I'll have it brought over. Unpack and we will meet in the mess at 10.00am in your P.E. kit."

I thanked him and he left abruptly. I perused my room, which was basic but adequate. Approximately ten minutes later there was a knock on my door and the corporal typist entered carrying my bags. Handing me my keys, he stated that my car was parked outside. He saluted and twisting round and marched out the door. I was left entirely alone in an army barracks!

'What the hell am I doing here? Yesterday I was a doctor in Cambridge and here I am in the middle of a highly active army training college. How the hell did this happen?'

I had half an hour to unpack and get to the Officers' Mess.

I just made it again and suddenly found myself in a group of about 20 similarly dressed individuals. We were approximately 70 % men and 30% women; aged in mid-20s to early 30s. We all mumbled or nodded hellos.

Then at precisely 10.00, the Sergeant-Major, who was earlier in the guardroom marched into the room and said, "Good morning ladies and gentlemen, I am your Sergeant-Major. My job is to help you to get back into shape and prepare you for the harsh outside world where you have chosen or have been selected to work for Her Majesty the Queen. I realise that many of you are very gently disposed and academic people; but you may not be dealing with similarly disposed people where you are going.

"What I teach you here may help you to survive outside against the animals that you will encounter when you leave the safety of this military establishment. So pay attention, do what I say an' do; don't waste my time and we will get on very well. At the end of this brief course, if you pass, you may be invited as my guests to the Sergeants' Mess, where you may show me your appreciation for the skills, I have taught you, in the usual manner. If you would like to follow me outside, we will start with a little run to gently warm you up and painlessly ease you into fitness training."

With that, we followed him out and into a two-mile warm-up run followed by twenty minutes of P.E. on the parade ground. Gasping for air and dripping in sweat, we then stopped, were instructed to shower, dress and meet at the Officers' Mess in thirty minutes for the Colonel's welcome speech.

This proved to be a more verbose version of the Sergeant-Major's speech but with much more camaraderie, which made us feel more welcome. Following that, we broke for an hour lunch break served with a huge mug of very sweet tea. We sat on long benches at long tables, where we consumed ham, egg, beans and chips.

The conversation was stunted and mainly about where we had come from and the overcrowded roads in Britain. There was a woman from Oxford, the city of dreaming spires. I was the only one from Cambridge, in my case the city of perspiring dreams. There was a couple from London and several from different places around the country.

Exactly on the hour, the Sergeant-Major reappeared and led us down to the armoury, where we were lined up for a brief introduction to weaponry protocols. The armourer, another sergeant, appeared from his office and the Sergeant-Major introduced us to him as a group of specialists sent by the defence department to become familiar with the use of hand guns, for our own personal security.

The armourer gathered us around him and said, "Right then ladies and gentlemen, welcome to the armoury, Weapons are a serious business and there are several rules you will follow while you're here under my instruction."

We stood in silence, listening intensely as he explained the need for strict adherence to the armoury rules. I imagined that they must have had some serious accidents in this building, judging by the serious demeanour of this weapons specialist.

He started by telling us that people may only enter and leave the building when a green warning light is on and no-one can shoot during these times.

He instructed us on where to stand to shoot behind a counter, when to shoot, only when specifically told to do so, where to stand when not shooting, so as not to distract the shooters. He showed us how to handle the pistols and how to hand the pistols sideways on to others with the safety catch on for automatics and with the barrel open for revolvers and told us when we could go and collect our target sheets.

He was also very particular about counting out the number of bullets, collected from the armourer and the number of empty shell cases returned to the armourer.

"Follow these instructions and we will get on very well, like a house on fire, if you'll excuse the pun!"

We each had to sign for the loan of one of a selection of various types of handgun and for the ammunition. The guns we were shown had different characteristics.

The Webley army service revolver had two sizes; – a point 38 had a powerful kick back and the smaller point 32, with slightly less kick back and which was the standard British Army officers' pistol.

We tried out double action pistols where pulling the trigger actually cocked the hammer, which fired at the end of the pull. Having fired its bullets, you had to release the revolving cylinder to empty the spent cartridge cases and reload with fresh live bullets. This emptying and reloading was very tedious because the cases were very hot straight after firing and it took time to slot fresh bullets into the cylinders! This wouldn't be too convenient in the middle of a firefight!

We also tried out the American semi-automatic Colt point 45, which was a much faster weapon. When fired it has a cover on top of the pistol that slides back, exposing its barrel and ejecting the shell. This sliding casing also cocks the hammer and loads a new bullet into its chamber, from the magazine clipped into its handle. The magazine (or Clip) holds 7 bullets, so it was much better in a firefight with a quicker push button to drop out the used magazine and clip a new one into its handle. However, it was heavier to hold and had a hell of a kick from its larger bullet with a bigger amount of explosive propellant.

The armourer enthused about a different pistol called the Walther P.P. (Police Pistol used by the East German Police and copied in Britain). This was a precision engineered automatic double action pistol (its trigger cocked and fired the hammer). The PPK was made famous as James Bond's favourite weapon. The sergeant recommended the PPS model for us, where the pistol barrel was bored out to 0.32 inches. This pistol was light to carry and highly accurate to shoot with very little kick back.

He added that, using bullets with a hollowed-out head and a little extra charge to the shell, this pistol would stop an elephant. No wonder James Bond liked the Walther P.P. range! We tried it out and no surprises, we liked it too. It was far superior to the Webleys and Colt pistols that kicked back and deafened you at the same time, despite wearing our ear mufflers.

We were taught how to strip the hand guns into their constituent parts, clean them thoroughly and then re-assembly them. We did this repeatedly until the various parts of the weapon were shining like new and we could do it in less than thirty seconds.

The afternoon seemed to pass rapidly; I suspect because we had to concentrate intensely on what was happening. I was somehow quite pleased when I collected my high-scoring targets at the end of the afternoon and discovered that I might be quite good at shooting people, should the need ever arise!

I wondered how this new responsibility set me apart from my medical peers, who were no doubt busy up to their ears in learning how to treat patients, with in some cases, the intention of saving their lives. Here was I, at what seemed like a world away from their world, learning the best way to save my life by the taking of another's. I perused the possibility that I might like to pop off those incompetent nurses who kept waking me up, but thought the GMC might not concur!

We were politely dismissed and retreated to our officer's accommodation to shower and ready ourselves to meet for dinner at 19.00 in the Officer's Mess.

Dinner was not quite as opulent as the fare at Downing College, but it was a close second. However, the conversation was somewhat stunted, with no-one giving away much about their individual circumstances and it mainly centred on the pistol shooting afternoon and guesses at what was to occur next day. We decided it was best to retire early as one of the waiters let it slip that we were expected at breakfast at 07.00. We thought the Sergeant-Major was probably planning an early morning surprise for us. We agreed that we'd forestall him at this and be ready for action "on parade" at 06.00!

We mustered as planned and sure enough were waiting in the Mess at 06.00, when we heard him rapidly marching across the parade ground.

We rushed out and greeted him in unison with a loud, "Good morning Sergeant-Major!"

He looked surprised to see us but rapidly responded with, "Good morning ladies and gentlemen, it's good to see we haven't dented your enthusiasm! Right then, let's start with a warm up jog to get you in the mood for breakfast."

Outwardly smiling, but no doubt inwardly grumbling, we set off and covered the same route we took the day before, which certainly warmed us up and we appreciated our breakfast all the more on our return.

This was followed by a morning of personal combat, demonstrating to us how to respond to physical assaults from all angles in surprisingly simple but effective ways. It involved unarmed and armed combat, without and with sharp and blunt weapons.

The Sergeant-Major stated we would repeat these lessons over and over again until we became expert in their application, so that if the moment ever arose when we had to use them, it would be second nature to us and insure our survival.

The afternoon continued with another trip to the armoury for more weapons and target practice. We duly signed for our guns and I had the Walther PPS point 32, but without the hollow bullets. Again, I was pleased with my results and the armourer was pleased that we seemed to have listened about the regulations and he didn't have to remonstrate with any of us about screw-ups.

And so the course continued daily with a warm up run, and hand-to-hand fighting in the morning and shooting in the afternoon. I was so busy, that I didn't have time to miss Annie and actually forgot to call her on the public phone outside the guard house.

On the Friday evening, the Sergeant-Major invited us to join him in the Non-Commissioned Officer's mess bar after dinner, to show him our gratitude for his part in our training to make us safer operatives. We took this task very seriously and created a kitty, from which we ended up treating all the non-coms in the bar to a free night of boozy excesses.

I have no recollection of going to bed that night and the first thing I knew was being shaken awake by the mess corporal.

"You better wake up sir, you're a bit late, your fellow trainees are all at breakfast and they sent me to fetch you, so you'd better shake a leg!"

I leapt out of bed and the headache then hit me right at the crown of my head like a beating hammer. What was I drinking last night? We medics had a reputation for boozing but non-coms were something else!

I walked into the shower the corporal had turned on for me which was cold and blasted me back into consciousness. Within 15 minutes, I was dressed and sitting down to a plate of bacon, beans and eggs and gallons of piping hot coffee.

14

We received no certificates of passing or failing. We finished breakfast, shook hands with our trainers, said adieu to our colleagues and in no time, I was on my way back up the A30 towards London. I was assessing what I'd learned from the experience and the reality was that here was I, a quite newly qualified doctor, set apart from my peers by being highly familiar and in deed comfortable with the use of a fully automatic deadly pistol and various ways to quietly kill people! Unless you were there, you wouldn't believe it.

As I slowly progressed up the overcrowded Saturday traffic of the A30, I started working out what I was going to say to Annie about the medical conference that I'd attended for the last 5 days. I needn't have worried; Prof's secretary had been in contact with her at Addenbrookes and briefed her on the conference. I called in at the hospital and picked up her note debriefing me on how I'd spent the week, so I was up to speed when I arrived back at Annie's house.

I felt anxious as I let myself in just in case some other young man had moved in on her while I was away. I walked through her hallway and called out as I got to the foot of her stairs and looking up, there she was smiling down at me. I charged up the stairs and embraced her deeply and passionately, squeezing her as if I never wanted to let her go. She was wearing a mini-skirt and silk shirt top, which showed off her classic fulsome figure, prompting my ardour and amplifying my hard-on. She dragged me across her landing straight into the bedroom.

We didn't take the time to undress, I fell on top of her and reaching down pulled up her skirt, pushed aside her thong and slid into her depths lustfully drowning in her juices. I thrust my pelvis against her so vigorously that I felt my testes bashing against her fourchette, being dragged in by my jousting lance. I ached for her and likewise, she for me. She was gasping and crying in joy with her legs and hips gyrating in time. I couldn't help myself screaming to a massive climax and filling her full of my semen. We fell apart onto our backs, sighing in unison, as we lay in a steaming heap of spent flesh. I imagined she must have been pleased to see me!

We slept to early evening, when I was awakened by her nibbling at my neck, while her hands were encircling my scrotum and her middle finger gently massaging my prostate. This brought my manhood back to attention and seminal fluid leaked out of my urethral meatus as lubrication in anticipation of our imminent love-making. We didn't need that lubrication as she stretched her body, thrusting her abdomen against me. I stretched too, extending my penis proudly upward.

She felt it and closed her left hand around its length pulling her torso down until her head was over it. She lowered her head and swallowed my glans penis, she was licking off her earlier dried juices and probing the opening with her darting tongue. A million-nerve ending in my glans started firing and I moaned in responsive expectation. She was wantonly moaning too and I reached down to feel her. I parted her buttocks with my right hand from below and slid my left thumb into her.

She gasped as I entered her and flexed and extended my thumb back and forth as she simultaneously imbibed at my manhood. The movements of my left arm rocked her over my phallus, amplifying her ecstatic squeals and bringing us both to a mutual crescendo. I came saturating her mouth to overflow, while her love nest gyrated on my extended digit. As they almost say in baseball, we were home and wet! We laid there and I realised I hadn't eaten since breakfast and asked her if she was hungry too. She replied she felt quite full up, and we roared with laughter.

I know, I said let's go out to dinner to that pub where we used to punt to in Granchester. We haven't been there for ages. We used to have great laughs when we were students in the college punts heading out to the meadow below the pub. We'd gorge ourselves with food and drink, then try to punt back to Cambridge, without sinking ourselves or any of the tourist punts we bashed into along the way.

We had a lovely meal in the Red Lion Pub there, recalling all the things we got up to during my student years and I diligently managed to steer her away from discussions about my previous week away at the 'Conference' on innovations in the Treatment of Infertility.

As we drove home, I explained that I had really missed her while I was away and I really had. I must have been a bit distant as in the back of my mind I was trying to relate where I'd really been with my other life as a doctor with her. I decided I'd better talk to the Prof or to Paul Bradley about these sudden misgivings and doubts in my mind.

After gynaecology clinic on the Monday morning, I waited to collar Mr. Bradley about my various concerns, but he pre-empted me, walked up to my desk and suggested we have a coffee in the Faculty Offices on the Addenbrookes 2nd Floor. The secretary made us coffee and we retired to a tutorial room.

"Well Mike, how did you get on? I imagine it must have been a bit gruelling for you. All that running and training, couldn't have been what you've been used to up till now. Tell me all about it. You must have lots of questions and maybe a few worries. We are all here for you, a bit like the Musketeers' all for one and one for all. I remember when I was in your position, I was very anxious about what I'd got myself into and whether I could cope with that extra and secret responsibility."

Again, he had foreseen my doubts and had kind of "magic-ed" them away with just a few brilliant reassuring words.

I told him about my concerns about being taught to kill people and how to kill them quietly; when I was a doctor, hated violence and had spent my whole life trying to eschew it and now, here I was needing to carry a gun for my own protection. Was I likely to be assassinated?

He assured me that in the several years he'd been in the service, he had never killed anyone or ever been in any danger of being assassinated. He re-iterated that we were really just Watchers, looking out for various people in the interests of our country. The course I'd just returned from was simply a precaution, because the world was a dangerous place anyway and, in our service, there were statistically slightly more risks. He repeated that the jobs he'd undertaken had all been medical ones, as a doctor.

Well, actually, they had mainly been surgical roles, when he was in no danger whatsoever. The courses and weapons were simply prophylactic, just in case and for our own protection. He urged me to think of it as merely part of training, probably skills never to be called on. Like those Cardio-Pulmonary Resuscitation courses you have to go on each year; you undertake them to keep up to speed, in some remote case that you may one day have to use them to save a life. Well these skills are very similar, except if you ever have to use our special skills, the life you'll be saving, will probably be your own!

I told him about the training and weaponry and how simple the Walther PP pistol was to handle and shoot and was in my humble opinion by far the best pistol we tried there. I asked him how often I could expect to go for military re-training and whether and how I should prepare for this.

He suggested that I might like to join a gym and attend it regularly, as some of the different specialists we will be working with have to keep very fit as part of their job and they couldn't be expected to slow down to compensate for any inadequacies on our part. Whereas we only encourage our patients to keep fit as a desirable ambition, while many doctors may often tend towards physical inactivity as they pour much of their energies in pursuit of academic achievements within their chosen professional fields.

"Don't wallow in obesity, keep fit! I use the gym at the Social Centre on campus here. Our faculty have corporate membership there! That will keep you in tune for your military training, that you will be undertaking on a regularly irregular basis, a bit like atrial fibrillation, so nobody notices you disappearing for regular few days at a time. As a rule, you may expect to go around 2 or 3 times a year or more if you need it, but you must make it your business to stay fit."

I thought about my love-making with Annie and knew just how fit I was, but I thought I'd better comply, as I didn't want to rock any boats. I knew when I was well off and was sufficiently amenable to taking good advice when I was given it.

He added that on top of the training, we might be called to undertake a job at relatively short notice and when called, we would be expected to go without fail as the safety of others would be depending on us. He did say that there were enough of us that such calls should not usually interfere with our lives too much. If we were away, then we were away, and others would be called.

The Prof has asked me to inform you that your personal medical professional development plan was discussed at our faculty meeting, while you were away last week and your progress in the department has been assessed as excellent and you have fitted in exceedingly well. We are of course aware that you are not a normal trainee in the department, but what it means for you is; should you consider applying for a training post in the next August academic intake, your application would be considered favourably to join us officially.

You should of course, pass your Cambridge Surgery finals and then complete your year in the house to become fully registered with the GMC first though, before you can apply to us. On this matter I need to tell you that next Wednesday is the 1st of the month and you will be moving from your job in gynaecology at Addenbrookes Old Site to the second half of your job in obstetrics at the new Rosie Maternity Hospital, at the back of the new Addenbrookes site.

I was delighted with this news, which rapidly took my mind off my worries in my other role and brought me right down to earth with a bump and back into medicine mode, where the concerns for us, were less pertinent to external lethal dangers.

"By the way, the Prof has also requested whether you and all the other SHOs could pop down to the old Mill Road Maternity Hospital to help transfer some of his lab equipment up to the Rosie for him asap."

I reassured him it would be done and we set about it the next afternoon. The old Mill Road Maternity Hospital was being pulled down, so lots of precious medical equipment needed to be moved to a new home in the Rosie Maternity Hospital on the Addenbrookes Campus.

When we got there, we noticed that where the bulldozers had been digging up the car park by the front gate, there was a huge great black stain in the soil. One of the site engineers identified it as iron in the soil, but he couldn't figure out how it there.

One of we SHOs immediately suggested it was probably rust, where the maternity patients had thrown their iron tablets away, which at that time, were routinely given in pregnancy. This practice had been stopped when research showed that excessive iron in early pregnancy could affect the baby's eye sight. The pregnant mums-to-be had pre-empted science by stopping them on their own accounts, but for different reasons.

15

I was excited to be starting obstetrics, that branch of medicine concerned with the science of pregnancy and usually the happy delivery of a baby at its end. I was about to discover that there was so much more to it than that.

Obstetrics is naturally communioned with gynaecology, because its only women that have babies, but not all women can have babies. It was an increasingly common part of our job to help naturally infertile women overcome this very emotional problem.

We all make a range of hormones in the fatty tissue parts of our skin, ranging from oestrogen, the female hormone, at one end of the range, to testosterone, the male hormone, at the other end, with several others in between, with structures that made them either male or female in action. Mankind depends on our gonads to supplement and dominate the skin hormones in order to support the sexual characteristics of our genders and make us who we are.

In men, the testes makes large amounts of testosterone to achieve this, while in women, it's the ovarian follicles growing each month that secrete oestrogen and progesterone in amounts large enough to support female anatomical characteristics, facilitate ovulation and if the ovum (egg), is fertilised to promote implantation, the development of the placenta, the maintenance of the pregnancy and the initiation of labour.

The cutaneous sex hormones are predominately male in nature. That's why post-menopausal women, who have used up and run out of follicles, may become more physically and even psychologically male like.

Our department of Obstetrics and Gynaecology, among other things led the world in undertaking infertility research, promoting ovulation for infertile women and also undertaking in-vitro fertilisation techniques for them. These were exciting and path-finding times and I was fortunate to be a tiny cog in this department's huge researching wheel.

The patients' emotions in undergoing IVF were gigantic, to say the least. The result of a failed attempt at IVF could facilitate a bereavement response of epic proportions and was so moving to the extent of being overpowering! Patients quite often felt it was so stressful, that they couldn't bear to try again. On the other hand the immense joy of achieving a pregnancy was such, that somehow it would quite often seem to reactivate their ovarian pathways and patient couples would commonly go on to achieve further pregnancies with no scientific intervention at all.

I settled down very happily into obstetrics and baby deliveries on the labour wards and by Caesarian sections for emergency deliveries. One Saturday evening, the labour wards were very quiet, with no-one in labour, so myself and the Australian Locum duty anaesthetist told the midwives that we were going to walk down to the hospital canteen for some sustenance and they could reach us if necessary, on our long range bleeps. We didn't tell them we were heading for the clinical school disco that was in full swing.

We didn't notice the passing of time until I left the dance area for a pee, only for my bleep to go off. There was a panicky midwife shouting at the other end that a full-term lady had come in with an obstructed labour and that they couldn't get hold of us, so they'd called in the consultant for a Caesarian section. Ugh! Midwives, I thought to myself as I rushed back into the disco, grabbed the anaesthetist and sprinted back to the obstetric theatres.

Mr. Robinson, the on-call consultant was just scrubbing up.

As we burst into the theatre, he looked round and said, "So nice of you to join us, gentlemen. If you could possibly scrub up, we'll get this lady off to sleep and deliver her baby." The lady and her four kg baby were fine and Mr. Robinson a gentle intellect and fantastic surgeon never mentioned the incident again.

I was fortunate to witness the intensely high emotions of pregnancy and the birth of many babies and the joy it would bring to its parents. I also witnessed that quite commonly in up to 20% of women, the joy of parenthood might be followed by periods of severe depression, commencing on occasions, in late pregnancy or more usually within a few days following delivery of the baby and its placenta.

The placenta is the source of the very high levels of female hormones during pregnancy. When the placenta is delivered during the 3rd stage of labour, the levels of oestrogen and progesterone decrease dramatically by the 3rd day after delivery. There are several areas in the brain responsible for mood elevation and fluctuations in these reproductive hormone levels, particularly progesterone, trigger depression in susceptible women, by inhibiting nervous transmission in the relevant brain centres.

It is similar to but more severe than the Premenstrual Tension Syndrome that many women may experience when the female hormones fall at the end of the second half of the monthly menstrual cycle.

We have seen many women In our department, suffer tremendously from both the Premenstrual Syndrome and the more significant Post-natal Syndrome. The post-natal syndrome may range from a mild 'Baby Blues', to a more serious depressive state and in extremis, to an overt 'Puerpural Psychosis'.

Psychotic post-natal mums may often need admission and a psychiatric input to their care, with sedation by major tranquillisers. This may lead to disastrous consequences for the post-natal mums and their families. In our unit, we are researching treatments with various dose combinations of Oestrogens and Progesterones to put right the imbalance, with promising results.

On the whole, obstetrics was mainly a gloriously happy time, but with occasional tragic mishaps. One day in the antenatal clinic I saw a pregnant lady, who was also a midwife, whose pregnancy had reached forty-two weeks gestation. It was policy not to let pregnancies go beyond forty-two weeks as the babies might out-grow the placenta, which becomes unable to deal with the oxygen, nutritional and excretory demands placed on it by the size of the baby.

All was fine on that Thursday afternoon. I said I would admit her to the ward and start up her induction to commence her Labour. She refused this with much indignation. I asked her to wait while I discussed her with the Professor, but she became quite agitated. The Prof came over and advised her to come in to be induced but she steadfastly refused and stated she wanted to do it naturally and left the clinic.

The following weekend when I was the SHO on call, we received an emergency crash call from that midwife's midwife to say she had collapsed with a massive bleed 'per vaginam'. Myself, together with the same on-call Australian anaesthetist were waiting at the Rosie, when the ambulance arrived. The pregnant midwife was in an acute stage of shock with her blood pressure un-recordable.

We took her straight to theatre, Mr. Bradley, with myself assisting and the anaesthetist, undertook an emergency Caesarian section, but the baby had died in utero some time earlier. The indignant midwife who refused to be induced lost her baby and her uterus.

I had settled into this obstetrics specialty and having given up my college flat, had moved in completely with Annie, when again I was brought down to earth by the approaching May Cambridge Surgery re-sit exams. The Prof, true to his word, gave me ten days paid leave, which was more than enough to swot up my old surgery revision notes.

I revised from 09.00 to17.00 each day, taking evenings off to enjoy myself and sailed through the written paper and the long and short cases with relative ease. This time my internal examiner was the highly esteemed Mr Rafftery, who asked clear but nevertheless very comprehensive questions.

When I finished my Viva, he patted me on the back and said, "Well done laddie, now go and become a surgeon!"

Three days later, the examination results were posted and I finally became a graduate doctor from Cambridge University. This prompted a great deal of celebrations from my family and friends, my college tutor and my clinical school supervisor Dr Walker as well as my colleagues in the Department of Obstetrics and Gynaecology.

I went back to work the following week in jubilation. The Prof and Mr. Bradley were delighted and said, "Very well done! You're still not quite a legal SHO, but at least you're a proper doctor now with proper university's degrees!"

With that, Mr. Bradley said, "Come and join me in the tutorial room, we have a job for you."

As I followed him out of the faculty office into the tutorial room, he turned, asked me to close the door behind me and said, "Tomorrow, you and I will go the Cambridge airport to meet a plane carrying four scientists and their families. These people have been rescued from inside the 'Iron Curtain' by some of our specialist friends from the military. When we meet them, they will be accompanied by armed police officers from Special Branch. Unhappily some of the military and some of the civilians sustained injuries during their extraction. The military are being dealt within their own hospital in Hereford."

"These scientists are very important to the NATO alliance and those on the other side of that curtain would dearly love to get them back or eliminate them. So they need specialist and very private care and attention. They can't go to a normal hospital, because they're under wraps, so they're coming to us. You and I will be collected from work by Special Branch detectives at an appointed time, and will proceed to the airport to pick up the subjects and carry them to the manor house inside the grounds of Fulborn Psychiatric Hospital. We will re-assess their injuries there and undertake appropriate treatment. The manor house has been equipped with operating facilities, should the need arise. Oh and by the way, we will be armed, just in case anyone tries to interfere with our plans. Don't look so worried Michael! Do you have any questions?"

"Oh right, oh fuck, you are serious, aren't you?"

"Yes, I am; very serious," and he looked straight at me with a huge grin.

"Yes, how will I get my weapon and what will it be?"

"Leave that to me, it will be a Walther PP point 32, with two spare clips and one in the handle; just in case!"

"Oh right," I almost gasped.

"OK, see you tomorrow," and with that he left the room.

I watched him go and stood there for about a minute, taking it all in.

"Holy fuck!" I shouted inside.

Here was I, a quiet academic scientist, about to go to undertake an armed mission as an agent of my country. Throughout the whole of my life I'd always tried to avoid conflict situations. I remembered during the Falklands War, when each night in the clinical school, we medics had watched the TV news channel for updates on how our troops were doing against the invading Argentinians.

I'd felt sorry for our soldiers, risking their lives, in the freezing weather, to get our islands back. I'd thought how lucky I was to be safe from national conflict situations and now here I was a doctor about to set off, armed to the teeth with a deadly weapon, but not just any old deadly weapon, just one of almost exactly the same type, used by James Bond!

I thought any minute now, I might be eaten by crocodiles or have might head knocked off by 'odd job' and where was Miss Moneypenny?

16

The next day as I was finishing a ward round with the senior midwife on the labour ward, my bleep went off summoning me to the faculty office. In anticipation, I almost ran the distance between us, to be greeted by Mr. Bradley and two very large gentlemen who turned out to be Special Branch detectives. The largest was Detective Inspector Robin Greenwood and the other, slightly shorter, but still tall was Detective Sergeant Martin Roberts.

"Good morning, sir," they opened in unison.

"Good morning gentlemen," I responded and as I did so, they handed me a pistol, sideways on, as we had learned at the armoury. They also handed me two clips of bullets, informing me that the shells were snub nose for extra impact.

Paul Bradley interjected, "Right, let's be going. We've got to get to the airport and be parked within thirty minutes."

We rushed down to the ground floor and out of the Casualty entrance to climb into a large black Mercedes minibus, with shaded windows, which they'd parked on the double yellow lines there. A warden was scribbling in his ticket pad as we arrived at the car.

The sergeant flashed him his warrant card and the warden backed away, begrudgingly tearing up the parking ticket. We jumped into the minibus and made the airport in time to see the private jet taxi up to the perimeter fence and turn off its engines.

We drove through the security gate, where the Special Branch man flashed his card again and drove straight round to the plane parked by the fence. As we pulled up below the plane door, it opened and another large man, who looked like a copper peered out. Inspector Greenwood who was out of the car first, hung his warrant card in his top pocket and the large copper visibly relaxed with a brilliant smile across his face.

He called back into the plane and slowly one by one a group of people disembarked apprehensively from the inside of the plane down the steps and onto the tarmac. Sergeant Roberts opened the side door of the minibus and encouraged them to get in. I noticed that three of them appeared injured including a young teenaged girl and all of them looked very frightened.

Roberts beaming from ear to ear helped the injured girl, who was about fifteen or sixteen, climb aboard with, "Come on miss, this way."

She answered, "Thank you," in a perfect English accent.

Within five minutes, we were all on our way to the Fulbourn Manor on the edge of Cambridge and got there speedily very soon afterwards. On arrival, two special branch officers, also with their warrant cards hanging over their top pockets, came out of the manor house and ushered the families into the massive entrance hall, where more special branch officers ticked the families off from a register.

Military nurses took the injured people into a medical area to one side of the entrance.

There were three armed officers assigned specifically to act as guards for each family. I thought these scientists must be pretty important to our government for it to go to all this trouble for them.

Mr. Bradley and I followed the injured into the medical area and on the way, I noticed that he also had a shoulder holster with a pistol clipped into it. He had said that we would have these precautions about our persons whenever we were on one of these special duties, just in case. He had clearly meant it! I tapped mine re-assuringly but feeling slightly uncomfortable and we proceeded to see the patients and triage their injuries.

It was apparent that one elderly man who looked rather grey was the most seriously hurt. He'd been shot from behind in his left shoulder, the bullet had gone straight through, with a small entry wound at the back and a bigger exit wound at the front. An army medic had placed a pressure dressing on both sides of his wound, which looked like it was holding the blood loss.

The nurses, who seemed to know what they were doing, had left the dressing in place, uncovered his upper body and inserted a canula into his other arm and were running in some normal saline fluid. Some of his blood was sent off to Addenbrookes for cross matching just to top him up if necessary, as its very important not to allow the elderly, whose cardiovascular system might be precarious, to become hypo-volaemic (low in blood volume).

The second man said he had lacerated his left leg rushing through a hole cut in a wire fence. The wire had ripped horizontally across the lateral aspect of his left upper thigh. The nurses had removed his dressing, as his laceration was no longer bleeding. They had cleaned his wound and one of the nurses was about to stitch him up, when I got to examine him.

I wrote him up for appropriate antibiotics and a tetanus shot, which came mixed with polio and diphtheria vaccines, though these are no longer prevalent in the West, they might have been highly relevant to these Eastern block's citizens. Another military nurse stabbed him with the vaccines and commenced the antibiotics connected via the drip, having checked him for allergies.

The young teenage girl had a laceration on the lateral aspect of her left lower arm, which was less severe than the second man. Her injury was amenable to closing with skin glue and suitably sized adherent dressing strips, which her nurse applied, having cleaned the wound thoroughly. She was given a tetanus vaccine as well as suitable oral antibiotics.

Mr. Bradley and I were both concerned about the elderly man and decided we ought to explore the wound. He got on the phone to the Prof and asked for anaesthetic help and we prepared the man for theatre. I clerked him and discovered that he, spoke better English than most of the locals, in fact, they all did including their children!

He was normally quite a fit man, who regularly jogged around his native city of Leipzig, where he worked as a missile scientist. So, that's why the government wanted them; they were into that sort of stuff.

This erudite and highly intelligent man, described to me how he and the others had been meeting socially for some time and had talked about their jobs, their conditions and lives in the East. More importantly, they believed that their ambitions for their children would never come to fruition behind the 'Iron Curtain'. They decided to take action and planned that one of their wives, who knew someone working at the British Legation in East Berlin, would approach him about their feelings.

Quite soon after she did that, a man called at the home of the woman and identified himself as a member of the Legation staff and stated that he could help them with their plans to move to the west. That man was probably an MI6 agent, from that branch of our security service that promotes our country's intelligence abroad.

They're also called 'spies' and are usually information gatherers. The MI6 man told them he could help them, but also asked them how they might be able to help him in return. The scientist described how delighted our agent was to find out that they and their friends were scientists working in rocket and missile technology.

After that initial contact and the realisation of how important and useful these people might be to the West, the scientist happily described how there must have been a great deal of intelligence activity on the part of our secret service in East Berlin. There were several debriefing meetings with a lot of surveillance and even drop boxes for message deliveries. He imagined there was also probably a great deal of actual spying, going on probably with listening devices and the like to verify that these people weren't being planted as "double agents and were sincere in their intentions to defect to the West."

About a half hour later, our conversation was interrupted by the arrival of a doctor, who announced himself as the requested anaesthetist. I thought he looked familiar and realised he was out of Addenbrookes and I had operated with him on a number of occasions, without really noticing him working away in the background to keep the patient asleep, sometimes paralysed and ventilated and most of all, pain free. So, he was also one of our Prof's group!

It just goes to show how you never know! Happily, the man's wound was cleaned on exploration and only one small artery had been severed on the surface of his rotator cuff, in the shoulder, which was easily repaired and left to recover. His wound was left to close by second intention, i.e., naturally from the inside outwards. This meant that it would require monitoring and regular post-op care, with dressings and antibiotic cover. It would mean follow-up by the team, which I guessed meant me.

Paul Bradley advised me about this. He said it would usually be very simple follow-up. I should attend daily to monitor the patients and their care by the military nurses, who by the way, were possibly more expert at wound care than I. More particularly, I should not forget the other rescued people, who were after all ordinary people themselves with the usual ills that might need doctoring and should attend to their requirements also.

Special Branch were still in attendance, trying to look like administrators and blend into the background. This was pretty difficult with their Israeli 'Uzi' machine pistols tucked under their armpits, projecting out of their suits!

Mr. Bradley also advised me that I needed to remain armed and on alert, as not everyone in the area were card-carrying supporters of the government. He didn't want anything to happen to me or to the government's guests. They'd come so far, hadn't they? It would be a pity for all of it to go 'Tits up' now.

There had apparently been a leak abroad, and someone on our side, over there had actually gone over to the other side, as there was no accounting for taste! This was how some of the extraction force and one of the scientists had been shot. Happily there were no fatalities on our side, but the specialists from Hereford had laid waste to a large number of eastern border guards. This would definitely be bound to play havoc with their Mayday holiday rotas!

Of course, none of this ever made the press. Nor did it when sometime later the deserting turncoat was found in a back alley of East Berlin, exsanguinated, with his throat cut from ear to ear. I thought Karma strikes again!

I was mightily relieved that this operation was entirely successful from our point of view, with all the casualties making full recoveries and all the families being successfully relocated with new identities in safe areas under the supervision of the Home Secretary and MI5, "the Watchers" of our home security force.

Afterwards, we were debriefed and the Prof was very pleased with our results. He congratulated me on my professionalism throughout the operation. Marion, his lovely secretary informed me that my account had already been set up at Coutts Bank and retainer payments had already been paid into it and that I would be receiving a further payment for my part in the latest exercise and the ongoing care of the families.

She gave me details of the account and my bankcard, should I need to access the account. She advised me to keep those account details and the card as part of the secret world of espionage and skulduggery that I had recently entered. I did see her point of view. I did tend to keep my finances close to my chest and it wouldn't do me any good to let anyone know I was now a paid undercover operative for Queen and country.

17

August was approaching and I felt sad that I was about to leave my job as an SHO in the department of Obs and Gynae, to go back to the bottom of the pile as a house surgeon in a peripheral district general hospital.

I made my goodbyes, to the team and turned up very ready for action on the first of August at 08.00 on a one in two rota. This meant, I lived at the hospital and was on call every second day for twenty-four hours and every second weekend from 08.00 Friday morning to 08.00 the following Monday morning.

I was to learn that this was quite a gruelling and exhausting rota, but I did see a lot of really fascinating cases which varied from the disastrous and tragic for normal human families, to the gloriously happy wonderful outcomes where deadly diseases were turned and defeated by human intellectual and surgical interventions. I was allowed a great deal of freedom in the operating room and as a result of this I learned a great deal of surgery.

I was awestruck by the skill and devotion of these surgeons who laboured for unbelievably long hours, saving people from the brink of death. Combatting not only fatal diseases, but also struggling against hospital administrators, who were constrained by impossible budgets, imposed by an uncaring government and its NHS.

Surgical lists were cancelled at the last minute on untold numerous occasions, so that patients might attend early in the morning of their operation starved and ready for surgery but keep their lifts waiting outside because they expected to be cancelled at the last minute.

My days were a mixture of clerking, operating and learning. I saw so many patients that my clerking skills had been honed and had become very slick. I could meet, question and examine a patient, gleaning all their necessary information and take their blood sample for transfusion in under fifteen minutes. I became intimately familiar with surgical anatomy and the various surgical techniques that we performed each day.

One day, I was called to A&E to see a lorry driver who had referred himself via casualty, with a raging fever and a very sore red left knee. He was clearly unwell, so I admitted him to the ward. I sent off his blood for screening which showed signs of a severe bacterial infection. However, the only very noisy complaint he was making was about his very sore knee. He was a very difficult patient, always complaining a great deal and generally making the ward nurses' jobs very difficult.

Although I started him on the usual broad-spectrum antibiotics, by the next morning his knee was swollen to almost twice the size of his other one. My registrar decided to drain his knee, which meant that I would be doing it as part of my training. I anaesthetised the skin, inserted a large white needle on a 20ml syringe and pulled back on the piston.

The liquid I withdrew revealed a very cloudy joint fluid, which should have been clear. This was sent off to the lab and we were very surprised when his knee fluid sample grew the gram stain negative bacterium diplococcus of Gonorrhoea.

He hadn't complained of any genital problems, so I hadn't bothered looking. When I examined his genitalia, he did have a very sticky infected purulent penile discharge which we treated with the appropriate antibiotic preceded by investigations to make sure he didn't have any other nasties hiding in his pelvis.

As this obnoxious patient had parked his huge lorry in the hospital car park, where it was causing an obstruction and he hadn't paid for a ticket to boot, the police had investigated his vehicle and discovered the driver was a wanted fugitive. A policeman approached the ward sister and then me to see if he was well enough to be arrested. However, because a hospital is a place of safety, he couldn't be arrested, while he was a patient. He was fast turning out to be a moron, complaining all the time and making the nurses' and his fellow patients' lives a misery.

So one day, when he was as usual, complaining about the care he was receiving, I suggested that he was now cured and as he wasn't due for anymore treatment, he could discharge himself, by simply signing a self-discharge form. He did so immediately, releasing us from keeping him in a place of safety. As he walked from the ward, two police officers, that we'd arranged, came, one from either side of the exit and placed him into custody. The look on his face was a picture to behold!

One Sunday evening, I was again called to casualty, this time to remove a foreign body. On this occasion I was shocked to find none other than my mother's parish priest in the A&E cubicle. My mother being very religious was a frequent attender at the local Catholic Church, so they knew each other very well.

As I introduced myself, the priest visibly pallored, but he later blushed profusely as he explained how he had accidently slipped in the bath and fallen on a bar of soap, which had entered his bottom and disappeared. He had been unable to retrieve the bar and neither was I despite many attempts on my part to retrieve it and save him further embarrassment.

Furthermore, when I called my registrar, he also couldn't remove it either, despite several more attempts with a long pair of Ali's forceps to hook the bar and land it. My registrar who was also quite a religious Irish man, was concerned about the priest's health because soap being highly alkaline, can be very toxic. So after a call to Guy's Hospital Poisons Unit, it was decided that it had to come out one way or another.

In this case, the other, was a trip to theatre and a quick laparotomy to excise it from where it had jammed at the junction of the rectum and sigmoid colon. Although it was quite a slippery little bar, it had managed to become wedged there, but its toxic nature meant we had to remove it.

It was most ironic that when we cut out the offending soap bar, which had been carved into the shape of a phallus, it turned out to have been fashioned out of a large bar of green Fairy soap!

Sister commented that his, "Tight arse must have been squeaky clean!"

I believe the trophy is, to this day is on a shelf in the surgeons' room at the hospital. The priest was removed from his office some years after this case. I suppose his vocation wasn't quite as strong as his sex drive. I wondered how many other priests had been stifled by the church's unnatural attitude to celibacy in their ministers.

I am informed that celibacy only became the rule when the church realised that married priests would want to pass on their possessions to their families rather than to mother church. The Pope at the time avariciously changed the rules to keep the church's cash balance firmly in the blue.

The one in two rota with this post really was quite wearing to we house surgeons and very inconvenient to our love lives. On my days off, I just tended to sleep a lot to replenish my stores of ATP. My life with Annie was one of passing in the night. I was almost always at work and I never got off on time, as there were always more patients than doctors and always more to do than there were hours in a shift. When I wasn't at work, I tended to be sleeping. Doctors' partners needed more patience than their doctors' patients! Sleeping was just simply a survival "modus operandi".

It wasn't just me, the other house officers were affected the same. One day, I was called to the ward, on a late afternoon, by the sister, who was a highly experienced surgical nursing sister. I wasn't on call that day, so I was surprised to receive the call. When I got there, I found my opposite number curled up in a ball in the treatment room. He was a Rugby Blue for Cambridge, as hard as granite on the rugby pitch and someone whom you wouldn't want to meet in a dark alley, and there he was crying like a baby rolled up in a ball.

He was highly intelligent and also most sensitive. His anxieties about the job and probably his fatigue had caused him to over-breath.

This hyperventilation had resulted in him blowing much of the carbon dioxide out of his blood. Carbon dioxide is highly soluble and if you breath too much it dissolves out of your blood back into your lungs and is breathed out. This makes the blood more alkaline and so the calcium in our blood comes out of solution and precipitates. The loss of calcium from the blood causes the muscles to go into spasm. The muscles at the front of our bodies are usually more powerful than those at the back and as they go into spasm, they bend us over and cause us to roll up into a ball.

I injected my friend and colleague with an anxiolytic called diazepam and gave him a plastic bag to breath into and out of. This rebreathing of carbon dioxide-rich exhaled air, raised its level in his blood causing calcium to re-dissolve back into his blood plasma. This and the muscle relaxing effect of the diazepam caused his muscles to relax enabling him to unbend. This fit young man's level of exhaustion made him unable to deal with the stresses of modern medicine.

Neither the good ward sister nor I mentioned these events afterwards and I'm glad to say that my colleague survived his year in the house became a firm friend and went on to much higher things in medicine.

My six months as a house surgeon proceeded very happily without any further too embarrassing incidents for me at any rate.

One morning, I was operating in the main surgical theatre assisting my registrar, when I received an urgent call from A&E about a man in severe pain with a rigid abdomen, a fever and no bowel sounds. He had been fine, the previous evening but suddenly stopped in his tracks by the unbearable pain.

My registrar asked me to de-scrub and to go and assess him. I did so and discovered the Casualty doctor had done a thorough job and the man needed an emergency laparotomy to find out what had suddenly paralysed his bowel. He was delivered to theatres and anaesthetised while the surgical registrar and I finished the previous case.

We re-scrubbed and prepared to operate. The anaesthetist was going to take a while, as he would have to paralyse and ventilate the patient, because his abdomen needed to be relaxed for us to cut into it. He was given a hypnotic to send him off to sleep, pain relief, a gaseous anaesthetic to keep him asleep as well as being paralysed and ventilated.

We then opened his abdomen and discovered there had been a blockage and that the bowel in front of the block had burst open emptying its contents into the abdominal cavity. There was tea, tablets, Weetabix, toast and marmalade all floating around in his abdominal cavity. There was a hard mass blocking the small bowel with a distended and wafer-thin torn ileum in front of the block. His bowel had literally burst open.

My registrar, who had only recently joined our team proceeded to expose the hard mass which we thought was cancer and to excise the frayed ileum, which had exploded proximal to it, leaving a smooth undamaged piece of proximal ileum to join up to the small bowel beyond the lump.

That was when the registrar said, "I've never joined two pieces of bowel before and really, because of the way, this man's bowel has exploded, he really should have a de-functioning ileostomy to give the bowel time to recover and I've never done one of those either. We will have to get the boss in to do this. Can you call him sister?"

She de-gloved and disappeared, returning later to say the boss Mr. Townsend was in a clinic in the next town and would be at least half an hour. The boss, who was a highly respected, old school excellent surgeon did duly attend and the suspect piece of excised bowel was sent off for an urgent histological diagnosis.

We had to wait a bit longer because, if the cancer diagnosis was right, we would have to extensively dissect out the bowel and the relevant abutting areas and draining lymph nodes to assess any spread of the disease. Happily, in about twenty minutes, the histology diagnosis arrived back and revealed that the blockage was caused by a granuloma or area of scar tissue, which had contracted, closing the lumen of the bowel and blocking the transit of food.

Somewhat relieved, the boss rapidly and expertly undertook an ileostomy, bringing the ileum out though the lower abdominal wall. He then washed out the distal and terminal end of the ileum and sowed it up with a purse-string suture.

He then sent the registrar to the theatre next door to continue the rest of that morning's operating list, asked me to close up the patients abdomen and left the theatre. This wasn't the actions of an abrupt man, but was those of a highly professional, an expert in his field who assessed and knew what needed to be done to make things work.

I proceeded to close the abdomen by its peritoneum first, then followed by its muscle layers and was just about to staple the skin outer layer when the sister said, "We're one swab short!"

I asked, "Are you serious, sister?"

She replied assenting.

"Try a recount, sister," I replied.

She did and came up with the same answer. In exasperation, I reopened the patient and found that the boss had placed a swab under the liver to absorb any blood oozing from various veins that had been diathermied earlier. He didn't tell anyone what he'd done and nobody had noticed. I cursed out loud and duly closed the patient's abdomen. He was wheeled to the recovery room and I went next door to join my registrar with the rest of the list.

All was well until the next morning when the boss, the registrar and I were doing a ward round. We reached the exploding bowel man's bed and he thanked us all for what we had done for him. We were very gracious about it, reassured the patient and moved onto the next bay. As we moved away, the patient put up his arm and indicated he wanted talk to me. I mouthed to him that I'd be back in a few minutes.

We finished the ward round and I returned to his bedside, where he told me that he'd been entirely awake throughout the whole operation. He was paralysed and couldn't move but could hear everything that had gone on through his procedure. He proceeded to prove the point by repeating verbatim all the banter that had gone on throughout the operation, the music that was playing in the background, the theatre sister's interruption about the missing swab, how I'd sworn when she interrupted and how I'd found the swab under his liver.

He was clearly telling the truth.

The anaesthetist had made a very big error and not given the patient enough hypnotic, enabling him to wake up during the procedure. The poor patient had heard us talking about the likely cancer diagnosis and must have been really frightened. Unhappily, the anaesthetist didn't notice him awakening, or the obvious changes in his heart rate and ECG, that would have occurred when he heard us discuss the diagnosis.

I was very polite and reassuring to him and said that sometimes when people have pain like he had, it may take more anaesthetic to keep them asleep and that no harm was done. Happily he never sued us or the hospital, for this serious blunder that could have ended in disaster, if he had a heart attack from the possible anxiety he suffered, particularly when we were waiting for his histology results.

In those days, there were less wretched ambulance chasing lawyers and patients were far less litigious than they are today and he never even considered that he was anything but lucky to have been cured by our rapid surgical intervention. He was very happy when I saw him in his follow-up appointment in our outpatients clinic.

On another happy occasion one Sunday morning, I was called to casualty to see an Arab gentleman, who was in a great deal of pain from a large sore on his rear end. On examination at that time, he had an exceedingly large perianal abscess, which edge to edge was almost five centimetres in diameter, very hot and very fluctuant, expanding in different directions when pressed in the middle. We took him straight to theatre, as he was in such severe pain, he would not be able to stand its drainage while he was awake!

After a proper amount of anaesthesia, I incised it, with the registrar and it was like an erupting volcano. We could have almost filled a small bucket with the amount of pus that erupted from it, on incision. We washed it out, packed it with paraffin gauze, dressed it and left it to heal by second intention (from inside to out), with daily dressings and intravenous antibiotics.

At the time, we were unaware that he was a Saudi diplomat. It wasn't until several days later that we discharged him during a ward round; when we noticed that a driver arrived on the ward to pick him up. He thanked us profusely for the help we had given him and handed myself and my surgical registrar a large brown envelope. This contained several other white envelopes inside, each with a series of pure gold stamps on them and addressed to him in Saudi Arabia.

He told us they were very valuable and that any serious collector would pay a four-figure sum to buy them. He also said that if we ever came to his part of the world, we should look him up. Mr. Townsend stared at us in incredulity and complete ignorance of what we had done so expeditiously to be rewarded so generously.

18

At the end of my surgical house job, I moved to a literally brand new hospital in Huntingdon for my post as a house physician. I had thought to myself that physicians know a lot but don't do anything, so the job might be boring compared with my surgical jobs. How wrong could I have been!

I was in a new style hospital structure of a huge one storey square, that would have made a good stadium with a large lawn and gardens in the centre. Medical Personnel was also very different, there were just house officers, senior house officers and consultants. This meant one less tier of registrar doctors and more work to carry out by everyone but also more experience to be gleaned for everybody.

I worked for a Gastroenterologist, an Oncologist and a Geriatrician. This meant that I dealt with bowel medicine, cancer, and elderly patients.

The gastro-intestinal medicine was very interesting with a great boss, who was an expert in endoscopy, putting telescopic cameras into the gut from both ends, to see things, photograph them and if necessary, remove them surgically. We would also inject dyes to help radiology make diagnoses and capture things in nets to extract various obstructions like gallstones and polyps, as well as dealing with all the other general medical conditions in our days and weekends on call. This was really a true mixing of the traditional medical and surgical roles.

The Oncologist was also a brilliant chest physician, he was also a physician to Royalty, though, he used to see them privately at home, so I never got to listen to a royal chest. Most of my work for him meant investigating and treating lung cancer patients. Mainly, because it was so common, I drained pleural effusions when the two coating membranes around the lungs were invaded by cancer, causing them to leak a fluid build-up around the lungs.

This fluid build-up, pressed against the lung's balloons (alveoli), and prevented them from expanding on breathing. I used to drain them and simultaneously inject a really nasty anti-cancer drug, called Bleomycin. As well as attacking cancer cells, this drug caused inflammation and scarring of the pleural membranes, sticking them together and prevented the build-up of fluid. This enabled the balloons to expand better.

Lung cancer was the most common cancer we saw, almost always secondary to smoking, I felt pity for the patients, who were usually in early middle age and invariably died, either from shortness of breath and exhaustion or from secondary cancers sprouting up in other strategic places, like their brains.

Geriatric medicine was very interesting, with elderly patients who were usually delightful, very wise and very helpful, as well as being very grateful for their care. Unhappily many of them knew the score and were very in tune with their illness and their disease outcomes. I was to have many a disturbed night, called to pronounce death on a patient I had come to know and like in the days before.

My life as a house physician wasn't always sad. The hospital wasn't too far from Cambridge, which meant my nights in the doctor's mess weren't always lonely. Annie was only twenty minutes away, so we very rapidly became familiar with every part of my single bed there. Our enthusiastic love-making became legendary among my medical colleagues, who despite being totally worn out by their on-call rotas, still moaned about our passion disturbing their sleep.

There was also a keen sense of camaraderie among the junior doctors there. It was us against disease, as well as us against our employer, the NHS, whose managerial incompetence inflicted such onerous working conditions on us, without any exceptions, we had very little respect for the hospital managers who again rarely bothered to hire locums in time so we could take our leave. They were clearly just interested in making their books balance and to hell with everybody else!

At some stage later, I questioned this obvious doctor shortage with the Prof at our debriefing session and he was quite forthright about it, saying the government and the medical profession were in the death throes of a bloodied relationship.

The government couldn't afford to train enough doctors, so they disguised this by restricting the numbers of university places and the numbers of doctors graduating in British universities. It was far cheaper to import doctors from the Commonwealth, who all wanted to come here for the more stable better life and the wealth of post-graduate experience.

It didn't matter to the government about the differences in culture, language and values concomitant with these clinicians. The government may have considered that the British population were tough and grateful enough to withstand such cultural differences, or maybe they were simply broke.

The shortage of doctors was thus by government design and a truth ridden with deception. However, the Prof rejoiced that the lack of university places meant that the medical university entrants were academically "La crème de la crème" and the top of the university pile! This saw to it that the NHS would mainly be in the safe hands of the chosen few home grown graduates, mixed with the cream of foreign graduates, with equally safe hands.

These stresses down to doctor under-staffing bound us together irreversibly in the fight to save our patients despite the government. We met together as often as possible, with weekly cocktail parties in the doctors' mess. Our various medical teams hosted these events, taking it in turns to concoct different potent cocktails to tempt our palates. On one occasion when my team were the hosts, having consumed a number of large alcoholic beverages, I'd forgotten we were also on-call.

We were in the mess at one corner of our square hospital, when we were suddenly interrupted by the cardiac arrest bleep in the Casualty department at the opposite corner of the building. We had to sprint down the two sides of the square building to reach Casualty quickly, which caused all sorts of upset to my gastric lining. I decelerated just in time to be able to stop at the now deceased man's trolley. The paramedic who had brought him in and was undertaking chest compressions with the Casualty sister, who sent out the arrest call both looked up.

The paramedic said, "Doc you look awful" and the sister added, "worse than the patient!"

We took over the resuscitation and commenced administering intra cardiac adrenaline, straight into his heart muscle, which made his arrested heart ventricles start contracting very rapidly in an abnormal very rapid rhythm known as 'Ventricular Fibrillation'. In this state, the hearts chambers don't have enough time to fill with blood before they weakly contract and pump it out. Effectively, in this rhythm, patients have inadequate cardiac output.

However once in this state, we administered a very powerful 300 joule electric shock with a defibrillator machine, which happily changed his heart beat back into its regular rhythm, correcting his cardiac output and facilitating his recovery to consciousness.

There is probably no greater thrill for a doctor than bringing a patient back from the dead. It makes you feel that all that effort to qualify and practice as a doctor has been worthwhile.

Having shipped the patient and his now happier wife up to the coronary care unit, myself, my SHO and the anaesthetist (who was in charge of the resuscitation), marched back to the doctors mess in an elated and victorious state, to be toasted by our peers, who were by that time, somewhat "cocktailed out."

It was some minutes later, that one of the senior housemen asked if we'd heard about one of the medical students in his year, who had left the clinical school and medicine as well, just weeks before taking her finals. She was a very popular and highly academic girl, who also happened to be a member of my own Cambridge College. Myself and several others there, had been unaware of this tragedy and we wondered what might have happened. We knew it wasn't the stresses of the "finals", because she was brilliant!

Another lady doctor filled us in that the student in question had been in a relationship with another medical student, a mature student in her year, called Peter Bass. This man, an American, was considered to be a very arrogant and a loud-mouthed braggart, who continuously boasted about how tough he was and how he'd done military service in 'Nam'.

It was apparent that he was very unpopular with every one present in the room. The lady doctor continued to elucidate the tragedy and reported that Bass had systematically bullied and undermined our fellow student. She had discovered that he had repeatedly cheated on her in their relationship and that this betrayal, together with his persistent bullying and systematic undermining of her character is what moved her to feel she had to get away, leave the clinical school and her career.

As we pondered this, over a game of Bar Billiards, someone among us whispered, "Wouldn't it be nice if we could teach that bully a lesson!"

Almost unanimously, we acclaimed, "Yes, let's get the bastard."

Within minutes we'd come up with a plan. It was known that he was currently an SHO in neurosurgery at Addenbrookes Hospital, just down the road. We called the operator there and sure enough he was on call for neurosurgery that very night.

After a few minutes, one of us called him pretending to be a clinical assistant in A&E and stating that he had just seen a retired Indian Army Colonel, who had only one eye and had fallen and bashed his head. The Colonel was slipping in and out of consciousness with a low Glasgow Coma Score and that now, his only eye was beginning to become less reactive to light and had become slightly dilated.

"Jesus Christ!" Bass gasped, "We'll have to Cat Scan the son of a bitch."

Our comrade continued, "Well, hang on a minute old man, we're just waiting for Mr. Marshall, the on-call consultant surgeon to arrive, any minute now and we'll be sending him over to you for a possible CT and an evacuation of his possible brain haemorrhage."

"Ok, Jesus, I better call in the neuro-team and my boss. Thanks a lot, we'll be waiting!"

We waited five minutes and another houseman colleague then called him back pretending to be his boss, the said Mr. Marshall and said, "Hello laddie, Marshall here, I've seen this chap and we're sending him on his way to you now. He should be with you in twenty minutes."

"Yes sir, thank you sir, we'll be here waiting for him!"

With that, we finished our game of Bar Billiards and went to bed, sworn to secrecy and eagerly awaiting the outcome in the morning.

We didn't have to wait long, at 07.30, the hospital junior medical staff were bleeped to attend Mr. Marshall's office at 08.00.

We duly gathered outside his room at the appointed time. We waited anxiously before the consultant marched in, placed his brief case on his desk and walked up and down his office staring us each in the eye as he passed.

Finally, he said, I don't know what went on here last night. I don't want to know and I don't care, BUT, I don't want it to happen ever again! Have I made myself clear to everyone?

We nodded agreement.

"Off you go and get on with your jobs, there are enough real patients out there to deal with, without inventing anymore, so get on with it. We skedaddled out of his office like greyhounds out of their starting gates!"

We never heard a thing about it after that. However, sometime later, in a different hospital, I had just returned from a weekend off and was doing a ward round to acquaint myself with the patients admitted over the weekend. The locum doctor acquainting me, was a Cambridge man from the year ahead of me.

Out of the blue he said, "Did you hear what happened to that arrogant bastard Peter Bass?"

"No," I replied.

"Well, someone played a trick on him, which resulted in him calling in the whole of the neurosurgery team at Addenbrookes. He had a blazing row with his boss the neurosurgeon, Mr. Hardiman and with the neuroradiologist, who was also the dean and got himself suspended. The arrogant bastard got the hump and promptly resigned. We think he left the country. That's a result isn't it?"

"Oh dear, oh dear, oh dear, shame!" I replied smiling to myself inside.

19

Sometime after the imaginary one-eyed patient events, in the middle of one afternoon I was bleeped by sister on our medical ward. She wanted me to attend to the man, that had previously had a cardiac arrest and who had been resuscitated in casualty, when I was on call on the night of the Mess cocktail party. He had just been transferred back to the ward from the Coronary Care Unit (CCU).

He was a farmer from the nearby countryside. The sister on the ward was very worried about him because she thought he might be in urinary retention. She told me that my senior house physician (SHO), Dr Sandra, who was quite a hard lady and strictly speaking, my immediate superior, had insisted that the farmer should have his catheter taken out in order that he should pee under his own efforts. Four hours after, she had removed the catheter, he still hadn't been able to pee and was in quite severe pain from trying.

Dr Sandra hadn't really considered that he was just recovering from a heart attack and he also had a huge prostate obstructing him from peeing and draining his bladder! The good sister asked me to re-catheterise the farmer, drain his bladder for him and ease his pain; then to take the catheter drain out immediately and not mention it to my senior.

To the farmer's delight and great relief, this is exactly what was done. The sister, who'd been nursing for many years, had much more experience of post heart attack patients' abilities to pee, than Dr Sandra, the SHO. This procedure was quietly undertaken when needed, for three days until our farmer patient was again able to pee on his own.

A few days later, during a ward round with our consultant boss, the farmer was being discharged home. He thanked our boss, thanked the sister and the SHO and turning to me, he passed over a case of excellent Claret, saying with a wink in his eye.

"That's for you doc, for all the extra care you gave me!"

The sister and I remained silent and quietly shared the claret later.

Sometime after, in the middle of a Sunday night, I was called by a GP who was sending in a middle-aged man with liver failure. Having a really busy weekend on-call, I was shattered and reluctantly dragged myself out of bed to make my way down to casualty to receive this patient.

I was shocked to see the poor man. He was in a dreadful state, a huge luminous yellow mass. The whites of his eyes and his skin were coloured a bright mustard. He was being assisted onto a trolley by two paramedics and two nurses. He could hardly move on his own, with his abdomen and legs distended and swollen with fluid called ascites.

This had arisen from his failing liver's inability to make the blood protein albumin. This protein holds the plasma in our blood vessels under osmotic pressure. His low blood albumin allowed his plasma to leak out of blood vessels filling up his tissue spaces and turning him into a giant human wobbly yellow jelly.

He had huge breasts and shrunken testes, because his liver could no longer breakdown the female parts of the range of sex hormones, we all make in the fat in our skin. He was very drowsy, almost unconscious so I quickly examined him and asked the casualty sister about him. She said his wife was in the waiting area.

I walked out to the area expecting to find his matronly wife, but was most pleasantly shocked to discover a young lady of great beauty, with olive brown skin, long dark hair and jet-black eyes. She was about thirty years his junior and was visibly trembling with anxiety about the prospects for her husband. I led her into the doctor's office and gently asked her about my patient's history.

Until he had become so seriously ill, he had been the owner of a large hotel in Huntingdon, to the East of the area, but had slipped into alcoholism and drank much of the profits. In doing so, he had effectively drunk himself into this state.

I tried to be as reassuring as possible to this lady, who was Brazilian and had come to work in his hotel, where she had quickly been promoted and wooed to her present status. I asked her to wait while I arranged for her husband to go up to the ward. I called my Senior House officer and presented my patient to her. We agreed to give him some intravenous fluids with extra albumin to try and osmotically suck some of ascites back into his blood vessels.

We also arranged to tap and drain some of his abdominal fluid in an effort to make him more comfortable and wrote him up for a sedative, just in case he went into alcoholic withdrawal and got the 'D.Ts.,' (Delerium Tremens), as his alcohol sedated brain woke up and went charging into over-activity.

I was then called back to Casualty to see another patient and was quickly taking the opportunity to again reassure the patient's lovely wife, when suddenly a cardiac arrest alarm sounded off on my bleep, for the ward I'd just left. I ran back there in time to see the duty team, who had just taken over, working frantically on my yellow patient. The nursing staff were describing how they were on a drugs round and hadn't reached him, when my patient, who was quietly withdrawing from alcohol had developed 'Delirium Tremens'.

He had started imagining dreadful flying insects bombarding him from all directions, attacking him over his body. He was rolling all over his bed lashing out with his hands and then suddenly went into a convulsion, during which he suffered a cardiac arrest. This was observed by the on-site nursing team, meandering in their routine drug round, between the patient beds in no particular hurry.

They were as usual, just anxious to record it in their "handover notes," but probably didn't realise that if they spent less time talking among themselves and more time facilitating their drugs round, this patient might not have developed the 'DTs' and gone into cardiac arrest. Instead, they did nothing constructive, other than call the cardiac arrest team.

Although allegedly trained, they didn't attempt any resuscitation as that required them to complete layers of health and safety reports. They just initiated the cardiac arrest call. Unhappily, the duty team was unable to resuscitate this man and he died, in the place that was supposed to help him!

I was faced with the prospect of telling his wife what had happened to her husband. She was seated in the waiting area and fixed her gaze on me in anticipation as I approached her. I gently took her arm and again guided her into the doctors' room and broke the news that regrettably, her husband had had a cardiac arrest and had died. She almost collapsed in despair and was sobbing uncontrollably.

I felt I needed to hug this woman in her genuine grief, human-to-human. Lord in my exhaustion, I thought, how lovely she felt and how overpoweringly seductive was her perfume. I was becoming quite faint from her clinging on to me, with her hot tears running down my neck, her perfume's bouquet and my fatigue, when suddenly I came back to reality, as sister came into the room with a pot of tea to save the day.

I regained my self-control and advised her that the Coroner would have to be informed about her husband's death. Also, there would have to be a post mortem examination to ascertain the exact cause of his death and that if she contacted the hospital bereavement office in a couple of days, I would arrange for her to be able to collect a death certificate from the Pathologist and proceed with her husband's funeral arrangements.

The look of sadness on her face made me feel powerless to help her. How I hated death for the pain it inflicted on the bereaved. I left her in the room with sister and retreated back to the ward, thinking that medicine was a difficult specialty, where we peddled drugs to try and slowly influence the course of a disease. I preferred surgery where one could rapidly affect outcomes, mainly for the better.

I didn't have very long left to do in this part of my training, just a few weeks or so. I was thinking that I ought to start considering my future career again, now that I was about to become a fully registered doctor. I hoped I could go back to Obs and Gynae, at Addenbrookes and thought I would contact Marion, Prof's secretary, about a job.

Well now at least, as a fully registered doctor, I wouldn't have to keep bothering Paul Bradley to sign the scripts for the controlled pain killer drug Pethidine on the labour ward. Then just as I was thinking about Mr. Bradley, my bleep went off for an outside call and there he was on the phone to me.

"Morning Mike, how's it going? Prof's asked me to call you as he wonders if you can call in at the faculty office to catch up. What's a good day for you?"

"Wednesday's my half day, so, would Wednesday pm be convenient? I should be able to get there by three o'clock."

"Yes excellent, I'm sure that will be fine, we'll see you then."

Well, that's a reassuring co-incidence, I thought. They haven't forgotten about me and maybe I could still be part of their team. Two days later, I was driving down the A14 towards Cambridge, wondering what the day might bring to me.

Prof's secretary was as efficient and warmly disposed as ever. She asked after my health and inquired how I was dealing with the stresses of life as a house man. She showed me in to a seminar room to await the Prof and brought me tea and biscuits. I didn't have to wait very long. As I sampled her boiling hot tea, I heard the Prof heading in my direction from the other side of the door. He burst in as jovial as ever debating politics loudly with Paul Bradley.

"Welcome back, Mike," he called out with his hand outstretched to greet me like his long-lost son. "It's good to see you again. How are you coping with the strains of life as a house physician? Are you learning a lot and taking it all in? You haven't been tempted by any of those hot-blooded young nurses, have you?"

I thought of Annie and the deceased Landlord's new widow and smiled to myself.

"No sir, I haven't we don't have the time or the energy. When I go to bed, I usually fall to sleep very quickly these days. I'm just looking forward to finishing this medicine job, so I can get back to doing surgery."

"Well done, my boy, save your energies for higher things, which is why we've brought you back in here. Do you wish to continue your career in this department, that is, in this department of Obstetrics and Gynaecology? If you do, you can join us here on the Professorial Academic Unit. I think, I can talk for my colleagues when I say that the last time you were with us, you discharged your duties to everyone's satisfaction and gave an excellent account of yourself. Furthermore, should you choose to take up our offer, Mr Bradley here will be mightily relieved that he won't need to be countersigning your prescriptions, to his joy and that of the midwives, as you will now be fully registered. (3) What do you say Mike? Are you with us?"

"Well, sir, as you've put it like that, what can I say, but yes, I would very much like to be part of your department."

"Welcome then, consider yourself one of us. Now, I believe that Mr. Bradley wanted a quick word with you about another matter, is that the case, Paul?"

"Yes, sir, that's right."

"Mike, would you like to walk back to the Medical Research Council Building with me?"

"Certainly," I replied and we left the faculty office.

20

Once outside, Mr. Bradley said, "I'm glad you're going to be working with us in more ways than one. Things have been a little quiet for a while but Special Branch have been in touch and want us to see an IRA terrorist man who has just been captured by the 22nd SAS Regiment in Northern Ireland. They've brought him over here for the debrief by Special Branch and MI5.

"Unhappily, the prisoner has some horrible skin condition that apparently looks like the plague and Special Branch want him checked out, in case it's catching. Your file says that your tutor at the clinical school was a dermatologist, so Prof wondered if you might be in a position to help us again with this one, on the hush-hush.

"He's actually very fearful for his own life, not from us but from his own side. The SAS ambushed his little group of freedom fighters outside Belfast and killed all of them, apart from him. He was knocked out by the blast from a stun grenade and got away with a concussion. Since he was the only one who survived, he thinks, quite rightly, his cronies will believe he was spared to help us. They won't be too bothered whether he's helping voluntarily or giving us information under gentle persuasion, he'll definitely be on the IRA's hit list and they'll probably knock him off to prevent him doing either."

"You do know a thing or two about dermatology, don't you? Would you mind taking a look at this man's skin? We'll tell him you're a specialist. Apparently, the prisoner has been talking like a canary, asking to do a deal but his skin looks as though he's got serious burns, with it dropping off everywhere. We can arrange for our SAS friends to bring him from a safe house and meet you when and wherever you suggest."

"Certainly, I'll be glad to help. Where do you think we should meet up? Could they come to the Memorial Court at my college, in the evening as it is usually very quiet, especially as the students have gone down for the summer?"

128

"Yes, that's a good idea. You must remain quite alert and of course, you must be armed. The SAS will be escorting the prisoner, just in case. However, you must remember, the IRA are very devious and although every possible security measure has been taken with this individual, he will potentially be very valuable to us and will be on top of their hit list. They know that and will come after him. You never know where they get their information from, or when they might pounce.

"We don't want you becoming a casualty, before your career gets started, so be extra vigilant and remember what you learned down at Camberley. I suggest you get into their vehicle to examine him, it will have the armoured body and bullet proof glass and make it early evening so there's enough light for you to see what you need to see.

"Make your diagnosis, your treatment recommendations and then leave. Remember the patient is a terrorist, so keep your conversations minimal to extract sufficient information for your clinical requirements. You can collect your weapon from Marion, 24 hours before the rendezvous. Do you have any questions?"

"How soon do you need this to happen?"

"As soon as possible would be good, they need to start his debrief and he won't co-operate until he gets treated. It's easier to accommodate his needs quickly, to extract more information out of him. He's being moved into the guardhouse at the Hereford barracks at the moment. We could get him here in 24 hours, but you need to pick up your pistol. Let me call Marion now to sort out your weapon and the sooner we get on, the sooner they get the information that they need.

"Just for God's sake remember that this man is thick and dangerous and probably personally responsible for the deaths of several innocent civilians, soldiers and police officers. We can't use him as a double agent because of the way we took him, if we let him go back, they'll know we turned him. We just need to milk any information we can get before we change his identity and let him go and hide somewhere undesirable for the rest of his life."

"Okay then, let's get on with it," I left Mr. Bradley at the Medical Research Council building, made my way back to the faculty office to collect my Walther pistol from Marion.

She handed over the pistol and 3 clips of ammunition, which she made me sign for. She was highly efficient and seemed quite cool, but as she handed me the shoulder holster, a broad smile broke out across her face.

She said, "You be careful out there. We like having you around."

With that, she gave me a huge hug, with no doubts about her feelings!

I left the department and drove back up the A14 to the real world of my house job. I locked the Walther in the boot of my car and walked across to the wards to see my peers working away with their patients and once again considered how different my life had become, one minute trying to save lives and the next at war with terrorism.

Still, I thought, 'It's all for the best, for Queen and country.'

The next day, Mr. Bradley came back to me and said the meet had been fixed for 19.00 in my college's Memorial Court, which was dedicated to the fallen of the two world wars. I thought it was appropriate that here I was going to war, as a "watcher" for the secret service, mixing medicine with war. I parked my car at the rear car park of Memorial Court with a few minutes to spare and waited. Almost immediately a black mini coach drove up and parked beside me.

There were three very large men who exited the mini coach. I could tell they were military, and all of them were carrying uncovered automatic weapons. They weren't worried about the subtleties of any cover-ups. They looked very menacing! I suspected they were probably the SAS, armed in case anyone attempted to take their prisoner away from them. They asked who I was and I told them. They apologised for their abrupt manner and quickly ushered me towards to nearside back door of their coach.

I entered the vehicle and sat beside an unshaven man in the back, who looked much younger than I. He wore a t-shirt, shorts and flip flops. One of his hands was manacled to the handle above the car door. In the other was an almost spent cigarette, on which he was dragging deeply. He had steely blue eyes, very fair hair and pale skin.

Except that much of his skin was crimson, with large plaques of flaky silvery dead skin scale, falling everywhere. His fingers were nicotine stained from his chain smoking habit, but also had an obvious clinical sign, which was now most familiar to me. His fingernails had the lifted edges and were the flaky nails of Onycholysis. It was one of the classic signs of Psoriasis that I had seen on my first day of clinical medicine on the hands of my beautiful actress patient.

This young Celtic terrorist had severe and uncontrolled Psoriasis and was looking most uncomfortable. The severity of his psoriasis was no doubt due to the severe stresses he was under. Medicine had recently become aware that stress somehow exacerbates the autoimmune disorders of both eczema and psoriasis. How stress to the emotional area of his brain can activate his immune T-cells and B-cells that cause these conditions, we had no idea!

His excoriated scratch marks were clearly visible all over his exposed neck and his arms and legs, where his amoeboid T and B lymphocytes had settled under the force of gravity acting on them in his extra cellular fluid.

I said, "I'm a doctor and I'm going to give you some medications that will make you much more comfortable."

He replied, "Will yer hurry then doctor, dis is driving me mad, I don't think I can stand it much longer."

This was a highly dangerous enemy of state, who had, as I had been informed, killed a number of our armed forces, not to mention several civilian and police members of his fellow citizens of Northern Ireland. Here he was asking me for help and baring his weakness for all to hear and see, he was the most intimate of foes. He re-stated every detail of his family history, laced with multiple details about his family's frequent incidence of diseases, that I recognised as autoimmune; including Thyroid disease, Type 1 Diabetes, Eczema, Psoriasis, Rheumatoid Arthritis and Inflammatory Bowel Disease.

These diseases are far more common in fair-skinned light-eyed Western Europeans, including Celts, which he was and members of his family had them all. There was no need for me to make judgments about his credibility, he was a better historian than the tame and trained patients we had encountered in our finals. I thought to myself that Military Intelligence or Special Branch wouldn't have much trouble debriefing him.

I was pleased he had something wrong that I had become familiar with and said, "Ok, I'll arrange it for you," and I left the mini coach.

I wrote a private prescription for a short sharp course of oral steroids. This was probably the quickest way of treating him and relieving his condition.

I gave him a reducing dose in order to preserve his own steroid producing adrenal glands. Steroid treatment suppresses the patient's own body's steroid production, so you can't just stop these exogenous steroids suddenly; one has to slowly reduce them, allowing his own steroid producing glands to become active again and come back on board.

The steroids would quickly frighten off his lymphocytes that were running amok in the reproducing germinal basal layer of his epidermis, pushing the skin cells there into overdrive, giving rise to the thickened scaly skin he was shedding all over the place.

I knew this severity of his psoriasis was likely caused by the current highly stressed situation he was in, with no discerning way out. I've always been impressed by the way that the mind can cause a reaction in the body. This type of medicine, where the psyche (the mind), can influence disease processes in the skin is called Psycho-dermatology.

Lymphocytes (one type of the body's defender cells) are amoeboid white blood cells that can migrate all around the body to fight off invaders. Once they migrate into the extracellular fluid compartment, they tend to become subject to gravity and end up precipitating downwards ending up in low body recesses like the limbs and other dead-end areas where they can cause havoc. They often get stuck at places where the limbs bend, like the elbows and knees, so these autoimmune skin lesions like eczema and psoriasis are much commoner there.

As I left the prisoner, I said to his captors, I forgot to tell him that he should try to cut down on his chain smoking as it would severely shorten his life.

They responded with, "Don't worry, doc. He ain't got long to live anyway."

I discovered later that this prisoner had provided a great deal of relevant 'hot' information, which was quickly used by the security forces in Northern Ireland and averted untold tragedies to our soldiers and the general population.

Turning this IRA man must have led to a great deal of 'break-ins' undertaken by MI5, and the planting of listening devices in cars and houses all over Ulster in the massive surveillance operations, that went on quietly every day in the war torn North of Ireland.

I learned that they use lock experts to enter houses and teams of search officers to look in all the hideaways. I was told they planted surveillance devices in nooks and crannies to photo or film the whole operation, including all of the house contents. Only a tiny hole was needed to plant a listening device or camera to record subsequent subversive events and battery packs were disguised in floorboards to allay any suspicions.

Later, I saw on another operation, where a whole street was secretly being filmed by cameras buried in the grass lawns, with only their lenses and microphones exposed.

I was relieved to have accomplished the objective for this 'mission', without being shot or blown up by the IRA because subsequently I read that this valuable asset, in this adroit and dangerous game, had been assassinated, presumably by his old comrades in the IRA, but who knows? Clearly the safe new identity and discreet existence Special Branch provided for him hadn't quite been safe enough. How the IRA had found him, the lord only knows. Of course, it might not have been the IRA!

As Paul Bradley and the Prof had warned me, 'Walls have ears.' The more I worked with them, the more I came to realise that.

21

Afterwards, I made my way back to my normal hospital job forthwith, watching in my rear view mirror, to make sure I hadn't picked up an unwanted tail.

Then, a few days later, I was on the daily ward round, when sister said, "Oh doc, the widow of the yellow man came to the ward yesterday and left a parcel for you. She said you had been very kind to her and she wanted to acknowledge this."

She handed me a small parcel wrapped neatly in gift paper. When I opened it, it contained a letter. With it and wrapped in tissue paper was a light blue scarf made from fine Peruvian Royal Alpaca Wool. This wool came from the inner fur lining of young Alpacas and was highly prized and highly priced for its excellent insulation properties. My colleagues were all quietly commenting to each other but very audibly.

Until one of them blurted out, "Oh yeah, what have you been up to then?"

"Nothing!" I replied all too defensively. "I've just been nice to a lady in distress." I left the ward and shot back to the doctors' mess, to read her enclosed letter in private.

Once there in the privacy of my room, I began to read. She introduced herself as Claudia, the wife of my patient who had died. She thanked me for the kindness that I had shown her and also thanked the nursing staff for trying to save her husband's life; little did she realise that he might still have been here if the staff had done their job properly. She added that she prayed that he was at peace now, no longer tormented by his dreadful disease.

She said that she missed her husband and felt very lonely in this cold and inhospitable country. She had many questions that had been left un-answered and wondered if I might spare a little time to meet up with her to help put her mind to rest.

I was intrigued by her display of generosity, which was quite disproportionate to my actions on her husband's behalf. She'd included her contact details and finished by saying that she hoped I would indulge her with my time to assist her in this period of her loss and uncertainty.

I felt it wouldn't do any harm and decided to call her there and then, to quickly try to assuage her uncertainty. She answered almost immediately and she sounded very pleasant on the phone. She explained how she hadn't really understood about her husband's condition and wondered how his failing liver could cause a heart attack.

I started to explain about how his heart attack occurred and it confused her even more. She was very apologetic for not understanding the process of how his withdrawal from alcohol would exacerbate his already heightened anxieties and could precipitate his convulsion and heart attack.

I could hear myself saying that perhaps we should meet so I could explain it to her better as this would help her to get to grips with the details. I thought it was the right way to deal with her problems and set her mind to rest. I agreed to come to her hotel that evening and she offered me dinner in the hotel restaurant.

I thought the hotel food would have to be better than the hospital canteen where I was due to eat and her company would be far better than that of my colleagues. I climbed out of my doctor's garb, showered and set off for the Old Stone Bridge Hotel a few miles down the road in the village of St. Ives.

On arrival at reception, I introduced myself and explained that I'd come as a guest of Claudia. On mentioning her name, I was immediately shown through two very large oak doors into a private drawing room. The receptionist advised me that Claudia would be right with me and asked if I would like something from the bar.

I asked for a beer and she inquired, "Which sort?"

"A real ale would be nice!"

She reeled off 3 different respectable real beers, which impressed my Philistine tastes and I chose a 'Broadside', which is a strong dark ale brewed up the road in Suffolk. This was delivered *tout de suite*.

I'd just had time for two mouthfuls, when the door opened and in floated Claudia. I gasped as she entered, smiling warmly, dressed in a Chanel haute couture suit and the red-soled shoes, of Christian Louboutin. Her olive-skinned legs stretched almost up to her shoulders and were accentuated by the mid-thigh mini-skirt and the Louboutin four-inch-high heels. I wondered how much per inch it had cost her deceased husband.

My Lord, I thought, it was worth every penny. She was looking completely divine.

"Hello doctor, I am very pleased you have been able to come this evening. I have been so anxious to speak to you about my poor husband. May I suggest that we have dinner in town, so we can talk discreetly? With your permission, I have booked a dinner at an Argentinian restaurant, not very far away, where I know the manager and we won't be disturbed. I will drive us, as I know the way very well and I can park in the manager's private car park."

I was thinking, 'Discretion? No chance!'

With a woman like her on my arm, everybody in town will have their eyes well and truly focused on us. I kept trying to think that I'm only here to help her understand what happened to her husband and at the same time instil in her how we had done everything we could to save him.

I knew that I was feeling a bit hunted but didn't know whether I should be contacting MI5, my medical defence union or Annie. Yes, she crossed at the forefront of my mind. I hadn't seen her for nearly a week, delayed by my NHS job and my other one. We'd talked by the public phone, just outside the ward for brief moments between my daily rounds of patients and medical tasks, but I hadn't touched her for what seemed like an age.

Now, here I was, alone with this dark eyed, raven haired beauty, reaching out to me for medical explanations and re-assurances, while oozing physical messages aimed in my direction. She was reaching out to me, like the Yin to my Yang, altering my compass and changing my course.

Her eccentricities were hiding her concealed strengths. Her fabulous universal appeal and ubiquitous head-to-toe beauty was disguised by her obvious and exquisite singularity. She feigned interest and understanding of my physiological reasoning of her husband's demise and interjected with praise for our efforts to curtail his fatal illness.

I very quickly gleaned her hidden agenda, but as the evening passed, the powerful Argentinian succulent and fruity wine with 14.5% alcohol definitely began to cloud the sight of my alternatives. Her beauty enhanced her divinity and assiduously dissolved my resistance. When she suggested returning for a coffee, I concurred and rapidly found myself back in her suite at the hotel.

As soon as the room service left the room, she doffed her Chanel Coutured jacket, revealing her transparent silk blouse that displayed her perfect torso. She took a long deep breath, boasting the fullness of her physique and proudly accentuating the inflection points of her waist and breasts.

I swallowed, feasting on her body and she saw this, and was visibly appreciating my appreciation. She approached me without hesitation, took my face in her hands and kissed me passionately, almost devouring my tongue in the process and pressing her body into mine like a solvent interloping a solid, which my nether region was rapidly becoming.

She expired her long deep breath into my ear, as her lips washed their way down my neck on to my larynx and upwards as she sucked her way up again to find my mouth. She moaned as she explored every nook and cranny of my mouth with her tongue. She pulled away suddenly and looking up at me she clasped my hand in hers and led me away into her massive bedroom. She reached to my belt and quickly releasing it, delved inside to grasp my rigid phallus, which projected proudly upwards like a NASA rocket, hotly engorged from pubis to glans.

Stepping backwards several times, she dragged me with no resistance to her huge bed, releasing me only to unzip and kick away her very haute couture onto the floor. She wore no under garments whatsoever and pulled me forwards and into her like a key into her moistened treasure chest.

She gasped as I entered her, locking me in with her long muscular thighs and we commenced our rhythmical rocking gently to-and-fro. As we rocked, her needy moans gently arose louder and louder until she screamed into an erupting orgasm with her pelvis vibrating for several seconds like a bucking broncho. I felt like the cowboy, who got first prize at the rodeo, as I lay still for fear of drowning in her juices.

We lay together enraptured in each other's arms and I rapidly fell asleep. Awakened by the sun, I realised I had not only stayed out all night but was about to be very late for work. I rolled to the edge of her giant bed and stood up, looking down on her.

In her sleep, she laid serenely like a sleeping Venus, with her raven hair flowing over her pouting breasts and the quilt accentuating her perfect curves. I tore myself away from her, gathering my clothes before my manhood could rise again and departed quietly, sneaking out past the night receptionist who was asleep at his desk.

As I approached my car, the full realisation of what I'd done blasted its way into my mind. The primitive dereliction of my fidelity to Annie struck home deep into my conscience. I had abandoned the principles that governed my behaviour and given way to animal instincts. What would she say; what would the professor say; I had lost the moral standpoint and strayed away from the right and the just.

For the first time in my hitherto fairly honourable life, I felt that I had lost my integrity and let everyone down. As I drove back to the hospital, I switched off Radio 2 and in a pensive silence, made good time before the rush hour. I showered, donned my doctor's attire and made it to the ward in time for the early morning round.

Sister was eyeing me wisely wondering what I'd been up to since she handed me the parcel the day before. It seemed like an age away and so much had happened, I wondered if I would ever be the same again. I felt like I needed to confess, but how could I tell Anna, it would devastate her and risk ruining our relationship.

In one pico-second, I decided to speak to the Prof. He would know what to do and he was so very worldly wise. I recalled what he said about "Far better to have dyspareuned than never to have pareuned at all;" (better to have had painful intercourse than never to have had any intercourse at all). However, this hadn't been painful, it had been bloody marvellous!

I called Marion and arranged to see the Prof about a personal matter in his faculty rooms the next day when I could sneak off. The time in between passed very slowly indeed and my mind was racing, unable to focus on my work and steadfastly fixed on what I'd done and the overwhelming urge to do it again.

Finally, at last, the requisite hour had arrived. As I walked into the faculty office, Marion unaware of my burden of guilt, greeted me warmly and quickly showed me through. I was immediately welcomed by the professor, exhilarated and enthusiastic as ever, firmly shaking my hand in both of his. Again, I felt like his long lost son, arrived home from the wars.

"Sit down, Mike, welcome back. Marion, can you bring us some coffees? Now then, what can I assist you with?"

"Well, Prof, I've been a bit of an idiot." I told him the whole story and my feelings of guilt, without the intimate details and my fears about Anna discovering the whole affair.

"My dear boy, thank God for that! I thought it was going to be something disastrous, that we might or might not be able to remedy. I was very worried that you might be here to hand me your resignation. The first thing you must remember, if I can take you back to our first encounter, when I asked you not to mention to anyone a thing about how you had come across me in my office in a distressed state. As far as I'm aware, you've fulfilled my wishes and haven't revealed to anyone the events of that evening. I thank you again for that.

"Also, I recognised certain thoroughly good qualities in you that you have continued to display both in your professional life as a young doctor and also in your other life for Great Britain. I am aware that these qualities have endeared you to all of your colleagues and we have become very fond of you.

"I am certain that as you have explained, you went to help that beautiful young woman with her grieving process and unintentionally fell victim to her overpowering physical wiles. You would certainly have assisted her loneliness and even more certainly have expedited her bereavement reaction. It seems to me that she may have been getting over that a bit too quickly from my experience of such things. From what you've told me, I'm certain it won't take too long before she's surrounded by crowds of suitors eager to keep her in her haute couture and red-soled footwear.

"It's my opinion that you should not contact her again and if she contacts you, be polite and firmly make your excuses for being unable to see her again. Heaven knows how your common law wife would take it, if she were to find out any details of that liaison. How do you feel she might react to it. Would you want to find out something like that? Do you see my point?"

"You are quite right, sir. I hate to imagine how she might take it and certainly wouldn't wish to find out."

"Good, then file it away in your head where you file all the other state secrets and never mention it again. It never happened and certainly doesn't deserve further worry or concerns. I'm sure the good counsel you gave that young widow, provided her with some understanding and comfort. The intimacies you both also enjoyed, didn't do either of you any harm. Don't ever mention it to anyone, as you already know: Walls have ears!

"If ever you are questioned about it, you must lie with the strength of honest conviction. I'm sure what happened was probably very good for both of you, but mustn't interfere with your important works here and your career in medicine. You are about to finish your house physician's post and then you will be due to start as an SHO with us in O and G at Addenbrookes. We are looking forward to you coming back to us on the 1st of August.

"However, I have another job in mind for you and Mr. Bradley will brief you about it, when you join us. For now, continue in normal mode, be very warm and loving to Anna and don't think about the luxury of feeling guilty. It will affect the way you behave towards her, creating suspicion and doubt, which is not good for anyone."

"Thank you, Prof. I am very grateful as ever for your very wise advice. I will do my very best to follow it. I look forward to joining you in two weeks and until then, I won't let you down."

I turned and left his office, feeling very relieved.

22

Again, the boss had set my mind at rest, calming my anxieties and pointing me in the right direction. I drove back to Annie's feeling like a great weight had been lifted from my shoulders. I was one of the team again, absolved of my puerile wayward tryst and eager to go home to the woman I truly loved.

I couldn't wait, drove like the wind and was soon parking up behind her car and gave her a hoot as I left mine. Calling out as I crossed the threshold, Annie shouted down from the landing above.

"Who's that strange-voiced intruder that I spy at the front door?"

"It's me and I've really missed you," I exclaimed as I climbed the stairs two at a time.

She was waiting at the top and I sank into her arms with our lips melted together quaffing our mutual saliva, pausing only to exchange our love vows. I told her how the last week had seemed like an age and I had really missed her badly. I didn't want to be separated again and reassured her that my next job in Obstetrics and Gynaecology had a much less onerous rota.

She was very emotional and wouldn't let go of me, squeezing me hard into her, as if she sensed an impending doom. She let go and stepping back, she reached out pulling off my jacket and tie and began un-buttoning my shirt.

She whispered, "I need to feel you in me, I've been wet all afternoon waiting for you to come home. Hurry doctor, I'm gasping for you!"

With that, she unbuckled my belt wrenching my trousers to the floor. My penis leapt to attention and she knelt before me on the bedroom rug, dragging me into her deep throat sucking like a long rocking siphon. I had been anxious that my bearing might betray my guilt; well here I was bearing it all and I certainly wasn't going to interrupt the proceedings to think about guilt.

I was highly aroused by the sensations erupting from my manhood and coursing to the pleasure centres of my brain. She vacuumed my rigid penis in a slow regular motion, licking the end in a circular swirl, swelling the glans and increasing the pace until it erupted into a sensational climax. I fell onto her at the foot of the bed, locked in her arms with my spent penis crushed against her belly.

We lay there for a while, stuck together by our passion, panting from our mutual exertions until she exclaimed, "I'm so happy you're home, don't go away again, I feel so lonely when you're away, I love you so much!"

"I'm not going away from you again. Let's get married, I want to be with you forever."

"D'you mean that?" she replied, as tears of emotion filled her eyes and ran down her lovely face.

"Yes, of course, you make me so happy, I don't want anyone else but you, so let's do it. I'll ask your dad, we can visit them at the weekend. I think, I should do it in person."

"Yes, that would be wonderful, they'll love you as much as I do."

By this time, she was really weeping floods of tears.

"Hang on, you're supposed to be happy and here you are crying your eyes out. That's not right!"

She hugged me tightly and said that she always cried when she was happy.

That was it; I'd made up my mind and I knew what was important and what made me happy. The yellow man's widow was gone from my thoughts. Annie was all important to me and I wanted to be with her and I knew that was how it would be!

23

Next day, I left early and went back to finish my last few days as a house physician. I pondered my situation as I drove up the A14 road. I'd learned a lot of medicine in this job, but was frustrated that most of the patients I'd seen were mainly quite old, usually very sick and quite often died.

I'd certainly put to good use the cardiology that I'd learned on my elective, by dealing with multiple cardiac arrests. Unhappily, in fact once, in the middle of the night, we had two for the price of one. As we were dealing with one cardiac arrest, the patient opposite, who had had a clear view of the proceedings (because it didn't dawn on the duty bank nurse to draw the curtains round the 1st patient's bed), and he also went into arrest and unhappily we failed to resuscitate him.

That wasn't the case all the time; One night we had another patient, who had been a spitfire pilot during the Battle of Britain. He came into A&E in cardiac arrest and the paramedics had sustained him in the ambulance by Cardio-Pulmonary Resuscitation (CPR). We took over and I remember how grey he looked, down on the trolley.

My SHO who was continuing the CPR said, "Right, give him some adrenaline."

With that, the sister handed me a syringe and I thrust it between his ribs right into his heart's left ventricle, injecting the lot. His heart monitor which had shown a flat line, suddenly changed into the jagged spikes of ventricular fibrillation. Then my SHO shocked him with 300 joules from the defibrillator and his heart started pumping again. We adjusted it back into a normal rhythm and he soon regained consciousness and was back among us.

We moved him to coronary care. The next day when we went to see him on our daily round, he called me back and told me that when he was dead, he was above us and looking down on us, watching what we were doing. He retold me about the chain of events precisely as they had occurred. This was certainly very spooky!

I wondered whether when his heart had stopped, the paramedics had been maintaining his cardiac output by chest compressions and his blood oxygen level maintained with an airbag attached to a mask. So probably this kept the bits of his brain that dealt with his hearing still working well enough for him to hear what we were saying and doing to bring him back.

On another evening, I was called to the elderly medicine ward to see a diabetic patient who was having a hypoglycaemic attack (a low blood sugar). This was during the visiting period on the ward and members of his family were all around his bed.

I gleefully arrived with the ward sister and as she pulled the curtains round the bed I told his relatives not to worry and that I was just going to give their father/grandfather some glucose and he would be as right as rain in no time. I plugged a syringe of glucose solution into his I.V. line and as I was gently pushing the syringe piston down and being reassuring to the patient, he had a stroke and died on the end of the I.V. line.

I looked at the sister in shock and she mouthed to me, "Don't worry doctor this sometimes happens to the very old." She motioned me to leave his bedside, by the other end of the curtain. This I did very sheepishly, leaving her to deal with his bereaved relatives.

In gastroenterology, most patients had happy outcomes and our modern medicine made a difference to their treatment outcomes. My boss Dr Richard Richardson was an expert on the new art of endoscopy and undertook cholecystectomies through a flexible telescope with a powerful lens at the end.

He would pass the scope down the patient's throat, through their stomach and into the duodenum, into the pancreatic duct, up the bile duct, where he could snare any entrapped gall stones and/or gall bladders and take them out. This was far quicker than the previous surgical means. The patients had far less morbidity and the surgeon's assistant had far less back ache.

One of the things that impressed me about physicians was that although they were specialists in certain areas, when their medical teams were on-call, they still dealt with all the other medical conditions that patients would arrive with in A&E.

Often, the next day various patients would be passed on to the team which was most appropriate to deal with them, but I was surprised by just how much these physicians actually knew. Certainly, the old surgical saying about them knowing a lot but not doing a lot, didn't really apply at all. Not only did they know a lot, they really did do a lot as well!

These were my final few days as a house physician and I left the world of medicine with fond farewells to my nursing and medical colleagues. I rushed home to greet Annie and we set off towards the Midlands before the Friday 'rush hour' traffic caught us and slowed us to a crawl.

Needless to say on arrival in Birmingham, her parents' house was thrown into bedlam. They seemed highly impressed that their daughter's boyfriend was a doctor, fussing about regaling me with offers of tea, coffee, beer, wine and all sorts of different spirits, most of which I'd never heard of.

When I asked their permission to marry their only daughter, they were utterly delighted. Her mother burst into tears and her dad kept patting me on the back with one hand while shaking my hand off with his other.

They badgered us about our plans, but of course we hadn't made any; as the subject had only come up the day before.

Immediately, as if a starting gun had just fired, the debate was set off to a flying start with everybody talking at once, becoming louder and louder, with each putting their spoke in, countering the other's ideas.

I thought it best to reserve my opinions, but contributing intermittent nods of approval, when everyone turned and focused on me, seeking my acquiescence. By the time we left to drive home almost all the informal arrangements were established. All I had to do was consider my guest list, book the church, book the registrar and publish the Banns.

Although it sounded simple, the real situation was quite complex. Annie and her family thought the event should be local to the Midlands. Considering my family, I thought South East England might be better but, ever the diplomat, I suggested a wedding at my Cambridge College might be an excellent compromise, appeasing both parties.

As an alumnus of my college, I was able to reserve its facilities. It was both an exquisite and remarkably economical venue, to those few, who were privileged members. This dissipated their arguments and everyone submitted, agreeing on the college as the site of the ceremony and festivities. They applauded the fact that given enough notice, it could accommodate many of the guests over night as well.

On heading down the M1, we agreed that while we were at it, it might be expedient to call in on my family to fill them in on the pending nuptials situation.

Once again, on hearing the news, being a big Irish family, my familial menagerie took off into orbit like their counterparts 'OOP North'. My mother almost strangled Annie with her hug, inviting her into the family and she spent the rest of the evening enriching British Telecom by phoning every relative around the globe.

By the time we'd eaten, it was getting on a bit so we were invited to stay and my parents duly insisted that the sheets were changed on their bed, which they most willingly gave up for their highly spoilt son, the doctor. I thought how times and morals had hugely changed since my older sisters' were courting!

The next day, we left the house in joyous pandemonium, which was very contagious. As we drove up the A10 to Cambridge, I could feel the excitement fermenting inside Annie as she kept giggling to herself and purring like a kitten. She was oozing happiness all over the place and I have to admit I felt the same.

On arrival at my college, I left her in the middle common room, with a large mug of tea and headed to the general office to contact the college bursar. He was a giant of a man, very sage and patriarchal and a man of great dignity.

He asked, "Are you sure you want to marry so young and at the beginning of your career?"

When I replied, "Yes sir!"

He looked me in the eyes and bellowed, "So be it! Let's get on with it, stat" (immediately), wrapping his very large arms around my shoulders and walking me into his study.

Then he booked the next available date, on the 3rd weekend in August, right in the middle of the summer vacation, when the college was closed for students but very open for tourism and conferences. It was done and with just a few million other things to consider almost dusted! I rushed back to Annie and she leapt out of her chair with joy. We sped home to her house to give British Telecom an even bigger profit and celebrated in the only proper manner for very happy young lovers!

The next day, I couldn't wait to get off to work to spread my good news and I didn't have to wait long, as it was the consultant ward round first thing. I entered the Department of Obs and Gynae and one of the secretaries, who must have been new, showed me through to the common room, where five other SHOs were waiting. I recognised them from the year below me at the clinical school. The new secretary left us but came back with a tray of teas. She was immediately followed by the Prof, five other Consultants and three senior registrars, one of who was Mr. Bradley.

The Prof welcomed us to the department and then Mr. Bradley took over and briefed us about Rotas and what was to be expected of we new career trainees in Obs and Gynae. It was all old hat to me, having done a long term locum there just over a year before, but this time I was to be an academic trainee and had higher expectations to live up to. The first was the expectation to pass the Diploma of the Royal College of Obstetricians and Gynaecologists, the DRCOG, which is the first post-graduate examination on the way up the training ladder to be a consultant.

This morning, it happened to be the Prof, who descended onto the ward with his posse of registrars, SHOs and medical students.

As jovial as ever, he led the team around the pre-natal and post-natal wards, from bed to bed, we stopped and discussed the various issues of each patient. They ranged from the most common issues such as Gestational Diabetes, with its implications of the later development of Type II Diabetes in the mother and for the foetuses.

The immediate threat was huge babies that out-grow the placenta leading to sudden death inside the uterus or the prospect of an early deliveries by induction of labour or Caesarian surgical delivery.

Also common, was Pregnancy Induced Hypertension, where some as yet unknown factor caused the pregnant mother-to-be, to develop very high and difficult to control blood pressure, which again could cause placental abruption and foetal death in utero and not to forget a possible stroke in the young mother.

We commonly had a large number of pregnant women, who kept threatening to go into early labour. The Prof was particularly keen to prevent labours before 32 weeks gestation. It was after this period that foetuses are mature enough to be able to make a compound in their lungs called Surfactant that had been shown to lower the surface tension of the alveoli balloons in foetal lungs.

Lowering the surface tension in the walls of the balloons enables them to inflate on delivery, allowing for gaseous exchange and facilitates breathing in the newborn. Babies born before 32 weeks were unable to breath properly and suffered from Infant Respiratory Distress Syndrome, as the surface tension in the alveoli stopped them opening and prevented gaseous exchange. Such foetuses had to be ventilated and many died or suffered brain injury.

A New Zealander doctor called Graham Liggins had discovered that in sheep, giving the Steroid Cortisol to premature labour ewes would delay labour and induce the foetal lamb to make surfactant and prevent the respiratory distress. This was such an important discovery that the Prof and the obstetrics department, together with one of the paediatric consultants, were undertaking a controlled trial of this on such pre-term women.

This was a phenomenal discovery, which was to save the lives of thousands of such premature babies that would otherwise have succumbed to respiratory failure. I felt very proud to be working alongside such brilliant people in the fight against disease, where Cambridge was the hub of the universe for such innovations.

24

At the end of the obstetric ward round, we gathered in the tutorial room for coffee and further academic discussions. Mr. Bradley was grilling the medical students about the cases we had seen on the ward.

At an appropriate moment, I whispered to him about my forthcoming nuptial plans and he responded with, "Are you serious?" grabbed me with both his hands on both of my cheeks and proceeded to hug me with un-abounding enthusiasm, drawing it to the attention of everyone present. It immediately stopped proceedings and the Prof charged over to us exuding his own even more than usual enthusiasm.

"Well done, my boy!" he exclaimed. "I couldn't be happier for you! Who is this woman that's captured your heart? Do we know her, is she that neurosurgical secretary we've seen on occasions waiting for you and can I give you my approval? We don't want to be losing you as one of our highly selected trainees. You must come and talk to me about your plans! When's the happy day?"

Suddenly, I was the centre of attention with everyone congratulating me and patting me on the back. I wasn't sure I deserved any congratulations; all I'd done was ask a very beautiful woman to marry me. I suppose she might have said no, so I supposed it was sort of a personal achievement.

After a great deal of more pandemonium and after I'd named my bride to be, the date and site of the ceremony, the Prof congratulated me again and called his academic team back to attention. The registrars, SHOs and medical students set off to Addenbrookes Old Site to continue the ward round for the gynae patients there. The other consultants on the Professorial team departed for their various outpatients' clinics, while the Prof asked me to wait back for a word with myself and Mr. Bradley.

He led the way to his study and once all three of us were seated inside, Mr. Bradley leaned forward and opened proceedings, "I have had some rather disappointing news, and I know that you Prof are already aware. I have heard from Special Branch that the young daughter of one of the East German scientist families appears to have got herself mixed up with a gang of 'ne'er-do-wells' in Stevenage, in North Hertfordshire, where her family have been settled. It would seem that she may be involved with drugs, possibly emanating from the local secondary school which she currently attends. Local plod have been aware for some time that several of the natives there are majorly involved with the drug trade and addiction is a serious problem in the town and surrounding areas.

"It would appear that Stevenage, which was a bustling new and pleasant industrial town of the sixties has declined rather dramatically. A possible arrangement between the ruling local council and various London boroughs has filled the town with the overflowing poorer families of London, so that unemployment and under achievement has become more common there. That is despite the excellent living conditions and services provided by the town's efficient council." It looks like the London boroughs may have returned Stevenage's offer of help with housing, by dumping some of their worst tenants on them.

"The drug problem seems to have moved up the A1 from Welwyn Garden City, where it first came to light in the sixties, when there were several large pharmaceutical companies based there. They became the most likely sources for various widespread illicit drugs in that area. The pep pills of then have become the cocaine and opiates of now. It no longer comes from the drug companies of the Garden City, it now seems to come out of London, delivered and peddled by groups of mainly Afro-Carribeans."

"The girl's parents are aware that their daughter seems to have become a bit distant from her family recently. They thought it was an adjustment problem and contacted our S.B. liaison officer about it. Because of the scientist's importance, he arranged for her to be quietly placed under surveillance by the watchers of MI5.

"This was hardly one of the usual roles of Special Branch, but it reflects the scientists' importance to our space industry and the investment made by our government in extracting them from the East. MI5 have photographed her scoring a hit on one of the large cycle tracks that run under the dozens of giant roundabouts in that town. It seems that the dealers actually cycle around the town delivering drugs on their rounds."

"We wonder whether you, Mike, would like to re-connect with the family again and assess the situation for us. MI6 have put a great deal of effort into making the scientists' defection to the West work and it would be a disaster if anything occurred that might hurt these valuable people and scupper the process.

"The latest reports from our missile placement people state that the defectors are providing valuable assistance to our weapons research program and they wouldn't want anything to interfere with it. We know from their comments and our observations, that they liked you when you looked after them on their arrival and they've asked if they could talk to you. They, like we feel you'll be well suited to deal with this very delicate family situation with your usual extreme discretion."

"You will again be working with Special Branch and depending on your report, we may have to put some other resources in place. We need to know what they think the problem is, as well as your thoughts on it and the basis for your opinions, together with any ideas you may have on solutions. You can liaise with the family involved by commuting from here during your working day and no doubt I can find a reason for your absence from the wards or clinic. Can you make yourself available from tomorrow morning?

"You can work what hours you require, but we'd quite like you to report back here tomorrow with the current situation first hand and then we can formulate an action plan with our friends in S.B. and any of the other resources we have available. Hopefully we can settle this as expeditiously as possible within a week or two, if possible, so we can have this problem sorted out and tidied away, to enable these valuable assets to continue their lives and work in peace."

I rapidly ran the idea through my head and thought the prospect of meeting up with those very pleasant people again appealed to me tremendously. If they were having trouble, after all the risks they undertaken to get here, then I'd be glad to help them and our service as much as possible.

"I'd be glad to assist wherever I can, Paul. If you can square it with my colleagues and the wards, I'll go and see them in the morning. Where do they live and will they and Special Branch be expecting me?"

Prof stepped in with, "Well Mike, we've anticipated your response and made an appointment at Stevenage Police Station, with S.B. at 10.30 in the morning. They'll brief you on their take on the situation. We've also booked you in to meet the parents at their house in Stevenage and from there, the girl, as soon as is possible. This is their address and the S.B. will be there in the background just in case. You won't be in any danger, their house is under surveillance and S.B.

are nearby and tuned in, for your protection and so as to make sure that they're settling in without any second thoughts. We don't anticipate any trouble, so you won't need to be armed. The last thing we want is for this unexpected hiccup to rock the boat."

"I know you'll listen to their problems sympathetically and be reassuring. They are a most valuable asset and we want to keep them on board. Good luck and we'll look forward to our debriefing tomorrow afternoon. You can shoot off now to plan your discussion with the parent's tomorrow and how you might approach the girl afterwards."

I didn't need telling twice, I had lots to think about to enquire diplomatically about this sensitive family issue that mustn't result in the scientists suffering a disaster. I went to the clinical school library and sat and pondered my approach. I thought I'd hear what S.B. thought first and then listen to what the parents' concerns were and how together, we might sort them out as rapidly and quietly as possible. I went back to Anna's for a quiet evening before I set out to sort out this new challenge.

I was confident as I entered the S.B. room at the Stevenage police station the next morning.

They stood up as I entered and greeted me with a respectful, "Good morning sir." I introduced myself and asked if they could bring me up to date with the family situation and their detective inspector opened the briefing.

"Well doc, we believe that drugs are possibly being shipped into Stevenage from one or possibly two sources. We're aware that one source is a gang of vicious Afro-Caribbeans in London and the North East, who currently supply a vast network in the Met and home counties with drugs and other low life activities including gambling and prostitution. The drugs in this case are then personally shipped from the Met up to Stevenage by carriers, who come out of London by rail to distribute them to various addresses in the town.

"They're being stored locally in the homes of various young girls, who invariably seem to be single mothers, who are thought to be open for cash inducements by the dealers and very easy to intimidate. The drugs are then passed to the delivery boys who actually cycle round Stevenage on the town's cycle tracks, that way they tend to avoid Plod, who are all in cars nowadays.

"They meet their customers and make their deals on the cycle underpasses. They also pass on the goods to local teenage dealers who sell them in the schools to their fellow pupils. This is how we think young Frieda became involved, as part of her integration into modern British teenage life. This seems to be the current pattern over South East England and across the home counties.

"However, we know of another possible and even more sinister source. We've recently had a case of a young man who died of an overdose of heroin, who doesn't fit the bill of the usual local blighters that commonly end up dead. He was a local boy from the town and a highly academic law student at the Hatfield Polytechnic. He didn't have any kind of connections with the places or people in the drugs world.

"Local police have screened all his student colleagues from the Poly and they're all very straight decent people. He was an athlete involved in a local running club. He didn't have a girlfriend and apart from his running, which was his only hobby, his other life was totally bound up in studying for his law degree. His tutor told us he was very dedicated and definitely heading for a first-class degree. We haven't spoken to everyone at the running club, as yet, so we've more to do.

"Those we have spoken to are also all very straight upright upper middle-class people, some professionals, others are his student mates, but all adamant about his honesty and all entirely ignorant about where he would have accessed the heroin. We think there must be another local source, getting their stuff from a different supplier, who might like making the hits much stronger. We now have enough local resources in place, courtesy of the Home Office and we think we have found a possible source involved at the athletics club.

"We are setting up a local surveillance program and will keep you informed of any progress. We have been made thoroughly aware of how important this is both locally and nationally and will be using all available resources to sort this out as soon as possible.

"I should add that we have been making some progress, whenever it gets out of hand our Organised Crime Team, which liaises with the Met and some other home counties Teams, gets involved. We have made several co-ordinated raids and arrested gangs of teenage dealers, who end up going to Crown Court. The youths don't know who those higher up the tree are. That's what we need to ascertain as soon as possible, to get them off the streets.

"Due to the importance of this case, we've had some help from the watchers at '5'. It would appear that the scientists hold some clout with the Home Secretary and MI6 have become involved, as they were part of bringing these individuals here in the first place. They've leaned on '5' who've very kindly supplied us with the "clout" to take this case right up the tree to the Home Secretary. No doubt that may be the reason you're here."

"Well inspector, I think you may be right about that, I'm here to look after the needs of the scientists, who are very important assets for Britain and liaise with you and or MI5. Thank you for the briefing, I think I'm much better equipped to speak with the relatives now. No doubt, I'll be seeing you later."

With that, I left them and went to find Frieda's parents.

25

I wasn't surprised to find the family set up and housed in a posh residential area of detached three to four bedroomed houses in the more affluent area of North West Stevenage. I surmised that they were there probably through the sponsorship of the Home Office, initially at least until they were settled. Stevenage had a number of very successful Aviation, Weapons and Space Science Industries based there so it was a natural site for them to settle.

I was also not surprised that major players in our country's security forces had become involved in this problem, which has to be said was pretty common around the country. Of course what made this different, was not only the contribution these highly skilled scientists could make to those industries, but the fact that during the combined efforts of our services to bring them here, several people had been killed and injured in the process. Our government was not going to let this situation go bad.

I was looking forward to meeting the Hoffmans again, as I'd built up a good relationship with them while they were recuperating at the Fulbourn Manor. I'd found them to be a very pleasant, outgoing, committed and highly intelligent family. They were most enthusiastic at the prospect of a new life in Britain. I was shocked when Frau Hoffman greeted me at their front door. She smiled but was no longer the charming and affable woman that I'd come to know earlier.

She looked tense and I very quickly grasped she was somewhat fraught with anxiety. She and her husband Herr. Dr Hoffman were at their wits end with worry about their daughter Frieda, who had changed dramatically since starting at her new school. Their young, charming and very bright daughter, who had been achieving an excellent academic record back in East Germany had become most withdrawn.

They described how she'd altered to be very sullen and was avoiding contact with her parents. In Germany, she'd had many friends who would be in and out of each other's homes on a daily basis. However, since joining the lower sixth form of the local school, she seemed to have only one friend, who never visited their house.

Frieda no longer came straight home from school and would no longer go to their study to do her homework. Although she still joined them for dinner, she ate like a mouse and made very little conversation. They started doubting themselves as parents and were self-blaming for over encouraging her in her studies.

A visit to the school Head of Year, confirmed their fears, Frieda, a former 'A' grade student was missing lessons, was late when she did turn up, was not completing her homework nor taking an active part in lessons. They were dismayed. What could have happened to their highly motivated scholarly daughter?

Reluctantly, on her teacher's advice, they searched her room and found the desolating answer. Concealed in a wash bag at the bottom of her wardrobe was all the paraphernalia of a drug addict!

They were devastated. All of their ambitions, their motivations and raison *d'etre* were broken to bits in the bottom of that wash bag. What could they do? Who could help them and more especially her? Who could they turn to, to sustain their family? Her father Dr Emile Hoffman, said he thought of me, but was uncertain how to find me and felt too ashamed to try. That's when he contacted the 'S.B.' liaison officer and so it went up the line to the Home Office, out to the Prof and back down to me.

I felt deep pain to see these lovely people in such distress. After all they'd been through to get to Britain for the sake of their only daughter and within eighteen months, she'd been turned and possibly destroyed by a reprehensible product of the breakdown of a modern British society. Her Head of Year told them the name of her guilty classmate, a failing non-attender, dragged up in a broken family.

I told them how sorry I was to witness their sadness and tried to give solace to their heartbreak and to reassure them that we would take appropriate steps to alleviate their situation as soon as possible.

Dr Hoffman expressed great shame about his daughter as if it was through his and his wife's failure that this had happened. He felt that he couldn't carry on in such an environment, in case his neighbours and work colleagues became aware of the situation. He wondered about the possibility of moving to another country in the NATO Treaty Alliance.

This sounded immediate alarm bells in my mind. I could see MI6 and the Home Office exploding at that suggestion. I asked them if they'd mind me seeing Frieda to discuss her personal situation, as I'd got on very well with her when she was recuperating at Fulbourn. They were at such a loss, in the helpless phase of bereavement, that they readily agreed to me seeing her if she deigned to return from School.

To negate the possibility of failure, I suggested we go and meet her at school. They were reticent and a bit anxious at the prospect, but conscious of time and the seriousness of the situation, I pressed the point and away we went. I was startled at the change in her appearance as she emerged from the school building. She'd lost a good deal of weight and frankly looked ill kempt. She looked surprised to see her parents waiting there and even more surprised when she noticed me.

She greeted me somewhat enthusiastically but almost awkwardly as well. I warmly shook her hand in both of mine and went on to hug her like an old lost friend, which I suppose she was. I said how glad I was to see her again and asked her to tell me what had been going on since we last met.

We piled into my car and on the way back to their house, I mentioned that her parents had been worried about her and that I'd suggested that the two of us might go for a coffee to talk about their concerns. I was surprised when she readily agreed.

As we sat at the back of the local Costa Fortune Coffee house I looked at her closely and noticed the pallor of her complexion, the dark rings around her once beautiful huge brown eyes. I looked straight into the tiny constricted pupils of a heroin addict.

"What's happened to you?" I almost implored of her.

She hesitated, looked up at me and opening up her school bag she said, "This."

Inside her bag, she revealed all the paraphernalia of a heroin user. There was a small bag of white powder, a lighter and a spoon for heating the heroin to liquefy it, a syringe, needles, and a length of elastic for tying off her veins to make them swell for injection. She said she liked to inject it as she gets a much better hit with an injection that sent her into a tremendous state of high.

She also had some drinking straws and aluminium cooking foil because she and her friend also liked to 'Chase the Dragon', where they would share a heroin bag and cook the heroin powder on the foil into a liquid and inhale the smoke or steam. If they had enough powder and if time was short, they would use the straws to snort a line of heroin directly into their nostrils for another quick high.

I said that I was sorry that she had become involved in this very dangerous habit and asked if there was anything I could do to help her.

She replied saying she thought she was hooked and if I could get her some more heroin, that would be a great help.

Her helplessness reminded me off the famous despairing quote from the Nazi Luftwaffe Leader Hermann Goring, when Hitler asked him what he needed to defeat the RAF and he replied, "Spitfires!"

I told her that it would be a tremendous waste of her talented life and if she carried on this path to her destruction, instead of using her wonderful abilities to do something good with her life, she would just be wasting it. I reminded her of all that had happened to free her from the evil repressive regime in the East and that several people had died just to make her free.

I asked her to think about that. I also said we could save her but that she had to want it to happen. We left the coffee house and drove in silence back to the Hoffmans'. Her parents opened their door as we approached it. I asked them not to worry and said that I would see to it that things were about to improve rapidly and that I would be seeing them all again very soon.

26

As I drove up the A10, on my way back to Cambridge I pondered about this desperate situation and what had happened to this man and his family. He was a high level scientist, who'd moved heaven and earth and risked everything to bring his family to the West. He had been totally naïve about the lower standards of family life in the UK, the depreciation of marriage and the inevitable concomitant loss of ethics and values. I wondered what he thought now.

I also wondered what Paul Bradley and the Prof would make of it. It brought home to me the differences between we in our Ivory Tower and the plight of the not so fortunate masses who have no way out of their tougher existence.

I thought how education had been my means of escape and here were these youths throwing away their opportunities for a quick hit and temporary escape that would rapidly hasten their downfalls and deaths. This needed to be stopped!

I pulled into the Addenbrookes staff car park and made my way to the faculty area, where I found marvellous Marion, who oozed warmth as I entered her office.

"Prof's not here. He sends his apologies. He's been called to theatre to do a difficult Pelvic Clearance for endometrial cancer; but have a cup of tea with me and fill me in on how you've faired today. How did your briefing go and how did you get on with the Hoffman's?"

I quickly did fill her in and thought to myself, Did she really mean a double entendre, as after all, she was a very attractive thirty-five year old beauty, in excellent shape. In any other circumstances, she'd be a prize, but the vision of Prof's face very quickly re-focused my mind!

She added smiling broadly that the Prof wanted me to meet him in his study at Downing at eight o'clock. I quickly collected my thoughts and realised I'd have enough time to touch base with Annie, whom I'd left at home in bed earlier.

I rushed down to the department of neurosurgery and there she was holding court with some of the nurses from the ward. She looked up and gave me a very empathic beaming smile that made me remember why I wanted to marry her. They stepped aside and stopped their chatting as I interrupted them. We embraced now, in full view of everyone, as they all knew that we were now an official item.

"Do you fancy a Chinese take-away for tea tonight?"

In unison, the nurses clamoured, "Can we come?"

"Yes of course, I responded, but I've got to go for a faculty meeting at eight o'clock," I fibbed with the power of honest persuasion.

"I'll see you at home at sixish and I'll collect it on the way back, I better rush, I know what you like." They all shouted their various menu orders as I left the department.

I left smiling, before they might detect any mendacious tone. I didn't like lying to Annie and these respected colleagues, several of whom had recently become friends, but it was for Queen and country and my rapidly excused exit did have some truth and was quite close to reality, as the best lies are.

I also thought their presence for the Chinese must divert Annie away from my absences. As I sped away out of the car park towards the Mill Road for a take-away. I thought to myself that my life was fast becoming most secret.

Unable to remember all their choices, I picked up the 'Set Meal' take-away for eight, rushed home and put it in the oven to keep hot. Annie and her mates arrived shortly afterwards, saying they were ravenous.

"For me, I hope," I exclaimed wrapping her in my arms and embracing her, before she could get her jacket off.

"Mmmmm, later, I'm starving, bring us food and feed us," was her reply.

"Right, you all sit there ladies, relax and slip off your shoes and I'll wait on you." I stepped into the kitchen and served up the 'Haute cuisine Chinoise'. The girls were already pouring out some wine.

"Not a full glass for me, don't forget I've got a meeting at work. Save it for later."

We rapidly devoured the dishes and I stretched out on the couch and Annie slid up beside me in cuddle mode. Though very difficult to resist, I reluctantly and gently pulled away, kissing her forehead as I went for my jacket in the hallway.

Moments later, I was speeding my was back into the city, passing the back of Jesus College, along Jesus Lane, around Parkers Piece and into Downing College.

160

It looked massive in daylight. The duty porter recognised me and waved me through the gate and another showed me to a parking space nearby. As I got out of my car, I was greeted by the very large porter that I'd met the last time.

"Good evening sir, welcome back, let me show you up to the Prof's room. They're expecting you."

I thanked him as he stood bolt upright and with that, he marched me off around the quadrangle until he stopped with a thump of his feet, about-faced and led me into Stairway 11. I suddenly became nervous, as I climbed the oak panelled stairway; wondering just who were expecting me. I didn't have to wait very long as he banged loudly on Prof's door, opened it and announced me to the company.

As I stepped inside, the conversation ceased and the Prof opposite me, swung round to greet me warmly.

"Good evening, Michael and welcome, we've been waiting for you. Come in and join us. Can I pour you a drink?"

"Yes, please and hello everyone!"

Prof continued, "You know almost everyone here, the Master, Paul and I are old friends, but let me introduce another of our friends and colleagues. This is 'K', who is the Director General of MI5. You may be aware that his department have been actively helping us on re-settling our East German Scientific friends."

"MI6 are also aware of and very interested in our meeting today, because, of course, they had a great input to securing these assets for us in the first place."

"K, like the rest of us, you must be anxious to hear Michael's up-to-date assessment of the situation, but first, may we ask you what your department have been up to recently, to help with the situation?"

The tall man in the dark pinstriped suit stepped forward, shook my hand and turned ready to pass on his team's input so far.

"Yes Professor, we have today arrested three Afro-Caribbeans in their early twenties and removed them from the streets of Stevenage. They were all in possession of quite a substantial number of illegal drug packages. We are holding them separately and incognito. We have them currently travelling around the home counties, where they will be visiting various police stations for a couple of days at a time, before being moved on to another. They have not been booked into any custody facility anywhere. For all intents and purposes, their arrests have not taken place. They have simply just disappeared.

"This is known in the trade as 'Ghosting'. No doubt, this will be causing some disquiet among their relatives, their colleagues and not to mention to themselves. Their bicycles were left behind and the television surveillance cameras around the town, were switched off at Police Headquarters, for a few minutes during the arrests. To all intents and purposes, apart from their bikes, they've vanished. We're hoping to rattle them and their higher-ups, by creating a bit of mischief and watching for any developments. We will interview them at some stage, when they have become sufficiently destabilised, to tell us the details we require. What happens to them in ultimo, will depend on what they know, what they tell us and what we decide here this evening."

"So far, only one of them has coughed who he is, but the other two are keeping schtum. The talker has a long record back to his pre-teens ranging from petty theft to robbery, burglary and various assaults. His conviction for stabbing led to him serving 3 years in the Feltham young offenders facility. So much for their rehabilitation service.

"I suspect the others are similar upper level members of the criminal fraternity. We have wiped our enquiries about them from the Police National Computer, so again there are no traceable records relating to their arrests and effectively, they no longer exist. We have had discussions with our colleagues in '6', who are interested in using them to create more mischief for these amateur pharmacists, but that's the status quo so far sir."

Prof added, "Thank you very much, Director, for your swift intervention. That must be sending all sorts of messages up the line, to their various London suppliers. I gather that the local Borough Council have also launched eviction procedures against a number of their tenants, who have previously been identified as providing storage facilities for these dealers. The grounds for their eviction are their anti-social behaviours and local S.B. have spoken to their neighbours to create the necessary witness complaints.

"In addition, very large drug stashes have also been seized through local police searches of the tenants' premises. They have been similarly detained incognito at the moment and I think we may also have to continue to hold these degenerates to prevent any contacts between them and their suppliers."

"That would seem to stabilise the local situation for the meantime, while we decide on further actions. I'm also aware that social services from out of the County have been pre-briefed in obtaining protection orders for any children involved."

K nodded and then sat down.

"Now Michael, thank you for your patience, may we have your report on the situation with the Hoffman family?"

I was amazed at what had already happened in this case. I'd had no idea about how swiftly our security services could work when necessary. I stood and went on to explain the salient features of the current situation with the Hoffman family. I mentioned their considerable regrets about coming to the UK, their thoughts about leaving and to my mind, most important of all, Frieda's addiction to heroin and how she needed equally urgent intervention to save her. I didn't mention the other possible source of drugs in the area, figuring that K would be aware of this. I finished and sat down.

The Prof rose and thanked me for my sensitive and to his mind comprehensive report on the family. He said that we would deal with Frieda immediately and that I should arrange for her to be admitted to a private psychiatric hospital known as 'The Priory', in North London and that she would be admitted, under an excellent and thoroughly reliable psychiatrist Dr John McCabe. She would be a voluntary 'in patient', but forcibly detained if necessary under the Mental Health Act. I was to become her life-line and to care for her as a very private patient until she was most securely recovered to her old self, drug free and back into her former highly academic congenial life style.

"I know I can give you this very important role, as we need her to be completely on board, if we are to keep her parents and the other scientists with us also."

I wondered how much this new role would impinge on my O & G training and again how the Prof might square it with my colleagues and the wards. However, he was the boss and when Queen and country call, we can but follow!

Then Sir James, the Master interjected that we couldn't have such people wreaking havoc with British society, more especially when it interferes with our national security.

He turned to K and said, "I'd like you to get together with 6 and work out a plan to wreak some more serious havoc of our own and deal with these individuals as you feel appropriate."

"Let me see it first and I'll square it with the Home Secretary. You'd better get your team down to Stevenage to deal with the women storing the drugs in the usual process manner, depending on their willingness to co-operate. Your people have enough evidence to oppose bail on grounds of their own safety, I'm sure their colleagues higher up their greasy scale, will have taken a substantial hit by the loss of their confiscated supplies.

"They will be angry and won't want these women talking to the authorities. They need to learn what it means to act against the interests of their country. If any of them fail to appreciate their precarious positions and put up any resistance to our investigations or obstruct us in any way, permanently remove them from society and let information be released to their peers that their bosses have eliminated them.

"We will slap a 'D' notice on this immediately, as their relatives, friends and crooked lawyers will try to create an outcry if any of this is broadcast far and wide. I would be grateful if you would arrange this for us K. I think gentlemen it's best if we let the Special Branch, 5 and 6 create this bit of havoc and we can let our watchers monitor the local situation and we can reconvene on a meeting on a when-necessary-basis. Do we agree?"

We, unanimously, nodded agreement.

The Prof picked up his phone and asked if the porter could arrange some further refreshments. In a matter of twenty minutes, the large military porter appeared with a colleague carrying two large trays of cakes and sandwiches. The Prof produced three bottles of fine college claret and one of port and proceeded to decant them most carefully into three crystal receptacles, as if he was dissecting out a malignant tumour. No sediment escaped into the vessels at all.

We sat down around his massive oak table and demolished the lot.

Paul Bradley and I wisely shared a taxi home and in the back we very quietly discussed the evenings events. I was anxious about the implications for the fates of the three drug pushers already arrested. Paul's view was that when something threatens harm against the state and their actions did; then the state has to respond and wage war against that threat. It was as simple as that. The drug dealers in their greedy uncaring haste had simply picked on the wrong victims.

It reminded me of the kidnapping of the Prof's family in Somalia, where the primitive kidnappers thinking they'd be receiving a ransom had inadvertently let loose a storm that was going to blow them off the planet. So here I was, a fairly new medical graduate, with all those years of training in caring for people, now at war with some unsuspecting drug-dealing criminals. Who'd have thought it?

I slid quietly into bed beside Annie and she turned towards me warmly encircling my inebriated body, edging my thighs apart, stroking the back of my scrotum and massaging my prostate. Umm, that's really pleasant, I perceived just before I passed out.

27

I awoke back into reality the next day with a thumping hangover in my frontal lobes. Annie was already up and I could hear the kettle boiling in the kitchen in the background. I walked towards the sound unsteadily and found her making breakfast.

"Good morning," I grunted.

She replied, "Well you appear to have had a good time at the faculty meeting; you were slaughtered when you got home last night."

"Yes, I'm sorry, a couple of us went for a few beers at the clinical school Student Union bar afterwards and the time just flew past, as did the Abbott ale." I quickly searched out some paracetamol from the kitchen cupboard and gulped them down with a long glass of filtered water.

"I'd better get going, we have a gynae ward round at 08.00 and I was late last night to the faculty meeting. Two in a row would not look good, especially as all the other SHOs are intensely keen and eager to be noticed by the Prof."

With that I slipped back into the bedroom, abluted, dressed quickly and slid out of the door.

I arrived on the gynae ward at Old Addenbrookes just before my over-enthusiastic colleagues and started a ward round with the staff nurse on duty. I realised that I'd not been briefed about my absence the day before, but the duty nurse very helpfully asked me how I'd got on at the Medical Research Council Labs yesterday, where I'd been helping Mr. Bradley with his infertility clinic.

"Oh, yes that," I replied, "I was taking bloods off the infertile couples, just checking their usual parameters and for any chromosomal anomalies and also checking them for this new disease called Aids, caused by the HIV virus."

In the afternoon, I had the honour of checking all the husbands' sperm counts. You'd be surprised just how many normal looking blokes have very low sperm counts, for loads of different reasons.

At that point, my other SHO colleague, who was doing six months of Obs and Gynae as part of his GP training, turned up and exclaimed, "Where the fuck were you yesterday, collecting brownie points, while I was here clerking all the patients?"

I replied, "You know that part of our MRCOG training is undertaking some research for a thesis. You can swap places with me next week if you want to spend half the day like a vampire, taking blood out of some very emotional infertile couples and the other half with neck ache looking down a microscope counting sperm."

"All right, I see your point, don't get flustered, I'll start the round at the other end of the ward and meet you in the middle," and he scooted off to the opposite end of the ward to strut his stuff.

Gynaecological surgery is a very academic discipline, being a mixture of up-to-date medicine often with major female abdominal surgery, in which we as surgeons often depend on helping each other out in our common fight against disease. I was glad to be able to find acceptance in my opposite number as to why I should suddenly be absent from my job as a junior member of the gynae team. I realised that the Prof or Paul Bradley had seen to it that I had a very good reason to be away and one that might be used again and again.

I finished the ward round checking all the post-op patients, who'd had their operations the day before when I was away doing my other job. Afterwards I made my way to Clinic 2A to help the Prof and Mr. Bradley with the Gynae outpatients. They nodded acknowledging my arrival and I slid into my position at the front of the clinic and the staff nurse brought me the medical record of the first patient of the day.

I scanned the notes and the GP's letter of referral. The patient was a lady in her late thirties, with a history of severe heavy periods, which had been so severe that she developed anaemia, which was making her life a misery.

The nurse showed the lady to my desk, who was a fair-skinned and light-eyed multiparous woman with three children. As she sat down, I thought to myself she's got a fibroid in her womb. For some very strange reason fibroids or leiomyofibromas (their proper name), are much more common in blond, fair-skinned light-eyed people and also paradoxically in black women.

She'd finished having kids, so I thought the best treatment for her would be a hysterectomy, via the abdominal route, which was much more straight forward than the vaginal route, which was easier for the surgeon than for the patient. I examined her bimanually and sure enough, I could feel a mass in the front wall of her womb.

To make sure, I ordered an ultrasound scan and ordered some blood tests to check her anaemia for the anaesthetist. I told her the diagnosis and reassured her that she would be cured by the treatment. I said she should continue the iron tablets from her GP and that she would receive confirmation about her surgery in the near future and she left a happy woman.

In the afternoon, I went to theatres with the Prof and Mr. Bradley and assisted them with all sorts of gynaecological procedures. These ranged from hysterectomies, both abdominal and vaginal, when the women's symptoms warranted such excisions. More common were Culposuspensions, where normally the tube draining the bladder, known as the urethra, was almost a reversed P-shape.

However, quite often, after a difficult vaginal delivery of a baby, the stretching the ligaments suspending the womb, caused by delivery, unbends the back to front 'P' shape, making it more vertically straight, causing urine to escape from the bladder, leading to leakage, particularly when pressure from the abdomen above by coughing or any other means, leads to such leakage.

To counter this 'Stress Incontinence', the urethra is supported and bent forward by sutures, elevating the first part forward. This slight bend in the tube alleviates stress incontinence, which is a very common 'Cross', borne by so many women after childbirth. We were researching a new mechanism for achieving this forward bend by introducing a tape that suspended the urethra like a hammock, and prevented its straightening and leakage.

The Prof liked to listen to the radio, so the afternoon proceeded very pleasantly. Between the records playing on the radio, the topic of conversation was my pending wedding. How were the plans going? Who would cover the wards on the day of the event and thereby couldn't come. I responded that I was leaving invitations to Annie. The Prof spared my blushes by suggesting that as long as he was there, he'd be happy and I needn't worry about inviting anyone else!

They didn't have to wait very long, as five weeks later there we all were in the College Chapel in the old court of my college. For completeness, almost all of the Obs and Gynae department, various other doctors, the relatives from both sides packed out the elegant ancient chapel to bursting point for an excellent ceremony joining myself and Annie as man and wife.

After a sumptuous feast in the post-graduate dining hall by the college caterers and champagne from the college's cellars, we left the throng and slid off for a three day honeymoon in Wells by the sea, in Norfolk.

I gather the weather was excellent, but of course, we didn't get to experience it, we were far too busy exploring our other's anatomies until we lay sleeping soundly. The three days seemed to fly by and suddenly it was Tuesday and we had to return to reality and make our way back to Cambridge, with work looming in the morning.

On the way down the A14, my new wife became quite emotional.

I asked her what was making her so sad and she said, "With doctors, the job always comes first. I see it all the time with the neurosurgical team. They're always at work and here we are, having to have a very short honeymoon because you have to be back at work. It's not fair, my friends have had two- or three-week honeymoons and all we can have is three days. It's just not fair."

"I entirely agree with you, but it won't always be like that."

The pressure of work imposed by government policy was truly a burden on those who followed a hospital career. It hadn't bothered me that much before, as I actually liked being a doctor and at the time, I was single, with no-one else to consider, just myself. Now of course, it was different; I had a wife who'd be at home alone while I was covering the on-call for A&E and general practice acute referrals, whenever the need should arise.

It was actually only going to get worse. As an SHO, on the professorial team, I was on a one in four rota, which wasn't too heavy, and on the next rung of the ladder as a registrar, the rota was also a one in three and then as a senior registrar, like Paul Bradley, it would have been a one in two, for several years until a consultancy vacancy arose for which, having completed the required training, one could apply!

However, at Cambridge, there was the additional benefit of a second senior registrar, entirely funded by the university. This meant that the senior registrars shared the teaching, which lowered their on-call to an actual one in three because the university paid for the extra third registrar, as well. However, it was the S.R.s who had to make most of the clinical decisions, rarely bothering the consultants, their bosses. This placed another heavy burden on their shoulders.

I thought about what Annie had said and of course, she was right. With any surgical career there would be loads of on-call days, with evenings and weekends lost forever.

I loved surgery and had always intended spending my career doing it. However, now things were evolving differently and I had other responsibilities. I had to take her point of view on board and heaven knows, there might be other little responsibilities coming along too. If she was as fertile as she looked and she did look really fertile!

Furthermore and after all, I was also working as a member of the top infertility research team in the world. I could foresee some possible heated relationship problems looming on the horizon. This made me start to consider other possibilities for other careers in medicine. What else could give me an eclectic broad ranging career that would provide me with the freedom to participate in both medicine, surgery and freedom?

For me the most important attraction in this world was freedom. All at once the path was as clear as daylight, for anyone with a normal brain, it was general practice. G.P.s were independent practitioners contracted to the NHS, but who could participate in whatever specialties they pleased and to whatever level they chose. They could be Hospital Practitioners and be working in Primary GP Care and also in Secondary Care, a certain number of days a week as members of various specialist teams, both surgical and medical.

They could be Clinical Assistants, working in clinics at a slightly less involved level. These activities gave them access as well as the freedom that goes with being independent General Practitioners, working as GPs in their own practices with their partners, and also in their own interest specialties in hospital, to suit them, their colleagues and their patients, for whom they held ultimate responsibility.

GPs had their own patient lists for whom they provided round the clock care for 365 days of the year, for which they were paid a capitation fees as well as items of service fees for various other treatments that had arisen since the formation of the NHS in 1948. Their contract was much more complex than Secondary Care Hospital practitioners, dependent on them making claims for all their work practices by certain dates, without failure, or they might not be paid at all. Despite this 24/7 commitment, primary care Partnerships provided GPs with more freedom than their secondary care colleagues, with less onerous rotas, on the whole higher pay and shorter daily working hours.

This suddenly sounded much more suitable for myself as a newly married man, with a wife to support. I decided to talk it over with Paul Bradley, on my return to work.

He was always a very kind mentor to me, in both my secret career, as well as being my superior in Obs and Gynae. I caught him alone in the surgeon's changing room after our afternoon operating list and told him about my concerns. As ever, he was totally frank and understanding and said that he and the Prof had wondered whether my marriage would alter the status quo. I defensively denied this and said that I remained as committed as ever to both services.

Paul quickly replied, "Well, I hope so. Those silent works we undertake for our country are a lifelong commitment, however, I do understand where you're coming from in respect of your career in women's medicine. The hours are prohibitive for a normal family life and that's why so many of us, like myself, are single.

"You'd have to find a very understanding woman to deal with the hours of being alone, the countless cancelled dates, the endless late arrivals because you've had to work over time because Outpatients had screwed up appointments, booking an impossible number of patients into your clinics or medical staffing haven't bothered to get a locum to cover your colleagues' vacations, so you can't go, even though you've already booked it with them, giving them an extraordinary notice of six weeks, which they totally ignore.

"You may have also made bookings with various holiday companies and paid several deposits that you won't be able to claim back, but that would be in the minutiae of your NHS contract, so you'll be screwed. God bless the impoverished and exploiting NHS and God bless the successive governments who haven't improved we doctors' terms of service, despite professing the opposite! I should also not leave out the BMA. Do not waste any money on their subscription fees, they are invertebrates, who appear to have lost their direction.

"I definitely understand and often thought about changing careers myself, except, I've almost made it to the top and my boss is just about the most wonderful person I know and the added bonus of our special job is just the icing on the cake for me. The emergencies of surgery, the risks of obstetrics and the thrills of our other secret work, have fixed my life forever. So, unless I go totally bonkers, screw that gay ex-nurse chief executive and/or all the surgical nurses, run naked around the clinical school with me leading them, and get well and truly sent to the nut house at Fulbourn, I can't picture myself in any other place or role."

"My advice to you, Michael, is talk to your wife very frankly about the burdens of working in a surgical career and whether she can commit herself to it and to whole heartedly support you. You won't of course mention our other role, which will remain confidential ad infinitum."

"If you are considering a life in GP land, the Prof has many contacts and I envisage no problems in us keeping in touch and being very able to cover any of your absences, we may in the future regard as vital for the public good. Indeed, it would be much easier to cover you as a GP, because of the current amount of professional freedom you will have there. Also, general practice can have a lot to offer in terms of financial rewards. We can talk about that later if you decide to go down that route."

"Think it over and discuss it thoroughly with Annie and then please come to speak to me and the Prof as soon as you've come to a decision. I won't mention it; it's up to you to come and seek us if and when you're ready."

He mentioned all sorts of professional incumberances the government were imposing on secondary medical practice, that the consultants at Addenbrookes were having to deal with on a daily basis. The government couldn't really afford the services provided by the NHS, as it had advanced. More importantly, nor could the NHS afford the thousands of very expensive over paid administrators employed. Its underfunding couldn't deal with the situation, and forced it to rely on the goodwill of we professionals.

I thanked him for his advice, his honesty and candour, which was truly his métier. I thought he was destined for greatness and it was no accident that he ended up completing his specialist training here at Cambridge, in a department with one of the greatest reputations in the world.

I left theatres and rushed back to meet Annie to discuss my career with her in earnest, wherever that was.

28

I arrived to find Annie lying in the back garden on a sun lounge in her black lace underwear exposing almost everything to all and sundry. She looked so beautiful, I totally forgot what I'd intended to discuss and leaning over, I embraced her with a passion that diverted my anxious sympathetic nervous system drive from my brain into a parasympathetic lust in my groin. Her hands reached up unzipping my pinstriped trousers and ripping them down to my knees exposing my rapidly filling extension.

I was trying to consider the feelings of the elderly retired civil servant lady, who lived in the maisonette below and who's living room window looked directly out onto the back lawn, but thought we only have one life and I can't waste mine, besides, watching us, might re-kindle her desires!

We fell onto the lawn and made love to each other as if the world was ending. My seminal vesicles rapidly exploded and we fell panting over each other with my knees covered in a bright green chlorophyll and my buttocks warmed by the afternoon sun.

Then with a clear head, I could speak to my wife about more logistical things than her lovely body and my desire to fill it. We showered and sitting in the kitchen over coffee I asked how she would feel about being married to a GP, instead of a surgeon. She suddenly smiled beaming with elation.

"Do you mean that, would you give up your ambition, for me, no I mean for us?"

"Yes, I would, I've been discussing it with Paul and also some of the GP trainees on our firm's rotas. To a man, they've reiterated that the government are yet to challenge general practice, because GPs are all still independent practitioners contracted to the NHS. The government doesn't know what to do with them. If the GPs go on strike, the NHS will collapse and the government will fall. The consensus of opinion was that for a while, general practice is temporarily safe from the destructive clutches of the government on the NHS.

"Patients like their GPs and primary care, as we know it and as yet, the government didn't have the balls to take them on! However, we don't know how long this professional freedom will continue. The primary care costs bill is nearly as expensive as specialist care in hospitals, so they're bound to come after it sooner or later. We've talked about it frequently at work and the Prof thinks that the professional freedom of primary care won't last for ever, they can't afford it and not withstanding any expensive wars, that they can rustle up to confuse the public, they'll be coming after it as soon as they can get round to it.

"They know that GPs on the whole have become quite introspective competing companies. They have no effective stewardship that could lead them against the government cut backs that the NHS will impose. In GP land, it's no longer, doctors against disease, it's become more like competition between GPs! The BMA tends to co-operate with whatever the NHS imposes on the profession. The government may control it by ennobling GP leaders and thereby, avoiding confrontation. For now, however, general practice is probably the place to be.

"I can specialise in any area that interests me. Obstetrics and Gynae, Surgery, Dermatology are my main interests and I can seek and obtain further qualifications in these specialties and see all those patients in GP land. If it becomes difficult here, we can always move elsewhere."

I wondered to myself how that might fit in with my other role with the Prof.

"Well, what do you think? Shall I opt into general practice and come home at night, or continue in surgery and see you as often as it allows?"

She looked up, stood up and slowly walked towards me, loosening the cord on her dressing gown, which cascaded to the floor as she reached into mine and gently slid her hand under my infusing penis, pulling it towards her. I guess that sufficiently answered my question and she led me erect up the stairs and into our bedroom, where she proceeded to clear all doubts in my mind.

The following morning, after a gentle word with Prof's secretary Marion, I was standing before him, rather anxious about how this impromptu meeting might go. He was not only my clinical boss, who could see to it that I never worked in medicine again. He was also my boss in a secret service that no-one knew about, but which existed in long oak panelled corridors, un-heard of by the public and controlled by single-minded quietly-spoken academics, who held sway over the normal echelons of power and seemed to be irreproachable in their ethics and intentions to protect the realm.

I was somewhat overawed, but couldn't figure out why. I knew this immense man of ultimate surgical, intellectual and compassionate sensibilities and was feeling that I was letting him down by wishing to leave his academic team.

However, I knew that I didn't want to leave him or his excellent team. I just felt the current career structures in secondary care medicine and surgery were outdated and destructive to normal family life.

In the back of my mind I was weighing up my career in O&G against the lovely Annie, as she laid on the sun lounger in her lace underwear. I felt sure that he above all others would understand the dilemma.

"Hello Prof, thank you for seeing me, I know how busy you are, I think you may be aware that I've been talking with Paul about my career plans, following my recent wedding. I want to let you know that after a great deal of thought, I've decided that my future career may lie in general practice. I love surgery and I've thoroughly enjoyed every moment of working here with you and your team.

"However, I feel that the intense pressures levied on surgeons by the NHS will be to the detriment of my new married and maybe family life. Whereas in general practice, the burden imposed on practitioners is far less, I do hope you will understand this dilemma."

"My dear Michael, I absolutely understand and I must applaud your decision. You have been fortunate to have found a lovely wife and I am completely aware of the stringencies of surgical training, imposed mainly by the NHS and to a lesser extent the Royal Colleges.

"In fact, we here at Addenbrookes have a relatively light burden compared with other peripheral general hospitals around the country, as we are partially financed and cushioned by our teaching of medical students in the university, which endowers us with extra senior surgical staff compared with our colleagues in the provinces.

"In general practice, you may well have much more freedom for the time being. I'm also sure that as a GP, you may be free to develop various disciplines that you choose for yourself within primary care. You may opt to partially work in secondary care as a clinical assistant or more formally as a hospital practitioner. You can rest assured that you are welcome to continue here at whatever level you choose. I can also let you know that I will help you in whatever choice you make.

"You should also know that your choice of career will not influence your other career in our national interests, which of course is for life."

"I know, you're aware that young Frieda Hoffman, the daughter of one of our new scientific assets from East Germany, has been our guest as a patient of one of my old friends at the Priory Hospital in Hampstead. She had to be sectioned in the end, but has done very well while she's been detained there. Her parents are very pleased and she was able to detoxify very rapidly. She was totally sedated for seventy-two hours, which prevented any convulsions and she has been free of all opiates for some considerable time.

"I'm aware of how busy you've been for the past few weeks, but I'd be especially grateful if you could make her care your priority, especially as you may be moving on in the future. Although in fact, you may be better placed in general practice to look after her."

"I suggest you look into various GP schemes around the country and select the one that suits you and then come back to me with the details and we will see what influences we can bring to bear to get you sorted out as expeditiously as possible.

"Go and see Miss Hoffman again as soon as you can and we will speak as to how you can proceed forthwith. Keep this career information between you, your wife and us, who are your other friends and advisors in this matter."

With that, he got up, walked around his huge desk and shook my hand with the grip of a wrestler. As usual, I was overwhelmed by his unsurpassed generosity of spirit. Leaving his department in mid-post, could cause him and the faculty some inconvenience and extra work, though I was also certain that there were thousands of career obstetricians, who would leap at the opportunity to join the professorial team at Addenbrookes, as it would be a huge boost to their career prospects and was most highly sought after.

I left his office and spoke with Marion on the way out. She looked sad and was bereft at the prospect of my leaving, but obviously knew the lie of the land.

"What's our loss is general practice's gain. I hope your new patients realise how lucky they will be to have you as their family doctor! Can I come and join your surgery, wherever you are? Can I recommend the local GP training scheme? The Prof knows the people that run it very well and can assist you there should you need his help."

"Hang on a minute, Marion. I've got a long way to go before I go anywhere. I need to find a GP training scheme near where we're going to live which suits me and Annie and we're not yet at all sure about that. I suspect we'll probably stay where we are and try to join the local Cambridge scheme, which I gather is very good and very competitive to get onto, so in fact you may be absolutely right and you may be able to be my patient after all, depending how things pan out. I think I may need two chaperones if I have to examine you."

"Oh, that's very good then, because I'm sure the Prof will be able to help you there a great deal. He knows everyone you need to know and if he doesn't, the Master does. So, you are bound to get on the local scheme easily. That's brilliant, because my GP is pretty useless and writes out useless prescriptions even before you tell him what's wrong with you. He must be psychic I reckon, except he gets it wrong all the time. I know you won't be like that."

With that, she enveloped me in her arms, hugged me as if it was the end of the world and kissed me fully on the lips, taking my breath away.

Blimey, I thought, it's the quiet ones you have to watch out for! Her chest was heaving when she released me and my nether regions were twitching appropriately to this new and welcoming stimulus.

"That's brilliant, Marion, I'll look forward to examining you." Can't I get struck off for that I said looking her up and down appreciatively?

"We'll have to see about that. Please keep in touch. We'll miss you around here. Though, I'm sure we'll see you with your other job. If I'm not around, when you're back here promise me, you'll look after yourself, it's very dangerous out there!

"I promise, and don't worry, the team will look after me," and with that, I turned and left the department.

I took my outstanding leave and used the time to examine the schemes up and down the country. There was no competition really, the Cambridge scheme won hands down, I was accepted on to the training scheme and a few weeks later I was embarking on twelve months as a GP registrar, with three lots of six months in various disciplines pertinent to GP doctoring. I chose A&E, Psychiatry and Paediatrics, which I felt were highly relevant to the type of medicine and surgery that I'd encounter.

The Prof engineered it with the head of the scheme so that I didn't have to do six months of Obstetrics and Gynaecology, because he considered that I'd had more than enough past experience on the professorial team and no-one was going to argue with him.

29

My first six-month attachment was in Paediatrics, away from Addenbrookes in a peripheral General Hospital. Paeds was a whole different ball game to adult medicine. Children don't lie to doctors, don't exaggerate their illness or invent their symptoms. They can become very ill very quickly and recover very quickly, but when they are ill you know it and their signs and symptoms show with a mountain of evidence what's going wrong inside them.

The post I was to work, was a one in two rota, which meant that I was on call for twenty-four hours every second day and from eight o'clock Friday morning until nine o'clock Monday morning every second weekend, which usually worked out to be over 80 hours of duty in a row, and you could be awake working for most of that time, with snatched minutes napping between calls from GPs and the various wards and Special Care Units we covered.

I wondered what Annie would feel about this new part of my G.P. training. We didn't realise quite how onerous the training could be. We had imagined that it would be easier than hospital medicine and I'd been used to the lighter burden of the professorial team, not realising that we were actually buffered by Cambridge University providing extra doctors to the professor's teaching role at the clinical school.

Still I thought, 'Hey ho!' It was all new grist to my mill and a new useful experience and knowledge to soak up for use later in general practice.

I saw a great number of seriously ill children in this discipline and had to cover a ward of forty sick kids, a special care baby unit with ten incubators, obstetric theatres and the labour ward to receive the new born babies from the obstetricians. These babies might be of all gestation periods from twenty-four weeks up to full term and beyond to a maximum of forty-two weeks.

That's when the foetal placenta could become inadequate placing the mother and baby at serious risk, so if the mums hadn't gone into labour by then, the obstetricians would induce them artificially to start the process and get the baby out before the placenta failed with accompanying disaster. I'd already experienced that disaster while working for the Prof, when that arrogant midwife refused to be induced, went home and lost her baby, her fertility and almost her very life, but for our timely intervention.

Paediatrics was not a job for the faint hearted. We had bleeps where the operator could speak to you and on a number of occasions, I'd be awakened by the operator, who'd tell me to rush to obstetric theatres and to dress myself on my way. I had no time to delay, needing to resuscitate a new prematurely delivered baby, that hadn't started breathing, post its delivery.

I could never understand why the midwives, who were a law unto themselves, would never call me, when they saw a labour wasn't going well, but always waited until the last minute when they'd wasted precious minutes trying to get the baby to breathe, before they'd realise they'd failed and then call me! I wondered just how many babies had been affected by the anoxia (no oxygen to their brains), that's caused by these delays. We doctors thought they'd probably grow up to be midwives!

There were two consultants in this specialty, both highly experienced Paediatricians. Their posts shared them between two hospitals, so that while one was on call in our hospital, the other was on call elsewhere. Their leave was covered by senior registrars, based at Addenbrookes.

One consultant was a Welsh Paediatrician, Dr Edmund-Jones, who was considered to be very arrogant and didn't really inspire our enthusiasm. He always insisted on turning up late on Monday evenings for his ward round keeping we SHOs hanging around, which was particularly gruelling for the one who'd been on call since Friday morning.

He'd bully the new mothers into breast-feeding. Although we all agreed that breast was best, we junior doctors believed it was a personal choice and unanimously thought he shouldn't have been forcing the post-natal women to do anything. The post-natal periods for women may be highly stressful with all the hormonal changes, their new roles and the responsibilities for new mums.

Once the baby has been safely delivered, the midwife will assist the mum to deliver the placenta, which had carried nutrients and oxygen to the baby throughout pregnancy. It also maintained the blood level of the two main female hormones oestrogen and progesterone for the gestation period. Three days after the placenta's delivery, the hormone levels in the blood drop precipitously and this drop, particularly that of progesterone can affect the mother's emotion area in her brain and induce post-natal depression.

One day, I was asking Edmund-Jones about this depression delaying the onset of lactation and he took exception to my opinion, especially when I also mentioned to him that I also thought breast milk should not be pooled and used to feed other mothers' babies on the post-natal ward, as it could carry the HIV virus, if the donating mother was HIV positive.

At that time, pregnant mothers weren't being screened ubiquitously for this infection, so no-one had any idea about this potential catastrophe. This opposition to his view, did not go down too well with him, I'm afraid and I was not his favourite junior doctor for most of my attachment.

Sometime later we had a baby admitted over the weekend with a severe obstructive croup-like wheezy upper respiratory tract infection. He was admitted by a brilliant locum doctor, who was from the year above me in the Cambridge clinical school. As we went round the ward to familiarise me with the patients he'd admitted over the weekend, we talked about our student days at university.

As I mentioned earlier, he took great delight in regaling me lavishly with the story Peter Bass, the arrogant doctor, we'd hoodwinked one night as junior house doctors, with the story of the comatose one-eyed Indian Army Colonel. He'd ended up arguing with his neurosurgeon boss and lost his job.

'That served him right,' the locum doc concluded. I feigned total ignorance about the prank but agreed vociferously with his conclusion.

The locum was concerned about the child, who had only arrived in the country a day before from Bangladesh, and hadn't responded to any of the usual treatments for his croup-like illness.

When we approached the child's cot, we could hear the rasping sound of stridor coming from the obstructed swollen airway in his throat. I went through the baby's notes and spoke to the child's parents and was assured by its father that the baby had received all of its baby vaccinations in Bangladesh, so I concluded that the child just had very severe croup and reassured them that he would improve in time.

Just after that, Dr Edmund-Jones walked onto the ward and although he wasn't on call that day, he asked if I had any concerns about any of the patients. So, I told him about the unresponsive severely wheezy baby.

He rushed off towards the baby's cot with me in hot pursuit.

He hastily lowered the sides of the 'Croupette' steam tent, looked at the baby and within one second declared, "This baby has diphtheria! Isolate him immediately. Where are his parents?"

I led him to the child's parents and informed him confidently and possibly patronizingly that his diagnosis was surely unlikely as the child had been fully vaccinated!

"Didn't you hear that stridor as we approached him? Never forget that sound, my boy! When I was a junior doctor, if we heard that sound, inevitably death would follow in its wake! Remember that sound as long as you live, so you won't miss it should you come across it again!"

I was still slightly confident as Edmund-Jones reached the parents, at whom he screamed an interrogation, reminiscent of the mad judge, who presided at the sham trial of Hitler's would be assassins! The father visibly shrunk as he was berated by the consultant.

"How dare you lie to my doctors? This child hasn't been vaccinated! He is seriously ill with a deadly disease, precisely because he hasn't been vaccinated. You may lose this baby and cause the deaths of many others, because of this and you will be to blame."

The parents didn't respond; they looked at the floor sheepishly without comment.

He turned to me and in a similar tone said, "Get the on-call anaesthetist up here to get this child asleep so we can examine him properly. I'm going to sister's office to get onto public Health, so we can start preparations to get a possible nationwide epidemic under control before thousands of people can get this dreadful disease. Then get hold of every member of the team that's been in contact with the patient and get them up here so they can have some relevant treatment to stop them developing this disease!"

I contacted the young on-call anaesthetist, explaining the situation and requesting his urgent presence in side room 5, on St. Julian's paediatric ward.

"Jesus Christ, you don't see that every day," he replied. "I'll be up there in 3 minutes. Get sister to contact the CSSD (equipment centre), people and get a chest cut down kit sent up there asap, just in case he arrests when we look down his throat. I've seen this before, in the Abborigines back home in Oz, when I was a medical student.

"They don't often take advantage of our vaccination scheme and we still get a number of Diptheria deaths among them every year. They're too busy dreaming about "Dreamtime" to take advantage of our public health system. You can't be too careful when you look at the back of the throat. If you touch it, it can cause a cardiac arrest, via the autonomic nervous system, especially when its massively inflamed as it would certainly be in this child." (5)

I thought to myself, why are all the anaesthetists I meet, predominantly Australian?

Sister, who was next to me nodded agreement and picked up the other phone to call CSSD, the instrument sterilisation department.

Five minutes later, the child was gassed and asleep, just as Edmund-Jones gently eased open the baby's mouth with a tongue depressor and in the pen torch light, it was there for all to see, the thick grey leathery pseudo-membrane, which was the patho-pnemonic sign (specific reminder sign) of the killer disease diphtheria.

It lay across the back of the baby's throat, a thick carpet of dead mucosal cells, dead red and white blood cells, mixed with grey colonies of the diphtheroid rod shaped bacterium of diphtheria; blocking the airway and causing the dreadful obstructing and rasping wheeze of severe stridor, as the baby gasped for breath.

Edmund-Jones was right! He might be an arrogant bully but he was sure good at his job and had aeons of experience. My early overconfident and slightly arrogant assessment of the baby showed how really inexperienced I was in the real world and in paediatric medicine.

I had to step back and remember my place. I should have been glad that Edmund-Jones got the right diagnosis because it just might save the baby's life and that did actually please me, because we were a team against disease after all, despite his strange narcissistic belittling ways.

Diphtheria, is very rarely seen in the UK nowadays, as we have an extensive programme of vaccines across the country. As a result we no longer have the huge death tolls, caused by such diseases in earlier times, due to the expertise of public health in prevention. So doctors in the UK may not get the experience in seeing and diagnosing these diseases that our antipodean colleagues may see down under.

When such cases do occur, it is usually found in immigrant patients, who haven't had the benefit of vaccination in their countries of origin, or in cases where for various peculiar reasons the ill-informed parents of children have denied them the protection of the vaccine programme. Instead they rather shortsightedly rely on their children being protected by 'Herd Immunity', conferred by the vaccination of their peers in the community, preventing disease spread to the denied unvaccinated few.

It has often been proposed that the UK adopt a system available on the continent, whereby unvaccinated children are excluded from attending government schools, in order to encourage a universal approach to protecting our communities. I thought this policy may at some stage reach the UK, as our laissez-faire and liberal attitude to immigration became more imposing on our native communities.

While I was busy tracking down all the hospital staff that had been in contact with the child, a much bigger logistical programme was getting under way to deal with this highly infectious patient.

The ward was shut to all further admissions and it's cot and ward areas, where the Banglabeshi child had been were thoroughly fumigated. All further patients to be admitted were sent to a neighbouring hospital.

The baby, his parents and siblings were isolated to the Coppetts Wood Hospital for Infectious Diseases. All the hospital staff including myself, the locum who admitted him, Edmund-Jones, the anaesthetist and all the nurses were given a course of Rifampicin to prevent the disease from developing in us. This drug turns the urine purple, which frightened some of the staff who hadn't been fully briefed on it.

All the passengers who had flown on the same plane from Bangladesh and any other contacts had to be traced and treated with Rifampicin. The whole exercise must have cost the UK's NHS, a fortune.

We clinical staff were all interviewed by public health. I took the opportunity to discuss the practice of pooling breast milk, with the public health consultant, who assured me he would speak with Edmund-Jones.

Shortly afterwards, the milk-sharing practice was ceased, following a message sent down to Maternity and Paediatrics from the Hospital Chief Executive. Nothing more was said about it, but I smiled to myself, just imagining what was said by public health to my boss. He never mentioned it, so I thought it best to let it go.

30

Paediatrics was a very full on experience, where I'd learned to deal with some really sick children. I considered it to be the most emotional discipline of all, where I saw children suffering from all sorts of different cancers and to whom I had to deliver dreadful treatments with concoctions of different toxins. Several of them caused symptoms far worse than the cancer itself.

I was very upset by one such baby, whom we had treated and then had to send to Addenbrookes for radiotherapy. The child had subsequently died and was sent back to us, as the parents were unable to get to Cambridge, through logistical mobility problems.

When the child arrived, I had to remove all the tubes that had been inserted into her tiny emaciated body and stitch up all the holes they made in her, before her parents could see her. This was a very disturbing experience for me, dealing with a dead baby, whom I treated earlier when she was alive. It made me wonder seriously whether I could cope with that specialty.

I also found that I was hardly ever at home and that the NHS got far more than its pound of flesh out of us, as we continuously worked far more hours than we were legally supposed to work. Somehow, the hospital managers relied on the doctors sense of duty to run the service and took it to the extreme to balance the books in their world, not concerned with the effect it was having on we, the doctors who kept the service running with the overwhelming odds stacked against us!

One early Monday morning, in the middle of the night, a highly premature baby of 28 weeks gestation in the Special Care Baby Unit (SCBU), somehow managed to pull out the canula that was hydrating her and delivering essential nutrients and drugs to keep her alive. The child had just one single usable vein large enough to accommodate the re-insertion of the canula into the skin of her scalp, which was barely the size of the canula itself.

I scrubbed and gloved up in my theatre blues to be as sterile as possible to attempt to re-site the canula. I cleaned the baby's tiny skull and attempted the re-insertion. Unhappily, I failed miserably and the needle went through the wall of the tiny vein and straight out the other side, filling the scalp with leaking blood. At this stage, my two bosses were on leave, so I had to call a senior registrar to come out from Addenbrookes to rescue me and the tiny baby.

The SCBU staff and I were all in tears until about forty minute later when the senior registrar arrived. He entered the SCBU like the 'Caped Crusader', looked at the baby, then at me and the SCBU nurses.

He said, "Don't worry, you've all done very well. He doesn't seem to have much in the way of access veins. Come and help me, Mike, I think he'll need a cut down. Let's re-scrub and get on with it."

With that, and after with me holding the baby's tiny head firmly but gently, he opened his kit bag, extracted a sterile scalpel and incised the skin above a tiny vessel which had magically appeared and slotted a fresh canula straight into it. He then proceeded to sew the canula in place so that it wouldn't fall out again until it was no longer needed.

The whole process took about ten minutes from his arrival and was so impressive that the nurses fussed around him like he was deity. I, who was equally impressed, just said how very grateful I was to him for rescuing the baby and me from my lack of ability!

He packed up his equipment and left, smiling at everyone.

He said he remembered me from my Grand Round presentation and hoped to see me at the next paediatric one and left with "It's all about having confidence, so keep up the good work!"

I was thinking how much I wanted to be as good as he was!

Sometime after that, I was called to A&E by the surgical registrar who was dealing with a four year old, who'd reached up to his mum's cooker and pulled a saucepan of boiling water down over himself. As the water landed on his head, he inhaled to scream, which in the process had caused some of the scalding water to be sucked into his mouth.

The surgeons had tried to insert a canula to get some fluid into him to replace the plasma that was oozing out of his burned skin, but they failed. The anaesthetist had also tried to intubate his swollen throat to keep his airway open, but he also failed. As I entered the A&E like the paediatric senior registrar/caped crusader had done a few weeks earlier, the team there looked mightily relieved.

I picked up a tiny pink Venflon canula and the surgical registrar held the child's arm extended as I slid the plastic tube straight into his only remaining visible vein. It was as if I was the world champion of inserting canulae. I then proceeded to intubate the child using a small laryngoscope as a guide and slid in the tube in one easy motion.

I was applauded by everyone and felt great. The child was transferred straight to Addenbrookes.

On another occasion, I was called to A&E to be confronted by some members of the Travellers' community. A large group of them had descended on A&E, jumped their place in the queue and demanded that two children, called O'Connor (who they had declared as seriously ill), be seen by the doctor!

The A&E SHO who was quite a timid young man had quite correctly called me as the appropriate specialty to examine the two children and retreated "tout suite"!

As I arrived in the department, I was greeted with a cacophony of demands by a group of traveller women, more than two of whom claimed to be the children's mothers, though there were only two children; but especially also by a number of surly males who were demanding that I admit the children into hospital for investigations, as they were seriously ill.

The nurses forcibly ushered the adults out of the children's examination room, enabling me to examine them, which I undertook as comprehensively as possible. I could find nothing wrong with either of them and appeared out of the curtains to confront the posse of the O'Connor relatives.

I declared to all and sundry, who gathered round me, in a fashion slightly closer than usual, that I was very happy to state that the children were both very fit and well with no signs of any illness whatsoever. With that, the O'Connor's launched into an extra-terrestrial orbit of acrimonious abuse.

"These children are ill," they clamoured almost in unison.

"I don't believe they are. Happily they are very well, except their teeth are full of dental decay. They ought to see a dentist as soon as possible, which we don't have here."

With that, a very large man with Fitzpatrick type one very fair skin, a shock of red curly hair stepped forward and demanded, "Does dat mean you ain't gonnas take 'em inta hospital?"

"Yes, happily, they don't need to be admitted. You can take them home with you." With that, I walked straight through them down to the casualty office and proceeded to write up their A&E records sheet.

The sister who had led my way down there accompanied me into the office and with the door firmly closed she exclaimed, "Well, thank God for that, doctor! The last time these travellers tried that, the kids were admitted and their parents all pushed off to Ireland for a holiday break. They leave the little buggers here for us to look after them to save them the costs of taking them on holiday. They also leave a couple of the old women behind to keep an eye on them, while they're gone. They visit periodically and nick anything they can from the wards that isn't nailed down. I was praying you wouldn't give in to them."

"Well, they won't do that this time. Those kids are fine but with rotten teeth and just a little dirty." With that, I left the room and again was confronted by the mob outside.

The surly red-head stepped forward and declared, "If any ting appens to dose kids, I'm gonna come back ere and get yer docta."

I was thinking why Edmund-Jones wasn't here to deal with these bullying morons. I was tempted to tell the traveller, he was free to try but felt it might provoke a further mess for the cleaners to deal with in the early morning, so I walked round my would be assailants and exited quickly back to our paediatric ward with controlled access and egress, to have a coffee with the staff.

I began to wonder what sort of society we were living in where these ne'er-do-wells could come into a hospital and take precedence over people going about their peaceful business. I wished they'd get an autoimmune disease and considered the logistics involved in fitting a holster in my white coat for my Walter PP pistol and thought I might discuss it at my next meeting with the Prof.

Apart from dealing with the death of a baby, I had treated and being threatened by the travellers, I very much enjoyed my six months in paediatric medicine. The one in two rota was highly demanding but the medical educational experience was phenomenal.

I learned so much about these little people's ills. I thought it was a whole different world of medicine, which it was. I felt confident going into my next attachment in A&E, if any kids would dare to present, then, I knew I could deal with them.

Another sad thing about this attachment was my enforced separation from Annie, which wasn't really compensated by the nights when I wasn't on-call. I would go home, have dinner and usually collapse on the settee and sleep till the early hours, when I'd wake up and slide in beside my wife and rapidly fall asleep again. The Prof was aware of my one in two schedule and didn't burden me with any new calls for my other job. I just continued my task in watching over Frieda Hoffman, who I tried to visit weekly. She had made exceedingly good progress and had been relieved of her compulsory detention order at the Priory.

She was due for release and follow-up as an Outpatient, the week after I finished Paediatrics, so it had been a long haul for her, her parents and my A10 commuting. We and she were all feeling confident about her future. The local drug dealer had been dealt with, her school drug user friend had also been detained in a Youth Offenders Prison, so Frieda was freed to follow a rapid 'A' level GCE course at a local college, where paradoxically, she would be closely supervised at a distance. I was confident she would be able to deal with that easily and I was temporarily free to concentrate on my private family and career life, with my wife and my new A&E job.

I had a week of leave owing to me which I'd booked at the end of my attachment, so Annie and I were able to fly off to Crete for a week in the sun, where we ate olives, warm bread, soft white cheese, pork chops and drunk Retsina, the local pine resinated white wine.

We walked along the deserted beaches and made love in the sand, which got everywhere, so we washed in the warm Aegian sea, walked back to our beach villa and made love again, collapsed sweating in each other's arms and fell asleep until the cockerel in the garden woke us up in the morning.

We were decadent and abandoned all thoughts of decency. We completely descended into wanton love-making almost all day and almost every day, when we weren't sleeping or eating. By the end of the week, I was exhausted and needed to get back to Accident and Emergency medicine for a rest.

31

For my attachment in Accident and Emergency, I moved back to Addenbrookes where the rotation for we Casualty Officers was a one in four and much lighter than Paeds. There were six of us working during the day and two of us working at night, but with the backup of the medical and surgical specialties teams. We were in a very busy job and never had the time to take our meals away from our posts. We became used to munching sandwiches in between patients.

Half of us were GP trainees, gaining valuable experience for when we were to be let out into practices The other half of us were in specialist trainee jobs aiming to become consultants in A&E medicine or surgery. These doctors were very dedicated specialists, who seemed to be motivated by the buzz of the life-threatening situations they encountered in the Casualty Department.

I realised that the lighter rota we had, meant that the Prof might sooner or later give me "a call to arms" and sure enough it came in the form of Paul Bradley, who'd been called to casualty to see a gynaecology patient. As I showed him to the relevant cubicle, he enquired whether I'd like to join him and Prof for lunch in the clinical school. I accepted this invitation and for the first time engineered it that I could leave casualty for a quick lunch.

I made my way back there via the underground passage way that permeated the Addenbrookes site so one could travel through it without surfacing above ground. I emerged at the allotted time and entered the senior common room to see the Prof and Paul Bradley seated in the corner immersed in conversation. As I approached they both got up and greeted me warmly.

The Prof was enthusiastic, as usual and was the first to burst out, "Hello Mike, long time no see. We've missed you! How are you getting on in the world of serious trauma and the misinformed who turn up because they don't have anything better to do? Do you like the vast range of patients and their sometimes bizarre presentations?"

Paul stepped in with, "No, I'm certain he's missing us in gynae where the histories and follow-ups are much more thorough for our patients."

"Well, we're so busy, I haven't noticed whether I've missed anything so far. We're never empty, 24 hours a day, 7 days a week, there always seem to be patients waiting to be seen. Some are genuine people who need to be seen, but many are complete idiots, who spend more time thinking about their take-away pizza topping, than they do before they roll up here. They don't seem to mind waiting ages to be seen, probably because they have nothing better to do with their lives.

"They clog up the department and prevent genuine cases from being seen in a timely manner. Prof, if we were able to make a small charge for seeing them, they'd think twice before attending and it would sort the seed from the chaff, but at the moment, the un-controllable waste of resources continues. I do miss the department though and the orderly flow of things, but I have to say at least we know when our shifts start and end and discounting a major disaster, we know that we're going to be free on our nights off".

Paul Bradley interjected, "Michael, we're sorry it sounds like A&E hasn't changed a lot since our day, except that in our day, admin staff, the public and nursing staff had a great deal more respect for doctors, than they do now, so we appreciate what you must be going through at the moment. However, a situation has arisen that requires your exceptional abilities to contain in our country's interests. With that in mind, would you be able to make yourself available for a briefing at Downing College next Tuesday at 18.30 in the Prof's rooms?"

I immediately replied, "Yes, of course," not even considering whether Annie had arranged anything social for that night. Internally, I questioned whether I was becoming obsessive about my role in the Other Service, or whether I was just honestly more patriotic about the cause.

With that, the Prof and Peter, got up and departed with the usual salutations and I made my way underground back to A&E. On my way, I diverted towards the neurosurgery Department on the Ground floor of Addenbookes and dropped in on Annie to let her know that I would be going to a lecture at the agreed time.

It was useful to be able to use my Personal Development Plan as an excuse for my absence from home. She seemed to accept that without question and I didn't feel guilty for leaving her at home as after all, it was for a very good cause. Also, it made me miss her all the more and seemed to make me enormously horny, on my way home, where she reciprocated like for like.

I felt elated as I made my way to Downing the following Tuesday. The large porter greeted me in his usual respectful manner, marched me round the quadrant and up the oak staircase.

"It's good to see you again, Doctor, how are you getting on with your new life in medicine? The Prof's party has only just arrived so I don't think you've missed anything."

I thanked him politely as he knocked on the large oak door of the Prof's quarters. Paul Bradley opened it with a welcoming smile. The porter stepped forward and announced me like a very important person at a posh wedding.

Paul stuck out his hand, shook mine vigorously and said, "Come in Mike," and I stepped inside.

There were six other people present in the room. I knew five of them, the Master, the Prof, Paul Bradley, K the director of MI5, Inspector Robin Greenwood from S.B. and another spectacled gentleman that the Prof introduced as M, the director of MI6. This situation was beginning to look rather serious.

The Master opened the discussions.

"We have assembled here today to discuss a somewhat embarrassing situation for our government. Mr. Greenwood's officers have for some time been running a number of informants from the Didicoy travellers fraternity in his area, more specifically, from the Chimney-top Dids, who have taken to living in houses. I should point out that because of a number of local mistakes, accurate and pertinent information has sadly been ignored, resulting in a situation, that were it to become exposed to the public, might result in our government's downfall."

This immediately focused our minds completely and I looked towards Robin Greenwood, who I imagine at this moment was regretting his promotion to Chief Inspector, so that he now bore responsibility for the screw-ups we were about to discuss. He stood up and addressed the meeting.

"Let me summarise for you gentlemen. Our local special branch officers were briefed by our colleagues in CID about a member of the Didicoy Community, who had information about the theft and whereabouts of a number of heavy machine guns from the Royal Ordnance Stores at the Leathersfield Centre in Sussex.

"The background to this is that our ordnance people have been testing a machine gun for NATO, on loan from the South Korean government, with a view to engineering a better cooling system for it. The gun in question out-fires the

191

NATO weapons currently in use by our forces. It would appear that, the chief government inspector at Leathersfield, a Mr. Mark Thomas, who has been testing these weapons to destruction, has been somewhat over-enthusiastic and destroyed rather too many, writing off several more than is usual."

"Our team has passed this over to our MI5 Watchers and it seems that this bounder, who was testing the very high powered Daewoo K3 5.56mm machine gun, has allegedly by him, destroyed about a two dozen of them, together with approximately 100,000 rounds of their particular ammunition off the Sussex coast. No-one has had the temerity to question his practices or ask where the delivery crates for this weapons went, nor discuss with him the unusually high rate of failure he found in this model, which came to us as most highly recommended by the South Korean Special Forces.

"What's worse is that somehow, we believe that he and others have also managed to steal a Challenger FV4030 prototype tank as well as its transporter! This tank is the one with all of that new ceramic Chobham armour, made at the Tank Research Centre in Surrey, which would be invaluable to our enemies in the Eastern block. Come to think of it, it was worth just over £65,000,000 to us, for the tank alone!

"We have been watching him for several months and believe he has somehow got in with the Bosnian faction in the former Yugoslavia and a network of illicit Moslem weapon dealers from Albania. May I hand over to you, Sir James?"

The Master stepped forward. "Yes, of course and thank you for your candour. In other circumstances, we would remove this traitor, but we've decided to spare him for the moment and leave him in situ to gather and use his information and possibly re-use him later for future activity in the Balkans, where of course, you are aware that we have our troops on the ground with both the NATO forces and the U.N.

"We have interviewed him and made him aware of the dire situation for him and his family and I gather that he is co-operating fully with our ongoing inquiries. Is that still the case, K?"

K stood and replied, "Yes, Sir James, he couldn't be more helpful."

The Master continued, "As a result, of two years of enquiries by MI5 and MI6, we are about to serve a large number of warrants across Britain, Europe and the Middle East. I don't have to tell you how secret this operation is. If it got out, the ramifications for our government would be unthinkable."

"Charles, our medical role in this will be to deal with the informants. I mentioned earlier, they are an interesting couple of former travelling people, who somehow got wind of the whereabouts of some of the so-called "destroyed" machine guns and a great deal of its ammunition, in a lock-up garage in St. Albans."

"As Robin has described, the traveller gentleman offered this information to the local CID for a small consideration. I believe he was after being hidden in a safe house in a new area, with a new identity for him and his girlfriend and a subsisting salary for the next few years. Unhappily, the CID controllers were a bit too slow in coming forth and dealing with his request.

"As a result of the delay and him letting information leak out to the wrong people, he and his girlfriend were thrown out of a second floor hotel window. As luck would have it, they landed below on a very large garden planter, which had just been planted and which to a certain extent cushioned their drop so that neither of them actually died. However, they did sustain severe injuries.

"Robin's team let it be known to the underworld that they did actually succumb to their major injuries but, we currently have them in hiding here in Cambridge.

"As you can imagine Charles, they are both very frightened and still very badly injured individuals. We have them under guard at Fulbourn, so we'd like your team to look after them, if possible until 5 can sort out the requirements for their future and 6 can get to work on finding our lost Challenger Tank and its trailer and round up the rest of the gun running enterprise, before any of this can get out."

I looked at Paul and the Prof and they both beamed warmly as I caught their gaze. I thought 'Wow', what an amazing and extraordinary situation and how lucky I am to be part of this incredible group of people (the watchers I mean, not the informants).

I wasn't certain how I could contribute anything worthwhile to the informants' further care, but no doubt I was about to be informed. With that, the Master finished his briefing and within a few moments, the large military porter knocked on the Prof's door. The security men and the police excused themselves and were led out by the porter.

The Master turned to us and explained that the didicoys had been treated by Orthopaedics down at the SAS Hospital in Hereford. It was felt they were now stable enough to be transferred out to Fulbourn, which was secure enough to accommodate them for their ongoing treatment.

32

The Prof said that he and his team were happy to contribute in any way they might be able, then with that, he suggested that it might be time to retire to high table for dinner. We all agreed and proceeded to the post-graduate refectory. On the way Paul asked whether I thought my current job would provide me with enough free time to be involved in the treatment and rehabilitation of our new house guests at Fulbourn.

I replied that I would consider it a pleasure to be an active part of the team again and that my shift pattern was very flexible and if they actually let me know reasonably in advance, I would arrange to be free to be involved again.

So, the following afternoon I found myself wending my way to the old psychiatric hospital at Fulbourn, to assess the two injured informers that had fallen foul of their criminal colleagues, and fallen foul from a second floor window. They ended up with multiple near-mortal injuries, despite which, they'd escaped death by the skin of their teeth and the cushion of a garden planter.

It was good to see the old S.B. officers again, Chief Inspector Greenwood and D.S. Roberts who were both there, with several of their underlings, guarding our distinguished informants, who still had a long way to go to full recovery.

The lady's pelvis had been smashed with all sorts of damage to her urogenital system (renal and reproductive anatomy), there within. She had to have a hysterectomy removing her womb with her fallopian tubes, an ovary and her pelvis had to be wired together.

Her chest had been compressed with multiple rib fractures, but it wasn't completely detached from its hinges on her upper back bone, so she could still breath as long as she had adequate pain relief. Her left kidney and renal artery had also both been ruptured by a rib, requiring their removal. However, although in a great deal of pain and highly compromised, she was against all odds still alive and able to complain vociferously, which, though a pain in the neck, was medically reassuring.

Her partner however was slightly more worser for wear. He had broken his back and had had to have several of his Thoraco-lumbar vertebrae screwed together. His paired spinal nerve routes needed to be decompressed to allow his nerves to exit the spinal pathways to innervate his lower body.

He was initially unconscious and paralysed for ten days and had also fractured the occipital bone at the back of his head causing a severe concussion. This had been treated by wiring together the plates of his skull and with a strong intravenous steroids to reduce the brain swelling inside his head.

Happily, he had regained consciousness and now required tapering off his steroids to prevent him developing a steroid psychosis, that could alter his state of mind into a pandemonium. This had to be done slowly in a controlled way, to enable his own steroids to come back on board, as they would have been turned off in response to the high doses in his therapy.

The care of these two patients was allocated to me, a fairly new and inexperienced G.P. trainee. However, I had connections and the Prof gave me a list of doctors' contact numbers from our group that I could access at anytime, should I need to do so. I wondered again how big this secret organisation was and never failed to consider just how redoubtable was our unassuming professor!

However having assessed our two new patients, I found that as their health improved, they became more demanding. They both independently presented with statement after statement of lies between them, demanding special attention and especially opiate medicines, when clearly they were no longer in that much pain!

At one stage, being a practical man, rather more than of theory and in a state of exasperation, I impressed on them that in my view they were out of order and that if they didn't co-operate in a timely manner, we would withdraw all treatments and throw them out to fend for themselves. I didn't know how the Prof might consider this, but it immediately had the desired effect. They backed off and behaved themselves. They had nowhere to go and if their ex-colleagues got wind that they were still alive, they would in no time reverse that risky situation.

Never-the less, they were both making steady and inevitable progress, until their main medical input was only physiotherapy, I managed to reduce my visits to twice a week and concentrate on my new life in A&E, where we were continuously busy in the front line of hospital medicine.

They say exercise is very good for you but I very quickly lost count of the numbers of 'Brought in Dead' unfit middle-aged golfers, that I had to go out to the ambulances to pronounce dead. I ended up advising several survivors that perhaps 9 holes might be better than the full 18!

An interesting case I saw was when Annie's GP was brought in by ambulance having collapsed during his morning surgery. His wife, who was also his practice nurse, told me that apart from a bad back, he was usually very fit. She said he had prescribed himself some pain killers and a quick examination of his 'pin-point' pupils, confirmed his opiate over-dosage.

We quickly reversed this with an injection of the opiate antagonist Naloxone and the good doctor woke up as I slowly injected the medicine into his left ante-cubital vein, at the front of his elbow.

He became rather embarrassed, when I advised him against inherent dangers of treating himself, without being usefully monitored by his own GP. I made him promise in front of his wife, that it wouldn't happen again before reassuring him that it wouldn't go any further. He was very grateful for this, because the General Medical Council strongly advises against it, in their Guidance booklet, 'Good Medical Practice'. Although this is presented to doctors as 'Guidance', that title is actually a euphemism. GMC guidance is far more like the ten commandments and the council take such breaches very seriously in deed.

I learned a very good lesson one day, when I arrived early for my shift, my colleague, who took my arrival as a timely opportunity for her to go to lunch, said, "I'm glad you're here, I'm starving. Can you see the patient in cubicle 5? He just needs his lacerated hand sowing back together!"

"Ok," I said heading off in his direction.

When I entered the cubicle I came across a very distinguished middle-aged gentleman, with his left hand painted with Iodine and extended over a sterile field.

He introduced himself as a retired Royal Navy Captain. He had cut his hand with a Stanley knife while laying a new carpet at home. He explained that the lady doctor had numbed him up and was about to sow him back together.

I explained that she had gone off to lunch and asked me to repair his wound. I checked that the local anaesthetic had worked and proceeded to stitch his palm back together.

He was a delightful man regaling me with tales of his life in the navy and was very apologetic for being a nuisance. I reassured him it was a pleasure to have met him and asked him to return in 10 days so we could remove the sutures for him. I also advised him to return immediately should he feel there were any problems with his wound. This is what we call safe-netting and accompanies every medical consultation between doctors and patients.

Sure enough, ten days later he returned for removal of his sutures, which revealed a well-healed and clean wound. However, when the casualty nurse asked him to make a fist, he couldn't flex his hand or fingers.

I was called to see him and had to explain to this decent man that I'd sown him back together without actually properly assessing the damage to his hand. The result of my negligence was that we had to operate on him in theatres to explore his hand and lower arm to pull down and rejoin his sliced flexor tendons. These had retreated back up into his wrist. We managed to re-attach them and after several weeks of physiotherapy, he was able to use that hand again.

This man had a clear case of negligence against me which he serenely acknowledged wasn't my fault because I was just following the instructions from my colleague. I learned from this that in medicine, you must always undertake your own examination and never just follow some other doctor's opinion, without examining the patient yourself and considering your own findings.

I never heard from that gentle man again and took great delight in impressing on my colleague that she shouldn't just abandon a patient in the middle of treatment to another doctor, when she wanted to go to lunch.

I learned a great deal of emergency medicine during my A&E training and particularly became highly experienced in CPR as we had to deal with multiple cases of cardiac arrest, which occurred on an almost daily basis. The lead doctor in such cases was usually the medical registrar on call, but we all took an active role.

I remember one case where a depressed man that had been cuck-holded by his adulterous wife, had set his house on fire while his family was in the house with him. He then locked himself in his loft. He came in as a cardiac arrest in progress and the crash team on his arrival went into automatic resuscitation mode on his partially burned body.

When the registrar lifted his eyelids to check whether his pupils weren't fixed and dilated, both his eyeballs were sizzling, having been cooked to a frazzle. At this, the registrar announced "Let's call it a day team I think this patient has left the planet"

On another occasion, I was with the crash team was in the middle of a cardiac arrest when a particularly beautiful ambulance lady, walked past the crash room, pushing a wheelchair patient down the corridor. It all went silent when our resus' efforts spontaneously ceased and the whole team stopped and watched her, with their mouths salivating, as she slowly floated down the corridor, and went out of sight. Then they returned to the procedure re-invigorated and the patient survived!

Once I had to suture a burglar's head, who had fallen through a skylight window while breaking in through the building's roof. I spent two hours sowing his scalp back on, while he was handcuffed between two police officers. Happily for him, my consultant boss, Mr. Williams decided to walk through casualty on his way to clinic and looked in on what I was doing. He examined the burglar's scalp, called me to one side and said he thought that the wound looked and felt a bit boggy.

When we had him unhand-cuffed and took him surgery later that evening, we discovered that in my haste, I missed a small pumping scalp artery, which had slowed to a trickle by the time we opened his scalp up again and drained the hundred and twenty milli litres of blood that had caused the bogginess.

One Saturday night, number of police officers brought in a well-known violent drunk with a history of Paranoid Schizophrenia. He was punching, cursing and spitting at everyone in the casualty vicinity. I approached him very calmly and while gently reassuring him; to my horror, he took a swing at me, as I tried to clerk him.

He was very angry and violent. He was so violent that while the police held him down, I injected him through his trousers with a large syringe full of the major tranquilliser Chlorpromazine (also known as the liquid cosh), and within two minutes, he was sound asleep. He woke up the following afternoon safely detained on the psychiatric ward.

My six months in casualty rapidly flew by and I learned that Accident and Emergency patients could be both surgical and medical. We might often switch from suturing up a trivial laceration or reducing a fracture to a rapid medical intervention to reverse a cardiac arrest or diagnose and treat a tension pneumothorax, by releasing the air compressing the lungs after a penetrating injury.

The thrill of these life-saving experiences will stay in my memory 'ad infinitum' and they taught me huge amount about being a doctor and our privileged position we have with our patients. The dean was right about the huge faith that patients have in our capabilities, especially so in the emergency situations that were an everyday occurrence in A&E.

I certainly enjoyed the 'Rush' I experienced there for the six months I was in the front line, during which time, I happily became used to knowing what my duty shifts would be and when I'd be free to enjoy life.

33

I was excited to move on to my final GP training attachment in psychiatry, a discipline I came to realise was essential to the life of every GP. This post was a light one, with a one in four rota, being on call for 24 hours every fourth day and fourth weekend. The work was based partially at the Fulbourn Hospital in a building about a quarter a mile from the manor house, where the Prof had our secret guests.

We also attended paediatric psychiatry clinics in the centre of Cambridge, where I rapidly became aware that the vast majority of children's psychiatric illnesses were entirely caused by their unbalanced parents, usually one but sometimes both!

The rota in this post gave me a lot of time off and I arranged with the Prof to continue monitoring our two informant patients, who although finished with medical follow-up, were still housed on the Fulbourn Campus.

As a former wannabe surgeon, I always thought that psychiatry was quite relatively straightforward. To my inexperienced mind there were only six different conditions to consider: Schizophrenia, Anorexia Nervosa, Depression, Bipolarity, Learning Disability and a range of Personality Disorders.

As far as I was aware, psychiatry couldn't cure any of them. The only positive factor I knew about that discipline was that the government allowed practitioners to retire on a full pension several years before all the other practitioners in the other branches of NHS medicine.

However, I rapidly became aware that there was much more to this discipline than was apparent to my biased eyes! The complexities of the human psyche (the mind, the part of the brain in the frontal lobes that thinks and makes us who we are), are individual to every person. The factors that repress us or motivate us to act are similarly as different as the experiences we encounter throughout our lives.

One of my consultant bosses taught me psycho-analysis, after Professor Sigmund Freud, who taught that analysing a patient's unconscious thoughts about various subjects and situations can give doctors insight into what motivates or represses their emotions and goals, inhibiting or exciting their life activities.

I practised this with several patients that were unable to function properly in society. I would partially sedate them, with an intravenous sedative, keeping them only just conscious and then quietly ask them about their worries and motivations, and the reasons they felt about things the way they did.

This procedure provided doctors with some of the reasons for some of their totally bizarre behaviours. This was very useful for dealing with some very common Obsessive-Compulsive Disorders. I would discuss this admitted information with the patients the next day and help them to release the brakes on their self-imposed repressions or impose the brakes on their various obsessional neuroses.

I also learned that quite often, psychiatric patients, who commonly see things entirely from their own particular point of view, will often try to manipulate situations to suit themselves and their views. In our weekly ward rounds, where the doctors, psychiatric nurses and psychiatric social workers had open discussions with our patients and where part of the treatment would be to persuade the patient to accept the realities of life and how they had misinterpreted them to justify their own behaviours and deviations from the norm.

Many psychiatric illnesses are chronic in nature affecting patients for many years and causing them long term hospital admissions and treatments which may only control symptoms, but not cure them.

In depressive illness, it had been found that nervous transmission is low in several areas of the brain that control mood.

Antidepressants work by increasing the levels of transmitter substances between nerve cells in these areas, as well as by promoting the new growth of nerve fibres. This increases nervous communication in mood controlling areas and thereby elevates the mood.

However, antidepressants didn't work for every patient and sometimes it takes ages for them to help, possibly owing to the slow growth of new nerve fibres, which help to bump up key nervous activity.

I was concerned to see that when medical treatments failed to help these patients, Electroconvulsive Therapy was sometimes used almost as a last resort to alleviate symptoms. Unhappily, this induced unpleasant seizures in the patients, but did rapidly improve their depression, but only for a short while. It is uncertain how ECT works precisely, but it is thought by some, to be due to multiple neuro-physiological mechanisms, i.e., we don't really know!

In the ECT sessions that I undertook, the patients were anaesthetised and given muscle relaxants (to prevent severe muscle spasms). Then an electric shock was passed between electrodes on either side of the head over the patient's temples. This caused them to fit in the same way as occurs in epilepsy, where patients would go into a tonic muscle spasm and then move into a state of repeated rapid muscle spasms followed by relaxations, which was called clonus.

This is usually followed by a period of no breathing or apnoea, during which the patient may turn blue, However, they quickly recovered by dint of chemoreceptors in their neck that rapidly responded to the rise in their blood carbon dioxide levels, making them breath again. It is important to maintain the airway and to insert a mouth guard to prevent the patients biting through their tongue during the tonic and clonic phases of the procedure.

As brutal as this may seem, to observe the improvement in the mood of these patients was incredible, sadly the improvement was short-lived.

In the Bipolar Affective Disorder, the mood of a patient may oscillate from profound depression to periods of extreme elation. The depressive phase of the illness is treated by antidepressants. While the periods of elation are treated by mood stabilisers, such as Lithium. This drug has to be monitored to maintain it at the therapeutic level to facilitate maximum efficacy.

This condition has a genetic element to it where several family members may have the same symptoms, but, it may also be induced by severe stress in certain individuals. It is a very interesting illness where during elation, the patients may display very rapid pressure of speech patterns with flight of ideas, loss of ability to concentrate and outrageous behaviours, such has spending huge amounts of money where the patient actually had no access to such funds. This is also a chronic condition debilitating the patient's lives and quite often leading to dependency in hospital.

The commonest cause of acute psychiatric admissions to the lock-up ward on the top floor was schizophrenia, where often young isolated male patients presented with an altered perception of reality, reduced social interaction, strange speech patterns and behaviour and weird delusions that may be with visual or auditory hallucinations.

There is a genetic element to this disease but several environmental factors may play a part in its development.

The usual cause of this, during my attachment, was a drug induced schizophrenia, in addicts who invariably lived in isolation and had chronically altered their perceptions with illegal cannabinoids and/or opiate drugs bought from illicit suppliers off the streets. These patients often developed paranoid delusions of persecution about various other individuals in their lives.

I saw one such patient who I was asked to detain, by the police, under a relevant section of the Mental Health Act. He had just murdered his next-door neighbour, by stabbing him multiple times, because he thought the neighbour had been talking about him. During my examination of him, I told him that after I had examined him, I would have to discuss my findings with police officers waiting in the room next door. I asked how he felt about that and he replied that he would like to kill me also for talking about him. Happily, he was detained in Rampton psychiatric prison shortly after that.

We treated such patients with major tranquillisers, counselling and rehabilitation, but unhappily only a small percentage of patients, made a full recovery, with the majority deteriorating and having lifelong impairment, dependency and in some cases confinement.

I found my training in psychiatry was frustrating because of the chronicity of the diseases and our failure to be able to cure them. However, it was very useful for general practice in facilitating diagnoses and treatments of the many psychiatric patients cast out into the community by the government's closure of psychiatric hospitals.

34

I left psychiatry enthusiastic to be starting my period as a trainee in general practice. The good professor, true to his word arranged a place for me in a small two man practice in the Chesterton Road in Cambridge. The head of the practice was a very kindly old school gentleman called Dr Geoffrey Ramsbottom, whose partner was a slightly younger Dr Thomas Bailey.

Geoffrey was to be my trainer, for the twelve months I was going to be there and I was to have a weekly tutorial with him, during which he was to teach me all he knew about life as a GP.

In my first tutorial, I discovered that we GPs were members of independent business partnerships contracted to the NHS to supply our patients with twenty-four hour care, for three hundred and sixty-five days a year. I learned that the partnership paid a private company, called Health-on-call, to cover the out of hours.

This was a good bonus for me, which meant that I didn't have to be on-call through the nights and weekends and could spend more time at home enjoying my time off with my wife. The two partners in the practice had decided that it was worth the costs to have the luxury of the nights and weekends off, knowing that such costs were tax deductible.

Although we were independent businesses, we were quite highly subsidised by the government, who paid for our surgery's rent and rates and at the time, our waste disposal as well. If the practice building was owned by the doctors, the NHS would pay the practice a rental for such use of their building. This was good news for those doctors who, like Geoffrey, were fortunate to own the surgery premises and be in that position.

These subsidies meant that new practices were able to start up in areas of GP shortages, where the government's subsidies facilitated getting the practices off the ground. However, it also meant that the GPs were unable to accrue goodwill to be sold on if or when doctors left the practice. Their patients would simply pass on to their successors at the practice.

I was taught that as a GP, I could at the end of my trainee year, take the examination for membership of the Royal College of G.Ps. However, at the time, as long as you had completed a traineeship satisfactorily, then you didn't have to take this M.R.C.G.P. examination to set up practice as a GP. I decided that, as I already had several other qualifications including the M.R.C.S. and I didn't know the lie of the land, I would postpone any further exams until later.

On joining the practice, I was paid a trainee's salary and was not paid a share in the practice profit, although my labours in Obstetrics and Gynaecology did earn income for the partnership. I didn't mind that because I was gaining valuable experience and being educated to boot!

At that time, GPs were paid on a per capita basis, but also received payments for various items of service, such as Contraceptive and Maternity Care. These were services that at the time of the NHS being set up were provided by secondary care in hospitals and not in the remit of GP primary care. Over the years, to save money, the NHS moved much of this work into primary care, where it was carried out by suitably qualified GPs. As a former Obstetrician and Gynaecologist, I took responsibility for this work and earned a substantial income for the practice by undertaking these services, exclusively for women.

As a surgeon I also undertook various surgical procedures. As a Member of the Royal College of Surgeons, I felt that I was well qualified to do this. However at that time we didn't receive payments for such procedures, as the government considered these as part of our General Medical Services, included in our contract.

Despite this, I enjoyed surgery and the patients liked procedures to be done much quicker by their own GPs locally, so I undertook surgical procedures to keep my skills up to date and to save the patients having to go to hospital. However I was peeved that we surgically qualified GPs didn't receive payments for these skills and weren't recognised as such. It also helped patients, cut waiting times and saved the NHS a great deal of money.

I was very pleased when later in my trainee year, the government relented and created a new contract where more items of service including surgical procedures, were recognised and GPs were paid a fee, albeit a miserly small one for undertaking them.

Our contracts were negotiated between the NHS and the British Medical Association. "very badly," we GPs considered, as the general perception of many GPs was that the BMA were merely lackeys of the government, perhaps more concerned with getting their own public honours than the interests of their members. This was possibly well borne out by the ever decreasing numbers of GP members at that time and since.

Despite these service fee disappointments, I felt happily settled into my new life as a trainee. I found the patients very respectful and generally happy to be seen by myself as the new trainee. I thought that many assumed that as I'd joined the practice, straight out of hospital medicine, I was up to date with the latest developments in practice, which I supposed was more or less quite true!

Initially, it took me a while to get used to having booked appointments and having the constraints of keeping on time. As part of that, there were signs all over the walls of the waiting room and doctors' offices refraining the patients from reporting more than one problem during a single appointment. I wasn't too fussed about this though, as I felt we may as well deal with any worries at the time rather than waste the patient's time and our precious appointments by making them come back again. I didn't mind running a bit late in order to sort things out there and then.

Also, as a trainee, I had the luxury of 15-minute appointments, when my two colleagues had only 10 minutes to sort out patient ills. Despite my longer consultation slots, I soon realised that GPs are working under siege, with fewer doctors going into general practice, than had been in the past. I noticed, because it was blatantly apparent, that the government were steadily encouraging the public to increase their demands on their doctor's time.

Home visits were another bane in GPs lives. This process had somehow passed into the GP's role at the formation of the NHS in 1948. Prior to this time, GPs would happily visit their patients and charge the patients for the convenience. However, the expectation that GPs had the responsibility to see patients in their own home carried over into primary care and stuck there.

Patients often consider themselves too ill to get to the surgery and yet the UK is the only country where patients may expect to have a GP visit them, when the alleged severity of their illness, in their eyes, precludes their travel. This commonly wastes a great deal of the doctor's time in the process, where a surgery slot would enable more really sick patients to have been seen.

I well remember several occasions when I called at a very sick patients' house to discover they had gone out, having miraculously got better and gone without remembering to let the surgery know.

Along the same lines, I discovered that many patient appointments are missed daily when patients don't bother to turn up to surgery or bother to cancel their booked appointments. Unhappily, the NHS in its false wisdom doesn't allow GPs to charge patients for this negligence and imposes yet another burden on primary care, whereas Dentists are somehow allowed to correctly impose such fees.

One day, having finished morning surgery, I was about to start my tutorial with Geoffrey, when a lady approached the front desk and enquired whether the practice would see any patients privately. The receptionist turned to us and Geoff stepped forward and invited the lady to come through and join us in the treatment room, which she did. Once inside, Geoffrey introduced me and explained that we did have private patients and asked her about her problem.

"Hello, I'm Janet Goodall and I've come about my husband Phillip."

She explained that the patient, her husband, was a racing driver in Formula 4 Motorcar Racing and that he had a crash at the Donnington Racing Car track in the Midlands. He had been admitted to a local hospital overnight and the doctors there had patched him up and were anxious to release him. However, he was not registered at a practice and this had thwarted their plan and his wishes to get home.

Geoffrey interjected that we would happily register him as a private patient and that we would glad to see him as such the very next day at his home in the nearby village of Granchester. I quietly pondered at how easy it was to have a home visit, when the boot was on the other private foot. I wondered whether Geoffrey would want me to go with him as no doubt my up-to-date surgical experience, slightly out ranked his and Tom's.

Sure enough, after next morning's surgery Geoff approached me and said that he wondered if I would like to accompany him to Granchester, to see and assess the practice's new private patient. I immediately acquiesced and we were rapidly on our way out to the village where Paulos and I had earlier entertained our Scandinavian language students in those long hot halcyon days as students. I was eager to see how Geoff handled his dealings with a private patient.

The patient was Phillip Goodall, who was the proprietor of a well-known and large chain of luxury car dealerships, as well as outlets for a vast range of motor parts, tyres and exhaust fittings. Geoffrey reckoned he was probably worth several million pounds. Certainly, the huge Manor House just outside the village, bore witness to that. We parked Geoff's old 'S' type jaguar and alighted to be greeted by a middle-aged butler who opened the large oak front door to let us in. We were shown into a great hallway and a few moments later, Mrs. Goodall greeted us there very warmly.

"Thank you so much for coming, doctors. I've been very worried about Phillip. Those hospital doctors were very keen to discharge him. It was all I could do to get them to keep him overnight. Once they knew he hadn't been unconscious, they wanted him off their hands. They hardly looked at his injuries. He's in a lot of pain with his left leg, which has a large wound and he has several others too. They just had a simple dressing put on his leg in the Casualty Department and didn't look at it afterwards."

Mrs. Goodall sounded like she was a bit manic as she blurted out her husband's injuries, hardly pausing for breath. She was obviously very anxious about him.

"Let me show you upstairs, Phillip is in our bedroom", she rattled off leading the way.

We duly arrived at the relevant bedroom about five minutes later and would never have found it had we not had his wife as a guide. The place was a massive Victorian building, in extensive grounds as well, both of which no doubt warranted a staff of several in-house servants and gardeners. I looked out of the huge landing window over the vast expanse of lawns and beddings and thought I wouldn't want to look after that lot.

We were greeted by a man of about forty-five years old, with an open friendly face, who thanked us for coming.

Without further ado, Geoffrey introduced us took his patient's hand to measure his pulse (so much for eyes first and most), and said, "Tell us what happened and where it hurts."

Mr. Goodall expanded on how he had rolled his racing car trying to avoid another "F…g idiot," was thrown out of it and ripped open his left buttock, which was "Very f…g painful!"

Geoffrey asked him to show us all of his injuries, starting with the worst ones and finishing with the less severe. He duly did so and I proceeded to examine them all carefully. He had several suturable lacerations and a very large infected injury on his right buttock, with a full thickness skin tear and about an eight centimetres wide layer of missing skin, which appeared very red and highly contaminated by soil and other debris.

I explained that most of his injuries could be treated by us with cleaning and closure by sutures. However, where the large area of de-sloughed skin was, it would need a skin graft and possible intravenous antibiotics, as well as cover for tetanus infection, which is rife in the soils of Britain. I also stated that these measures should not be delayed any further that as he had to go into hospital any way, they could deal with all the wounds together, while he was there. Geoffrey agreed making it unanimous.

I immediately called my ex-tutor Dr Walker, who was by this time, a Consultant Dermatologist at Addenbrookes and he agreed to see Mr. Goodall that evening at the Evelyn Private Hospital, near the Cambridge University Botanical Gardens.

Mr and Mrs. Goodall agreed with our advice and we said that we would arrange for him to attend by private ambulance for surgery that evening, with a discharge agreed for the following morning, to be followed up by Dr Ramsbottom and myself. The Goodalls were both elated and expressing eternal gratitude for our prompt attendance and expert care. We were then politely shown out by their butler, back to Geoffrey's Jaguar which was put to shame by the Goodall's huge Bentley, parked outside their triple garage, to one side of their enormous house.

Geoffrey thanked me for dealing with the problem and said my expertise would be reflected in my next month's salary, after Mr. Goodall's condition had resolved.

He closed the discussion with, "Oh, by the way, could you deal with him for the duration of his injuries?"

"Yes, of course, it would be a pleasure," I replied, not realising how that response might affect the rest of my life.

We returned to the surgery and I embarked on the afternoon's booked list of patients.

35

The following day, I received another outside call, but this time, it wasn't for me as a GP.

I was buzzed through from reception saying there was a woman on the line, "Who wouldn't give her name, but was a very good friend, and she needed to speak to me."

I clicked on the line and was delighted to hear the gentle tones of the Prof's secretary, the lovely Marion.

"Hello, how's my favourite doctor? Do you know how much we're still missing you, well me really? When are you coming back for a visit?"

"Which question would you like me to answer first," I interjected.

"All of them starting at the end," she replied.

"OK, OK, to what do I owe this lovely surprise?"

"Oh, I see, straight down to business, and no time for small talk. Well, all right, the Prof ever watching out for your interests has said that it's time for you to go back to school for some more self-preservation exercises. He's asked me to give you the heads up so that you can give your colleagues time to accommodate five days of leave, commencing on a Monday in two weeks, which he presumes, will be more convenient for your colleagues."

She was right, Geoffrey and Tom, although quite flexible, were both quite serious about adequate notice being given for leave, as patients had to be seen and there were booked clinics that had to be postponed or cancelled and the nursing staff needed to be organised. Fortunately, both of my senior colleagues were not away during the proposed leave period and I was able to go without causing any chaos.

I was able to cover my departure with my colleagues and Annie by saying that I was going on a week's study leave for my Post-Graduate Training Allowance which had recently be introduced as compulsory for our continuous professional development.

GPs were to be paid an allowance for attending 30 hours of recognised or approved post-graduate studies. Marion had searched out this cover for me. The Prof had procured all of the necessary paperwork, from a course being run at the Brighton Hospital for that very purpose, including notes on the lectures and the relevant handouts. Nothing had been left to chance.

I didn't relish the thought of leaving Annie for a week, but lately my life as a trainee had given us much more time together than we had when I worked in hospital medicine. Nevertheless, we did our best to make up for the week away by being together literally, for as much as possible. It was good stamina training for the trials the Sergeant-Major would have in store for me in the coming week.

The time together passed quickly, and it didn't seem long before I was calling into the Department of Obstetrics and Gynaecology to pick up my orders from the totally efficient Marion. The Prof was as usual in theatres when I arrived, and Marion taking advantage of his absence, rushed round her desk and hugged and squeezed me till I was breathless from the contours of her breasts crushing me between them.

"Please, please be careful down there, we want you to come back hale and hearty. Don't let them injure you and watch out for those weapons! Slip-ups with them can be fatal and that would be unbearable for me."

She was a very lovely lady and truly concerned about my welfare and I was becoming concerned about her level of concern. As I looked at her, liking what I saw, an elegant most attractively refined lady in her late thirties, I pondered that it could be delightful, but I was a newly married man, with enough complexities on my agenda.

I kissed her gently on her cheek and quickly exited to set off on my journey down the A10 to London, round the North Circular, down the A30 again and on to Camberley.

After a tedious but slightly shorter journey of three hours, I pulled into the huge college car park and slotted my car into one of its tiny parking spaces. I picked up my orders and entered the guard room and approached the huge reception desk. Looking up, the desk sergeant smiled and jumping to his feet, he marched over, saluted me and held out his hand in welcome.

"Great to see you again, sir, welcome back! Do you have your orders?"

I handed them over and he quickly opened them.

"Your party is due to meet in the Officers' Mess for dinner at 19.00. You will be in your old quarters and here is the key. if you let me have your car keys,

I'll arrange for your belongings to be brought over later. Corporal, would you kindly take the good Captain to his rooms in 'A' block of the Officers' Quarters?

"Also Captain, as you have a few hours before you meet the others, you are free to leave the college should you wish. Here's an I.D. Pass, you can use if you want to leave, but remember not to discuss your business here with anyone and remember to be on time this evening, where the dress is smart casual."

I thanked the sergeant and left with the corporal to find my rooms, which were a short walk away.

"I remember you from your last visit, sir, are you back for anuver keep fit course?" enquired the corporal being friendly.

"I can't really say can I Corp?" I replied defensively.

"Don't worry Captain, you can talk to me, I'm the one oo's going to be looking after you while you're ere."

"Sorry Corp, I was just being cautious, it always pays to be cautious, doesn't it."

"You're quite right, I could be a spy, but I ain't. Ere's your quarters. It'll be me bringing your stuff over later, so I might see yer then, if not, it will be in the morning at breakfast in the Officers' Mess."

He opened the door letting me in and was gone in a flash.

Once again, I was alone in my adequate room. I thought about going to explore Camberley, but as most towns in Britain are very much alike, with the same facilities, same shopping precincts and the same boring shops, I decided that a quick kip would stand me in better stead for the pending tribulations ahead and duly fell asleep quickly on my small but adequate bed, on which I was rudely awoken later by the sound of several other of the army's 'guests' returning back to their barracks after their warm up morning run. With them making the most noise, I recognised my old friend the Sergeant-Major, who was barely in a sweat.

"Right then, ladies and gents, I'd like you to shower, dress and come to the Officers' Mess in half an hour to meet the Colonel." This brought back memories from my last visit but today, I seemed to have been spared the cross-country part of my training.

As I looked at the runners, I thought one of them looked familiar. I recognised him as one of my fellow clinical students from Cambridge. Sure enough it was indeed Dr Peter Richards, a former good friend of mine from the clinical school and a thoroughly good man.

He had been in the army during his clinical training and at various stages of our course used to shoot off to this army college for various parts of his military training, including a phenomenon called Boot Camp. Where he was taught Basic Army skills, a process designed to turn a civilian into a soldier, have his head shaved, his individual character removed and swopped for a man who obeys immediately without questioning any orders that are screamed at him by any passing superior, but similar soldier.

Later that evening, when we met at dinner, I learned that in fact he was now a Major in the Army Medical Corps. He was about to go on a goodwill mission to South America, to deliver a grand piano to a group of former head hunting natives in the Amazonian jungle.

Although a slight publicity stunt, the exercise showed the locals how expert the British Army was at undertaking intricate trials in such difficult terrain. I was actually very impressed, when he later explained to me all the various precautions and secret political deals that had to be undertaken to achieve this goal.

Peter was exceedingly surprised to see me at that evening's dinner and enthusiastically exploded with loads of questions about when did I join the army and what I was doing there. I replied that it was hush hush and having expressed such complete surprise, he never asked again, throughout our stay. I liked this man a lot and it was good to see him and feel a sense of camaraderie with him again, even though our non-medical roles were enormously different.

I also recognised some of the other dinner party guests as returners from our previous course a year earlier. We nodded to each other but as per orders, our conversations were slightly stunted and rather confined to the challenges expected to be in our way in the morning.

The next morning, we all assembled on the parade ground at 07.00 and set off for the customary warm-up run followed by some close order P.E. The Sergeant-Major emphasised that this time we would also be concentrating on getting fit and staying that way. You could tell which group members were probably full time military as they were the first back from the run and had hardly broken out in a sweat. The rest of us were dripping and looking like we'd just run the marathon.

Peter Richards very astutely and quietly pointed out to me that he knew I wasn't military, by the physical state I was in after the run and by the fact that following our showers, we returners were separated from the others and had a coffee in the Officers Mess while they had to attend the Colonel's welcome speech.

We all met up for lunch and then adjourned to the armoury with its firing range. It had been expanded and updated from last year. The same sergeant welcomed us all and re-iterated the same speech we'd heard before. This time however we returners and some of the military types were again, separated and moved to an adjacent building. In it, there were about 20 indoor firing galleries, with baffled walls and ceilings. We were each allocated a target firing lane, approximately fifteen yards long, with overhead target retrieval carriers and short sound-baffled walls separating the firers from each other.

Each lane had a bullet trap to prevent bullets ricocheting back at the shooter. We were each given our own ear mufflers and handed a pistol. This time we were all given a Walther PPS, which had become standard issue, because of its superiority over the other pistols. I thought it ironic that our military was now using weapons copied from our former cold war enemies in East Germany.

This time, the ear mufflers were superior too and we were no longer deafened by the explosions of gunfire. I was pleased that I quite rapidly regained my former prowess, and did even better than I had done in my last firing experience from our previous visit.

After a stint in the firing lanes, this time round we were taught to draw our weapons and fire at targets, while moving around a simulated residential area. This involved targets suddenly popping up out of nowhere and we having rapid reactions and the ability to distinguish between innocent bystanders and dangerous individuals trying to shoot us.

We very quickly used up our allocation of bullets and the sergeant was very pleased with all of us.

I fantasised that if the NHS failed, I could always become an assassin, but very quickly put that thought right out of my head. That evening I ate with Peter and we compared his job in the medical corps with mine in general practice. We also discussed our target scores over dinner and he complemented me and suggested I might like to join him in the military, if general practice didn't turn out to rock my boat. I smiled inwardly to myself at his invitation and thought I wonder what he'd say if he became aware of my other job in our country's security.

The week rushed by very quickly and I enjoyed the company of my alumnus from Cambridge, which interspersed with my calls home to Annie made it pass rapidly. I managed to keep up the cover of the week of lectures and was confident in the knowledge that the Prof had covered all the paperwork, including the attendance certificates.

I survived the Friday night session in the Sergeants' Mess without too much of a hangover and was quickly up and out for breakfast in the morning. I was most impressed because the corporal who was assigned to watch over me actually came to my quarters with a large mug of tea, to make sure I didn't oversleep. In no time at all and with appetite replete on a large plate of eggs and bacon, I was on my way back home, looking forward to my quiet life with Annie.

36

Apart from leaving the bedroom for meals we spent the rest of the weekend entwined in and around each other. By Monday, I needed to go to work to get back my senses.

On reaching my overcrowded pigeon hole, I found a letter from none other than Mr and Mrs Goodall. They were very grateful for the medical care that I'd given Phillip following his rapid admission into the Evelyn Private Nursing Home. They thought I was an expert for sorting out his injuries and post-op recovery.

Obviously, my old tutor must have put in a good word for me, after he had grafted the lesion on his right buttock. They were inviting Annie and me round to their mansion for dinner. I thought to myself that they couldn't have received Geoffrey's bill yet and that might dampen their gratitude a touch.

I was due to see Geoff for a tutorial that lunchtime and passed on the good news and I was pleased but not surprised to hear that he and his wife had been invited too. Geoffrey also mentioned that Phillip had not only been sent a bill, but he had also promptly paid it as well.

Geoffrey was beaming from ear to ear and pleased me by saying I was now due for a generous bonus at the end of the month. I wondered just how much he'd been paid to provoke his beaming and looked forward to see just how much I was going to receive for doing my bit.

The work at the surgery was enjoyable and I didn't notice the days fly by and soon enough the day of our dinner date at the Goodall's mansion was upon us. I felt it was important to impress, these our private patients and had suggested that Annie might like to go into the city to buy a posh new evening dress, with the shoes and handbag to match.

She readily complied with my idea and shot off to indulge herself. She wasn't looking forward to dinner with some of our boring patients, but was readily persuaded by her sojourn in the couture shops of the Grafton Centre in Cambridge.

She did look the part when she appeared in her designer gown that almost coalesced with her skin, so that in a dim light, you wouldn't be able to figure out where one stopped and the other began.

Her new lingerie, left little to the imagination as she emerged from the bathroom. My God, I gasped to behold her. She looked so incredibly beautiful that I had to steel myself to keep my hands off her.

Geoffrey and his wife Jacqueline arrived to give us a lift and I let them in just as Annie descended the stairs to the hallway.

"Well, you look absolutely lovely my dear," exclaimed Jackie. "You're a very lucky man Michael."

"Hear hear!" proclaimed Geoffrey.

"Yes, I know I am," I said proudly.

"Mike told me to push the boat out. So, what could I do?" Annie replied self-consciously.

I wondered how boring this evening was going to be and how long I had to wait to sink between her luscious thighs. I thought that I might burst in anticipation and couldn't wait to get back home.

Jackie pulled me back down to reality when she interjected with, "Well, come on then, we can't hang around here all-night admiring Annie, when we might be missing a millionaire's feast."

With that, we clambered into the back of the 'S' type and were on our way to Granchester, where we were greeted by the butler at the huge front door and shown into the vestibule.

Mrs. Goodall joined us almost immediately with kisses and bonhomie all round.

"Do come in and join us for drinks and meet our other guests with Philip."

We followed her into their huge dining room, which was almost the size of the Great Hall at my college. Philip bounded up to greet us as enthusiastically as his wife. He introduced us to his two guests as his medical saviours, who had rescued him from severe injuries.

Geoffrey introduced our wives and I could see our host's eyes almost devoured Annie as she floated across the dining room floor. Janet Goodall's mouth dropped wide open and her eyes almost popped out of her head at Annie's natural beauty. She outshone all of the women there, radiating her elegance and glamour to all around.

The other couple there turned out to be a local politician and his wife, who also lived nearby. We learned that he had some notoriety as an author. They also gazed in admiration at the sight of my beautiful wife. I felt so privileged to have her as my partner in life.

I have to say that although I was looking forward to getting home to be with Annie, the evening went very well as we feasted on the finest wines and exquisite food and very entertaining conversation. Although I'd never read any of his books, the politician was a very skilful conversationalist and storyteller and kept us all entertained for the whole night.

Our host Philip was also very charming and wasn't to be outdone by his politician guest. He insisted on telling us his life story, how he started off as an apprentice car mechanic and selling cars from the first garage where he worked.

He boasted on how he'd had to work seven days a week fixing cars to build up his savings enough to lease his own first premises and then the car sales business took off to become the huge empire he owned today. He thought it must definitely be better selling luxury cars than fixing them.

All in all the evening flew by in hedonist self-indulgence and in the car home, we roared with laughter at the amusing anecdotes we had enjoyed earlier as Geoffrey's wife Jacqueline drove us back, in her starchy indifferent and cold sobriety.

I noticed her face in the interior mirror, which looked remarkably preserved. She had hardly any Crows feet laughter lines in the outside corners of her eyes. She'd probably never laughed much in her sedate and objective world of academia.

I thought this part-time lady doctor must have had a very cloistered upbringing, which was really quite common among practitioners of her gender. I'd become aware during my training that the female medical students, who by this time in the history of the profession, made up over fifty percent of our number, were almost all very serious academics by nature.

They didn't seem to have much of a sense of humour, compared with the traditional male students, nor certainly compared with the vivacious female medical students we'd met from Israel. Jacky's female colleagues had surely been inculcated with the government policy of strict obedience to the rules and the importance of Whistle-Blowing on those who broke them, which bore a very uncanny resemblance to Nazi Germany, Mouist China, Pol Potist Cambodia and Stalanist Russia, where even children would often inform on their parents to ingratiate themselves with government lackeys.

I imagined that they must have been selected like that so they could compete in the tough predominantly male world of medicine. Jacqueline definitely portrayed that very earnest type completely and I wondered how she had floated Geoffrey's boat, if she ever did, or if she ever let her guard down at all. I couldn't imagine her ever initiating rampant sex anywhere in her relationship with my G.P. Trainer. I certainly felt some pity for Geoffrey and wasn't at all surprised he was almost homiletic in my tutorials with him.

When we were finally dropped off at home, and I followed Annie up the stairs, I cleared them in record time, almost pole vaulting up the stairs on my erection. We proceeded into the bedroom and there in the half-light from the landing approached each other, almost savouring our moment of contact. We kissed passionately as I ran my hands over her shoulders, along the prominences of her clavicles and down on to her sumptuous breasts, lingering over her areolae until her nipples engorged into proud and rigid erections.

For almost a pico-second, my mind wondered to the images I saw when I visited the Camberley Army College and we were shown an army documentary on East Germany, where the Communist government posted adverts all over East Berlin stating, 'We salute the erections of our workers!'

My whole being was saluting her erect nipples and her other accoutrements that came with them. I was already wet with the anticipation and the pre-ejaculate, that I'd nurtured throughout the evening, from the stolen images I'd gleaned of her hypnotising our fellow diners, lubricating my engorged glans penis and saluting my own erection.

We fell into each other on to the bed, oscillating rhythmically into a crescendo of mutual frenzied come. I collapsed exhausted in exaltation and slept where I lay inside her.

I woke up as the sun came up and she moved beneath me to restart the flow into my flaccid and spent phallus, which awakened, responded accordingly pressing fervently into her pelvis. She gripped me with her vestibular muscles that locked onto my manhood and almost wrenched me into her, drowning wantonly in her welcoming love pool. I sunk to my pubis and filled her again, erupting till I was empty.

We lay there stock-still, with hearts racing and skin soused and slippery. I drifted back off to sleep until Annie woke me, bubbly and enthused with superlatives about the previous night's dinner with the Goodalls.

"What a fabulous evening!"

"What a fantastic house and what a delectable dinner!" she ranted as I lay there totally knackered and azoospermic.

"Yes," I barely managed to pronounce with all the remaining ATP in my body.

"I enjoyed it very much, and I take it you did, too."

"Yes, I did, I loved their brilliant house. Fancy living in a place like that! I thought they were marvellous and that author bloke was really funny as well. It was a really lovely evening. I don't s'pose they'll invite us again; we were a bit boring compared to them!"

I thought about my role as a doctor and what it involved, and my other secret role, hidden at the back of my mind. Neither was boring, in fact, I thought both were absolutely and thoroughly thrilling. I'd never been bored for one second since I entered medicine. Mind you, I'd never had time to become at all bored. I'd been busy since day one.

For the first time, I wondered what it was that motivated my new and beautiful wife. I didn't want to gainsay her view, but clearly, I felt that we might have different viewpoints from very slightly different backgrounds.

She had been overwhelmed by the worldly possessions, success and financial freedoms of the Goodalls. She bet that they didn't have to cut short their honeymoon in rainy England to get back to work. Indeed, wherever they had their honeymoon, it would probably have taken the length of our honeymoon to get back home!

I was too knackered to take an issue with what she'd said and understood why she'd been so impressed by the massive exhibition of wealth and privilege, displayed in that calossal house 'chez Goodalls'. I just turned over and fell back asleep.

I woke up later to the sound and aroma of sizzling bacon and eggs and forgot about Annie's earlier envious comments.

We had a peaceful weekend and I was ready to go back to work on that Monday, where Geoffrey was equally vociferous about the Goodalls' life style.

"I reckon they must be multi-millionaires," he enthused during the after lunch coffee, as we signed the repeat prescriptions.

"Yes," I almost reluctantly agreed, jealous of Annie's earlier enthusiasm, "but I rather be a doctor than a mechanic"!

"Yeah, you're right, I suppose we make a slightly bigger impact on mankind than he does," Geoffrey begrudgingly added. "Let's go and sort out these home visits; it'll bring us back down to earth."

So off we went together delivering medicine into the homes of our sick patients and the afternoon passed with no further envious banter.

When I got home that evening, I was greeted by Annie who rushed up and hugged me boiling over with excitement.

"You'll never guess what! I got a call today from Janet Goodall inviting us to go with them to the Henley Regatta on Saturday. We'll have to dress up, I'll have to get a different posh dress and you have to get one of those striped blazers, boater and posh flannel trousers. His company goes there every year in the firm's coach and they have a table in the Stewards' enclosure. It's a very posh do and the Royals often go there too. I think Phil must have been a rower when he was younger!"

She was so excited, she was almost manic hardly pausing for breath, as she jabbered out her news. I was thinking to myself, probably the only rowing he's ever done is in dispute with his customers.

"I'm not sure I can go because I'm due to take a Saturday surgery this weekend," I barely managed to interject.

"Oh, we must go, it will really be great and I've never been before. It will be marvellous! You must get Geoffrey or Tom to swap the surgery with you. We can't not go, it will be such fun!"

"Ok darling, I'll ask them in the morning. I'm sure they'll help if they can," and I did ask and they did help and we did go to Henley, with Annie dressed up to the nines and myself in a new striped blazer and Geoffrey's borrowed boater. It was a very posh event and we feasted on champagne, strawberries and Beluga Caviar. I even enthused about some of the rowing.

Annie was glowing with delight as we laughed and joked with the Goodalls all the way back to Cambridge. She was the proverbial Belle of the ball. How the other half live, I thought to myself in an almost stuporous state, as the coach meandered up the A10. I was replete in booze, strawberries and fish eggs.

As we approached the turn off for Granchester, the Goodalls invited us back to their mansion, but I was anxious to get back as I felt quite inebriated and I didn't want these people, who I didn't really know too well and who were now also patients at Geoffrey's practice, seeing me as such.

I thought going back would be bound to exacerbate my already slightly loaded condition. It was not very professional and I kept wondering what the Prof might think. We were dropped off back at Annie's and I was soon tucked up in bed unconscious to the world.

37

On the Monday after, I had a very good day in surgery and felt certain, pending investigating tests, that I diagnosed a really rare case of Phaeochromocytoma. This is a scarcely seen but usually benign adrenaline secreting tumour of the suprarenal glands, which sit on top of the kidneys.

These glands secrete our body's endogenous steroid from the outside of the gland and also adrenaline from its middle part. Sometimes areas of this gland become autonomous and start secreting either or both of these hormones in excess.

Something clicked in my brain from my University Histology class many years earlier, when I remembered that patients can present with high blood pressure, a racing heart at rest and excessive sweating, even when they're cold.

I felt so excited when I discussed it with Geoffrey. The patient had to go to the hospital to retrieve a pot to collect her pee for 24 hours to see if she had excessive adrenaline products in it, which would be diagnostic of this condition.

That evening, I drove home very pleased with myself and eager to boast my diagnostic prowess to Annie. As I burst enthusiastically into our home, I was somewhat deflated to discover a note from her saying that she'd gone for a massage with Janet Goodall at her gym club and would I like me to join her with the Goodalls for a Chinese meal afterwards.

Fed up, I drove to the designated Chinese restaurant to find Annie and the Goodalls ensconced at a large table with a huge Lazy Susan revolving tray at its centre, almost overflowing with every sort of Chinese dish imaginable.

Annie got up and greeted me with a peck on the cheek. She railed with enthusiasm about her wonderful massage and how she must do this regularly, like her new friend, as it has to have great benefit for her well-being.

Philip also got up, leaned over and shook my hand.

"I hope you didn't mind me ordering before you got here, only I know the owner, who recommended this large bargain choice that has everything on it to satisfy everyone's tastes. So, we should all eat a hearty meal."

I thanked him and exchanged pleasantries, feeling somewhat miffed inside that I'd been manoeuvred into spending my evening eating Chinese food, for which I had mixed feelings with an arrogant multi-millionaire, for whom I also had much more negative mixed feelings.

We spent the whole evening talking about Philip's successful business strategies and how they intended expanding their already large enterprise. He explained that while their luxury car outlets were quite widespread nationally, they were somewhat restricted by the actual car manufacturers, as to the size of their operation, what they could sell and where they could set up.

However, that wasn't the case for the other sector of their business. They enthusiastically described how they'd had to employ a business manager, whose job it was to travel around the country seeking out potential sites for new outlets for their motor parts, tyres and exhaust systems. He would contact the local councils and chambers of commerce, looking for any profitable opportunities to be seized in the particular local business economy. He would set up the purchase of the site and the Goodalls would supply the money to make it happen.

Janet Goodall said they were very excited by how well it was going and how they envisaged expanding hugely. The only bad side she could think of was that it had meant that Philip quite often had to go away around the country to planning meetings to sort out the details of the deals.

I managed to survive the evening in close proximity to this super-wealthy self-indulgent businessman, who spoke incessantly with his mouth jammed open with large portions of sweet and sour everything, sowing it like seed ubiquitously across the table. I hate to say it but I didn't feel at all sorry for his slight inconvenience of having to travel away, in the grand scheme of his things!

Next morning, over breakfast Annie was again bubbling about the evening's feasting and then how it would be a good idea if she joined the Goodalls' gym so she could keep in shape for me and enjoy an occasional massage when the NHS got under her skin. She thought it would be good for us both.

I did feel it was a good idea to keep fit but didn't necessarily agree that it had to be in the most expensive gym club in the area. Still once I'd agreed with the principle, it was a small step before her membership card dropped through the post and she became a member of the same club as her new best friends, the Goodalls!

Before long the massages and Chinese feasting started to become an almost regular thing. Happily, my practice commitments precluded me from some of their gastronomic soirees. I would turn up late or on occasions, miss the whole evening. I'd get home late and Annie would be dropped off sometime after. There were other girls' events from the gym club that didn't really involve me at all.

After some time, I noticed that Annie no longer seemed to mix with her old secretarial friends from Addenbrookes. They certainly no longer seemed to come round and we no longer socialised at the hospital do's. I asked Annie about this and suggested we might organise something but she declined stating that they were boring and didn't mix in the circles that we now enjoyed.

I was disappointed by her response, as I actually liked several of her former mates and didn't appreciate, like she did, the social attributes of the members of her new circle of friends, who struck me as being a bunch of shallow overpaid sycophantic nerds.

Then one night out of the blue, Annie suggested that she should change her hours in the neurosurgery department as Philip Goodall had suggested she might like to work for him in his local headquarters for a much higher rate of pay than she we earning with the NHS. She thought it was a good idea, because it would help us to save more for a bigger house and have more funds to enjoy life.

I reminded her of the benefits and security of working in the NHS and that his job offered her none of these, just the chance to earn a bit more. I had to admit I felt uneasy in my gut about him, who was the sole arbiter for the rights of his employees. I'd also heard some strong rumours about his company from some of my patients. She clamorously protested that this was unproven hearsay and I sensed that she might be protesting a little too much!

Notwithstanding my advice, my wife went ahead and reduced her NHS work to three days per week and commenced working for the Goodalls for the other two.

I expressed my misgivings about this new arrangement but Annie dismissed this as cynicism on my part. She was right, I was cynical. No business man I ever knew, got rich by being philanthropic, despite his surname. I could only advise her and she would have to see things for herself. Until she did, I would have to live with her ill-advised decisions. I would confine my views to my work, both as a GP trainee and for the Prof.

I didn't have to wait very long, the next day, I received a call from Paul Bradley, with a request from the Prof that we urgently meet up the following Monday at 17.00 in his rooms at Downing, as a serious development had occurred that required urgent intervention. He asked if I could make that day and I agreed.

I felt excited that I was once again back in action and it certainly rapidly focused my mind on the issue of national security, temporarily relieving me of my worries about my wife's possible infatuation with the life style of wealthy business men, and/or the wealthy businessman himself.

The next day, I was also pleased, to discover that my patient's 24 hour urine collection was positive for high levels of catecholamines (the breakdown product of adrenaline). This would prove the diagnosis of a Phaeochromocytoma, which happily was treatable. So I referred her to the surgeons to excise her adrenal gland with the adrenaline secreting tumour and presented this case at my GP school, because it was such a rare disease.

The following Monday, I made my way to the Old Court at Downing, was shown up to Prof's rooms and led inside to be greeted by Paul, the Prof, Chief Inspector Greenwood from Special Branch and K from MI5. The large porter brought round a tray of college claret, which softened the atmosphere and Prof asked the chief inspector to bring us up to date with developments.

Robin Greenwood rose to his full very tall height and started his report, "I'm very sorry to tell you that the level of substance abuse among the young people of England, particularly from our point of view but not only in the home counties, but all over Britain, has increased massively. It would appear that our criminal justice system is just not coping with the level of activities of the criminal fraternity.

"Organised Crime gangs have now set up country-wide for the importation and distribution of drugs from London in the South, Glasgow in the North and Bristol in the West. From these three centres it is being spread across the country, via networks of commuting Mules, who use the roads, the railways and national coach networks to move their supplies around and into towns across Britain."

"Professor and you doctors may be interested to know that locally the dealer who compromised your German Scientist's daughter is back in business, spreading her wares across educational establishments of North Herts. She was let out for good behaviour, after serving half her sentence. It seems that she didn't heed the warnings our local Plod gave her and went straight back into business.

"We are a bit concerned about our situation locally, as it seems more and more likely that there may be another major source of opiate, cocaine and crack supplies on the scene nearby; other than the historic West and North African operations. We have had several sources of information concerning various local Athletic and Sports Clubs being in the market place for supplying illicit medications, using their sports club as a cover. There have also been two drug deaths among local youths, where they have emanated from normal decent upper middle class family backgrounds, who have out of the blue over-dosed on cocktails of various non-prescribed drugs.

"We are currently monitoring a local suspect, with a very long criminal record, who runs a boxing club, where there have been a number of whisperings about him assisting his boxers with anabolic steroids and other stimulant drugs. However, this man has always been a petty criminal and doesn't have the wear with all to finance a big operation, so we are a bit perplexed about the financier behind him.

"So in summary gentlemen, we are faced with a serious escalation of the country's drug addiction problem, possible based on two sources of supply; one from criminal Africa working with some known elements from the Caribbean islands and more likely another, as yet unknown from some other local major supplier. This is having a huge and detrimental effect mainly on, but not only on the youth of the country. That's the conclusion of my report gentlemen."

The Prof stood and began his response, "Thank you, Robin, for that very comprehensive and sombre report. Well gentlemen, it seems the measures that we've put in place have not really achieved the objectives we set for ourselves some months ago.

"K, what do think about this situation? It seems that the normal law and order resources haven't made much progress with dealing with these melancholy events. Do you have any ideas about how we might intervene more positively?"

K rose to his feet and looking slightly forlorn, as the head of our country's main security network, he opened with, "Gentlemen, I have to agree with our esteemed colleague from S.B. We seem to be failing miserably with our efforts to maintain the security of our country. However, I have to say, it is not for the want of trying. Between you and me, I would deny it outside of this room, we have been majorly hampered by government policy."

"In the Criminal Justice System, it seems that there is a permanent policy to impose extreme leniency in sentencing as much as possible; so that even suspects with seriously long and persistent criminal records obtain ludicrously light prison terms, that are far more reforming and remedial than punishing and deterring. So they simply do their little stint of Bird and come out to go straight back into their former criminal enterprises, encouraging their peers to join them without the recourse of effective punishment. In short Professor, our hands are tied by home office and in ultimo, existing government policy, which seems to be restrained solely by expense."

"As Detective Chief Inspector Greenwood has just admirably demonstrated with the case of his local dealer. Our resources although stretched, are very successful in monitoring and nicking these degenerates when necessary, but the local courts have to impose useless sanctions that do nothing to deter them! We need to impose far more substantial controls on these anti-social animals to send a message to their heartland that imposes no doubts as to what will happen if they persist in their ways."

"That's the view of my department. We have many more serious security matters we could be dealing with for the country's welfare that could have more practical and beneficial outcomes than dealing with these worthless reprobates. We are frustrated and feel we need to act substantially to reverse the status quo and rescue our society."

The Prof rose again and thanked K for his forthrightness.

"I am grateful for your professional opinion. It seems we may have been lackadaisical in the sanctions we imposed on the individuals involved in these activities. I feel we need to redouble our efforts. May I suggest that we reconvene in 28 days and in the interim might I suggest that you K liaise with D.C.I. Greenwood, to institute what measures that you deem appropriate to investigate these individuals and in particular to track down all the sources of these drugs and round up all the deviant drug dealers.

"In the meantime, our team will consider the situation and make recommendations to the P.M. to thoroughly deal with those concerned in a more deterrent way. Gentlemen, I look forward to seeing you all in four weeks' time."

At that juncture, we all rose and left down the old oak stairs, dutifully walked round the quadrant and joined our cars.

Paul stopped me leaving and said, "This is likely to mean that the Prof will want to discuss these developments with us, to gain our views. Will you think about this and get back to me. I'll let you know when Prof wants to meet. What's your best day?"

"I can take Thursday afternoons as my half day. Shall I come to the department?"

"No, I'll let you know when I know."

With that, I jumped in my car and drove off through the Cambridge rush hour traffic back to Annie's house. She wasn't home. Instead, I found a note telling me she'd gone to meet up with Janet Goodall at their gym and did I want to join them for a Chinese again? Did I fuck?

I called the gym and left a message saying I couldn't make that as I'd had to go to a last minute meet up with some of my old O & G colleagues and I had hoped she might come with me as she knew them too. I felt that I'd transmitted my feelings in my reply and set off to the pub at the roundabout on the A10 near the museum, where I knew I would find some of my former colleagues.

38

I walked into the overcrowded bar and sure enough was confronted by a noisy posse of my ex-Obstetrics and Gynaecology colleagues, who were as exuberant as ever and let out a huge cheer as they spotted me bursting through the side entrance. Mine's a pint, I clamoured, making my way through the crowded tables where people were looking up wondering if I was anyone famous.

That's when I saw her out of the corner of my eye, like a mirage in the hottest and driest desert, I stopped to stare and yes it was her, the beautiful Sally Rawlings, sitting with a group of young women and staring directly at me. I stopped deadly still and caught her gaze, as her look of surprise extended into a warm and delicious smile, designed to melt the hearts of all those who beheld her.

I ignored my enthusiastic former colleagues and the pint of Abbot Ale that was being passed in my direction and made a beeline towards her. She stood as I approached and I held out both of my hands, which she took in hers and I pulled her towards me enveloping her tightly in a huge hug, which she reciprocated.

She was even lovelier up close and I felt my ardour responding as I clung onto her, drowning in the exotic bouquet of her expensive perfume.

I didn't want to let go of her, but she gazed up at me saying, "Well fancy meeting you here! I've often thought about you and wondered how your medical life must be going."

"And I you, I kept watching out for you on the TV. How are you? You look totally wonderful."

"So do you!" she exclaimed looking me up and down.

I felt I had so much I wanted to say to her, as I was still holding onto her hands, before being rudely awakened by the raucous clamours from my mates at the bar. We turned looking at them and she laughed out loud.

"Aren't you going to introduce me then?" she coyly asked.

"Yes, of course!" I retorted dragging her away from her three friends, with one saying, "Don't mind us!"

I replied, "I'm sorry. Where are my manners? I'm Mike and I'm an old friend of Sally's. Why don't you all come over and meet my mates? Don't worry, their bark is much worse than their bite."

They looked at each other, then suspiciously at my mates and then at me and then one of them exclaimed, "Sure, OK, you don't look too dangerous!"

I thought, if only they knew, and still holding Sally's hand, I dragged her over towards the bar with her friends in hot pursuit. My chums welcomed me and them warmly and we spent the whole evening having a really enjoyable time, chattering along, discussing medicine and the trials and tribulations in the lives of junior doctors.

I hadn't told her anything about the developments in my personal life and simply joined in the general good-humoured stories my colleagues and I had brought up about medicine and this fully entertained them.

I never once thought about the whereabouts of my beautiful, but possibly errant wife.

Gradually, my friends and hers drifted off leaving the two of us together stirring our coffees, talking the small talk and occasionally pausing to steal an inquisitive look at each other.

"I did wonder about you, Mike," she said looking down towards the table, "But I didn't want to interrupt your important studies. I knew how hard it must be studying medicine, as you and your mates have let us know this evening. I didn't want to distract you or get in your way. Also, where I come from, it's usually the man who pursues the woman and I thought that had you wanted to, you would have called me. I guessed that you just probably didn't want to."

"No, that's wrong, I did want to. I understood your dedication to acting and devotion to your responsibilities in your acting roles. I respected that and though I wanted you so much, I could understand why you wouldn't want to be swayed from your devotions by a mere student."

I could see the irony of it that we clearly had very similar views from our diverging recollections.

Looking at her now, I had to admit to myself, that anyone in their right mind would want her; she was absolutely lovely and I could hardly keep my hands off her. I stole a quick glance at my watch and thought, hell I have to go.

"Can I give you a lift home, as it's rather late?" She declined saying she'd take a taxi, but I couldn't let her do that and insisted she let me drive her and I did!

When we got back to her place I said, "Look, I've got so much I want to say to you. Can we meet and talk together? We can't leave it like this."

She agreed and we arranged to meet in the University Botanical Gardens a week later. She gave me her telephone number, just in case something cropped up and we had to change arrangements.

I bent down as a friend, to kiss her goodnight and she clung onto me with a gentle but enduring kiss that again stirred awake my intense passion for her. I turned and left her, without looking back and was totally confused in my head. I drove home to my wife, who was asleep when I got there, so I quietly slid in beside her, with my mind elsewhere.

I couldn't sleep and lay there thinking about the day's events. I thought about my disappointment on discovering that Annie had assumed the opportunity to go off and meet up with her new wealthy friends, with very little regard to how I felt about it. I had to admit that I felt damned annoyed about it!

Then my mind quickly moved on from an irritable mode into one of total pleasure as my memory perused the delightful face of Sally Rawlings, who out of the blue had just sidled back into my life and mind, releasing a rush of endorphins on the way.

I mmmed out loud without hesitation, as I reconsidered her lovely face looking up, holding me in her gaze as her lips homed in on mine, for that long goodnight kiss. I had to see her again and couldn't wait a whole week. With that thought in mind, my rapid eye movement dream sleep gave way to non-rem deep sleep and I drifted off with a mile-wide grin all over my face and that beautiful thought in my mind.

Next morning, we awoke with the alarm clock and Annie turned towards me in our bed. I was still highly miffed about the evening before and the way she just ignored any feelings that I may have had about yet another Chinese meal.

She moved across the bed towards me, reaching out with her left hand across my chest, and started to stroke me gently back and forth over my erogenous zones, engrossing my attention, softening my ire and arousing an urgency in my nether regions that vanquished any thoughts of liaisons in the Botanical Gardens.

She pulled my arms over her and I rolled onto her soft womanly belly. My engorged phallus pressed against her pubis and she grasped it, pulling me into her and I sank into her already moistened love cave. We reeled violently as I repeatedly thrust into her, harder and harder until she cried out in pleasure into my ear. I quickly came, filling her with my copious ejaculate.

I was uncertain whether the substantial volume of my seed may have had something to do with the unsatisfied arousal I had felt with Sally the evening before or whether it was entirely due the sexual delights of my beautiful wife lying beneath me. Still, I didn't want to provoke a debate and lay there drifting back into a perfectly satiated post coital sleep.

I was awakened soon after by Annie, who with the rapidity of my performance, possibly hadn't been as satisfied as I was. She rolled over a few degrees and I slid out of her onto my back beside her. She flung off the quilt, bent down over me and almost devoured my sticky glans, quaffing and licking off our love juices until it was like a newly pink painted flag pole. She drew up and separated her knees and pulling my left hand behind her, over her buttocks, she extended my left thumb and slid it fully inside her.

She rocked back and forth taking pleasure from my digit pressed hard against and repeatedly rubbing her clitoris. She moaned louder and louder sucking with all her might on my bulging glans until we burst forth writhing involuntarily, with her soaking my hand in her flow of love juice, until she rolled off leaving me floating in the pool of her emissive climax.

We lay there in silence, before she moved to the edge of our bed and immersed herself in a silk dressing gown, which clung to her like a purple rash accentuating her body curves.

"I must rush," she said, "I have a busy day at the hospital today."

With that, she rushed off to the shower, leaving me there alone immersed in my endorphins. I was coming back down to earth when she returned and started dressing in front of me, slowly pouring herself into her lingerie, her black thong pouting over her pubis and her unwired gossamer silk translucent bra, which she filled to overflowing.

She unwrapped her black hold-up stockings which she unfolded over her long legs up to her thighs, smoothing them off with the palms of her hands. That was the horny-est adornment I'd ever seen. In an instant she was gone rushing off to her work place, where she would light up the frequently tragic neurosurgical wards with her divinity.

Left in bewilderment, I finally got up and showered removing her essence from my sweaty body, dressed and drove off to morning surgery. As I made my way through the rush hour, my mind raced through the events of the last eighteen hours. In the previous evening, despite our love-making, I started off thoroughly annoyed with the thoughtless behaviour of my lovely wife, who had deserted me with no real thought about my wants and needs.

I'd needed to speak to her and should have, to air my grievances and this morning, had missed the opportunity, in a repleted exhaustion. I then un-expectantly and in the middle of a huge huff, met a most beautiful woman from my distant past, who had melted my anger, re-awakened my desires and having taken her home, left me totally bereft. I then returned to my marital home still in a bereaved but half excited mood, only for my passions to be awakened again, but this time by my lovely wife.

What an ironic world, and what the hell should I do. I couldn't get the lovely Sally Rawlings out of my mind and I totally desired to see her again, as soon as possible; but then again my fabulous wife had just blown me away and satisfied every possible desire known to man.

These delicious dilemmas were occupying my concentration as I called in my first patient, who was complaining of piles, which blasted my rampant cravings into oblivion and focused my attentions on a swollen and inflamed fat bottom!

That jarred me down to earth like an un-opened parachute and I worked my way through morning surgery. I was interrupted by a call from one of my ex-Obs & Gynae colleagues who was asking whether Sally Rawlings was available for a romantic soiree. I rapidly set him straight that she wasn't.

When I got home that night, Annie didn't seem to be her usual self. To my mind she was certainly in a state of almost panic, which she denied.

"I'm just worried and want to make a good impression in the morning with the Goodalls. I've only worked in the NHS, and private business is a whole different state of affairs."

I swiftly interjected that she would just have to be there to make such a good impression. She smiled at that and rushed off for a shower and a very early night.

The next day she was up and out, dressed up to the nines, before I lifted my head off the pillow. She must be really keen, I thought to myself, possibly a touch jealous, but in fact, very jealous!

Eventually I did lift my head off the pillow, showered and made my way to work in a melancholy mood. I staggered through my patients, trying to focus on Roger Neighbour, the Guru of analysis of general practice Consultation and to ignore the thought of Annie's curvaceous haute couture exposed to the business world of the Goodalls.

I couldn't block the thought of them salivating over her as she graced their profit generating milieu. It sickened me thoroughly into a trance-like state, from which I was awakened with a start, by the ring of my surgery room phone. I bounded back to reality by the voice of Paul Bradley.

"Morning, Mike, there have been several developments since we last met and there is to be another meeting which will be a big one. However, this time the meeting will take place in forty-eight hours at New Scotland Yard in London and I'm afraid this reflects the seriousness of the situation. The Prof and the Vice-Chancellor will be there.

"We need to get there by 10.30, at the Met Police Special Branch department on 17th floor of the Yard, which is closed off to the rest of the building. They will be expecting you and you can get inside the foyer, where we will be met and escorted to the 17th floor. I'm going to get there by 10.15, so we might meet up on the Cambridge Buffet Express, if not, I'll see you in the foyer."

"Thank you, Paul," I said, relieved that now something was happening that would lift me out of my domestic dilemmas and bring me back to concentrate on the important events of national security.

"I'll be there. I'm glad some thing's finally happening. I feel I may need to speak to you about a personal matter and I don't feel I should get the Prof involved while all of this is going on. Perhaps now we can sort these buggers out once and for all."

Annie had just been gently relegated to the back of my mind, as I was back in the mind frame for Queen and country.

Apart from a couple of calls from our district nursing staff, which often meant they were trying to transfer work from their desk to we GPs in primary care, the rest of the afternoon went without any other major incidents.

I returned home just after Annie, who was in the shower when I arrived. She emerged looking fantastic, with her tanned womanly figure bulging out in all the right places. She knew how to press all the right buttons, that would fill my extremities and she did.

This time however, she didn't rush to envelope me.

Instead she heaved to and sat at the kitchen table, saying, "The Goodalls would like me to go to Southampton for a couple of days as they're opening a new outlet there. Do you mind if I go? They said they'd pay me a big extra bonus for being away from home and that would boost our savings. You don't mind, do you? They're thinking of travelling down there on Sunday for a planning meeting with the local council on Monday. I said I thought it would be all right because I should be back Tuesday night and I won't have to change my work days at the hospital."

What could I say?

So I said, "Be careful, you don't know much about the harsh world of business and people don't get as rich as the Goodalls without having some ruthless qualities to get what they want."

I was beginning to hate the bloody Goodalls, almost kidnapping my wife, without so much as a 'by your leave'!

Still, it immediately occurred to me that it would mean that I could meet up with Sally and use the opportunity to discuss things and perhaps sort out the confusion that was keeping me awake at nights, since our chance meeting in the pub. The next day, I called Sally from the surgery and arranged to meet and go for Sunday lunch. We would meet up with her and drive out to the very nice country pub in the village of Little Shelford.

I was quite anxious about what sort of reception I might receive at this new turn of events, but very rapidly was relieved at the warm enthusiasm she exuded down the phone line. Sunday it was to be then. I put the phone down and felt very elated, which powered my way through the rest of my working day. I arranged to meet in the Botanical Gardens, which shouldn't be too crowded at this time of day and Little Shelford was far enough away, out of town and we weren't likely to run into any of my patients, colleagues or Annie's friends in either place.

Strangely, I thought that I didn't feel guilty for making this liaison. After all, we were just old friends, meeting up to discuss our lives in the period between now and our last brief encounter. Yet why was my heart thumping with excitement? I was a married doctor temporarily at a loose end. Why shouldn't I meet this old friend? It was all above board, yes it was, wasn't it?

39

In the world of government secret services, it was second nature for its members to keep things to themselves, but the new feeling of the blood coursing through my veins and the resulting obvious glow on my face, following that phone call was like a huge advert of intense euphoria. Patients kept commenting on how well I was looking.

I thought, 'Oh crap, I hope Annie doesn't notice me sending off any clues that I now no longer deplored her shooting off to Southampton to work with the Goodalls. In fact, I had fallen into an eager anticipation of the weekend.'

Still, I didn't get to enjoy the euphoria for very long. The next day, I was on the early train to London to New Scotland Yard for the meeting with our colleagues from the security services, the Vice-Chancellor of Cambridge University, the Prof and Paul Bradley. My path didn't cross with Paul's on the train, which gave me some time alone to reflect on the issues arising at our last meeting.

The security services had been tasked with tracking down the other source of the drugs flooding the English countryside. I imagined that they must have done just that, to give rise to this meeting. That was what I was expecting, as I exited the Embankment tube station with just enough time for a bacon and egg sandwich in the snack bar on the way out.

I crossed the road to enter New Scotland Yard, past its world famous sign post into the foyer as Paul Bradley came in from Charing Cross, in the opposite direction. As we checked into reception, with me using my university membership card as I.D., a very large police officer approached us from one side and requested that we go with him in the lift, to be shown to our meeting.

We both complied unquestioningly and went up with him in a very rapid lift, directly to an unlisted floor, designated by a single button on the wall panel. As the lift door opened, we walked out and into the plushest office I could have imagined.

We were greeted by another very large policeman who ticked us off his clipboard checklist and said, "Come with me gentlemen."

We followed again and were led along several long corridors until he stopped, stood to attention and banged on a large door marked 'The Committee Room'. It was opened and we were shown in. As we scanned the room for signs of friendship, our ever demure professor stepped forward and with a gentle wave of his hands, silenced the throng.

"Ladies and gentlemen, may I introduce two of my esteemed medical colleagues, Mr. Paul Bradley and Dr Michael Taylor. He continued and introduced us to the others present that included the Home Secretary, the Metropolitan Commissioner of Police, K from MI5, a Chief Superintendent from Special Branch and Detective Chief Inspector Greenwood and last but not least, the Vice-Chancellor from Cambridge University and Master of Downing College, who, we gathered later, had just been made a Lord of the Realm, for his services to medicine and as the Queen's Physician."

I quietly thought to myself, 'I wonder what might happen if he ever got her diagnosis wrong, but he probably never did.'

The Prof continued, "Gentlemen, we've invited you here, at such short notice, as we have become aware that there have been some very serious developments concerning the security of our country. I'd like to again call on Chief Inspector Greenwood of Special Branch to bring us up to date with these events. Please continue, Chief Inspector."

Robin got to his feet and commenced his report.

"Ladies and gentlemen, I have to report that we have invested considerable man power in our efforts to track down the importation and supply of the massive flow of illicit drugs into Britain."

"We have had several major successes in stopping and seizing drugs from the huge operation supplying the shipments into the major city centres from where it is networked everywhere via the national transport services, young school age traffickers and Mules all over the country. However, I must re-iterate that we are being hampered by the central government's rehabilitative sentencing policies.

"We frequently see that known drug dealers, who being caught in operations, undertaken at great risk to the police service and then after a successful prosecution, are being given very trivial prison sentences, at the behest of the government. These are un-reforming and quickly free them to revert to their former drug-dealing trades."

I saw the Home Secretary grimace at Robin's censure.

"Unhappily, one such case that will concern you and your team deeply Professor, is the daughter of the East German Missile Scientist. As you are aware, considerable effort was undertaken to shut down the local drug line that infected the area where she and her parents lived and the dealers involved were banged up for period deemed appropriate by the courts."

I could feel myself welling with anxieties for the dreadful news that he was impart, I thought I would explode waiting for him to tell us all!

"I am very sorry to report that, as soon as the local dealer had been released from her rehabilitating and reforming prison sentence, she immediately re-contacted her suppliers and got straight back into her local trade, supplying all the schools in her local area, including the college of Miss Hoffmann. It is with deep regret that I have to report to you that Miss Hoffmann was again persuaded to partake of her former habit and as a result of this, succumbed to an overdose of opiates.

"She was discovered by her parents, where she was lying beside her bed, with the opiate hypodermic still embedded in her arm. Her parents, understandably were broken and as a result have left their employment in the British Weapons Industry and moved back to West Germany, where the government and the courts have a different attitude to combatting illicit drugs. Dr and Frau Hoffmann feel they can no longer bear to live in the West that took their daughter away from them and shattered their lives.

"They are hopeful that a new member of the Russian hierarchy, Mr. Mikhail Gorbachev might have a different attitude to the post war carve up of Germany. They hope that one day they might be able to return to their homeland in East Germany and forget what happened to them here in the free West. I fully realise gentlemen that this must be a great disappointment to your team and to you in particular Dr Taylor, as we are aware of your personal input to her rescue and rehabilitation. I am very sorry to have to pass on such news."

I was totally shocked and devastated, how could this have been allowed to happen. She was in the fullness of youth, a girl who had so much promise and so much to offer. I couldn't imagine what this had done to her parents, who had come here for a better life, for themselves and their daughter and with so much to offer us in the West.

Their rescue had cost the lives of a number of people and now it had all been blown away by a number of scum bags who had no values in life apart from their own particular narcissistic needs, impervious to the greater need and good of others.

I blamed the government who had reneged on law and order, oblivious to the effects of financial cuts and feeble punishments. I could see the horror in the Master's, the Prof's and Paul Bradley's faces. We were all traumatised and I felt particularly let down by the weakness of our judicial system and its ineffective sentencing policies.

We knew that the judiciary wasn't really separate from the executive arm of the government, probably much influenced by the treasury too, that probably persuaded the red silk and white Irmined judges, (7) so that the rest followed without debate.

Mr. Greenwood continued, "We are aware of the main suppliers of this major import line and in our view, we are prepared to undertake a comprehensive operation to shut it down in perpetuity.

"However, with respect to the second source of major illicit supplies in the home counties, as yet we have made little progress. We think that the main dealer is a former British Athlete, himself possibly highly involved in the shipping of drugs from Europe on a grand scale and supplying them through various athletics club outlets across the country. He is well-connected in the sports world and travels over the country to various British club venues and events.

"He's also sometimes involved in organising events; where his disciples spread the drugs gospel. There have already been several overdoses across the country as the strength and efficacy of this new drug source is not well known. However, as yet we know he is quite a small fry and has a lifestyle as such. We don't know who is financing his operation and paying him for his distribution services.

"We know he is a petty dealer and that he, his family and friends have done time and have the connections to distribute their trade. However, we also know that they don't have the necessary funds to bankroll this big-time operation. We know his is definitely not the financier. We are currently tailing him and his associates to try and find where the cash is coming from and how they are getting drugs into the country. We are sorry to bring you these bad tidings, but hope our intense surveillance of these perpetrators will reap some benefits in the near future."

The professor thanked Mr. Greenwood and then relinquished the floor to the Home Secretary who uneasily admitted the government's policies for dealing with the illicit drug industry was failing absolutely. He ended with the promise that he would see to it that it would be part of government agenda for the next session of parliament.

At this point, the master rose to take the floor and demanded what we, the guardians of Britain's security, were willing to do more imminently, to fix the situation and protect the public interest.

Then, K rose to his feet and said, "At the moment, we know who some of the perpetrators are, and I feel that the time is right for us to take the necessary steps to retire them permanently from active duty. This will slow down the drug trade immediately and give our colleagues in Special Branch and MI5 an opportunity to find the 2nd source."

The Chief Superintendent from S.B. loudly applauded this, stating that in emergencies in the past, such sanctions had frequently been undertaken to bring security issues back under control.

K proposed that a team of experts be set in motion to permanently remove the known guilty individuals completely from circulation. This was readily unanimously agreed and vociferously supported with 'hear hears'. The whole idea was thereby decided. Britain could no longer entertain the idea of waiting for justice from the judiciary.

We were a quasi-arm of the executive and had to deliver it swiftly and with extreme prejudice, to save our society. The Home Secretary took up the offer to convey these conclusions to the Cabinet and expedite the necessary arrangements as soon as possible.

The meeting was closed by the Home Secretary, stating that we would all be informed as to when these Sanctions Operations could commence and Paul and I left to make our way back to Cambridge where we were to watch and wait, to witness the results of this decision, whereby considerable numbers of somewhat shady people would suddenly disappear without explanation.

Our journey back to Cambridge was for the large part in silence. Both Paul and I were utterly shocked that an important government action to rescue the scientists had been thwarted, by such moronic criminals, who were totally in the dark about the security implications of their drug dealing, the disastrous effects on the rescued East German families and the dire consequences that were about to befall themselves.

They would probably never know either, as for them retribution would be swift and relentless. It was war, albeit undeclared war and the government would now be acting decisively to defend its citizens.

'So be it,' I thought to myself remembering the fate of the lovely Frieda Hoffmann. I hated these animals and thought the sooner our society was rid of them, the better. The regular rhythm of the train's wheels then led me to slip into a light REM sleep, where I dreamed that I was walking in the country in conversation with Sally Rawlings, until I was suddenly awakened by Paul Bradley shaking my arm on our arrival.

"Do you mind if we walk for a while?" he asked. Michael, "I don't know about you, but I feel like I need to discuss the implications of what we've just witnessed and agreed in that meeting. I'm slightly uneasy about a Star Chamber kind of approach to dealing with the drug problem in Britain today. I have concerns about what might happen to our society when we bypass the rule of law. Who decides where it will stop and who watches over the watchers?"

I understand that society is under siege and we are at war with these perverse forces in society; but it is an undeclared war and should we not be trying to achieve the same results democratically though our representatives in parliament.

We were walking towards Mill Road, where I'd taken Sally Rawlings to the Chinese restaurant all those years before, which brought her pleasantly back into my mind again. However, this wasn't the time for such pleasantries, as Paul needed to talk, so I answered him.

"Have we not been briefed by our security service about the dire situation our society is facing. The Home Secretary confirmed this and that our democratic processes are not coping with the situation. These are the experts we empower to watch our society's back. I suspect it has to be we who decide in ultimo. Yes, as silent guardians of our society, we guide the executive into this action and it will probably be us who will decide when Britain is safe and call off the war."

I surprised myself by what I was saying, convincing Paul and possibly myself that it was time to take a much harsher stand. It must have been the thought of lovely Frieda that fuelled my unusual impromptu verbosity.

We walked on through the busy Friday afternoon, until I realised I ought to get back home in time to greet Annie on her return from work. I hoped we could enjoy the evening together before she inevitably had to pack and prepare for her time away with the Goodalls. I said farewell to Paul, hailed a cab and arrived home just in time to greet her on her return from Addenbrookes. She was her old self, rushing up the stairs to where I waited on the landing and hugged me tightly, allaying any jealous doubts in my mind.

"How was your day?" she enquired, mine was hectic. "The wards were packed with neurological disaster patients, admitted and awaiting surgical interventions, to stave off their deaths."

"You mustn't let your work make you unhappy. You know your neurosurgeons quite often pull their patients back from the brink. Let's have a relaxing evening here tonight and make it an early night, I want something to remember you by, when you shoot off with them on Sunday."

I was determined not to let my horrible morning at the in Scotland Yard or her pending departure, interfere with our home life. We had until Sunday before she was due to depart for Southampton in her new role in the Goodall's employ.

I instinctively had some considerable misgivings that my wife of under a year's duration, was very enthusiastic and possibly a touch over-enthusiastic about going away to work with people she and in fact we, knew very little about. She seemed infatuated by their huge amount of wealth and their obsession for accumulating even more. I wanted to warn her about the nature of the business world and how on the whole, it lacked the nobility of a vocation.

Certainly, we in medicine, especially working for the NHS, might through a lifetime of very hard work, obtain a reasonable standard of living. However, it would never in a month of Sundays, reach the levels or life styles of the Goodalls of this world.

Still I bet they never enjoyed the unique and immeasurable pleasure of diagnosing and curing a very ill patient or restarting the heart of a cardiac arrest victim. These capabilities and rewards could not be found in business and were more usually located in the hearts and minds of we in the medical profession. I thought to myself, I'd rather be a poor medic than a rich arsehole.

Annie might be slightly covetous of their existence, but I was reasonably certain she loved me more than their wealth and she showed this regularly, giving me her whole self when we made love. I knew for certain she wasn't faking that.

Yes, that was it, if I was feeling a bit jealous, I knew how I could re-boost my faith in my wife and re-nourish her love for me in the best way I knew how. I pulled her towards me, reaching down over her soft and curvaceous buttocks crushing her flat tummy into mine as I stood astride her. She lifted her face up and closed her lips over my throat, caressing gently as she advanced her mouth up to mine, locking together and pressing her tongue deep inside sucking the very air out of me.

We kissed with such passion, I didn't feel it as her hands began deftly to unfasten my belt and trousers until reaching inside, she enveloped my manhood coaxing it forwards, as she crouched down to gently suck on my glans while cupping my scrotum and massaging my prostate with her finger tips. She stood up and led me into our bedroom with me stepping out of my clothes on the way.

At the foot of the bed, she let go of me stretching both arms up high while I unbuttoned her blouse and unhooked her bra, shedding sunlight onto her breasts with their nipples pointing proudly skywards. They were challenging me to latch onto them. My mouth caught them briefly as she lay back onto the bed opening her legs to pull me deep inside her moistened labia, where I sunk completely up to her cervical canal, making her gasp out loud.

We rocked gently with her pelvic muscles gripping me in perfect unison, pulling me even deeper into her. She moaned louder with each rampant thrust of our loins, as gradually and steadily, we both reached a crescendo of orgasm flooding each other full of juices and collapsing into a hot sweaty pile of spent and literally overflowing love. After that, as we lay there, I knew I didn't need to question her loyalty; She was utterly mine, lock, stock and beautiful barrel.

We lay together asleep until our human sexual appetites gave way to the even more basic appetites of hunger. She disappeared to the kitchen and quickly delivered our supper, which we ate with our bodies as tables and my tongue mopping up any spillages that cascaded over her. Eaten to the full, we again fell asleep in each other's arms glued together by love juices and spilt supper.

We slept in almost till noon, when our consciousness regained, forced us to unstick and peel apart alighting to the shower where we bathed and pruned each other like royalty's ladies in waiting. I relished her perfect body and didn't want her to depart without leave from ablutions.

However, she had to go in order to pack for her trip with the Goodalls and again my mind sunk back into the green pool of jealousy. Was it so important to her to earn some extra cash? I needed her now not in twenty years when we'd paid off the mortgage a couple of years early and we were too knackered to enjoy what was left of our once athletic bodies.

Time seemed to gallop through our Saturday, no sooner had we shopped for food for me while she was away and a few odds and ends she'd need for herself, but the afternoon was suddenly gone, slipping away into the evening for an early supper and we retired early to bed where we hugged each other tightly until sleep finally loosened our clinging hold.

I slept soundly till the harsh barrage of the radio-alarm wrenched us back to life, with very loud Sultans of Swing on Radio 2. Annie leapt out of bed in a flash and was singing in the shower before I'd swung my feet to the bedroom floor. She was showered dressed and down stairs in record time. I came down to join her as she dished up a hearty Sunday breakfast. There is nothing better than a full English and I was determined to enjoy it rather than languish at the thought of her imminent departure to the South.

However, as tempus tends to fugit, it rapidly came round to her driving off to meet up with her new-found wealthy friends. I went to our bedroom window to watch her drive off down the road, round the bend and out of sight. This left me with a rather wary feeling in the pit of my stomach of some impending doom. The inevitability seized my mind that shit will happen and I didn't want it happening to my wife, at the hands of these over-bearing avaricious nouveau riche and self-promoting Baffoons.

40

All at once my wife was gone and I was there alone and feeling slightly downcast; however, that wasn't the case for long, as my mind swiftly turned to the prospect of my rendezvous with another beautiful woman. What a dilemma to have to face, another man would be exceedingly happy to be in my boots.

I wondered how I should deal with her, I was allegedly an intelligent professional man, happily married, but temporarily alone because my wife had gone off to earn some extra cash for our household. I shouldn't be in any way downcast; after all, here was another lovely woman and it had been my idea to meet up with her.

I had loads of things I wanted to discuss with this ephemeral old friend, who was also a very beautiful actress. She had suddenly and briefly brought such pleasure into my life and prematurely vanished and now unexpectedly she was here again.

This unforeseen situation had possibly been instigated by a moment of unreasonable jealousy about my wife's enthusiasm for going away with the Goodalls. However, I knew inside, I was also motivated by the totally delightful woman I was meeting in this hastily and half planned secret liaison.

My mood switched to joy as I decided on how I should deal with this precarious situation, with my mind almost retreating back into my days as a single student.

I decided that I had to tell her the truth, that in the three and a half years since our paths had fleetingly and passionately crossed, I had met and married a lady who was the love of my life. She'd understand, she was a highly intelligent and sensitive artist and there was no reason why I shouldn't meet her and discuss our life histories since our brief and fleeting encounter at the start of my clinical training.

With that in mind, I made my way down to the Backs in the middle of Cambridge, parked in my College Memorial Court and let the porter know I was there. Parking in the middle of the City was a valuable privilege of college members, not to be abused. I was about an hour early, but it was a good walk to the Botanical Gardens.

I thought, as we had been taught by Chief Inspector Greenwood, it's best to be early to assess the surroundings and any individuals who may not be as they seem. Today was different, this wasn't anything to do with security and no-one knew about it except me and lovely Sally Rawlings.

Having parked, I walked down Trumpington Street towards the Botanical Gardens Brookside Gate, I wondered whether she'd be there; after all, we hadn't really communicated for several years. Why would she want to go out of her way to meet me, when I'd ignored her existence for more than quite a long time.

All of a sudden, there she was, in her cashmere grey top, light grey mini-skirt and Chanel Pumps, her blond hair up and tied neatly behind in a bun. My God she looked fabulous! Other mortal men were walking past with their eyes locked on to her. I wondered how they had managed to avoid collisions or walking straight into the Lily Pond, but I thought their situations forbade them staring too long. I walked directly to her, entranced by her alluring gravity that pulled me towards her.

She looked up and said in all innocence, "Hello, I wondered if you'd come here today. I didn't know what to expect. I mean I'm glad you're here and very relieved because, I didn't know whether you'd actually be here. I mean I was uncertain whether you might not want to, after the other night when you were there with your noisy friends. I thought they'd spurred you on and maybe you wouldn't be terribly willing."

How could anyone be unwilling, as she stood before me clearly slightly anxious but totally gorgeous, oozing beneficence and overflowing with pure beauty to the nth degree. In one instant I was back at my very first days at the clinical school, when I first met her, with her huge grey-blue eyes staring up at me almost in anticipation that I might pull her directly into my arms, reminiscent of our first night together.

Good Lord, I wanted to but felt I had to say something in response to her anxiety.

"Of course, I'm willing. I seem to remember it was my idea to meet. I couldn't just let you walk out of the pub that night and let you disappear for another three and a half years. I have so much I want to say to you, like how frequently you've occupied my mind, stealing me away from my medicine or surgery, that should have held me without interruption."

I bent down and kissed her on both cheeks, like the continentals do and immediately succumbed to the ethereal esters of her perfume. My God, not only did she look a million dollars, she smelt like that too.

"I'm so glad to see you, I was also anxious that you might not show up, and here you are. You look lovely and put these gardens to shame."

"Stop it, you're embarrassing me!" she exclaimed.

"Let's walk," I interrupted, "I want to show you off easily outshining these fabulous exotic flowers." We turned and headed down the West Walk in silence, then in a moment, we both broke the silence almost simultaneously and stopped.

"You first!" she interrupted.

"Are you still acting?"

"Yes, I am. Are you still a medic?"

"Yes, I am. Well, technically, I'm a bit different to that. I'm now a GP in a practice not terribly far from here. Well actually, I'm a GP trainee, with some time left of my training, before I'm let loose on the public. Are these stunted conversations breaking the ice between us?"

"No, I don't feel there's any ice between us. We were very intimate and close, the last time we were alone together. I do feel happy to be here. I feel very safe with you and I can sense that you have goodness within you. I remember being very happy before, when I've been with you and you made laugh, by the things you said and the way you behaved.

"I've thought about you on many occasions since that time and it made me smile and miss you. It's just been the passage of time, where our paths didn't happen to cross, that has put some distance between us, but I do somehow feel very confident about you and that perhaps we could cut through that distance. I think that I might be able to be close to you again. That's why I came today; it wasn't just curiosity, I felt something tangible was there between us, not just the love-making we enjoyed that night we were together."

Somehow, here I was, a married man walking with a beautiful woman, who was not my wife and who was being totally open with me about her feelings.

I was slightly bemused by her frankness and yet I felt happy and relieved by her feelings. She displayed an integrity and nobility in the honesty of her words, when for my part, I hadn't reciprocated with any feelings of my own.

At that point a child on a small bike came towards us wobbling awkwardly. It looked like we might collide, so I grabbed her hand and pulled her in to me avoiding the crash. When it passed, I held on to her and we continued along our path around the lake, hands entwined like two young lovers. She didn't let go as we meandered along, oblivious to any finish line, just holding on to each other.

I asked her about her acting career and she enthusiastically extolled about her life on the boards, waxing lyrically about her parts and plays almost right back to that morning when she left me in my college flat, confining me to my life without her, but engrossed in medicine.

Throughout her story, she held on to my hand as if it was the natural thing to do, with our arms swinging between us in unison, as we walked towards the Hills Road Gates of the gardens.

We stopped as we approached the gates, with a group of Asian tourists flooding in before us. In stopping, with our hands still entwined, she swung round towards me and face to face, I couldn't stop myself and pulled her forwards, closing on her mouth and we embraced.

It felt like the right thing to do, like an overdue reunion of the long-lost lovers that we were. It was a hard, enduring and consuming kiss, with neither of us eager to finish. She felt divine with her pelvis enveloped by mine and our lips locked like limpets in a low tide. She smiled up at me as she stepped backwards.

"I'm sorry," I babbled, "That was very forward!"

"I didn't protest, did I?"

"No, you didn't, but it was forward! Why don't we try it again? We can do it better," as she stepped forward looking up into my eyes.

I couldn't resist her overwhelming beauty and sunk into her, totally forgetting my earlier intentions and abandoning all hope of redemption. We kissed most passionately, with utter surrender, unhurried and sensuous, our tongues delving deep inside, urging each other's senses to a complete arousal.

We were lost in each other, impervious to others, until the Asian tourists burst into a spontaneous and tumultuous applause, wrenching us back to reality. We both turned towards them, gave a polite bow and exited the gardens laughing to the sound of their cheers.

Once outside in Hills Road, she turned to me and said, "Let's go back to my place, it's not far from here and we can talk. I'd like to make lunch for you and we can eat in together, without the publicity of a pub lunch in Shelford."

"Ok, that would be great," and we walked the short distance hand in hand, immersed in each other, once again like two carefree young lovers, which was, of course, what we weren't!

Along the way, people we saw smiled at us, as if we were a perfect couple. I didn't understand how my mind wanted us to just be that couple and live for that happy moment of existence. I was ignoring the startling truth, that I couldn't have her, I wasn't free. I had a wife, who was away, working on our behalf, helping to build our life together.

In a matter of minutes, we'd reached her flat and she exclaimed, "Here we are, don't be put off, it's not a palace but it's my place and you are very welcome to be here."

She slipped a key from somewhere and opened the door to her maisonette, on the top half of a house, which had been converted to a two bedroomed flat, with its own entrance and stairway. She bounded up the stairs in front of me, charged into her living room and spinning round towards me, enveloped me in a tight hug and another ravenous kiss that again raised my ardour by its intensity.

Against my overpowering urges, I pulled back and said "This is very cosy, is there more?"

"Yes, of course, come and have the guided tour!"

I felt I had to distract her and ignore my tremendous natural intentions to be dragging her off to her bedroom. She'd already noticed my tumescent response to her passionate embrace and was homing in for un coup de grace.

Against all my animal senses, I rushed off towards what I took to be her bathroom and heard her head off into another room behind me. She shouted after me that she often wondered what I might think about where she actually lived. While I pee'd, I shouted that I thought it was great.

I washed my hands and swilled tap water around my dried mouth, which slowed my rapid heartbeat and unstuck my tongue. I opened the door to step out and there she stood, dressed entirely in black silk lingerie that clung continuously to her moistened skin and holding me in her beautiful wide steely blue eyes.

She calmly said, "I hoped you would like it. Would you like to come and see some more?"

"Yes, I think I would," and with that, she took my hand and led me through to her bedroom.

My mind was totally focused on the rear curves of her exquisite body, as she flowed across her floor to the edge of her bed before me. She still had that same grace that bewitched me that first day, when I met and examined her at the hospital.

She turned and gently pulled me into her arms, holding me against her soft and succulent breasts, abdomen and pelvis. She pushed her nose and mouth gently into my neck, caressing me as she 'ummmed' into my ear. Her hands slipped behind to the back of my waist band and she clenched both buttocks massaging them up and down.

I felt them slide round forwards into my groin, where she unzipped me and sliding inside, she gripped the length of my manhood, releasing it from captivity to stand headfirst against her belly, moistened by my leaking seminal fluid, it slid down into her wetted and welcoming cave. She gasped as I sunk into her until the waist bands of our coverings dragged me back.

We fell onto her bed and her legs separated and sinking inwards, I brushed past her labia with my pulsing glans and she let out a gasp. She reached out ripping down my obstructing briefs releasing the ultimate depth of my phallus as we rocked back and forth onto her G spot on the anterior wall of her vagina, making her cry out with joy.

My mind was awash with total pleasure as we rocked together as one. I couldn't focus on anything else, just the intense release of overwhelming endorphins driving us on harder and harder, depolarising the millions of penile and vaginal nerves until we erupted together sensationally, leaving us floating in our wash of fluid, silent in mutual exhaustion.

41

After a while, Sally broke the silence with a giggle and she laughed out loud saying, "Now, that was really, really very forward."

"Yes, it was," I replied, "But forward or not, it was sensational, no you were sensational. I have thought about you many times over, during our time apart. Now though, it doesn't seem that long, being so bound up with my life in medicine that time has just flown by so rapidly."

I thought now was the time I must tell her about my personal and private life, that I'd become a doctor and how I was now with my wife Annie. Somehow, I just couldn't; she was so happy and so lovely, lying there in my arms, happy, wide-eyed and wonderful. I couldn't ruin it and wrench her back to a terrible reality.

She looked up at me and exclaimed, "I don't know about you but I'm starving. I couldn't eat this morning, I was so anxious about meeting you, or I mean possibly not meeting you! What can I get you to eat? I have a fridge full of food. Come and see!"

With that, she leapt out of bed and ran off to the kitchen, with me in hot pursuit. She opened her fridge and started pulling out her provisions.

"What about a nice steak with salad and chips and a lovely wine? I want to feed you up, so I don't wear you out."

"Don't worry, docs have to have a great deal of stamina; but I do feel a bit peckish and that sounds really good," I replied as I sneaked back to her bedroom and started to put on my clothes.

Once more, I was utterly replete, totally satisfied and totally guilty. How had I let this happen? It wasn't fair on her. I should have stopped it, as I'd meant to do when I came out of her bathroom earlier.

Yes, earlier, now suddenly an unredeemable time ago; but how could I stop it, for that matter, how could anyone? No individual with "X and Y" chromosomes could have resisted her lovely face and the sight of her body, as they opened the bathroom door to experience that vision of a perfect and sensual feminine anatomy.

I was a man, with normal male hormones and responses. It wasn't all entirely my fault, she was the one who was forward, but I'd involuntarily shown her that I was up for it too, by my physical responses to her advances. I should have stopped it then, without responding at all; but I just couldn't help it she was just so irresistible and gave my shrinking resistance no mercy.

Furthermore, it was well known that an erect penis has no conscience. She is a highly sophisticated adult and must have surely known that. I felt bad about feeling good about these sexual events and didn't know how to proceed, but all those endorphins sure felt really good inside me.

I took what I thought to be her silk dressing gown though to the kitchen with me and she slid into it in one graceful movement, filling it to perfection. Like her lingerie which enhanced the sensuality of her olive tanned skin. I could have eaten her where she stood and probably might have done but for the sizzling steak on the pan. She spun round and caught me gazing at her, smiling at my blatant adoration.

"Be a darling and get some wine opened, there's a Faustino 1 Rioja in the larder, which will be perfect with the steak if we let it chambré for a while."

Blimey, I thought, she really was sophisticated.

She shook up the salad, deep fried some chips and in a moment Tournered and Glissered, like a ballerina to serve up lunch onto her table in one graceful floating movement.

I stumbled in opposite her and poured the red wine as my humble offering to the proceedings. We ate and drank heartedly, clearing the plates and devouring the fabulous Rioja.

Afterwards, she leaned back in her chair, fixed me in her gaze and politely posed the question, "Well, I've told you all about me, may I ask about what other things you've been up to for these past few years?"

My mind suddenly raced back to extraordinary events of my clinical course, my world in the security service, my life as a doctor and finally and reluctantly my thoughts halted at my wife and my married life. Yes, now was the time. I had to come clean. I dreaded the effect it might have on her. I didn't want to hurt her and had very strong feelings for her.

She had been so straightforward and open about her feelings and with no hesitation she'd exposed a tremendous vulnerability about those feelings concerning her career and about me in particular.

I hurriedly blurted out, "Sally, I have to tell you that I'm actually married."

She stopped in mid-motion, rigid to the spot. Her face paled while her pupils dilated and tears welled up glistening her eyes and flowing over her cheeks.

"I thought that you may be, I didn't think someone like you would stay alone for very long. Millions of women would chase you and strive to get you into their arms. You have what women want, and look at me, I came to meet you today, already realising that you probably wouldn't be free; but I came any way and I was right, you are taken and not free. This is not your fault, I'm here also. I invited you up here because I wanted you, no more than that, I hungered for you and needed to make love to you passionately!"

She had certainly achieved that, every muscle in my body ached from her passion as I stood there looking stupid, still in my boxer shorts. I wanted to rush forward and hug her, as she looked totally serene and eloquent in her total acceptance of my situation. I stepped forward but she stretched out her hand to thwart my advance towards her.

I stopped and muttered, "I'd better go," retreating to her bedroom to finish dressing in a fruitless effort to regain some self-composure.

She remained where she was, motionless in the impotence of her sudden bereavement of my loss in her life. I dressed quickly and in leaving said that I hadn't meant to hurt her and that I had been overwhelmed by my desire for her and that my feelings for her had been genuine and heartfelt. She remained silent and stared ahead as I passed her and made my way out down the stairs to the outside.

I walked back towards the city centre, past Peterhouse and Kings to Senate House, where I'd graduated oh so honourably, so resplendent with my cap and gown and ermine hood, just a few years before. That was not how I felt now, I was ashamed that I had clearly injured this lovely woman, who had lifted my emotions to extreme heights and shaken my marriage to its foundations.

I thought about Annie and what my infidelity would do to her, how my behaviour would affect my position within the practice and what homiletic Geoffrey and his stuffy wife Jacqueline might think. Finally, I thought about letting down the Prof, who was ever a very honourable man. I walked through my college Old Court, crossed the Cam and back to my car and drove home in silence, unable to look in the car mirror as my image would nauseate me.

I couldn't get her image out of my mind, she was so beautiful even in her sadness, I wanted to go back and hold her to myself and not let her go, but I couldn't. I'd made my proverbial bed and now had to lie in it.

Annie would be back in a couple of days and I had to get on with my life in our home and wait for her arrival. I had plenty to keep me busy and though I went to bed weary, I couldn't sleep at all. The images of Annie and Sally kept flashing across my dream REM sleep mind, denying me any hope of restful sleep.

The alarm wrenched me up in the morning and I went off to the surgery utterly confused about myself and my feelings towards the two women, stored firmly in the front of my brain. They screwed up my thoughts and aborted any hope of objective medicine. I went to my room and sat at my desk staring ahead as one of the receptionists brought in a cup of tea and my box of patient notes.

"Are you all right?" she asked observing my silent unresponsiveness.

"Er, yes, of course, just rather a hectic weekend, Annie was going away so we had to prepare for that," I replied assuredly. "Can you send in my first patient?"

She did and away I went into first gear, working my way through multiple signs and symptoms across the Monday morning. I found I was pausing between patients my mind racing back to the intense pleasure I'd experienced not twenty-four hours before.

I found I was quietly hyperventilating just thinking about Sally, her sensuous body and silky-smooth tanned skin. It was true that ultra violet light was good for her psoriasis, as there were no signs of it that I could see. She must have been away, probably lying on a beach somewhere.

Lucky beach, I thought to myself, then quickly re-focused on my patient list. I called in the next one, desperately trying to put Sally out of my head, to be more professional and consider my patient and their presenting complaint, rather than a beautiful, highly intelligent and sensitive woman who would make any man happy for the rest of his life.

I thought back to my days in psychiatry and immediately decided I'm madder than the patients that I used to section for being where I was, rather than with that woman I should really be with!

42

By the end of morning surgery, I didn't feel like talking to anyone, so I made my excuses and headed off into Cambridge and quite by accident, found myself in a café at the end of Mill Road, near the corner with Parker's Piece sports field. I sat alone staring ahead in a trance, over a coffee.

It was about a ten-minute walk from Sally's place and I was seriously mulling over whether I could go back there to try to somehow ameliorate the diabolical situation that I left there, less than a day before. I was lost in thought blindly staring out of the window looking through the traffic, as it queued up outside to get onto the roundabout joining Parker's Piece, the huge green in the centre of Cambridge.

That was when I saw her, there in the queue, in the huge open topped Bentley. Yes, it was her, you couldn't miss the Bentley, but what was she doing there? Was I mistaken? It couldn't be Mrs. Goodall, she was supposed to be in Southampton at a planning meeting with the local council. The car was gone in an instant and suddenly my world was in total confusion. Was that really Janet Goodall? Had they come back early?

I needed to find out what was going on. She was supposed to be with my wife and her husband on the South Coast. Why was she here? I rapidly left the café and headed back to where I'd parked my car in the new health centre, that used to be the old Maternity Hospital. I jumped in my car and drove off in the opposite direction towards Addenbrookes Hospital to head South on the A10 towards Granchester.

I wanted to get there to park up somewhere in a vantage point and out of the way. From where I could wait and watch the entrance to the Goodall's Drive, to see if it really was her and if so, what was she doing there and why was she not in a meeting in Southampton.

I soon got my answer. It was her and here she was turning into her drive, in her massive luxury car without a care in her world. I was suddenly overcome with paranoid doubts and suspicions. Perhaps she never went to Southampton, leaving my wife with her husband alone together. No, it can't be that, they'd probably achieved their objectives early and Annie was back as well, waiting at home as I sat there.

That was it, Annie was at home eagerly waiting for me. All thoughts about Sally Rawlings were suddenly whisked away, as my own shameful vulnerability came into focus and I had to get back home to check up on my own family life, to see whether indeed there was a threat to it.

The thought that Annie must be at home relieved me as I sped off back towards Cambridge where I'd find her waiting. I put my foot down heading North up the A10 back into the city, ignoring the speed limit, urged on inside me to find my wife where she ought to be. I pulled up outside our home and there was no sign of her car. I let myself in, still believing that she must be inside.

I called out, but there was no answer. I walked up the stairs in case she hadn't heard me, but she wasn't there.

Again, I was plagued by the unknown suspicions running across my Watcher's mind. Where was she, and where was that Goodall man? I wondered what my options were. I could get my Special Branch friends to track down her car for me, but I didn't want anyone knowing about my own deserved insecurities. Why was I so suspicious? Was I being unnecessarily paranoid?

There was no real tangible reason to be so. The only possible reason was perhaps her slight over enthusiasm for going away to help them and maybe her "a bit too frequent" wishes to join them for those repetitive heart burning Chinese meals.

When in doubt, I considered that doing nothing was my best option, after all, she was due to return the next day and she surely would do so and it wasn't that long to wait. However, on my way back, I decided that the more information I could acquire the better, that's what my Watcher colleagues would quite rightly advocate and that would be the better option!

I planned that I would go back to the Granchester after dark, keep a watch on the Goodall's house and look to see if her husband was there or even wait in case he'd show up. This I did, parking in the local Red Lion Pub car park, next to the meadow where we had spent many a perfect afternoon picnicking, having punted up the Cam in my college punt laden with food, wine and a posse of lovely ladies.

From the car park, I quietly made my way to the Goodall's, walked up the drive to their house and spied through their huge windows. I could see Janet there inside all alone, but there was no Philip to be seen anywhere. In frustration, I left and made my way home most perturbed by what I hadn't found. I didn't sleep at all, floating in a sea of self-doubts. I felt maybe it was some sort of irony, paying me back for my earlier em-passioned love-making with Sally.

The Red Lion pub just above the picnic meadow

As the sun dawned on Tuesday, I dragged myself up and out the door to work. Again, unknown to my patients, I was totally unable to concentrate on their various problems or diseases. This was terrible, because my totally selfish sexual indulgence with Sally had left me ridden with guilt and unable to deal rationally with my wife's absence.

I tried in vain to clear it out of my head and decided I would go back to Granchester and wait for Annie to return later, as expected. I calculated how long they would take to cover the journey and left my surgery in time to get to my hidden vantage point and watch out for their arrival.

Again, I didn't have to wait too long, and in the distance, I saw Annie's Golf car approaching. I could see her and Philip Goodall laughing inside. They passed my position and slowed to a stop quite close to his driveway entrance. They both got out of her car smiling and chatting and walked round to open its boot.

My heart was thumping rapidly in my chest and I wanted to rush out and greet them, but I froze as he leaned forward, pulled her into him and kissed her passionately enveloping her in his arms, crushing her into him like he didn't intend to let go. From where I was standing, neither of them wanted to let go.

I was suddenly devastated, paralysed in silence, as if I'd been shot, purblind by emotion. I was left breathless by its duration. Suddenly, he turned away, reaching into the boot to extract his luggage, he turned and strode into his drive. She in turn climbed into her Golf and reversing her car, she turned it back towards me and passing, headed back to Cambridge.

A man with his dog walked towards me and must have seen how shocked I was. He asked me if I was all right. For a moment, we stood in silence, then my eyes filled with tears and I sobbed there in front of that complete stranger. He approached me possibly about to try to comfort me, but I waived my hand back and forth, shaking my head to say no.

Instead, I just said to him, "Don't worry, I've had a bit of a shock."

With that, I returned to the pub car park, got into my car and left, feeling totally broken.

I don't remember my drive back, but I ended up in the Memorial Court car park of my college, staring ahead of me and not seeing the students walking past nodding hello to me and thinking how rude I was to ignore them. That was until one of them came up to my driver's side and tapped on the window.

"Are you alright doc? You look a bit lost."

I recognised one of my patients, who was also an undergraduate medical student member of my college. How right he was, I thought. He'd be a good and observant doctor one day.

"Yes, I'm OK, thanks. I was just on my way home gathering my thoughts making sure I hadn't forgotten anything."

With that I started my car and headed out of the college, onto the Backs and off to home. I didn't know what I might encounter there or how Annie was going to be, or what she might want to say, or have to say, or whether she would stay or leave or what?

Ten minutes later, I arrived back home and sure enough there was her car. I pulled in behind her, walked up the path and let myself in the door. Somehow this time it felt different. There was no longer the urgent anticipation I felt the last time, when I'd just returned from Camberley.

I shouted out, "Hello, where are you?"

It felt something like that the first time, when I felt a bit anxious in case some other young man had moved in on her while I was away. This time when I looked up the stairs, she wasn't there looking down on me. She called out from the bedroom and I climbed the stairs expecting I didn't know what. On the landing, she approached me smiling to greet me and we embraced on the lips but this time, without passion but with the brevity and affection of a fond friend with the lost urgency of a past love.

I stood back to gaze at her veritable beauty, but this time she didn't elevate her eyes towards me. Instead, almost looking at her feet, she embarked on a diatribe of the details of a planning application, which was totally incomprehensible to me and inappropriate for the moment.

I moved forward and stood in front of her again, causing her to look up at me eye to eye.

I stepped back and said, "I know."

She looked like she was about to speak, but froze in mid-breath, lifting her head, she moved towards me and mumbled that she was sorry. I lifted my right hand to stop her in her tracks and she flinched as though she thought I might strike her. I had the presence and clarity of mind to drop my arm, not that I would have struck her anyway.

I turned and walked away into our bedroom, sat on the bed with my head in my hands totally bereft and at a complete loss as to what to do. She was left standing on the landing and I heard that about one second later, she must have dropped to her knees, erupted into tears and rapidly degenerated into a sobbing mess.

I didn't know how to respond to this, but I had to do something. There I was, a dishonourable adulterous doctor, feeling broken and destitute having discovered that my exquisitely beautiful and loving wife had also been dishonourable and adulterous too!

It actually was a very ironic situation, in which we both co-existed, which had it not been quite so far-reaching, would have been quite comical, like a West End farce.

I walked out onto the landing, knelt down in front of her and wrapped her in my arms and patted her gently and reassuringly. After all, what kind of pot was I, to even consider calling this kettle black and feeling distinctly like I was living in a glass house, after my activities over the last forty-eight hours, I wasn't going to be throwing any stones at anyone.

Between her sobs and my pats, she looked up at me dolefully and unthinkingly I asked, "Why?"

That started her sobbing loudly again and then in between breaths she said, "I don't know why; his wife decided she didn't want to come with us and yesterday, we were alone all day at the meeting and later again, at the hotel in Southampton. The meeting with the council, had gone very well. We had dinner and probably had too much to drink and when we went up to our rooms, he asked if he could come in for a coffee. It seemed alright, so I said Yes.

"After that, it all just seemed to flow along. Then without realising it, one thing led to another and in the next minute, we were kissing and fell on to my bed and that was it. I didn't set out to sleep with him, it just happened and at the time, it felt like it was the right thing to do. I didn't set out to hurt you and didn't want to, it just happened. I don't love him, I love you. You're my husband, I don't want him, I want you and I want to stay with you as my husband, if you still want me."

What could I say to her? My clothes in the laundry box possibly still had the bouquet of the beautiful woman I'd left just about forty-eight hours before. My head was full of mixed feelings. Some were sound and forgiving and some were totally uncivilised, aimed towards the arrogant, rich and unethical tosser, who had been screwing my wife.

I wanted to kill the bastard very painfully and make him suffer for the way he had used Annie and de-stabilised my marriage; notwithstanding my own despicable and undisclosed behaviour in this very sad and ironic scenario.

I was still uncertain as to what to do. I felt betrayed, but had I not betrayed her? Yes I had, and here I was with a beautiful woman in my arms, who was my wife, partner for life with whom I had planned to procreate. Was I going to let this arrogant semi-illiterate oaf close a curtain on my life plans? No, I bloody wasn't. My stubborn working class values wouldn't let that rich moron have his own way with my family!

I held her face in my hands and elevated her chin up towards me and said, "I love you, too. He doesn't deserve you. You're far better than he is. You're mine and you belong to me, not that moron."

With that, I lifted her face up and kissed her.

"If you want; we'll avoid these 'Oyks' from now on and we'll be together, like we should. Are you up for that?"

She looked up again and said, "Yes."

At this stage, I didn't have any idea as to what I should do. I knew that I didn't want to lose my wife to this rich patronising bastard. I knew that I definitely felt tremendous animosity towards him for sleeping with her, but I knew it took two to tango. Annie went off to shower and left me contemplating how I was going to deal with the moronic lothario.

She returned after a while and we went to bed where I held her all night, some of which, she was weeping and repeatedly saying she was sorry.

I actually believed that she was. My stint as a psychiatrist had equipped me to read people and to know when someone was lying and she definitely wasn't. To this day, I'm sure she was overwhelmed, possibly by his immense wealth or may be the way he negotiated with the Southampton Council to build his new business outlet there, or possibly by his overt overconfident and crass behaviour, promising her almost anything to impress the common sense right out of her.

Some people may be impressed by such a devious display of narcissistic power. Well, I was about to show him that I could be powerful too and I laid awake all-night planning on how I was going to deal with him.

I thought I was well aware of how to use weapons and could just buy a gun and dispatch him to hell, one dark night after he arrived back at his house. Then I remembered, hell I'm a doctor and I've spent all my adult life learning how to heal people and I wasn't going to betray my ethics and beliefs for that miserable specimen.

I decided that in my position, all I could do was to let him know that I knew and that my wife had confessed everything to me and never wanted to see him again and if he tried to go anywhere near her, I would see to it that he would be ruined financially. I couldn't really do any more than that without degrading myself.

In the morning, I told Annie what I'd decided to do and she didn't take any persuading to agree. She didn't want him to come between us and be able to ruin our way of life. She had no idea of my secret life and the level of influential connections that I could call on to prevent this individual from preying on society. I left it like that, as it was far better to be seen as a gentle and conscientious doctor than some gun-wielding killer.

I found Philip Goodall's contact details from his surgery notes and called him. I could tell he was totally surprised to receive a call from me, but feigned pleasantries, which I didn't exchange with him. I informed him that Annie had told me what went on in Southampton and didn't want anything further to do with him. I heard him gasp and he went silent on the end of the phone. I also said if he attempted to contact her again, I would ruin him and that I was in a position to do so. I was tempted to threaten him physically, but in my position, I felt that it would bring me down to his level and I wouldn't do that. I felt we needed to get on with our lives and didn't need to consider this dullard again.

I felt strangely relieved afterwards and somewhat superior, that I wasn't bothered by the fact that he would get away with undermining our marriage and private lives. He might be looking over his shoulder for the rest of his days wondering what kind of revenge might befall him. I just didn't want to waste my time and energies with a twat like that and had my very busy life to get on with, besides, I never really liked Chinese food anyway.

In the next couple of days, I went straight home from work and spent the evenings in, being with Annie. We never spoke about her stay on the South coast and gradually, it slipped out of my mind relegated by all the other everyday issues in our lives. She never mentioned going to the gym again and happily in my view, increased her commitment to her working hours in the neurosurgery department.

Our life together somehow quickly became somewhat routine we'd arrive home, dine in, discuss the day, I'd do some surgery work and then we'd retire to bed, where we went to sleep. Somehow, our desires for each other slipped away. I thought that perhaps, she was very anxious about displaying her physical desires after being with Goodall.

On my part, I became thoroughly involved with my life as a G.P., immersing myself into practicing medicine and didn't broach the subject of making love. Instead, I was rapidly becoming a respected member of the local community. It was during this time that I discovered what life in general practice was really about.

43

Not very long after, I received a call from Chief Inspector Greenwood of the Special Branch. He asked if we could meet, as he had some new information that I might be very interested to hear about. He suggested I might like to get out of Cambridge to somewhere I wouldn't run into any patients or anyone who knew me. So we agreed on a pub I knew on the A10 on the Southern corner of the village of Harston.

I arrived there with a few minutes to spare and bought a couple of pints of real ale, took them to a spot in the corner of the pub and sat down just in time to see Greenwood's shock of curly red hair burst into the bar and make his way towards me in hasty enthusiasm.

"Hello doc, thanks for coming. I thought I'd give you the heads up on what's been going on and let you know what's about to happen in the not too distant future. You may not be aware that following our last meeting at the yard, MI5 and 6 have been liaising with each other, for a change and with various police drug agencies over the UK. They've come up with surprisingly very large numbers of illicit dealers across this England's Green and Pleasant Land of ours.

"The agencies are about to embark on the biggest peace time clean up job ever undertaken across Britain to help rid us of this evil trade interrupting our peace and legitimate ways of life. You would have gotten wind of it, when people suddenly start disappearing from around your neighbourhood, commencing in the next couple of weeks. We're intending to start hitting them where it hurts hardest and without mercy. So, I don't need to tell you how there is a need for extreme discretion about this.

"Some of our local teams, on a need to know basis, have been asked to nominate their most serious and unpleasant offenders. We are aiming to eliminate the worst drug sociopaths from around the country in an attempt to redress the balance, save a lot of lives and provide our various forces with time to re-group and eliminate the rest of the massive illicit drug trade throughout Britain.

"In our part of the country, we have been watching a number of locations in London and South East England. We believe we have located a major outlet for imported shipments from Africa, in the Dagenham area of South East London. The drug-dealing operations have occupied a group of houses there, but where all the run-down houses in the block are held by one owner. We have acquired the Land Registry documents and building plans and it seems that the owner is a Nigerian Baptist Minister.

"His ownership is in the name of a Housing Charity for the homeless in the area, which is ironic in that most of the highly vulnerable drug victims around Britain are homeless. However, it appears that without planning permission, this minister has knocked down some of the party walls between some of the buildings in a terrace, providing enough accommodation for a major drug processing, packaging and distribution centre. We know that they are the source of the drug delivery systems supplying towns all over the country.

"During the past month or so, we've managed to install quite sophisticated surveillance equipment in some of the rooms in the houses, including the cellars. We've been quietly monitoring what's going on there, collecting the necessary evidence on the responsible scumbags running it. You'd be surprised at how profoundly decadent some of these animals are.

"There aren't any homeless locals living there at all. Instead, they have several young addicts, mainly females, coming and going and fixing up there, sometimes sleeping over in various degrees of semi-comatose states and sharing their sexual favours with whoever supplies them with their drugs.

"The good Baptist Minister has been seen frequenting the building, occasionally staying overnight, no doubt to pray for the souls of the young people trapped there, and no doubt also partaking of their favours in moments of spiritual weakness. In fact, he is Emmanuel Norton-Brown, well known to the police for dealing drugs and pimping within the black community of East London. He has no ministerial qualifications whatsoever.

"We plan to move in en masse and purge these degenerates permanently, as part of a country-wide operation. I know how personally you'd become involved through the death of that young Hoffman girl and I thought you might like to see hands-on how this was going to be done."

I immediately baulked at the prospect of actually watching the wholesale expunging of these parasites and wasn't really certain about how they were exactly planning to do this. However, I remembered the Hoffmans and felt that I'd been in at the decision to sanction these removals and if I objected, I should have done so at the time. The degenerates had taken over and it was no longer safe for ordinary people to walk the streets.

I could hear myself in the distance, saying, "Yes, thank you. I would be gratefully reassured to see these morons get what's coming to them."

"Right then doc, can you be at Scotland Yard at 08.00 next Friday week? So, we have enough time to get there, see what's been going on from our teams in place and get the ball rolling or to be more precise, get their balls rolling."

"Thanks, Robin. I appreciate your sensitivity about this issue and I feel I ought to be there on behalf of the East German family, who lost their daughter because of these anti-socials. Unofficially, at some stage I may be able to let the Hoffmans know that justice has been done for their daughter, to give their minds some peace."

"No doc, this must never come out, because our actions are entirely illegal and despite our good intentions, the Do-Gooder Liberals in society would paradoxically demand our blood! It could even go all the way up to the top and bring down the government. So, although its entirely necessary for the sake of our society, I have no doubt that our executive will file this away in the public records office until long after we've both shuttled off our mortal coils."

Then, with that rapid but thorough briefing, we both finished our drinks, exited the pub and went our separate ways. On my way back up to Cambridge I wondered whether the Prof and Paul Bradley were aware of these pending operations. They had to be, as they were there at the last meeting in Scotland Yard. Though I still thought I'd better contact them and brief them about the current details and also seek their help in arranging cover for me to witness the operation on the weekend after next.

I thought about Annie's current fragile state and decided it might be politic if I took her away for some time commencing that weekend so we could talk together, recuperate from the present circumstances in our lives and re-kindle our marriage, at least, re-kindle it as much as possible. With this in mind, I did contact them and sure enough, they were both aware of it.

As if he was reading my mind, the Prof suggested that I take some leave from the surgery, commencing the week before the security's operation, to give me some time away with my wife. I suggested to Annie we visit my parents for the week where she could be spoilt and distracted. Then I could invent a reason to escape on the day of the operation and get into Scotland Yard for the action and be back at my parents in the evening without creating any concerns.

The days quickly passed, leading up to me playing witness to part of the national clean up. I made my way on the early train to London, attending a fertility lecture symposium in London as an excuse. I took a taxi to the Yard. We gathered on the special operations floor for the briefing. There were thirty or so officers seated in the hall. I imagine some were from Special Branch, some from MI5 and possibly some from MI6, some were from the Firearms branch of the Met and many I assumed were CID.

We fell silent while the Commissioner of Police embarked on his speech reminding us of the importance of our mission for the security of our country and safety of our people. He reminded us of the vital permanent secrecy of this operation and those who were being bound by the Official Secrets Act for the duration of our lives and for the protection of our families. He wished us luck, thanked us for our participation, asked for 'Any Questions' and walked off the stage, to almost unanimous applause. It was almost like a briefing taken out of a war film, and I suppose we actually were at war.

Robin Greenwood and I made our way South-Eastwards out of London towards Dagenham in an unmarked police car. We arrived at the dismal terraces of what had at some time been a row of council houses. We parked around the corner and were let into a house just out of view of the target terrace.

Inside were several rather mean looking large detectives, who looked like they were packing (carrying weapons). We were approached by one of them, whom I recognised as Detective Sergeant Roberts, from our previous meetings when we dealt with the East German scientists at Cambridge.

He nodded with a welcoming smile and said, "Hello Doc, it's good to see you again; exciting times eh!"

He turned to Robin Greenwood and said, "Robin, we've had an amazing lucky break through. This Vicar bloke, seems to be working with us, He's got hold of a geezer, who he seems to think is a drug-dealing competitor. His buddies have been knocking seven bells out of him for some time trying to get him to spill the beans on his rival operation. So far, the bloke, who looks very well heeled, isn't talking, but we've got bets on how much longer he can hold out.

He's been getting a fairly thorough beating so far. Our chaps are keen to go in there, but they're enjoying watching the bastard suffer."

Greenwood, got very enthusiastic about this, very rapidly.

He responded with, "Say that again Martin. Are you saying that this drug dealing, pimping, imitation vicar has managed to locate and nab another main drug operator in the home counties, when all of our police resources, all over England have come up with zilch? Did he have some sort of divine intervention or something? Come on doc we've got to see this. Where's the video screen?"

We charged through the house with Greenwood in the lead and then all of a sudden, Roberts branched off to lead us triumphantly into a dimmed bedroom with a large bank of television screens. They showed various rooms in the target terrace of houses, one with piles of boxes in what looked like a store room. In another was what looked like a laboratory, with a bench, piles of small plastic bags and a mountain of white powder, which I took to be heroin.

In a third room were a group of men, standing around a seat in their midst, on which was seated another man whose face was looking very swollen and battered. The men were taking it in turns to hit him around the head, with what looked like brass coloured knuckle dusters on their fists.

As I approached the screen, I could hear a man whimpering in pain and begging them to stop. Apart from his extreme distress, his voice timbre sounded somewhat familiar, yet his puffed up, swollen and misshapen face frustrated any recognition.

Then as they struck him again, he cried out, "Alright!" and there it was, that familiar patronising and so condescending posh voice of no less than Phillip Goodall himself.

Except, this time he wasn't so smug and full of himself, he was spitting out his teeth, blood and mucus, spraying his tormentors before him with his bits and fluids.

"My God! It's him," I exclaimed for all to hear.

"Who?" retorted Robin Greenwood.

"He's a patient, I've dealt with in the past, a very very bad man. I personally know what an evil piece of work he is."

"Clearly, I can see how right you are, doc. Let's watch for a while and see what Norton-Brown's interrogators can find out; a lot more than we could, if we had to interview him with his solicitor. It looks like we got here just in time, he's about to blab and give them what they want to know."

With that, we sat back and observed how interviewing was being undertaken outside the regulations of the Police and Criminal Evidence Act(6).

Goodall was crying and begging them not to hurt him again. Through his split and battered mouth, he half-whispered, "What do you want to know?"

"How d'you get your Horse (heroin) into this mother fucking country?"

"In my cars!"

They hit him again and he screamed out, "In the cars I import!"

"Where are your suppliers?"

"Columbia!" he screamed.

"How?" they shouted as they struck him again.

He passed out and his head dropped. They encouraged him again with a bucket of water, which rapidly seemed to bring him out of his stupor.

Greenwood interjected with, "It's a shame we can't use these guys in our interviews for Special Branch."

Goodall responded that pouches of Horse were taped inside the various parts of the cars which he imported for his business, before they were sealed into containers in the Port of Antwerp. The containers are shipped to Kings Lynn in Norfolk, unloaded and carried to his warehouses, where the cars are stripped of their illicit cargo.

He was sobbing as they pressed him for details of drug shipments, how they were distributed around the country, the names and contact details of his main dealers and where he kept the loot generated. For a while, it sounded like a police interview.

Except that this time, when they demanded information, Goodall hesitated for a second, and a hail of blows descended on him, again rendering him unconscious, but this time round, the bucket of cold water failed to return him to consciousness.

His interrogators summoned the Reverend Norton-Brown, who appeared wearing only a dressing gown. While the questioning had been proceeding, the reverend had clearly been helping himself to the fruits of some young addict. When he saw his unconscious rival dealer, he ordered two of his men to bring in the white bitch, he'd just left back in his room.

A few minutes later, the men returned dragging a hysterical woman who was none other than a very bedraggled Janet Goodall, definitely looking very much the worse for wear. She was naked and had sustained bruising to much of her face and body, as well as telltale severe bruising to her thighs, where they had been forced apart for non-consensual sex. The vicar must have been questioning her, while treating her to some of his own romantic rape and pillage.

Norton-Brown said, "This should get the bastard to tell us where all his cash is hiding."

Goodall was gradually recovering consciousness with a further bucket of water assisting in attracting his attention. The vicar stood behind Janet Goodall, who was held from each side in front of her husband. The torturers repeated their questions about where the cash from his operations could be found.

Goodall looked up and smiling towards his wife, mouthed, "Sorry," and at that, the vicar pulled out a knife and slit the woman's throat from ear to ear.

With that, in our distant observation room, I shouted out, "For God's sake, take him out!"

In the corner of my eye, Robin Greenwood nodded and there was suddenly a cacophony of sound as all hell was let loose. Detectives had burst into the rooms firing everywhere and they did take him out, with everyone else there as well.

I looked up and muttered to myself, "I didn't mean that."

I was stunned by the pandemonium and din let off by around a dozen handguns firing off into the rooms on the screens in front of us. The place looked like a battle zone with distorted and bleeding bodies littered all over the place. I'd seen many dead bodies in my training and career, but on the whole, they had died peacefully and very few of whom died violently. These drug dealers died suddenly with the grimaces of horror on their faces, where as yet late post mortem muscle relaxation hadn't had time to intervene.

The law and order service had taken no prisoners and no quarter was offered or accepted. These were intentional executions, once and for all, ridding the world of these inhuman degenerates, who had preyed on their weak and naïve customers. They didn't deserve justice and had paid the ultimate price, which was measured and inflicted without mercy in an overwhelming but succinct manner.

Silence filled the room and I thought about perhaps going to check whether any of the targets were still living, but the ones I could see looked definitely bereft of life. The SB shooters had probably used those special heavy-duty cartridges to wreak physical havoc and make sure no-one lived to tell the tale.

I felt like I was going to throw up, nauseated by the scenes of carnage.

"You look a bit pale doc, are you feeling alright?" a large detective proffered, looking me in the face. "Don't worry, doc, that's a common reaction in these bloody situations."

I wonder if he had any idea of the emotions I was experiencing. I was a doctor had just been part of a planned fatal ambush of about fifteen of my fellow humans. I didn't think there was anything common about it, at least not in my life's experiences!

A few minutes later, a large black van arrived and several white-coated men began to remove the dead bodies, piling them into the back, including the Goodalls'.

I walked out of the observation room door, rushing headlong along the corridor trying all the door handles for a toilet and just in time found myself outside throwing up all over the small back yard.

A cold sweat enveloped me, making me shiver as I pulled myself back together and rejoined the others, to be greeted by the large detective who had asked how I was feeling. He was probably right; it was the bloodshed that had overwhelmed me.

Inspector Greenwood approached me advising me not to look so worried because specialist cleaners would shortly be arriving to be tidying up after these proceedings. In the long term, the terraced properties, which included the houses in this row previously owned by the good Rev Norton-Brown, would quickly be demolished, redeveloped and sold off. The confiscation of the rest of his property and that of any others involved, would then very quickly ensue, going some way to balance the costs of law and order.

We quietly left the scene and walked to the car he'd parked some way from the carnage, leaving the team behind to clean up and remove all the evidence.

I thought to myself, the powers of the state are mighty. Meanwhile, I was in a different state of shock; I knew something bad was going to happen that day, but I never thought I would be party to a mass execution. I wondered if the Prof and Paul Brady knew the precise details of this and whether they'd actually been present at a similar event.

Inspector Greenwood must have seen I was upset by the massacre.

I must have looked like I was going to throw up again so he broached the subject with, "That was pretty horrific, wasn't it?"

"Yes, it was, I wasn't sure that was about to happen. I thought they might be arrested and held somewhere."

"Don't be too upset doc, just remember what they did to Frieda Hoffman, that young student. Did she get any mercy?"

That crushing truth of his question, cut through me to the bone! No, that precious and brilliant young woman, who was about to explode into womanhood, had been cut down by these heartless morons without any mercy or a thought to the far reaching results of their reckless business.

I rapidly re-focused on why I'd been there and why I voted for action with the others, back in the Prof's study. This was a war to save our civilisation and we able people, were fighting it to protect our society and save other young victims like Frieda from such pending disaster.

I looked up at Robin and could see he was deadly earnest about what had happened and also certain it was the right thing to have done.

"Can you take me back to Kings Cross? I need to go home and think about today. You are probably right that it had to be done. We were losing the war against drugs and up against the dealers with an ineffective rule of law. I need to mull this over and talk to my fellow members of our group."

With that, we jumped into his car and in no time I was on a fast train back to my wife at my parents' place.

I closed my eyes, still rather nauseous and my mind was racing about the scene. I thought back to the Sandhurst Armoury and the sergeant who taught us about weapons and how to shoot them. He moaned a lot about modern crime novels where authors, in ignorance, muddled up bullets with cartridges and quite often wrote inappropriately about the smell of Cordite when there had been gunfire, when it hadn't been used for years.

Prior to 1900, cartridges consisted of a brass casing, containing a primer, at the back, then some gunpowder and then a bullet (the projectile usually made of lead) at the front. The primer is struck by the gun's hammer and explodes sending hot expanding gases forwards to ignite the gun powder, In the confined brass casing, the gun powder ignites expanding and propels the bullet forwards at high speed (approximately 1700 mph in most handguns).

In the early 20th century, Cordite took over the job of the gunpowder because gunpowder produced a lot of smoke, both displaying the position of the shooter and impeding his vision. Since the end of WW2, it was used less and less. Modern ammunition propellants use saw-dust soaked in the high explosive nitroglycerin encased in Graphite. It is the more powerful nitroglycerin in today's "ammo" that explodes and expands projecting the bullet forwards with more force and also producing a very pungent smell that permeated the air and might possibly have contributed to my earlier nausea.

Somehow today's overwhelming smell was not quite like that of the Sandhurst Armoury. It must have been all that bloodshed in the area.

44

Suddenly I was brought back to reality as the overhead speaker announced we were approaching my station and I quickly alighted the train. I decided to walk the mile or so back to my parents to get some air, regain my colour and refocus my mind on my day's cover story of a fertility symposium. Being the current centre of family attention, they'd be bound to grill me on how I'd spent today. They'd be bloody shocked if they knew!

As I walked through the stream woods where I thought back to my earlier existence there. Where, as a local lad, I'd played with school friends, embraced my first girlfriend and experienced my first sexual encounter with a 6th former from the local Girls Grammar School, though I'm fairly certain it wasn't hers.

How cheated I had felt when my parents almost forced me to put aside my very social 'social life', to concentrate on my studies in order to overcome the intense competition for getting into university to study medicine. I did knuckle down and studied hard while many of my mates took full advantage of the laissez-faire freedoms of the Swinging Sixties and Seventies. I wondered what they were doing now. Had they been successful and got on well?

How simple and uncomplicated life was then, compared with now and the debacle I'd witnessed that morning. I bet none of their lives were as complex and mind-numbing as mine.

I thought of them and my family and knew they wouldn't believe it, if I told them. Well, I couldn't tell them, so it didn't matter. At that point, I reached my parent's front path, walked up it and rang the doorbell. In a minute, Annie opened the door and whisked me into her arms.

My life might be mind-numbing but the feelings I was currently getting weren't numbing at all! I entered the house and my parents greeted me almost as enthusiastically, like a soldier returning from war; which in a way, I suppose I actually was.

They sat me down to huge dinner and bombarded me with loads of questions about infertility, IVF and whether what we were doing was interfering with nature and should we be doing it. I fenced off their questions with my view that our work was changing very desperate couples' lives from despair into happiness and that was a good thing in itself. Straight after dinner Annie and I retired for an early night, professing my exhaustion from a very long day.

Although I actually was exhausted, I couldn't sleep with my mind still racing over the horrors I'd witnessed that morning. Annie pulled me back into her lap but my fight or flight nervous system held me back from relaxation and I turned over and into her to just hug until I finally drifted into sleep.

We woke up relatively late for us. There had been none of my home's usual noisy morning banter, that normally shook the house awake. I imagined my mother threatening my siblings and dad if they made any noise that might waken those poor overworked NHS guests upstairs.

Annie crept off to the bathroom for a shower and moments later there was a subdued knock on the door.

I called out, "Come in," as if I would from my office at the surgery. My mother walked in laden down by a huge tray of every possible breakfast food you could imagine.

"I thought yous might be hungry, so I brought yous up something to sustain yers."

"Mum, we were about to come down", I countered guiltily and just at that moment, in walked Annie, with a small towel round her midriff, displaying what midwives describe as her "more than adequate feeding equipment."

My mother excused herself and retreated rapidly towards the door, saying, "Take yers' time, we'll see yous downstairs," and with that, the door was shut secure and we dug into her full Irish breakfast.

For a moment, her speech reminded me of the IRA prisoner of the SAS back at my college earlier, but the vast distance between her absolute innocence and his total depravity, re-enforced my resolute and unswerving devotion to my extra-curricular security duties. It focused why I was involved with this most unusual group of academic well-connected individuals, upholding the stance against evil.

Having rapidly consumed the most important meal of the day, my thoughts turned to the carnage of the day before and notwithstanding the carnal display of

Annie dressing, I felt I really needed to get back to the real world and speak to my mentors.

I asked my wife how she was feeling and she said she had loved being in the warmth of my childhood home but was ready to go back and get on with our lives. I agreed with her and within an hour we'd said our goodbyes to my family, promising to visit soon and drove East to Hertford and up the A10 towards Cambridge.

I dropped off Annie at home, confident she would be fine, once she was back in her own house, where she could lock out thoughts about her previous sojourn with Philip Goodall and feel reassured there that she wouldn't be having to do that again! I was totally certain about it but of course, I couldn't tell her that.

I headed back to Addenbrookes and the Obs and Gynae faculty office. It was late afternoon, when I burst in on Marion, who swept me up, crushing me in her arms and demanding where I'd been for so long. I professed it was a state secret and asked the whereabouts of the Prof and or Paul Brady.

She complained they were still in theatres and ought to be back already, but no doubt had been detained by some emergency, which was prone to be a re-occurring situation in the surgical world. Suddenly they burst through the outer office door and rushed in among us.

Prof exclaimed, "Hello Mike, great to see you: won't you join us for some of Marion's appetising delights?"

"Excellent Prof," I replied, looking straight at Marion, with us both wondering what the great man was thinking. Marion took the initiative and rapidly produced a tray of tea and crumpets, which we sat down to enjoy in the privacy of the Prof's study.

"Welcome Mike," Prof opened, "How did you and Annie enjoy your break? I hope it helped to refocus your minds on the important things in your married life together."

I replied that it had and we had used the time to reinforce our commitments to each other, in the peace and tranquillity of my childhood home and family.

"I'm very happy to hear that my boy, we can't have our roles in medicine and homeland security placing a strain on the more important issues of our personal lives."

"Thanks for that Prof, I'm always grateful for your advice, I need to ask you about what I was called upon to witness yesterday. I went with Inspector Greenwood and a team of special branch officers to a planned raid on some drug dealers in the outskirts of London. I was uncertain about what to expect. I knew they were going to remove them from society, but not quite how that was going to happen.

"I was quite shocked and appalled by the carnage I witnessed there, they slaughtered all the criminals without mercy. No-one made any attempt to arrest anyone, they just shot them all. I'm not sure how I can live with that. It just raises serious doubts in my mind that we might be sinking down to their levels."

The Prof and Paul both looked straight at me in dismay, for a couple of seconds, but which to me felt like a couple of minutes, and then the Prof spoke.

"My dear friend, you may remember that evening when I spoke to you about the kidnapping of my family and what I told you about our forces having to intervene to rescue them and other innocent victims, those terrorists had taken, in their undeclared war on society.

"I know that you are a highly sensitive, skilled young doctor who has sworn an oath to preserve life; as have we two here, as well. However, you must appreciate that these are very unusual times and those folks you saw being shot, have also made undeclared war on us.

"This is a war that we have quite frankly been losing, as you have witnessed in the sad case of young Miss Hoffman and other unfortunates whose deaths have been caused by these degenerates. We have accepted the responsibility for carrying the fight to these enemies, in the names of those victims, because currently our justice system has failed us and we have the ability and responsibility to put this right.

"You were with us when we were appraised with the advice from our security experts, that the state of affairs is such that we have very little choice but to take the necessary steps to protect our way of life. I have great sympathy with your doubts and uncertainties, but feel most strongly that our usual high levels of sophistication and impeccable standards cannot apply to these perpetrators and must be put aside when faced with dire situations of national security. What do you think? Is that not so, Michael?"

I looked into both of their faces and could see they had no doubts or insecurities about our enforcers' methods to straighten out the imbalance of Goodness against Evil. When I quickly thought about what the good Prof had so eloquently said, I had no choice but to agree with him.

Once again, he had in an instant, confronted my doubts and allayed my fears, which evaporated right out of the window. Which was probably why he was a professor and I was a GP trainee! I thanked them graciously and Marion again passed round the remaining crumpets, which immediately eased the moment, and we munched them down voraciously.

45

The Prof broke the silence with, "Now, while I have you both here, I'd like to appraise you both about a situation that may arise for us in the near future, which our friends in 5 feel we might be able to help them with. They have for some time been cultivating relations with a certain Second Secretary at the Russian embassy in London. This diplomat's duties include being a close assistant to the Russian Ambassador himself and thereby he is party to a great deal of information which may crucially be to our country's best interests."

"It appears that following the last undiplomatic mutual tit for tat expulsions of their team in London and our team in Moscow, the Russian Secretary of State for Foreign Affairs, has sent us a new team of young and almost Pro-Western diplomats, from the Ambassador down to their Junior Counsellors. Of course, MI5 are being very cautious and undertaking their usual surveillance steps and scrutinising their loyalties and motivations.

"However, while this could possibly be a devious plant; on initial analysis, it appears that one of their second secretaries and his wife may have become disenchanted with their own government's political viewpoints. This information was first gleaned at the diplomats' arrival party at the embassy amid the usual cocktails and canapés. The invited other nationality diplomats exchange banter with their hosts, consuming vast amounts of champagne, while trying to appear very friendly and interested, without getting drunk and failing to keep their own state secrets to themselves.

"Apparently, we have had it from a reliable source, who is one of our friends at Langley (the CIA). He managed to stay sober at that event and learned that back in the past, the second secretary's dad was detained at some length by the NKVD (predecessor of the current KGB), which resulted in him being physically disabled and subsequently retired from his job, as a local village Commissar in the Kazakhstan area of Siberia. This had followed his betrayal by a colleague who had informed them that the individual wasn't quite as an enthusiastic Commissar as he should have been.

"It seems that the newly arrived diplomat has become somewhat disillusioned with his Communist ideals of service and may like to live here in the slightly safer climate of the decadent West. This seems to be the result of the treatment of his father and also some recent prominent murders of Soviet dissidents, who had considered themselves safe in the West, until their sudden and unexpected demise.

"It's early days yet, but this may quickly develop in our direction, so I thought I'd make you aware that our services may be in the frame for providing them with some rapid access to safe housing, which we are able to provide in the extensive grounds and facilities of our Fulbourn Psychiatric Hospital and Manor House. However, we are yet to see how this will evolve, and I will be back in touch with more details, as and when, so enjoy the rest of the afternoon and I'll see you anon."

With that, Paul and I left his study and headed out of the faculty to the underground passage back to the clinical school.

Paul said, "It's been a while why don't we pop back to the bar and have a chat," which was just what I was hoping we would do.

On the way, he said, "It sounds like you were subjected to witnessing a real battle in that S B raid. I imagine you were horrified, being exposed to that sort of debacle. I don't envy you at all. I'm sure it would have turned my stomach as well, but as the Prof has just said, we are at war with these dealers, who are posing a huge threat to our way of life.

"As we were made aware, it's a threat the powers that be are not in a position to deal with through the justice system, as it's not working. The executive (government) doesn't have a large enough Parliamentary Majority to make the changes necessary to sort this out and so we few have to go to war to defend the status quo."

We had reached the clinical school and came up the back stairs into the common room with its student union bar and I ordered a couple of pints.

"These are unusual times, Mike, do you think you can carry on in this service or do you want to call it a day?"

I must have alarmed them a bit, for him to ask me that. Clearly, the Prof had wanted him to sound me out.

"No, Paul I don't want to bail out. I know how important our service is. I was just a bit shocked by the utter brutality of the operation."

We picked up our beers and moved to a quiet corner of the bar, where my previous senior surgical colleague continued, "You weren't supposed to be subjected to that display of butchery. Inspector Greenwood should really have cleared your involvement through our usual channels. We only became aware of it the evening before. You should have been properly briefed and issued with your own weapon. Imagine what would have happened if you'd been shot during your presence there. I'm sorry you had to deal with that traumatic experience. Are you OK or do you think you might benefit from some of that rapid eye movement therapy for Post-Traumatic Stress?"

I answered that I didn't and let him know that in future, I would keep him and Prof in tune with any planned or unplanned extra-curricular activities on my part. Shuddering to think of the complexities of the ensuing situation, if I had been shot or had my throat cut from ear to ear. How would that have read in next week's B.M.J., or on the clinical school notice board? It was typical of him to show such care for my welfare.

I thanked him for his concerns, we finished our pints and I left to go home, slowly through the evening rush hour. I wasn't sure where Paul was going, but he turned off to the right on the Cherry Hinton road towards Fulbourn and the psychiatric hospital. I knew he lived somewhere out that way and felt a bit sorry for him, because he didn't have a partner and was probably going back to an empty house.

Maybe, I should have asked him back for dinner at our place, but in fact I wasn't sure what the lie of the land there would be, when Annie and I would be alone in the house again. A great deal had happened since that morning when she left to go off to coast with the Goodalls. Could we revert back to the marital bliss we had earlier, or would the Goodall's sojourn raise its ugly head?

I suddenly sensed a deep feeling of anxiety creep over me and could feel my heart thumping in my ears and chest, as heat and sweat ran down my face and body, sticking my shirt to my back. I was afraid and automatically I was physically reacting to my fears, which took over without me being able to control them. There was no reason for such anxiety, Goodall was gone permanently, there was just me and Annie.

I'd analysed the problem when I first discovered it and at the time, dealt with it rather well in my own mind. I hadn't over-reacted, using my spook connections in the watchers. I spoke to Goodall and dealt with it like a civilised doctor should. Although now, as Karma would have it, he got himself removed, rather dramatically, by his nefarious competitors in the narcotics market; to where he can't do any more harm. Now, all I had to do was to deal with Annie and enjoy my life with her. I knew just how to deal with that and follow my instincts.

I quietly entered our front door and made my way through to the kitchen where Annie was busy cooking the dinner. She was bare footed, wearing tight denim shorts, which looked like they were part of her, with one of my shirts undone at the neck and tied up under her breasts. She looked fabulous. She turned and walked towards me smiling and enveloped me in her arms.

I pulled her into me, with her abdomen against my burgeoning phallus, which was pressing itself into her like a medieval battering ram. My anxieties evaporated into the kitchen fan and out into the back garden with the aroma of the citrus sauce from the duck à l'orange, she had sizzling in the oven. Both me and my phallus were glad to be home, apparently very glad!

We stood there for several minutes with our tongues exploring every centimetres of each other's mouths and then she backed away pulling me towards the hallway and up the stairs to our bedroom.

In a last pico-second, I reached out and turned off the cooker, I didn't want the dinner to spoil, I might need it to replace the energy I was about to expend reassuring my wife that I really did love her and so I did for some time, in several ways that would definitely have spoilt the dinner, if the oven hadn't been turned off.

After this overt display of requited and unbridled mutual passion, we lay there, wrapped together, sliding over each other's moistened, perspiring skin, with our sweat soaked bodies cooling by evaporation. At some un-noted point, we slid, much cooled, under the duvet and slept till sunrise. I woke up to bright morning sunshine feeling again that all was right with the world.

I drove off to return to my normal medical role as a trainee GP, happy to be going back doing the job I liked very much. On arrival at the surgery, the practice staff and the GPs, Geoffrey and Tom were all, most welcoming to me, it was if I had been away for years. They were oblivious to the horrors that I'd witnessed.

I was keen to file the last 36 hours away in my memory banks and get back to the usually non-threatening business of seeing patients and learning the intricate roles of being a General Practitioner. I picked up my box of patient records strode into my consulting room and called in the first patient over the intercom.

After what seemed like an age, an elderly woman that I'd come across before, entered my room pushing a walking frame before her, and slowly negotiating her route to her seat.

"Well, what seems to be the trouble, Mrs. Tredget?" I enquired sympathetically.

"Well doctor, I've been coughing a lot lately and can't really get my breath. I think I may have a chest infection or asthma, like my husband, George," she responded anxiously.

I said soothingly, "Don't worry, we'll soon get that sorted out for you," remembering her late husband who'd had severe chronic obstructive airways disease, from smoking 40 a day since his childhood and had died of it.

"I'll just have a listen to your chest and find out what's been going on to cause this."

She opened her blouse and I watched her breathing, which she managed very well without any exertion. Then I percussed her chest wall, which was resonant throughout, indicating no signs of dullness or infective consolidation. I then listened very carefully to all the areas of her chest. It was as clear as a bell, with no signs at all of the tumbling air of an asthmatic wheeze. She also had no signs of heart failure, another common cause of shortness of breath.

"Well, Mrs. Tredget, I can't find any cause for breathlessness, your chest is totally clear!"

"It's much worse at night, doctor! Please can you give me a puffer? I need one and we've used up all the ones my George had, since he died and he can't have any more 'cos he's gone," she anxiously clamoured, more panicky than insistently.

"But, why are you using them when you don't need them? You don't have an infection nor do you have asthma. In fact, your chest is that of a fit young woman."

With that, she burst into tears and sobbed it was not for her but for her dog, a tiny Chihuahua called Sherry, who did have asthma, diagnosed by her vet but who's fees she could no longer afford since her husband George's demise. Through her tears, she whimpered how desperately anxious she was about Sherry's health and that she thought her last companion might die and then she'd be left all on her own, and she couldn't cope at all on her own.

I thought to myself that I'd become aware of her and her late husband since I'd joined the practice as a trainee and it was likely that he'd chosen to die, earlier than he ought, to get away from her and avoid her constant verbal battering!

What should I do with this perverse request for medication, which went against all the ethics of the NHS. Then I thought about how the NHS didn't give a thought to the fate of its junior doctors and exploited their goodwill in every situation it possibly could.

I balanced this against the cost of an inhaler to relieve Mrs. Tredget's little dog's tiny airways that were so easy to obstruct and how its demise would affect her mistress's existence and in a pico-second, I prescribed two inhalers for little Sherry, knowing that Mrs. Tredget would be greatly relieved by them, probably more than the dog!

The rest of the morning proceeded well with the usual collection of aches and pains, sprained muscles and relentless chronic smokers' coughs, until out of the blue, this very posh lady arrived, who I thought must be another of Geoffrey's private patients, who had somehow slipped into the NHS list.

However, I was soon to discover she had sought me out as I was considered among patients, as being a dermatologist. This most attractive, late, very well-coutured lady, presented complaining that she repeatedly suffered from broken fingernails, despite attending the best manicurist in town! Her nails looked alright to me and I wouldn't have asked her to scratch my back with them for fear of serious lacerations.

I thought back to all the time-wasters I'd seen during my time in A&E, held back my urge to tell her to get a life and despite her looking well and truly highly well-nourished, I found myself advising her on how important it was to have a balanced diet, rich in the various minerals necessary to maintain the intimate architecture of her fingernails!

She left the surgery reassured that her nails would soon be winning prizes and left me wondering why people take the NHS for granted. I thought I'd discuss that with Geoffrey in our next tutorial and ask him whether he agreed that the end-user of our service should have to pay a fee to make them think more before they abused it.

My days passed without any further notable events and I returned home for a hopefully peaceful evening, placing my faith in good providence and knowing I'd done my bit for medical science.

At home, I found Annie as enticing as ever, busily preparing dinner in the kitchen, which I passed through, quickly kissing her as I passed. I was aware that as a trainee, I had to contribute to various trainee seminars and I'd been asked to prepare a short lecture to refresh my peers on common skin conditions we were likely to encounter in GP land. I knew that if I'd stayed in the kitchen, I was not likely to get out without burning the dinner again.

So I excused myself and sloped off into the bedroom we used as a study. There I tried to concentrate on producing the talk for our next trainee session in the post grad' centre at Addenbrookes. I'd barely started to list all the commonest dermatological conditions likely to rear its head in the local population, when the house phone rang out to rescue me from academia. The caller was Paul Bradley.

"Hello Mike, have just had a call from the Prof, it seems that situation he referred to yesterday has just taken off in no uncertain terms. It's your afternoon off tomorrow, isn't it?"

"Yes!" I answered.

"Well, that's good because he wants us to meet him at Downing tomorrow for a briefing at 14.00 in his rooms on Stair 11."

"OK Paul, I'll see you there."

46

The next day at the allotted time, I was shown up to the Prof's rooms again by the porter. I was greeted by the Prof, Paul Bradley, D.C.I. Greenwood and "K" from MI5.

The Prof addressed us first, "Well gentlemen, some of you know why I have called this meeting, so I'd be grateful for your patience while I explain things briefly to you all. MI5 have been informed by the CIA, that last night at the U.S. Ambassador's office, a Russian lady, Mrs. Olga Zakharova, the wife of one of the new team of Russian diplomats, presented herself at the front gate of the embassy in Grosvenor Square, requesting asylum.

"She was in great distress at the time, which was not helped by the U.S. marines on gate duty, who wouldn't let her in and ended up arresting her for assaulting one of them. She must have been quite an able woman to have managed to assault one of those marines who aren't famous for their frailty. Eventually, an attaché there, managed to realise what was going on and rescued her from the marines. She is the wife of Dmitri Zakharov, the second secretary at the Russian Embassy, an important diplomat newly arrived in London."

"We have learned the reason for her distress is that Dmitri didn't come home from work yesterday, and the embassy have informed her that he left there at the usual time. Olga is insisting that the local KGB have probably detained him, because of the recent discussions they have been having in privacy at their home."

"D.I. Greenwood tells us that our Special Branch don't have him and K says nor do 5 or the C.I.A. That leaves a large question mark over where he is. She thinks their family flat is probably bugged and the KGB have been listening in, on their latter-day liberal views. She has insisted that she cannot go home and wants to claim asylum in the U.S., thus her approach at the embassy."

"The U.S. are saying they are currently in critical negotiations with Russia over gas supplies from them to the U.S.'s Middle Eastern allies; which could disrupt stability in local key areas there. They can't be seen to be getting involved with this situation, which to them is of relatively minor importance. They want us to take her in and hide her until a more convenient opportunity arises for them or us, their principal allies, to give her sanctuary."

"She is, of course correct, as we are aware that our Soviet KGB guests bug as many targets as possible and not only routinely bug their own comrades living quarters, but also employ a team of lip readers to monitor various conversations that occur during their embassy soirées. It's likely that Dmitri Zakharov has been compromised, due to his desires for Western freedom and possibly that either of these surveillance methods was used to trap him and his wife."

"Where he is at the moment is a matter of conjecture. K is of the opinion he is probably in an embassy freezer by now, awaiting his dissection and transport to somewhere in the North Sea. It's sardonic to note that after all his alleged wishes to spend the rest of his days living in the warmer decadent West, his DNA would end up being part of a plate of Cod, smuggled out of the North Sea by a Spanish fishing fleet and ending up as the main course in an Alicante restaurant. At least, it would be a warmer fate than retiring to life in an East Siberian gulag."

"Getting back to Mrs. Zakharova, as I mentioned earlier, our American friends would like us to accommodate her quietly in a safe area, where we or they could interview her at length, discover her true loyalties and also what Dmitri has told her; while we protect her from her own country's security men, who no doubt will be trying to do the same thing."

"K, what's your view on this?"

"Thank you, Professor, for your succinct analysis of the situation. Gentlemen, we cannot let her fall into the hands of the KGB, who will definitely not demonstrate the more subtle ways of persuasion. I entirely agree, she may have an intimate knowledge of several things pertinent to our interests, so we need to accommodate her securely and groom her for a debriefing."

"Does anyone disagree with K?"

No-one dissented.

"So be it then, we will pick her up from the US Embassy and carry her to a safe place, where her debriefing can be undertaken sympathetically. Chief Inspector Greenwood, would your chaps take on that task, possibly with some of our personnel along for a medical input should that be necessary?"

With that, the Prof concluded the meeting. K left the room, escorted by the porter, I thought to myself somewhat ironically, that the college security man was escorting our country's top security man off the premises. It just goes to show that you can't trust these spies!

Detective Chief Inspector Greenwood remained behind to be involved with arranging the details for Mrs. Zakharova's pick-up and rescue. I had correctly assumed that the Prof would want Paul Bradley and/or I to go as well. It was to be a military-like operation, as we were all aware that the Russians will have eyes on the US Embassy.

Their spying on and arrest of Mr. Zakharov an embassy official, had probably made them aware that by hook or by crook, Britain was the most likely place to where Mrs. Zakharova would choose to escape.

We were to be armed, I with an excellent Walther P.P.S., just in case, and she was to be protected by all means possible. She was unlikely to be the most popular colleague to her diplomatic peers. Her silence would be their priority, which was diametrically opposed to ours.

The pick-up was to be in the evening. Olga Zakharova was to be smuggled out of her safe haven at the US Embassy in Grosvenor Square, Mayfair, in a catering van, which was a frequent visitor to the site. She would be dressed in the Catering Company's dreadful livery of grey peaked cap, grey long Teflon coated cotton lab type coat, grey trousers and grey rubber Wellington boots. How fetching I thought, for this wife of a quite high-grade Russian Diplomat!

The van and its grey passenger would proceed Westward into Hyde Park and on to Kensington Gardens where we would pick her up in our convoy of large security cars, likely to be bullet proof Range Rovers, a bit of British car muscle, to deal with any threats from any scrawny Russian Marussias or LADAs.

Chief Inspector Greenwood thought it ironic that we would be transferring her into our care, just around the corner from the Russian Embassy, in the last place they'd be looking.

My cover for the operation was to be my attendance at a post grad lecture, which was a common occurrence among GP trainees and enabled me to be absent from Annie for the evening.

The CIA had not provided any details about the current condition of Mrs. Zahkarova, except to say how distressed she was on the night of her defection and her altercation with the U.S. marines. So apart from that, we had no idea what to expect.

Paul Bradley suggested we might take some sedation with us, on a just in case basis. The last thing we wanted was the local police attending what passersby had reported to be an attempt kidnapping, in the middle of Kensington Gardens.

I left the surgery early that evening, making my way to Addenbrookes to be picked up with Paul Bradley, by the Special Branch in a convoy of three black Range Rovers. These sped us down the new M11 road with lights flashing and sirens blowing at over 120mph. It didn't feel at all that fast and I thought these cars might be very appropriate for me as a GP, for home visits!

We arrived in our appointed lay-by at the appointed time, precisely 19.30.

Within seconds, the catering van pulled in behind us, causing our Rovers to have to shuffle along a bit. The S.B. cops driving the catering van, who were supposed to park in the gap we'd left in front of us, were not as precise as our S.B. drivers in our beefy Range Rovers.

Within seconds the fearfully anxious looking, bent over figure of Olga Zakharova, enveloped in grey Teflon was guided by her burly catering/cop colleagues into the middle rescue car and we were on our way East towards the M11 and North to her secure haven.

Paul Bradley and I introduced ourselves politely and reassured her that she was safe now and on her way to a very secure place where she would not be in any danger. We told her we were medical doctors, who would be looking after her and dealing with any problems that she might possibly have.

Mr. Greenwood offered her a drink and she requested champagne. Unhappily that wasn't available in the car's drinks cabinet. When he asked if she would like anything else, I was surprised when she asked for vodka.

I was even more surprised when the good inspector produced a bottle of Grey Goose vodka from a refrigerated deep centre console box at the front of the car and passed it to the back together with a tumbler glass. She accepted these and poured herself half a glass and knocked it back in an instant. By the time we reached the M11, she had demolished three more.

I looked at Paul Bradley and was imagining he must be thinking, 'So much for the suggestion of sedation!' After the vodkas, she seemed to relax. The next time I looked in her direction, she was sound asleep, snoring like what I imagined a Russian bear might do.

This gave Paul and I an opportunity to observe her. She was very tall at about 5' 8", clearly highly muscular, without an ounce of fat to be seen anywhere. She was statuesque with a sharply angled jaw, was slim, graceful and splendid. I thought to myself thank God we had rescued her from those KGB thugs. Heaven knows what they would have done to her. I made a note in my mind to ask Mr. Greenwood how these Special Branch cars would come to have a very expensive well-equipped bar inside their vehicles.

We arrived at Fulbourn Hospital in just over an hour despite the busy London streets, where we disembarked from the big Rovers, surrounded by burly but welcoming S.B. officers, with their Israeli Uzi machine pistols bulging out from under their even more bulging muscular arms.

Once inside, we were greeted by a team of army nurses, who were newly arrived that day from Hereford and whisked Mrs. Zakharova away to her suite of rooms, which had been especially prepared for her, planted with listening devices by MI5 and guarded by a team of armed S.B. officers.

The nurses briefed us that Olga had reported being exhausted by the emotional trials of her day, not to mention the vodka she'd put away on the journey, and wished to retire straight away, so Paul Bradley and I decided it was best for us to retire too and arranged to meet her formally the following afternoon, which inconveniently wasn't my afternoon off and caused me some concern. We both excused ourselves and sped off to our respective homes.

I locked my expensive Walther police pistol with its spare clip in the boot of my inexpensive car and made my way to my home with Annie. It was very late and she, as expected was tucked up in bed. I slid in beside her and pressed myself into the hollow of her lower back, just above her pelvis and orientating my phallus below and in between the walls of her buttocks' Gluteal muscles, which created a cutaneous sleeping bag.

Sustained by its warmth, my penis was soon enhanced into a responsive erection. She must have been exhausted as she didn't respond and laid there all night almost impaled on my fully warmed flagstaff.

Next day, having rushed through my patients in record time, I sped over to Fulbourn, picking up Paul Bradley on the way. We were shown by army nurses, up to Olga's quarters, a very large suite of rooms. This building was an annex of the old NHS asylum had recently been converted into an amazingly posh country Manor House.

The security service certainly hadn't stinted on their refurbishment budget. There was a mobile globe shaped bar, a large TV and were even fresh flowers on the centre of a coffee table.

Almost immediately, we were joined by Mrs. Zakharova, who had transformed herself from the fearful grey figure of the night before into the confident, elegant, charming and becalmed wife of a diplomat, standing before us.

"Good afternoon," we both opened simultaneously.

"Hello," she replied, "I'm very grateful for you bringing me here, but I'm so worried about my husband. Could you help to find him for me? I know he's at the embassy and the security men probably have him. Can your government help to rescue him?" "We are both very keen to live in the West." "Can you please help us?"

It didn't take a doctor to tell that she was clearly still visibly anxious, quite rightly about the fate of her husband Dmitri. I didn't think it would be helpful to tell her what K thought.

Paul responded that he was sure that our side would do all they could to find out the fate of Dmitri. I remembered that night in the Prof's room when I'd accidently walked in on him and how he'd hoped our side might intervene on behalf of his kidnapped son.

I knew that Britain had recently undertaken a fabulous military and logistical feat of taking back the Falkland islands from the "Argies", for the freedoms of its population, not to mention its rich oil and gas deposits under its surrounding territorial waters, but I just couldn't envisage a troop of SAS being helicoptered into the Russian Embassy to rescue Mr. Zakharov.

The embassy, in Kensington Palace Gardens was a different kettle of fish to the Somali desert and Mikhail Gorbachev might have something to say about that. Nevertheless, there was something about the serenity of this woman and the dignified way she clung onto her composure as she asked for our help to locate and possibly rescue her husband. She must have thought that it was unlikely that H.M. government could help him, but clinging on to hope, she had not yet given in to the impotence of bereavement.

I ignored those thoughts and quickly focused back on our job in hand and said that we, as doctors, had to ask her about her medical history and possibly undertake some various examinations and also probably test a sample of her blood for various things as she would for some time be a guest in our community, albeit in a possibly limited and isolated way.

She immediately understood what I was saying, and invited us to sit down with her and join her for coffee, while we asked her about her history.

I made notes while Paul Bradley asked the pertinent questions. She had no problematical illness history at all and I noted that she had told us about her record of all the usual public health vaccines that we also had in Britain, so medically she was not at all a risk to Britain.

We were not surprised when she revealed that she had been a highly talented athlete in her youth and had represented her country as an accomplished fast runner. Certainly, from where I was looking, I could see why.

She had the body of an athlete and a face that could also have sent another fleet to Troy. That Dmitri was certainly a lucky man and I couldn't quite understand how he'd become distracted by politics, with a woman like that at home!

Once again, I put that out of my thoughts and asked her if she would allow me to examine her with one of the army nurses as a chaperone. She immediately acceded to my request and retreated to her bedroom with the nurse and I close behind her. She very quickly and gracefully undressed and poured herself into a silk dressing gown, which she filled voluptuously.

I caught my stethoscope on my jacket pocket in my clumsy attempts to approach her, like a smooth and highly professional physician and ended up looking kack-handed. My examination very quickly revealed that Olga was physically perfect, so me and my nurse chaperone retreated to rejoin Mr. Bradley in her living room, while she redressed.

On her return to join us, Paul explained that while she was with us, she was not a prisoner, but she would have to be accompanied by nurses for her protection within her quarters and also by armed police officers in the surrounding grounds of Fulbourn.

She would later be interviewed, by other officers from our security service, but there was no need for her to worry about that, as long as she was truthful in her answers to their questions. In the meantime, our government diplomats from the Foreign Office, as well as Special Branch would be doing everything they could to locate Dmitri.

We also advised her that she could contact either Paul or I, should she find it necessary. She was very grateful and carefully filed away our telephone numbers in her bag for future reference. Paul and I excused ourselves and we set off back to Cambridge.

After a while, he broke the silence with, "Blimey, she's a bit of a stunner, isn't she!"

"She certainly is. I'm sorry I couldn't find anything physically wrong with her, that I might need to return to check. Hang on though, she was very anxious, but then, that's only natural given the circumstances. I think if she was a normal patient, it wouldn't warrant a home visit out to Fulbourn to check up on her.

"Mind you, the Prof did say that she needed our utmost consideration and we had to be nice to her and we don't want anything to happen to her that would prevent the watchers gathering her useful information. Right then, I've talked myself into it, I'll go back tomorrow to make certain that she's ok."

"Well done Mike, I thought you might," retorted Paul Bradley, with a smile from ear to ear. "It's always better to be safe than sorry."

"I'm glad you agree," I condescendingly replied, turning into the Addenbrookes entrance road. "I'll keep you and the Prof informed of any developments."

With that I dropped him off, turned round and headed towards home, leaving the world of espionage behind and that of medicine and Annie in front of me.

47

I drove home and put my feet up enjoying the tranquillity of our living room which backed onto a local deserted playing field and I quickly nodded off in the knowledge that all was hopefully still alright with the world.

Olga, the asylum seeker was safely stashed out of harm's way and I fully deserved to have a kip! However that was not to be, and in a very short while, Annie roused me on her return from work and I sensed she was not her usual vivacious self and was somewhat subdued. I asked if she'd had a rough day.

This sometimes occurred in the neurosurgical department, where patients were often facing death from some lethal disease only to be rescued from the brink by the skilful intervention of her surgical colleagues. The department staff, often aware of the histories and intimate details of those patients, could sometimes experience a bereavement reaction by proxy when those patients would, despite the best efforts of the neurosurgeons, succumb to their illness.

Annie said she was all right and her day had been OK, but she clearly wasn't. Perhaps it was fatigue, but I knew she'd slept soundly the night before. My instinct told me not to press her too deeply for the cause of her apparent low mood and I left her to open up to me when she felt able or inclined. I didn't want her to feel like she was being interrogated so I left her to it.

As a previous member of the good professor's gynae team, I was keenly aware that occasionally women's behaviour may be influenced profoundly by the levels of different hormones coursing through their blood and influencing their emotion centre in that part of their brains.

During dinner our conversation was somewhat stilted and devoid of the usual high-spirited exchanges. After eating, she quickly adjourned to our bedroom. I sat there alone thinking how she had usually dominated the conversation with all sorts of news and views but tonight I sensed the need for me to intervene and lead the chatter.

I followed her and asked specifically about work as that usually led onto various animated reports of various patients and their cases, but she replied it was OK but didn't respond with her usual open opinions of her colleagues or events in the department. I was trying to scan and scrutinise all my activities to see if I caused this low mood response, but came up with a blank. I was rapidly getting fed up with this almost silent atmosphere.

I didn't come home for this performance, so I shattered the tranquillity with my slightly insensitive, "What the hell is the matter with you? You haven't said more than two words to me in the last 24 hours."

She looked up and blurted out, "It's not the same. I don't think you love me anymore. You can't do, after what's happened. You're different and I can feel it!"

Feel what? I thought to myself, I'm totally the same, that is apart from being completely knackered with all that had gone on over the last few days, the shootouts, mass killings, and high speed international rescues, she's lucky I'm not hiding in the cellar from fear of being bumped off by some Russian sniper or hired hitman!

Oh, that was it, the penny dropped, she was feeling guilty, which led her to introspection and transfer of her guilt feelings onto what she imagined must be a change in my behaviour towards her. Where she got that from, I could only guess.

Someone must have turned her mind, after I had been certain that I had convinced her of my feelings.

I knew I had to quickly reverse those destructive thoughts and reassure her of my love for her. I rushed towards her and held her tightly in my arms and kissed her, recounting how I would never let something so menial come between us. She sobbed as I held her and I could feel her tears running down my chest as I gently turned her head and wetted face upwards from my throat towards my mouth.

I kissed her passionately on the lips and face, draining her saliva and drooling it back all over her. I could feel her gasping at the intensity, arousing me to rigidity as I pulled her to our bed and forced my phallus into her, thrusting against her pantied labia with my unbridled desire. Within a minute, I had burst forth and soaked her in my seminal emission like a hot spring and we lay there stuck together at both ends, panting and soaked from top to bottom and we fell asleep there, glued together.

We woke with the dawn and having unstuck during the night, we rolled over to our respective bedsides. She got up and shortly, I could hear her fill the kettle and put it on to boil. I lay my head back on my pillow enjoying a few more minutes of semi-sleep, satisfied that her routine activity of boiling the kettle, meant that I must have soothed her woes, as it certainly had mine.

Moments later, she returned with a large mug of green tea to rouse me back to reality. I immediately knew she was lifted out of her previous unhappy doldrums. She was humming a tune and had a definite spring in her step. She put my tea on the bedside table, skipped out of the door and I could hear her singing in the shower.

'Blimey, my uncontrolled and enthusiastic rapid climax must have really impressed her.'

I got up and our paths crossed on the landing, with her on route to the bedroom and myself heading to off to shower, which was very quick as Annie had drained most of the hot water! I missed her erotic dressing ritual, which was probably a blessing as I had a full surgery, overbooked as usual and being late would have agitated the patients and reception staff to boot.

I ploughed my way through my morning list until with 3 patients or half an hour left to go, I was buzzed from reception to tell me I had an outside call and should they put it through to me. I accepted the call and it was the Prof's secretary, Marion.

"How's my favourite doctor?" she whispered down the phone, which woke up the whole waiting room. "The Prof realises it's short notice, but he would like you to attend Mrs. Zakharova at Fulbourn as soon as you can today as the security services are planning to let her know the outcomes of their investigations into Mr. Zakharov. That sounds like it's not going to bode too well for Mrs. Zakharova. I imagine they'd like you there in case she takes it rather badly."

"Oh dear, that's bad. I do feel sorry for the woman, she was quite desperate when we saw her the day after she arrived. I hoped we would find him for her. They don't deserve this."

"Well, at least she will have you there to help her deal with whatever the news will be. You can comfort me if ever I get bad news. Special Branch are due to get to Fulbourn at 2 o'clock. Can you get there by then?"

"Thanks Marion, I'll remember that, if you remember I'm now a married man. I'll make sure I get there by two. Pass on my regards to the Prof, bye, bye," and with that, I hung up the phone, got back to my remaining patients and finished surgery in record time. I had to admit it to myself that I felt quite excited at the prospect of going back to see Olga Zakharova and especially so at the thought of being able to comfort her in whatever fate had in store.

As I was technically on call for the surgery, I looked in the visit book and I saw that there was an elderly man, bedbound with an exacerbation of his chronic obstructive airways disease. He lived out on the Madingley road, along from the massive American War cemetery.

This was right out of my way on the other side of Cambridge. Blast! I cursed to myself and drove off at speed, wishing I had one of those Special Branch Range Rovers. Happily the traffic was light and I made the round trip including home visit in under an hour! Then I was free to concentrate on my next home visit on the exquisite Olga!

I just made Fulbourn by two o' Clock and sure enough there were my two old Special Branch friends, Robin Greenwood and Martin Roberts.

"What are you two doing here?" I asked happily.

"MI5 dumped this delicate job on us, as they thought we might be better at conveying bad news."

"Oh it is bad then?"

"Yes, it is," D.I. Greenwood replied. "Our contact at the Russian Embassy has confirmed that Mr. Zakharov died while being questioned by their security morons. They have been removing his remains, piece by piece, in their Diplomatic bags. We're tasked with breaking the news to his wife or rather his widow.

"We've been asked to stress to you that it's your job to see that she remains here under sedation if necessary, to see to it she doesn't do anything outrageous embassy wise and/or come to any harm or even self-harm. As you know, her presence here is of course most secret and H.M. Government doesn't want anything to occur that might endanger that secrecy. They don't need any other "faux pas" to embarrass them in the international community."

"That's good, I was aware of the secrecy, I was at Prof's meeting. What it really means is I get the blame if anything does happen to her then!"

"Don't worry doc you're surrounded by our blokes here. They'd have to be pretty determined to get past them!"

"I think they may be but it's not that I'm worried about, it's the lady herself, we examined her physically, but we have no idea about her mental health and however you frame it, what you are about to tell her will probably knock her sideways!"

"You'll be alright doc. You're highly experienced. You'll be able to sort her out and from what I've seen, I wouldn't mind sorting her myself."

Then with that, the three of us entered the vestibule of the annex and asked to see Mrs. Zakharova, who very quickly appeared with her two nurse guardians. Robin approached her and quickly re-introduced us and asked if we might find a convenient room where we could chat. She smiled politely and one of the nurses bade us follow them into an adjacent drawing room.

We'd just sat down and there was a very slight pause, which was shattered when Inspector Greenwood suddenly erupted with, "I'm sorry to inform you that we've discovered that your husband is dead!"

'That's subtle,' I thought, I'd hate to witness him being direct with anyone!

Olga responded by promptly collapsing; due to her shock dropping her blood pressure and making her faint. She slipped off her seat and fell to the floor, narrowly missing a marble coffee table with her head. The nurses leapt to their feet and rapidly re-ensconced her on a sofa, raising her legs to increase her blood flow to her brain. She soon recovered her consciousness and rapidly scanned the faces of us all around her.

I imagine she was trying to grasp whether what she had heard was real. Then on almost immediate recognition of reality, she burst into loud sobbing, interspersed with long gasps of breath. One of the nurses enveloped her in her arms, trying to comfort and sooth her utter state of loss and abandonment.

She was inconsolable so I felt it appropriate for the nurses to lead her off to her bedroom, where I intervened with a sedative injection. Within a minute, she was quietly asleep; rescued temporarily from the harsh reality of her news.

Myself and the two detectives retreated like three very unwise men. I left the nurses with some anxiolytic tablets to give her, should they feel they were still necessary and I asked them to call me when she awoke in the morning.

This they did rather early and I asked them to hold the fort until I could get there after morning surgery, which they agreed.

When I got there, I was shown into Olga's rooms, where she greeted me very sedately. The nurses had obviously recently given her one of the Benzodiazepine anxiolytic meds I'd left with them. Her face was swollen from the effects of her distraught sobbing herself to a disturbed sleep; which I imagined from the look of her, must have disturbed her all night.

She apologised to me for her dishevelled state. I responded that I was sorry for disturbing her and said that I was concerned about her and the terrible traumatic loss that she was having to endure. I told her I was there to help her and that she was safe and, in the end, the pain of her loss would pass and that she would be alright.

I pointed out to her that she could ask me about anything, but that I didn't have any information about what had happened to Dmitri, except for what D.I. Greenwood had said.

She replied that she understood and that the tablet had made her dizzy and would it be alright for her to sleep.

"Of course," I replied apologetically, "You rest, and I'll come back when you're a bit more restored and have had a chance to settle in and then we can have a talk about your future plans."

With that, one of her nurse minders helped her back to her bedroom and I asked the other one to let me know when she might be able to meet again to discuss her options. I then left, heading for the Prof's faculty offices to discuss just what her options actually were.

I was met by Marion. She told me the Prof was as usual in theatres; still completing his afternoon ops list. She called gynae theatres in the Rosie Maternity Hospital and left a message that I was in the faculty office and a theatre sister called back to let us know he was on his way.

On his arrival, I outlined Mrs. Zakharova's current condition. He thought it might take some time for her to acclimatise to her present situation, including her acceptance of her husband's death and her own present danger. He urged me to try to make her safety my priority and accede kindly to her requests pending her future debriefing by MI5.

"Mike, we will leave it to you to decide when that time might be, but be gentle with her and remember what she's going through and the courage she has shown to defect to the West. Also, bear in mind that she is a target for removal by the other side, who may do anything to prevent her debriefing, so carry your personal weapon with you when you're with her and be careful. You will have to be the ultimate arbiter of her existence until she is ready for debriefing."

I left the department and went home wondering how I might cope with this new responsibility for Olga's safety and how long it might take before her minders might get back to me. I'd never been a bodyguard before but felt confident that if I could deal diplomatically with my patient, Mrs. Tredget's asthmatic doc, then I ought to cope easily with various KGB assassins, after all, you don't have to negotiate with them, you only have to shoot them and I knew I was already quite good at that.

I arrived home to be greeted by my loving wife, who was back to her former lively and loving confident self. We spent the evening in a relaxed and normal married way, with none of the former stresses we had endured. We retired early, slept well and arose to a sunny morning. Annie got up first, showered and then dressed provocatively in front of me.

I think it was the way she drew her stockings up her outstretched legs, locking them into her suspender belt, that made me want to assist her with this intricate operation, leaving me eager and wet in the anticipation! I leaned forward, reaching out for her and she rushed away, saying she was late for work, so I retreated back to my bed, shot down in flames and heading for the surgery.

Four days later, I was called by the corporal nurse at Fulbourn. She thought that Olga Zakharova was now ready to talk to me. After my last visit, she had remained in bed for two days, refusing to eat anything or talk to anyone. I imagined that to have been the shock, total loss and impotence part of her bereavement reaction.

On the 3rd day, she'd asked the nurses for some food and started to communicate with them without prompting. They weren't sure what emotions she was displaying, but thought I'd better be called so that I could come along and assess her again. I went the next day to check her out.

The nurses said they were worried about her as she seemed very flat and spoke to them in a similar tone. She forced a smile as I was shown into her rooms but I quickly saw that they were right and she was clearly in a quite low state of mind.

I asked if there was anything that I could help her with. She immediately asked if I could bring her husband back. I remembered this could be her in the bargaining phase of bereavement.

I replied if only I could, but countered with, "Is there any other practical thing I could help her with?"

To which she said, "You could get me out of here. I'm going mad with claustrophobia in this place!"

I wondered what sort of place she had in Russia if the huge Fulbourn Manor House was making her claustrophobic. I suspected it might be the nurses surrounding her that was the cause and said, "I don't see why not, where do you want to go?"

"Anywhere, just out of here, somewhere normal," she replied.

"Ok, I'll discuss it with your minders," I blurted out without thinking, what if she ran away, or got nabbed by the KGB or even shot by them. I could imagine the look of disappointment on Prof's face if one of his men screwed up the whole operation.

I spoke to her nurses and the Special Branch detectives and we agreed that the S.B. would accompany us but at a short non-crowding distance in the background. I then squared it with the Prof, who as ever, expressed more concern about my safety than Olga's.

We settled on a short guided tour of Cambridge, with myself as the guide. I drove her into the city and parked in the Memorial Court. I didn't know where the four detectives who followed us planned to park, but I did catch sight of two of them as we left the old court of Clare and headed to Kings College Chapel, to impress her with the altarpiece painting of the Adoration of the Magi, by Rubens.

She was utterly stunned by its beauty and the chapel itself, built by Henry the VIIIth. She was also amazed that students actually lived in these beautiful historic buildings and watched dozens of undergraduates in their gowns exiting their various wooden staircases around the perimeter of the pristine lawns.

I then took her for lunch at the Airman Pub, which was very close by, and where she knocked back a ploughman's and two glasses of champagne, while I stuck to a cheese roll and a cup of coffee. She was fascinated by all the paraphernalia of the 2nd World War pilots' and the personal notes and letters that had been pinned to the walls by the airmen and various visitors.

Out of the blue, she asked if she could have a ride in a punt, I willingly agreed, but to keep it safe we went on one from a tourist company, where I could sit quietly and keep my eyes peeled for any unwelcome interlopers. She enjoyed the guide's informative lecture and became clearly relaxed at its slow progress along the river Cam.

She didn't notice two detectives trailing us in the punt behind. She was surprised at the fact that the heir to the English crown had occupied a ground floor room in the huge Trinity College for his student time at the university. After the river tour, she looked a bit exhausted so I suggested we return to Fulbourn so she could rest and be returned to secure surroundings, relieving me of her safety burden.

On arrival back, we were greeted by her nurses, who were happy to see her safe and sound. She thanked me profusely for my expert guided trip and hoped we could do it again soon! I said I hoped so too and approached her nurses, exceedingly relieved myself, but half looking forward to my next sojourn with the Siberian beauty.

Her nurses were anxious to ask me how it went and whether I'd perceived any danger throughout our brief outing. To which, I happily replied that I hadn't. I sensed a slight look of disapproval in their faces, which changed to a frown when I suggested we might go out again. I saw that Olga must have heard that as she turned back and gave me a smile.

Next day, as I worked my way through my minor ops list, my mind lost concentration and briefly darted back to Olga's wide eyes devouring all of the historic and tourist parts of Cambridge. Yesterday, they had almost hypnotised me and now led my mind to wonder away from my patients' symptoms. I began to fix on them and what she was thinking behind them.

Why had she so intoxicated me, I was a happily married man with a lovely wife, who was entirely my own. Annie and medicine had occupied my every waking minute of the day and I hadn't had time for any distractions, no matter how pleasant they were. And yet, I couldn't get this other most vulnerable and lovely lady out of my mind. She was becoming an obsession and I couldn't wait to get a call to go and see her again.

48

I didn't have to wait very long. The following day, I had a call from Marion. She said the Prof had heard from MI5 that they were anxious to begin Mrs. Zakharova's debriefing. She asked if I thought she was ready. I selfishly and unthinkingly considered that this would probably mean that I would no longer bear responsibility for her safety and she would be moved to some other safe location, where I could no longer fall under her spell.

Without hesitation, I heard myself say that in my view, she wasn't quite ready and that she had only had one trip out of Fulbourn to taste the freedoms of the West and I hadn't had an opportunity to fully assess her readiness. I proposed that we should expose her to more outings allowing her to experience everyday life in England so I could measure her readiness and commitment for life in the West.

Marion replied that she would pass on my opinion and reminded me that I was a married man and if I was to fall foul of other womanly charms, she thought they ought to be hers!

I thought, "Good old reliable Marion, always looking out for me."

That evening, Annie broke the news that she hoped to visit her parents that weekend to acquaint them with how she was adjusting to her newly married life and asked whether I wanted to come with her. I responded that I'd love to, but was far too busy and needed to use the weekend to catch up on outstanding surgery work.

I thought it would give her the opportunity to touch base with her parents without me there to distract them. She reluctantly agreed and hugged me desperately saying how much she would miss me and how she needed to make it up to me now. So she did and the early night did us both a power of good!

The stage was set and while Annie headed North, I had the weekend to engineer my more thorough assessment of Olga's readiness for life in the West and the MI5 debriefing. Next day, I called her guardians at Fulbourn and said I proposed a trip to the theatre to acquaint her with Shakespeare, by his play *The Merchant of Venice*, which was on at the Cambridge Arts Theatre. I was anxious that they'd agree as I thought the irony and the triumph over avarice in the play might distract her from her bereavement.

I'd actually noted that Romeo and Juliet, was their next production at the theatre and thought that would have been a complete disaster to expose her to that after the latest events in her life. I was happy and quite excited when the nurses agreed for her to go out for a bit of English culture and I arranged to pick her up early on Friday evening.

Her Special Branch guards agreed to wait outside the theatre as they'd both had enough of the Bard in their school days and it was unlikely she would fall victim there.

I picked her up after my surgery and drove to the Memorial Court with her guards at a discreet distance behind us. We parked, crossed the Queens Road and the Backs and walked through Old Court. On our way, we paused for me to show her the graduates dining room and chapel.

She laughed when I explained to her how once a month, we would walk led by the senior tutor, in twos in our gowns, from the post grad common room along the paths to bypass the sacred lawns to dine. On the way, tourists would snap our pictures enthusiastically.

We emerged from the college by Old Schools and Senate House and strolled down Kings Parade. where I suggested we have a drink and she leapt at it. We had over an hour till curtain up and she was already beginning to soften her sullen widowed affectations.

A bottle of Veuve Cliquot in the Airman pub helped her on her way and relaxed me a lot too. She was smiling a much more as we left the pub and within ten minutes we were heading for our seats in the Arts Theatre, in time for the play's opening scenario.

As we made our way through the auditorium, I was struck by the conspicuous gazes fixed on Olga, by the captivated males in the audience and who could blame them, she was totally beguiling. When she stepped out in Siberia, she must have personally caused local global warming, melting the snow and forcing the Yeti back to his forest. No wonder no-one could find him!

When the curtain went up, she froze, fixed in her seat and locked in a stare at the players on stage. She was enthralled and later, I could sense she was almost rigid with fear when the money lender insisted on his payment from the impoverished hero, Antonio.

She trembled from then on until he was rescued later by the intervention of the heroine disguised as the judge. Olga was so refreshingly naïve and I was almost convinced that she thought the plot was really a true story. I thought to myself she's actually very genuine and can't be a spurious plant sent to mislead us by the KGB.

The play ended with the good guy winning and the theatre erupted into standing applause. We leapt up to clap and she turned and wrapped me in her arms shouting, "Thank you, thank you, that was wonderful."

The lights came on and we stood there moulded together in appreciation as people filed around us.

I de-clamped from her embrace and said forlornly, "Well, you enjoyed it then; I think we'd better go or we could get locked in!"

We left the theatre with the crowd and made our way back to Memorial Court. The route back was almost deserted but happily I recognised the night porter and he remembered me allowing me to pass through Old Court on the way. She enthused all the way, over the bridge and through the grounds and she placed her arm in mine proceeding like a couple.

On reaching my car, there was a note on the screen from our friends in S. B. saying they'd gone back to Fulbourn as they considered there was no risk to the 'asylum seeker' at this point in time. How they knew that, I didn't know. I thought I was probably at more risk than her, but was grateful to be spared their surveillance.

We got in the car and she said, "Do we have to go back to that prison just now?"

I said, "Well, it is rather late but I know the night porter and could offer him a small bribe to let us into the middle common room for a coffee."

"Oh yes," she replied, "Can we do that?"

"Well, we can only try."

With that, we set out again, arm in arm back towards old court, where the night bell raised the porter and I gently persuaded him, with an appropriate and considerable gratuity, to let us into the middle post-graduate common room. She was amazed at such access, open to members of the college. I explained that it wasn't every member who were able and that many were not deemed worthy. That really impressed her.

We leisurely sipped the college coffee and I told her about my life as a doctor, omitting my other unusual job working for the Prof. She explained how she now felt abandoned by the loss of her husband, in this strange country, alone and frightened by her embassy chasing her and the prospect of interrogation by the British Secret Service.

I pointed out that she was not alone and she was under the care of our branch of that service, especially by myself in particular. We were not the KGB and no-one had ever died while being questioned. All she had to do was be truthful about her wishes and intentions and she would be protected and safe from the clutches of her embassy's security people.

I could tell that she was somewhat cynical about my last assertion and possibly knew more about our secret service than I did. My mind raced back to the corrupt Warren Commission's failed attempts to cover-up the executive conspiracy to assassinate JFK, but then, they weren't British and were definitely bent.

In the corner of my view, I saw the porter doing his rounds opposite and glancing up towards us in the lit-up middle common room. I suggested it might be time for us to go. At which, she reached out taking hold of my arms and pleading that she couldn't bear to be alone in the huge rooms of the Fulbourn country house.

I stood to extricate her hold on my sleeve and she rose with me, enclosing me in her arms, and pulling my head down gently, she kissed me fully and passionately on the lips.

I couldn't help reciprocating measure for measure, but retreated inches out of her enticing range, deeply inhaling her lingering expensive perfume and pheromonal bouquet, both of which were overpowering my objectivity.

She looked up at me and whispered, "Must we go? I feel safe here with you. Can't we stay?"

Despite the overwhelming urges that were storming through my loins, I was imagining the scandal, the night porter, the clinical school dean, the Prof, the GMC, the KGB and Annie, all of whom might not want to share the spirit of the occasion.

Without a word, I led her by the hand, out onto the old court square heading rapidly to the porter's lodge and entered.

The porter looked up and said, "Will that be all, doctor?"

I replied, "Thank you, Mr. Hodges. I wonder if I might possibly use your phone, and do you happen to know the number of the Varsity Hotel?"

I thought to myself, 'Well, the Prof did ask me to be nice to her.'

Addenda Notes

1. There are now recognised more than 80 autoimmune diseases, where a patient's immune system has been turned against themselves, leading to malfunction and disease. These include Ulcerative Colitis, Crohn's Disease, Thyroiditis (including Hashimotos Disease and Graves Disease) Type 1 Diabetes Mellitus, Multiple Sclerosis, Motor Neurone Disease, Rheumatoid Arthritis, Nephritis, Eczema, Psoriasis, Morphoea, Alopecia and Vitiligo, to mention a few.

These diseases are associated with inheritable cell membrane markers which are found on our cell surfaces and are prevalent in populations from certain regions of the world. They predominate in women.

2. Pathology is the study of disease and its mechanisms.

3. Surfactant is a compound found in the lungs that lowers the surface tension between liquids enabling air to enter the balloon-like lung alveoli for gaseous exchange to take place. The liquid lining the walls of the alveoli holds them together preventing inflation and gaseous exchange. Premature babies don't make surfactant in enough quantities to enable alveoli to open, obstructing air entry, so they can't absorb the oxygen in the air they breathe.

4. At this time, newly qualified doctors in the U.K. have to undertake one year of additional training, employed in recognised hospital in-house jobs, consisting usually of 6 months as a house surgeon and 6 months as a house physician. During this time, when on-call, the doctors live in the hospital (house doctors). After this year as doctors in the house, they can become fully registered with the General Medical Council (GMC).

5. This autonomic reflex cardiac arrest is more commonly seen in Acute Epiglotitis, in children, where examination of the throat, especially using tongue depressors, can cause a sudden cardiac arrest.

6. The Police and Criminal Evidence Act 1984 defined the regulations concerning, among other subjects, people detained in custody with respect to their safety and care by the police.

7. Silk and ermined judges are the law lords.

8. Oxford is also known as the city of dreaming spires, while Cambridge has been described as the city of perspiring dreams.